The Rejects

The Rejects

An alternative history of popular music

Jamie Collinson

CONSTABLE

CONSTABLE

First published in Great Britain in 2024 by Constable

1 3 5 7 9 10 8 6 4 2

A CIP catalogue record for this book
is available from the British Library.

ISBN: 978-1-40871-796-7 (hardback)

Typeset in Bembo by Hewer Text UK Ltd, Edinburgh
Printed and bound in Great Britain by Clays Ltd, Elcograf, S.p.A.

Papers used by Constable are from well-managed
forests and other responsible sources.

Constable
An imprint of
Little, Brown Book Group
Carmelite House
50 Victoria Embankment
London EC4Y 0DZ

An Hachette UK Company

www.hachette.co.uk

www.littlebrown.co.uk

For Chloe and Caspar

Contents

Welcome to the Worst Day of Your Life

On Sunday, 19 August 1962, a Beatles fan called Bruno punched George Harrison in the face. The band were playing a gig at the Cavern Club, and a story in *Mersey Beat* had broken the news that Pete Best had been fired. The crowd were chanting 'Pete for ever, Ringo never' and 'Pete is best,' and Bruno was very much a Pete Best man. Brian Epstein had presciently attended the gig with a bodyguard, but George Harrison was left with a black eye for the band's very first recording session the following week.

This most famous example of musical rejection provides a perfect illustration of its potency: kicking someone out of a band is always a form of betrayal.

I've frequently found it heart-breaking myself. From youthful shocks when members of favourite groups were suddenly 'disappeared', to closer-up fall outs I've witnessed in the music industry, these rejections often feel like tragedies. The original line up can seem as though it's somehow the only right one; excising a person from it breaks primal rules around never leaving anyone behind, and everyone deserving a second chance.

A great deal of each member is poured into a band and the burning effort to make it successful. Deep bonds are formed of the kind that outsiders can only marvel at, and which result in the chemistry that makes the music great. But within these bonds there are rivalries, dissatisfactions and resentments, and they can seep into the project's bloodstream and act as poison. Musical relationships are often forged in youth, and a breaking of them appears emblematic of a terrible, adult hardening.

Of course, by the time the end finally comes, the doomed bandmate might have had dozens of second chances. Often the rejection is entirely necessary. Sometimes, though, as we'll see, the loss of an original member can fatally wound even the biggest of bands.

One thing is always true: these stories tell us a great deal about the act in question. And about groups in general, too. Bands are strange, unique social organisations. They're formed from varying measures of friendship, creativity and business. Sometimes a member is included purely for their ability and despite their total lack of suitability in every other regard. Conversely, successful bands may tolerate a subpar player if they make the social group work better. Very often, bands are viewed by one or more of their members as a route to purely individual success — and damn the others.

As kids we put posters of these little gangs on our walls and imagine them to be just that. The best of friends, blood brothers and sisters with an unbreakable bond. The type of friendships we crave for ourselves. Often, this is sheer illusion, and those four or five people in the picture aren't friends at all. *How soon can I escape from these morons?* the singer might be wondering as he or she gazes coolly at the camera.

But what of the others in that picture? What about that inter-esting-looking character towards the back, standing a little apart from the rest? The one that got fired shortly after the photo was taken. Does that look in their eyes, that hint of a smile, suggest their mind was already on other things? What happened to *them*?

As a result of their dynamics, groups make for volatile brews. I remember a band I worked with many years ago, organised around a leader and performing under his name. They didn't make it very far, despite a lot of time, effort and money spent on their behalf. Before they fell apart, they briefly featured a skinny, livewire guitarist with a name that a screenwriter might choose for a stripper. He had short, reddish hair, a little moustache, a leather jacket and an intense, mischievous, slightly menacing gaze. I remember thinking that his edgy charisma might add to the band's appeal.

A few weeks after they set off on tour, upset broke out in the record company's office when a woman on a message board accused the guitarist of spreading STDs. Shortly after that, some sort of violent explosion took place on the tour bus, in the middle of nowheresville, USA (there might have been a knife involved) and the crazed guitarist stormed off into obscurity. As we'll discover in the stories to come, this is hardly unusual in the world of bands.

I've worked in the music industry for more than twenty years, primarily at record labels rather than management companies, booking agencies or publishers. We're the people that sign the artists, help them make their records, then market those records across the globe and try to get them consumed by as many people as possible. Talk of the death of labels has been greatly exaggerated. You'll have seen the headlines – the industry is expanding again, and record companies are doing better than they have been since the MP3 and Napster appeared like dreadnaughts on the late nineties horizon.

I've worked with a lot of different artists – singers, bands, rappers and electronic producers. They've come from all sorts of places and all kinds of backgrounds – middle-class England; brutal, underclass east London; Japan, Europe, Australia, all over America. The ones who succeed tend to be the most ambitious, and you won't need me to tell you that there's hard work and luck involved too.

There are self-destructive types, but also many highly self-controlled people – some frighteningly so. Nearly every time a group of musicians comes together to make a band, crew or group – genre deciding the term – someone along the way will be rejected. Some are destined for their own solo careers; others won't get with the programme in one way or another. Many don't quite want it enough to go through the hard years – the miserable touring and the hand-to-mouth existence, and the risk: the looming void of failure, the vision of themselves as a washed-up thirty-something with no home or pension.

I've always been drawn to the difficult, troubled characters, the people who are brilliant but flawed and fuck things up. I'll attempt to go easy on the amateur psychology in this book, but I think it's probably important to get it out in the open: I have these tendencies myself, and that's probably why I love these characters.

Regardless, I end up being friends with the troubled, warm second guitarist rather than the cold, controlled, ambitious singer. Graham Greene said that there's a 'splinter of ice in the heart' of artists, and this certainly applies to successful musicians. You have to be cold enough to shed impediments of any kind, and thus to reject your friends and bandmates. To be willing to break their hearts.

This book is about the people who are thrown out. It turns out that a perspective on bands from both the inside and outside is rare and uniquely revealing. These people were there, but they develop an objectivity by becoming outsiders, even if some of them never recover. And anyway, the people with the splinters of ice won't tell you anything they don't want you to hear. They need to control the narrative. The insider/outsiders might just tell the truth. In fact, through their stories, we can perceive an entire alternative history of popular music.

And this isn't a book about fuck ups – it's a book about bands, artists, players and people, united in their rejection but diverse in their stories and lives. For some of them, being thrown out of groups was an essential staging post on the way to finding their true callings – novelists, soldiers, towering solo successes.

We'll uncover stories from the fringes but look at the most famous ones too – those notorious rejections that everybody's heard of.

Like most writers, I don't like to tell people what I'm working on until it's finished. Partly, it's superstition – you think you might jinx it. But in the main it's people's reactions you're afraid of. If you describe an idea to someone and see a lack of interest – or worse, active dismay – in their face, it can crock the work for days.

But I felt more relaxed about *The Rejects*. I'd told a few people, who told other people, and I decided not to worry about it. Plus, I wanted suggestions for the cast, and a lot of music fans have a favourite kicking out story.

So at parties, bars, lunches, children's playdates and dinners, if someone asked, I would tell them what I was working on. The vast majority of people, if they had any interest at all, would immediately ask about what I came to think of as The Famous Ones. 'You must be writing about X?' they'd say.

In part, these stories stay with us because they provide the most striking examples, or the really painful ones. I think they're so notable, too, because they conform to recognisable archetypes:

It's just not working out.

This place ain't big enough for the two of us.

We've sucked you dry.

Your face doesn't fit.

I'm too good for you anyway.

And more than that, these stories stay with us because these are archetypes from *life*, not just from bands. Who of us hasn't experienced a rejection based on the above? I'd go so far as to say that we're lucky if we haven't experienced all of them: in love, in friendship, in work.

As we meet the cast, we won't stick purely to the rules and will interpret rejection broadly, partly because rules are dull, but also because we'd miss out on some great tales. Along the way we'll find glory, tragedy, chaos, failure and redemption, heartbreak, humour, violence, generosity and love. We'll discover surprising, life-changing connections between our cast of characters. We'll get a unique view on musicians and music and life, and we'll have a great deal of fun.

To the Rejects, then – a supergroup all of their own. Let's hear it for them.

1

Pete Best, the Beatles

He was a lousy drummer, you know? – John Lennon

Let's start at the beginning, and the deepest cut. Four young men in Liverpool, and the unlucky drummer who didn't make the grade.

Every group has to walk the line between friendship and ambition. The pack-like quality required for a band to gel is essential. An outsider can only gape at these bonds – the shared language, spoken or physical, the currents of energy, the way they seem to move together, to read each other, in person and on stage.

But to be in the gang you have to play your role. If you can't, the band has to go through the trauma of kicking you out.

Pete Best contributed to the Beatles. As the Quarrymen, they didn't have a drummer, nor a place to play. It was Best's mother, Mona, who set up the Casbah Coffee Club in her cellar. Pete had asked for a place his friends could meet up and listen to records. Mona had room – their house in West Derby, Liverpool had fifteen bedrooms and an acre of land.[1]

1 Mona Best was a character worthy of a book herself. She was characterised by her dogged support for her son's band, her gambling, her open-mindedness, and her affair with Neil Aspinall, who would eventually become CEO of the Beatles' Apple Corps.

Pete and some friends got together and started a band called the Blackjacks. He was the drummer, and liked to hit all four beats in the bar with his bass drum. Paul McCartney, who'd begun to frequent the Casbah with his and Lennon's band, the Silver Beetles, liked that – it was propulsive. Every band wants a drummer to be like an engine behind them, driving them forward. When their first (unofficial) manager, Allan Williams, cooked up an offer for the band to go to Hamburg, what had since become the Beatles asked Best to join.

The band's experience in Hamburg was vivid, shocking, wild. It comes to life in Best's autobiography. Even here, though, in his own book, Lennon and McCartney come across as the main characters. McCartney is careful with money, and jealous if another bandmate gets more attention. Lennon is like a proto-punk, *Sieg Heil*-ing or mooning at the audience, or calling them 'German spassies', indicative of his early obsession with disabled people.[2]

All of this appears to have gone down well, part of the 'make show!' instruction that the gruesome impresario and former clown, Bruno Koschmider, had demanded. The band leapt around, stamped, play-fought, screamed at the audience and rolled on the floor for seven hours a night. In part, it was a good release from the frustration of sleeping in two tiny concrete cells at the back of a seedy cinema.

There are early signs that Best stands apart, though they only appear in retrospect. In Craig Brown's *One Two Three Four: The Beatles in Time*, he writes 'while the others rag about, Pete

---

2 Best wonders if, beneath this fascination/repulsion, 'somewhere deep down he nursed a sort of sadness for them'.

remains sombre, drumming as though it were a chore, a bit like washing up.'[3]

'In those days we were all the best of friends at all times,' Best writes, 'and we would go through much together in the spirit of five rather seedy musketeers.'

They were still teenagers when they arrived in Hamburg – George Harrison hadn't even turned eighteen.

Hamburg: 'Making show' is a hit. The venue – lifeless and grotty on arrival – fills up nightly. Lennon pushes his act, appearing in his underpants, a toilet seat around his neck, a broom in his hand. 'Sieg Heil! Sieg Heil!' Anyone objecting is told to get stuffed.

Ringo Starr is in the city too, drumming for fellow Liverpudlian Rory Storm. He and Best pal up: 'It was in Germany that the friendship blossomed. We would lend each other drumsticks and go shopping for cymbals. It was an extremely pleasant relationship that would last a long time to come, but not for always.'

---

3 In researching *The Rejects*, I was lucky enough to exchange emails with Craig Brown. He told me about Florence Ballard (see Chapter 5) 'The Supremes definitely sacked someone . . . there's a good biography of them on my shelves.' Of Best, he said: 'He finally made quite a bit of money after he successfully sued Ringo, who'd said in an interview that he was sacked for taking too many drugs, as far as I can remember.' Actually, Best sued the Beatles as a group for defamation of character, and they settled out of court in January 1969. Brown told me he was 'using these musings as a work avoidance scheme', but he also mentioned his 'chapter on the guy who replaced Ringo on tour when Ringo was ill – he wasn't quite sacked, in that he'd only ever been hired as a replacement, but he took it that way, and never recovered.' This is the fascinating tale of Jimmie Nicol. As Brown says, he doesn't qualify as a reject, but that's one of many excellent reasons to read *One Two Three Four* – one of the best books about music that I've ever encountered.

The boys befriend the tough, well-armed Saint Pauli waiters, who double up as venue security when things get rough. They also get on well with the women – most of them sex workers from the Herbertstrasse. The Beatles sleep with hundreds of women in Hamburg. In their tiny, dark dungeons alongside the cinema urinals, they swap them (or are swapped), try out new positions and group up for orgies. The women never charge, and in fact become jealous if slighted.

'There were usually five or six girls between the four of us. During the proceedings there would come an echoing cry from John or George: "How's yours going? I'm just finishing. How about swapping over? I fancy one of yours now!"'

On the most memorable night, 'eight birds gathered to do the Beatles a favour. They managed to swap with all four of us – twice!'

Lennon, for his part, is also an enthusiastic masturbator. 'That was very good!' he reports, after five minutes locked away. He doesn't 'like sex to be too conventional', and regales his band-mates with the results. 'I tried position 68, with her standing on her head in the corner!'

There's a shocking moment in Best's autobiography in which he and John attempt to rob a sailor. The man has made use of his visibly fat wallet to treat the Beatles to a night of food, drink and friendship. According to Best, 'Paul and George weren't as keen, as they pointed out the dangers.' When it comes time to act, the pair duly melt away. John and Pete make their move, but are no match for the sailor, who fights back 'with all the tenacity of a man who had probably seen it all in the seaports of the world'.

After punching them, he pulls one of the locally ubiquitous tear-gas guns. John and Pete charge him, deflecting the first shot, and then turn tail and run away. The sailor retains his wallet.

I find it interesting that, after what happened later, Hamburg wasn't enough for Best. It was a rock 'n' roll lifetime crammed into two short years. But ambition is like that. The thing that got you there in the first place means it's impossible to give it up.

Koschmider never comes good on his promises to the Beatles, and doesn't reward them for having turned his new venue into a success. So, when a better offer comes in, they leap at the chance. A young venue owner, Peter Eckhorn, offers the band much better terms (and accommodation) at the Top Ten Club.

Despite Koschmider's threats – 'if you leave me, you won't ever play the Top Ten!' – the Beatles jump ship. The physical threats come to nothing, but George Harrison is abruptly deported for being underage, and disaster strikes when the others empty their old cells. McCartney seeks to illuminate his and Best's windowless room by setting alight a condom. In the process, some material on the wall is singed. In the early hours, fast asleep in their comparatively luxurious new digs, two 'gorilla-like cops' appear. McCartney and Best are arrested, and rapidly find themselves going the same way as Harrison.

Back in Liverpool, it feels as though it's all over. The band don't speak for weeks. It's Mona and Pete who spring into action and try to retrieve the gear, making 'frantic calls to Peter Eckhorn', who thankfully obliges. 'On the day of the ship's arrival in Liverpool, Mo and I booked a taxi – there was no family car at the time – and headed off to the Customs shed at Dingle.'

The crate the gear is in is massive, and they have to break it all down to fit it into the cab.

The band get back together and begin introducing British audiences to 'making show'. It goes down a storm, and something is really happening. *Mersey Beat* claims that the Beatles have 'resurrected original style rock 'n' roll music . . . when it had been emasculated by figures like Cliff Richard', noting in particular the 'mean, moody magnificence' of Pete Best.

Continuing in the spirit he showed in retrieving the gear, Best becomes de facto manager. The band – leaner, better, more battle-hardened now – go back to Hamburg.

It's at this stage that hair – always so crucial a rock 'n' roll signifier – becomes ominous. Until now, the Beatles have all worn theirs swept back, in the Elvis/Teddy boy style of the fifties. In Germany, though, they reunite with former guitarist Stuart Sutcliffe, who'd stayed behind with his girlfriend, Astrid Kirchherr. One day, Sutcliffe appears with his hair swept forward into a fringe.[4] Cue much piss-taking from the band, who 'fell about, pointing to the fringe as though it were something that had afflicted him during the night, like a rash'.

Nevertheless, George soon follows suit, and a few months later so do John and Paul. Pete, foreshadowing his doom, retains his quiff.

'No other member of the group ever made any mention to me of conforming and the style was certainly never an agreed

---

4 The origins of the Beatles mop top are much debated. Astrid Kirchherr has both claimed and refused credit. The true pioneer is probably Klaus Voormann, Astrid's original boyfriend. Described by Best as 'a cultured fellow from Berlin', he wore his hair in a fringe to separate himself from squares. He went on to design the cover for *Revolver* (as well as the interior of George Harrison's house in Surrey).

"must", he writes, rather defensively. 'No one suggested that I should fall in line.'

Drugs, another tribal signifier, also played a role. The band began to pop amphetamine tablets – 'making show' was exhausting. But Pete Best wasn't interested. For him, the booze gave him energy enough.

Back in Liverpool again, success beckons, but fault lines begin to show. Paul and John take a trip to Paris on their own. 'It seemed a little odd that they didn't tell us.' Brian Epstein, the Beatles' brilliant, tragic manager, comes on board. Mona and Pete are happy to hand over the reins: 'He was so keen and full of enthusiasm,' Mona said.

If anything, at first Epstein seems keener on Pete than the rest of the boys. He takes him for a drive to Blackpool one evening, and makes a pass at him: 'Would you find it embarrassing if I ask you to stay in a hotel overnight? I'd like to spend the night with you.'

'I told him that I would much prefer to go home,' says Best. 'There was no argument, no scene.'[5] There was 'nothing nasty about it, nothing obscene, nothing dirty. It was a very gentle approach.'

It doesn't worry Best. They have a manager in place, and the Beatles are now one of the hottest live acts in Britain. They have their eyes on a bigger prize though: it's time to start making records.

At first, this doesn't go well. A trip to London to audition for Decca sees the band nervous and hungover. It's New Year's Day,

---

5 A few years later, Brian would take John on holiday to Spain for a week. This trip would become the subject of intense speculation over a sexual encounter that may or may not have taken place between them.

1962, and they'd spent the night celebrating in Trafalgar Square. Dick Rowe, who would become infamous as the man who turned down the Beatles, doesn't attend, and instead sends Mike Smith, one of his A & Rs.[6] He and Epstein choose a set list consisting mainly of standards, which in retrospect seems a poor decision. A row breaks out between Lennon and Epstein, who critiques John's playing.

'You've got nothing to do with the music!' John rages. 'You go back and count your money, you Jewish git!'

It takes months to hear back from Decca. When they do, it's a no.

'The news of the Decca turn-down was kept from me for days to come,' Best says, a sense of disquiet perhaps beginning to set in.

Paul's father Jim complains when Best is beset by female fans at a performance, his hair pulled out, his tie pulled off and his suit badly mauled. Bizarrely, Jim's main concern is why Best didn't call the other boys back to share in this violent experience. 'I think that was very selfish of you,' he says.[7]

Epstein tries more labels, to no avail. Worryingly, they are running out of choices. There's only one imprint left within EMI: Parlophone. Its boss, George Martin, agrees to audition the band. Ironically, he's looking for something in the vein of Cliff Richard or the Shadows – the bands the Beatles would shortly turn into a thing of the past.

---

6 'Artist and Repertoire': perhaps the most glamorous but high-pressure role in the music business.

7 Later, when Best gamely attends a televised Beatles show after his sacking, Jim McCartney says, 'Isn't it great, they're on TV!' 'I'm not the person to ask,' Best understandably replies.

The audition seems to go well, but for months there's no word. In the early summer, something unsettling happens: 'A strange conversation . . . during a visit by Joe Flannery, manager of Lee Curtis and the All-Stars and a childhood friend of Epstein's. Out of the blue he said: "When are you going to join us, Pete?"'

'You must be joking,' Best replies. 'Why would I quit the Beatles when we're just about to get our big break on Parlophone?'

'Maybe I've jumped the gun,' Flannery says, backtracking.

Worried, Best confronts Epstein.[8]

'Eppy became very quiet, blushed as he always did and started to stammer. "I'm telling you as manager," he said convincingly, "there are no plans to replace you, Pete."'

This is a lie, and Best is not long for the band. In July, Parlophone offers the Beatles a contract, but again Best is kept in the dark. A couple of weeks later, they play the Cavern, and Best says goodnight to Lennon.

'Pick you up tomorrow, John.'

'No,' Lennon replies. 'I've got other arrangements.'

These are the last words that John, the closest Beatle to Pete, will ever speak to him.

The next morning, Best is summoned to Epstein's office. The manager is in an 'uneasy' mood and talks 'anything but business'. Finally, he plucks up the courage to deliver his message:

'The boys want you out and Ringo in . . .'

8 Best refers to Epstein as 'Eppy' throughout his book. The other Beatles preferred 'Mr Epstein', befitting the father figure he became to them.

Best is stunned, one question echoing through his mind: *Why, why, why?*

'They don't think you're a good enough drummer, Pete. And George Martin doesn't think you're a good enough drummer.'

Best is left 'numb'. In his shock, he agrees to play a couple of remaining dates before Ringo can join. Later, of course, he realises he can't go through with this.

Neil Aspinall, the Beatles' driver, friend of Best and by now Mona's lover, offers to quit. 'Don't be a fool,' Pete tells him, 'the Beatles are going places.'

Later, Aspinall asks the band why Best had been kicked out.

'It's got nothing to do with you, you're only the driver,' comes the reply. Best doesn't accredit it, but other sources point to it having been spoken by John.

Best is left hurt and confused. Mona phones George Martin, who claims the sacking is nothing to do with him. In 1980, the producer told the *Daily Mirror* that he was surprised Epstein let Best go, as he seemed 'the most saleable commodity as far as looks went'. But the drummer had 'seemed out of it at the audition. The others laughed and joked and talked amongst themselves, but he was silent most of the time.'[9] Anyway, Martin wasn't too worried about who drummed. 'Fans don't pay particular attention to the quality of drumming,' he said.

Petitions are raised by fans, dozens of whom gather at the Casbah. Mona camps out on the phone to Epstein and Martin. The band's fans seem obsessed with Best. Surely, they will never

---

9 It's important to be clear here that Martin meant out of the group dynamics, not 'out of it' on drugs or drink.

give up? But fans are as fickle as they are fervent, and eventually that's exactly what they do.[10]

Best joins Lee Curtis and the All-Stars, who evolve into Pete Best and the All-Stars, then the Pete Best Combo. Failure looms, then arrives. In 1965 Best finds himself married, a new father, living in three rooms in Mona's house. It all becomes too much for him, and he attempts suicide by gassing himself at the old-fashioned fireplace. His brother Rory smells the fumes, breaks down the door and revives him. 'Once I had become stabilized,' Best writes, 'Rory told me that I was "a bloody idiot."'

Something seems to strengthen in him, or perhaps he simply reaches a point of acceptance. He sues the Beatles for a libellous comment Ringo made – 'He took little pills to make him ill,' and in 1969 the band settles with him out of court. After a stint doing tough, manual labour in a twenty-four-hour bakery, he finally becomes a civil servant.

So, 'Whodunnit?' asks Craig Brown in *One Two Three Four*.

The official story became that George Martin had told the band they had to lose him, so what else could they do?

But it wasn't true.

'As in the denouement of an Agatha Christie,' writes Brown, 'it was the least likely suspect who finally confessed.' It was George Harrison – 'quiet, thoughtful young George'.

Harrison claimed that Best kept calling in sick, and that Ringo would sit in for him. 'Every time Ringo sat in,' George said, 'it seemed like "This is it." Eventually we realised, "We

---

10 Nevertheless, feelings about Best's sacking remain strong to this day. 'Of all the hundreds of names associated with the Beatles,' Craig Brown writes, 'his is the one that can still darken the atmosphere.'

should get Ringo in the band full time." I was quite responsible for stirring things up. I conspired to get Ringo in for good. I talked to John until he came round to the idea.'

George Harrison, the silent assassin. Perhaps he also understood that John, for ever hiding his sensitivity and hurt beneath a snarling, tough veneer, wouldn't be able to resist taking credit for the sacking.

It was Harrison, too, who understood the dynamics of the fans – that they'd get over it.

When a Pete Best fan called Jenny writes a letter of complaint, he replies: 'Ringo is a much better drummer, and he can smile – which is a bit more than Pete could do. It will seem different for a few weeks, but I think that the majority of our fans will soon be taking Ringo for granted . . . Lots of love from George.'[11]

He was right. Years later, a Beatles fan called Elsa Bredren spoke to the band's biographer, Mark Lewisohn. 'I used to love Pete and was heartbroken when they sacked him. But it soon passed, and it was as if he'd never been there.'

'It's like a cut,' Mona tells fans years later, when they visit her house, the site of the long-gone Casbah Club. 'It bleeds, it heals, but the scar's still there.'

It's just not working out.

11 In his attempts to understand the real reasons for his sacking, Best also considers the idea that he was 'sullen'. In this, he reminds me of Jason Everman (see Chapter 12), kicked out of Nirvana and Soundgarden for being too moody.

2

Steve Mann, the Mothers of Invention

He couldn't make the changes. – Frank Zappa

Steve Mann appears to have been blessed with incredible talent and cursed with awful luck. Not only did one of the very best guitarists in Los Angeles in the mid-1960s never fulfil his ambitions, but for a long time the world wrongly thought he was dead.

Mann was born in 1943 and grew up in North Hollywood, a suburb in the San Fernando Valley just over the hills from Los Angeles. A 'nice Jewish boy', he discovered the guitar in high school, and his talent was immediately evident. He quickly ticked the prerequisite boxes of favouring his instrument over his textbooks and incurring parental disapproval.

Making the hop over to LA to attend Valley State College, he began immersing himself in the city's folk scene, playing gigs at legendary venues the Troubadour and the Ash Grove. He befriended Hoyt Axton, Jorma Kaukonen and Sonny Bono. His reputation as a gifted player seems to have been established quickly, and he found himself very close to greatness on several occasions.

In 1962 he was introduced to Janis Joplin at the Troubadour, and the pair began working together and playing open mics around Los Angeles. This partnership ended when Mann briefly went north to San Francisco.[1]

Sometimes he performed as Little Son Goldfarb. He gave Kaukonen the nickname 'Blind Lemon Jefferson Airplane', and is thus indirectly responsible for naming the iconic psych-rock band.

Mann was gradually drawn away from folk and towards the blues. There are historical mutterings about doubts over how seriously a nice Jewish boy playing the blues could be taken. His talent was strong enough to overcome them. In 1967, at the pinnacle of his career, he played a solo show that was recorded and released as his best-known album, *Live at the Ash Grove*. On its cover, he grins out wryly at the camera, his hair black and lustrous, his face long, fleshy and handsome.

Despite the limitations of the recording, which was made direct from the PA system to a small tape recorder set on a table, Mann's virtuosity is unmistakeable. His playing on the album is bright and fluid, the finger-picked notes chiming and lingering in the air like musical sparks. Sometimes it's incredibly rapid, his technical skill astonishing. His voice has charm; it's mid-toned, soft, textured and occasionally hesitant. It's not absolutely first rate, though, which in music usually means unique, and that probably explains why he's best known as a guitarist.

The album consists of blues standards, including 'She Caught the Katy', written by Taj Mahal and James Rachell, and later made famous by the Blues Brothers. Interestingly, Mann's version contains a terrifying line that doesn't appear in the

1 Given what happened later, it might have been that he was running away from his problems. Certainly, the Bay Area was where he'd end up when his demons apparently defeated him.

original: 'If I don't get that good lookin' woman, I'm gonna take my switchblade and cut her no-good throat.' It seems doubtful that a man known for being gentle, as Mann was, would have written this himself, suggesting that other, lost versions of the standard might once have existed.

By 1966 he was a member of Frank Zappa's the Mothers of Invention, who were signed to MGM and playing bigger LA rock venues like the Whisky. The Mothers were known for their sonic experimentation and complex, jam-like live performances that seemed improvised but were actually very carefully planned and rehearsed. It might have been the failure to learn these difficult arrangements that spelled Mann's doom.

'Steve Mann, who was one of the best guitarists in LA, wanted to stay in the group but couldn't make the changes. We had to get rid of him,' Zappa said.

The problem appears to have been cocaine. In 1967, shortly after *Live at the Ash Grove*, Mann suffered some sort of catastrophic breakdown. He disappeared from LA, and due to an errant liner note on another artist's album, everyone thought he was dead.[2] Pete Frame's *Rock Family Trees* was still claiming this to be the case in the 1990s.

Mann had actually gone to the Bay Area, never to return. He resurfaced in the noughties, recording and occasionally playing live, accepting visits from pilgriming fans. He lived in care homes and was nursed by generous friends, heavily medicated, monitored for sobriety and never fully recovering his mind.

2 The singer and guitarist Stefan Grossman released an album around the time that was dedicated to 'the dear memory' of, among others, Steve Mann. This, combined with Mann's disappearance, gave rise to rumours that he'd died.

Hoyt Axton's 'Snowblind Friend' was written about him. Its lyrics tell the tale of a man who seeks paradise but, finding prayer too slow, instead buys a one-way ticket on 'an airline made of snow.'

The song became even better known when Steppenwolf covered it. Steve Mann's story thus found its way into musical fame, even if he never did.

3

Bootsy Collins, the J.B.s

Son, y'all the greatest band in the world, but
you just can't play. – James Brown

Pioneering funk bassist Bootsy Collins learned to survive his time in James Brown's band through laughter. But one night, the laughing went too far.

Brown was a paternal figure to Collins, if a tough one.

'He kept me real close,' Collins recalled. 'To show me things, as if he knew that I was going to be out there myself one day. He showed me as much as he could, without telling me anything.'

For an artist known for his towering ego, and for being ultra-demanding about the details, this was a generous attitude to take.

'He [told] me he'd called the radio stations and had them play his songs. He'd go there personally, and he'd take me with him. Not only did I play the shows, he wanted me to see him taking care of business.' It was an object lesson in the application needed to succeed: 'He was hard core, man. Hard core.'

But the lessons weren't always easy to understand.

'I mean, good Lord. Every night after we played a show, he called us back to give us a lecture about how horrible we sounded. Any time that you knew you'd played a great gig, and the people were loving it, he'd call you into his dressing room and say: "Haaargh! You just ain't on it. You just ain't on the one." I'd be like: "What? We ain't on the one?"'

No matter how hard they tried, the message was always the same.

'He was sweating profusely, his knees were bleeding – we just wore him out, and he would still call us in and tell us it wasn't happening.'

Collins and the band began to wonder if Brown was crazy.

'One night, we knew we wasn't sounding really good – we were off – and he calls us back there and said: "Uh huh. Now that's what I'm talking about. Y'all was on it tonight. Y'all hit the one." Sometimes you just have crappy nights, you know. He would call us in there and he'd be laughing, and he'd say: "You're killing it! Son, you're killing it!" That's when I really knew that this mother was gone. He was on another planet.'

Gradually though, the J.B.s realised that Brown just wanted to keep them on their toes, to drive them to practise harder.

'He knew what he was doing. You know how sensitive musicians are.'

The bandleader gradually honed his bassist, teaching him not to be too 'busy', to be more minimal, focusing him in on that near-mystical beat – the one:

'I was playing a lot of stuff. He loved all the different stuff, but if I were to give him the one – the one beat on every four count – and *then* play all that other stuff, he said, "Then, you my boy."'

But as in all master/protégé relationships, rebellion finally kicked in. At first, the unpredictable critiques were frightening. Brown appeared to be deadly serious, and these were sensitive musicians after all. Eventually, though, the J.B.s learned a coping mechanism.

'When we saw how stupid this stuff was that he was doing, we just started cracking up. Any time he would say something like "Errrgh! You're not on it, son," we would die laughing.'

It worked. The band had become confident: 'He stopped calling us into the dressing room. We knew we had it.'

And that, of course, was the first step in breaking away.

The father–son relationship had started to grate, and this being the early 1970s, LSD was on the scene.

'I promised myself I'd never do it during a show, but he pestered me so much not to do it that one day I just did. You had to be so tight with his music; there was no way you could play it when you were high. My bass turned into a snake, and I can't even remember playing.'

After the show, the call came for Bootsy to enter the back room.

'He was explaining how terrible I was – even when I wasn't taking LSD.'

This time, Collins took the coping mechanism too far.

'I laughed so hard I was on the floor. To him, that was very disrespectful. He had his bodyguard throw me out. He fired me, but I just couldn't stop laughing.'

It was time for Bootsy to leave home. Parliament-Funkadelic, and fellow cosmic experimenter George Clinton, were waiting for him.

'With him, you could just come as you are,' Bootsy recalls. 'It was perfect, because he allowed us to experiment, and he wasn't like a father figure. He was like, "If you wanna get loaded in the back seat, go ahead!"'

With Clinton, Collins and the band could 'wear whatever we wanted and fully express ourselves. There were no walls between us and the sky, you could just keep reaching and reaching.'

Eventually – and perhaps predictably – though, the experimenting itself led to harder years. Collins had a motorcycle accident when inebriated, resulting in a long hospitalisation and a fear he'd never play again. There was a subsonic plane journey when the engines blew out, and the aircraft plunged towards the Atlantic. To make matters worse, Collins had just watched *Jaws*.

'Now put that together,' he said. 'OK, I'm gonna crash. Then if I ain't dead, Jaws is gonna eat me.' Thankfully, 'one of the engines kicked back in and we were able to fly back to New York sideways. It was a crash landing, but we made it.'

These wake-up calls had the desired effect, and he got clean. In more recent years, it's been James Brown's lessons he's reflected on.

'A lot of things that we think are negative to us help shape our lives. Like the thing James was doing when he was saying I wasn't on it, that was a negative thing and that was why he was doing it to me. It helped shape my life and make me better. A lot of things come at you in a negative way, and it depends on how you accept it and respond to it. It can make you a better person.'

4

David Ruffin, the Temptations

Nobody is bigger than the group. – Otis Williams[1]

Ego is a well-established pitfall, but it can be very entertaining for fans. Initially a backing singer for Motown legends the Temptations, David Ruffin quickly became their star. Identified by co-writer Smokey Robinson as having the best voice in the group, he delivered their first number-one single, 'My Girl'.

Before long, he was riding around in a custom limo, dating famous women, and taking a lot of cocaine. His suggestion that the group change its name to David Ruffin and the Temptations did not go down well. Eventually, after failing to turn up to a show, Ruffin was thrown out.

Unfortunately for his replacement, Dennis Edwards, Ruffin proved capable of turning up to shows after all. He began appearing unannounced and crashing the stage, taking the microphone to perform his best-known songs. The popularity of this tactic among fans eventually got him rehired.

Immediately reverting to type, he showed up late to the first rehearsal and was promptly sacked again.

1 Technically, this quote comes from the Otis Williams character in *The Temptations* miniseries, based on his book.

Florence Ballard, the Supremes

There was something inside of her that was just pulling,
that she wasn't able to handle. – Diana Ross

A little girl is screaming.

It's February 1976, a winter's morning in Detroit. None of the neighbours comes to check what's happening. Maybe they're used to screams – they're not uncommon, apparently, on this down-at-heel street.

The little girl was called Nicole, and she was seven years old. She was screaming in horror because of how she'd found her mother.

'I always watched my mother. I came downstairs and she was slumped in the dining room, and I knew that something was wrong because she was foaming out her mouth. So, I climbed up in the chair and I called my grandmother, and I said: "Grandma, something's wrong with my mommy. Somebody help me."'

'She was so strong, even though she couldn't move, my mother said: "Just go back upstairs."'

Nicole's smarts in using the phone and raising the alarm weren't immediately rewarded. For hours, nobody came.

★   ★   ★

Florence Ballard was originally the leader of the Supremes, the Motown stars who were second only to the Beatles (see Chapter 1) in terms of chart success in the 1960s. In 1965, their music was transmitted to astronauts, making them the first group to transcend the planet.

Florence was one of fifteen children. She learned to speak up to make herself heard, and she loved to sing. One day, she was sitting on the porch of her house in the projects, singing with her sister Maxine.

'Milton Jenkins, the manager of a local boy group, the Primes, stopped his car, got out, and told us he was looking for a girl group,' Maxine recalled.

Maxine wasn't interested, though she must have liked Milton. She later married him and bore their five children.

Florence was definitely interested in the idea, and she quickly recruited two of her friends: Mary Wilson, from high school, and Diane Ross, from her church. The group were initially named the Primettes.

When it came time to talk about labels, the three young women looked at each other and said in unison: 'Motown.'

Berry Gordy's legendary Detroit label snapped up the group – on the condition they change their name. Suggestions included the Sweet Peas, the Darleens and the Melodees.

Florence said: 'I think it should be the Supremes,' Mary later recalled.

'Where Did Our Love Go', their second single under their new name, went to number one in the US. They'd already been together for six years and had released nine less successful songs as a group. It's notable in retrospect that Diane – by now Diana (the name, rather than Diane, that was written on her birth certificate purely as a clerical error) – Ross sang lead on the song. But just then it didn't matter. It was summer 1964, and success had arrived in dramatic fashion.

Over the next three years, the Supremes released ten number-one singles. They flew all over the world and became music stars of the highest order.

'Flo was thrilled when they first made it big,' Maxine said. 'There was a glow in her eyes. She said, "I feel like I'm on top of the world. I'm so happy."'

The three young women were so close that they all bought houses on the same street – Buena Vista Avenue in Detroit.

Among all the mudslinging and drama that came later, there are those who suggest that Berry Gordy decided Diana Ross would become the group's leader after he began a sexual relationship with her. That, however, doesn't seem to be definitively true. After all, she sang lead on that first number one. Perhaps Gordy saw something in her from the start, and the rest came later. In an interview with Barbara Walters in 2000, Ross bristled at the idea that her relationship had got her what she wanted, but not in the way you might think: she was defensive of Gordy, not herself.

'He probably believed in me more than I believed in myself,' she says. Her guard drops a little. A look comes into her eyes – the fierce, closed look of a lover when an external challenge presents itself. That was something special, her face seems to say. Don't presume to know.

There's no doubt that Ross was ambitious from the outset. 'Diane was aggressive,' Maxine claimed. 'She knew what she wanted and she went after it. Back in the projects in the early days, we would all start off walking down the street together, but Diane would always end up way ahead of us. She'd say: "You are all too slow. I'll see you all later."'

As so often, the seeds of the group's destruction were sown in its formation. Diana and Florence were destined to battle it out for leadership. Diana was more focused, her eyes firmly on success; Florence had a drinking problem and struggled with depression and her weight. Diana had a voice with a higher register, which Berry Gordy considered to be more distinctive[1] and commercial (some would claim more 'white'); Florence's voice was strong – a gospel singer's – but it was less unique.

'Diana had that pop sound,' Mary recalled. 'Which was something he was really going for.'

What Diana *didn't* have was the terrible trauma that had been inflicted on Florence as a teenager.

The Primettes had already formed when it happened. It was 1960, Florence was still in high school. She attended a sock hop with her brother Billy, but at some stage she lost track of him. A fellow student – a budding basketball star – offered to drive her home.

Instead, he drove her to a back street and raped her at knifepoint. Allegedly, the player was future NBA star Reggie Harding.

Florence locked herself away for two weeks and didn't return to the group for months. A change came over her, according to

---

1 As I said in Chapter 2, this is arguably the most important aspect of a singing voice in popular music, assuming that ability is there too.

Mary. She'd always been the strongest personality, but now she withdrew and was never the same.

'I had some pretty blue days,' Florence said in an interview recorded shortly before her death. 'I used to sit and cry for myself. I was sixteen turning seventeen. No birthday present really interested me. It all just hurt.'

Florence's dad, Jesse, was a heavy drinker. He kept it mainly to weekends and was always a good worker. Alcoholism runs in families, though, and there's been speculation that it did in hers. Either way, she turned to booze to make herself feel better.

Florence could never win the battle with Diana Ross. She was too damaged and unhappy, and her drinking increasingly out of control. Her weight was perceived as a problem. She had a sweet tooth and liked baking. In the Supremes, she started out as only a US size ten, but the others were skinny.

At first, she and Diana made a joke of it on stage.

'Thin is *in*,' Diana would say.

'Yeah,' Florence would reply. 'But fat is where it's *at*.'

The joke wore off. Diana became the clear leader of the group. Gordy changed their name to Diana Ross and the Supremes. He nattered at Florence about her weight.

'"Florence, you're too fat,"' she claimed he said. 'Well, I was a size twelve, and I guess next to Diane maybe I was fat, but as far I'm concerned, I was pretty damn stacked.'

Eventually, she threw a drink into the label head's face. There were screaming rows between her and Diana, and Mary Wilson later recalled that Florence could be 'explosive'. But according to a 2007 *Daily Mail* interview with Maxine, Florence's sister, rumours of physical, hair-tearing fights were unfounded.

The end came in Las Vegas in 1967. 'He [Gordy] kept calling me fat so much until I went on stage and I poked my stomach out as far as I could. Berry called me the next morning and said: "You're fired."'

'She only got $160,000,' Maxine claimed, 'was forced to relinquish all royalty payments and agree never to refer to herself as a former Supreme.'

Florence never recovered. She married Tommy Chapman, Gordy's sometime chauffeur, who became her manager too. He didn't do either job well, allegedly beating her. The couple had three children and divorced in 1973.

'She didn't have a very good life after she left the Supremes,' Don Foster, another former manager said. 'She was not a happy person, and I think the depression was magnified because she had no outlet at all.'

'She always had a look. She felt lost, like something was missing,' said Chris Cornelius, her nephew.

After money from her Motown settlement went missing, she accused her attorney of embezzlement and fired him. Her house was repossessed, forcing her to rely on friends. Her drinking and depression worsened. She was a smoker, and her weight was difficult to control.

'I drink under pressure,' she said. 'When I'm depressed and I drink beer, it gets all distorted. That's no cure for any kind of heartache. I guess I drink because I want to feel happy, but it only made it worse. I thought actually, I was an alcoholic, I gotta be an alcoholic, because I keep doing this.'

But it wasn't just beer: 'She drank Scotch and vodka,' Cornelius said. 'She didn't drink cheap liquor . . . When she bought liquor she bought good liquor, during these dark times in her life.'

By 1975, things appeared to be getting better. She had some money and a new house and seemed to be reconciled with Tommy. She made a guest appearance with Mary Wilson's the New Supremes in Los Angeles. But in the background, she was still struggling with depression and drink. She'd begun taking anti-depressants after a spell in the Henry Ford Hospital's psychiatric unit. Now she was taking amphetamine-based weight-loss pills, too.

On 20 February 1976, she visited her mother. She complained of feeling much too hot and began eating ice cubes out of the freezer. 'If something happens to me,' she said, 'take care of my babies.'

The next morning, Nicole found her in the chair, foaming at the mouth.

When no one came, Florence lay on the floor for hours, until her sister and husband came over and called paramedics. In hospital, it seemed at first as though she'd survive, but it was not to be. Her heart was too badly damaged, and she died in the early hours of 22 February. She was thirty-two.

'I think she died of a broken heart,' her nephew said.

At the funeral, another controversy broke out when Diana Ross turned up, and the attention was very much drawn to her.

The writer Mark Bego recalled the funeral in somewhat vindictive terms:

All of a sudden, in one grand and dramatic motion, Miss Ross catapulted herself into the church, flanked by two burly bodyguards. She let out a sobbing scream. She then appeared to swoon to the point of being seconds away from collapsing.

People were climbing, clawing, and hanging from the edge of the balcony to grab a glimpse of the black sable-bedecked and tear-soaked Ross.

It was Florence's funeral, and Miss Ross acted like she was out to steal the show, in much the same way – I feel – she stole The Supremes away from Ballard.

In my opinion, that Diana really is an unmitigated bitch! She won't even allow Florence to be the star of her own funeral!

Maybe. But there has to be a question over whether Ross really needed to do this to get attention, being the superstar that she was. Perhaps she simply wanted to mourn.

For Ross's part, the *Daily Mail* quotes her as having said that:

'Florence was always on a totally negative trip. She wanted to be a victim. When she left the Supremes and the money stopped coming in, it really messed up her head. She was just one of those people you want to grab and shake and yell, "Get your fucking life together."

'If I'd known how it was going to end with Florence, maybe I would have taken more time with her, fought her more, even though she didn't want my help. But she got to be a pain in the ass and I said, "Oh, forget it." Maybe I should have slapped her in the face a few times.'

She was more generous when interviewed by *Sounds* magazine. 'She was a good mother, she was talented, she had a lot of class, she carried herself very well,' she said, 'but there was something inside of her that was just pulling, that she wasn't able to handle.'

Since Ballard's death, lurid theories of murder have been circulated, not least by members of her heartbroken family: She'd threatened Berry Gordy, who'd done a funding deal with the mob. She was poisoned. It might have been Tommy – she cut him out of her will in 1976. What was the brown substance in her stomach?

The chances are it was just cereal, and that an undiagnosed predisposition to atherosclerosis had combined with depression, trauma, drinking, smoking and weight-loss pills to quite literally break Florence Ballard's heart.

Postscript

I was struck by that Barbara Walters interview with Diana Ross in 2000. The world of music – and stardom – has changed a great deal in the last quarter century.

Diana Ross was re-forming the Supremes for a segment of her tour, but without Mary Wilson (or Cindy Birdsong, Ballard's replacement in Diana Ross and the Supremes), who herself gave an interview, badmouthing Ross and naming the figures she'd been offered and considered insufficient.

Remarkably, in Ross's interview she discusses the 'accusations' – and the figures directly. 'We need to answer some of these things that are really not correct,' Ross says. 'I really didn't want to get into the numbers of the tour.'

But that's exactly what she does: 'She [Mary] was making – I heard her say – a million dollars a year. They [the promoters] offered her – for thirty shows – double that, and I doubled that.'

Walters asks Ross if it's true she's making fifteen to twenty million dollars for this tour.

'I wish,' Ross laughs. 'Most of my money is in percentages. If we do well, I do well.'

Ah, how much easier it was to get a juicy interview out of a celebrity in the year 2000. Diana Ross was a megastar then, an A-list legend. There isn't a chance in hell that someone in her position would answer these questions now – they wouldn't even agree to them being asked. Can you imagine Beyoncé responding publicly to LaTavia Roberson or LeToya Luckett (see Chapter 20) – her original Destiny's Child groupmates – and discussing their royalty splits?

It gets worse (or better, I suppose, from a celeb-hungry, TV viewer's perspective). Walters shows Ross footage of Wilson's interview and accusations.

'I think the unhappiness came when things started not to work that well in her life,' Ross responds. 'I think she's coming from a lot of pain. And I see such unhappiness in her, coming out of her.'

Ouch.

Ross, having exposed herself to this stuff, is impressive. She appears confident and honest, though of course she'd had a lot of practice with the media by then. Her eyes only harden when Berry Gordy is raised.

'She [Mary] said you were all equal,' Walters says, 'until you began a love affair with Berry Gordy. And she said that's the reason that you were made the star.'

'I'm not going to defend that,' Ross says. 'I think the audience knows that that's my voice on all those songs, it had nothing to do with my relationship . . . I just think he's a very special man.'

The turn of the millennium feels like a foreign country. Towards the end of the interview, Walters asks Ross if that's her 'real hair'.

'Should I ask you if it's yours, Barbara?' Ross quite reasonably asks in reply.

6

Brian Jones, the Rolling Stones

A kind of rotting attachment. – Keith Richards

If Pete Best (see Chapter 1) provides the tragic element of the Beatles' origin story, then it's Brian Jones who does so for the Rolling Stones. And like that band itself, his story is darker, druggier and uglier.

Something just turns in certain kids. I remember a boy at school, who almost overnight went from a diligent blond cherub to a frightening, cold kleptomaniac. No one knew what was wrong with him. Nothing left in changing rooms was safe, and there were rumours of dramatic scenes between parents and teachers. The former good pupil now appeared complicated and troubled. There was a dark glamour to this, a hint of adult sophistication. When we were all fifteen, the girl he was seeing told her friends of the bruises on her thighs, where his hips had slammed into her during sex.

Something like this seems to have happened with Brian Jones, who (like Florence Ballard) is part of an ultra-elite group of rejects – the sometime bandleaders themselves.

A middle-class boy from Cheltenham – quietly spoken and nerdy – Jones used to like trainspotting and took his grammar-school sport seriously. His well-to-do household was religious, frosty and conservative – characteristics that solidified when his younger sister Pamela died of leukaemia aged only one.

In his early teens, Brian's wholesome pursuits were hampered by asthma, which thwarted his hopes and made him resentful. It also meant he turned to music.

And something switched in him more generally in his teens. He became wild, irresponsible, obsessed and rather mean. By the time he was playing blues guitar in London clubs, at the age of eighteen, he'd fathered three children. Jones had a face that might have been cherubic if it wasn't for a streak of cruelty. It's a face that's almost enough to make you believe in physiognomy, because he was clearly a bit of a bastard.

His burgeoning obsession was with American blues from the Mississippi Delta and Chicago, with artists such as Howlin' Wolf, Muddy Waters, Robert Johnson and Elmore James. His transgressive behaviour cut him off from his family and community and meant that, like his heroes, he had no escape route from his music. He was driven – he had no choice but to succeed.

From awe to outright disgust – that's how Brian Jones went in the eyes of Mick and Keith. When they first came across him, they were a pair of unformed innocents, enthralled by this sophisticated, vivid kid who was really *doing it*. In the early sixties, Jones was already gig-hardened; an ultra-focused musical prodigy, living the edgy rock 'n' roll life of which Mick and Keith had only dreamed from their living rooms, where Mick sang Buddy Holly to neighbourhood mums.

They first saw Brian on stage, up there above them with his blazing blond hair and sharp clothes. He had the chops, the looks, everything. The others watched, wide-eyed with wonder, and then they began to learn from him. He knew the records and the songs, he knew the open G, D and E guitar tunings crucial to blues and rock – fatefully, he taught them to Keith.

Like John Lennon, Brian Jones sneered at and provoked the audience – a visceral thrill in the early 1960s.[1]

In the late 1950s, the tabloids were running scare stories about 'depraved Negro music' and 'the beatnik horror'. In his definitive book on Jones, *Sympathy for the Devil*, Paul Trynka speculates that Brian's parents 'would have felt they were living through a case study.' Other fathers were contacting his own to seek arrangements for the young girls he was impregnating. Unlike Keith Richards, he was not allowed to play music at home. This drove Jones out of the house, into the clubs and on to the stage. In another echo of the Beatles – Hamburg, and their 'ten thousand hours' – Jones likely amassed more experience than any other blues guitarist in Britain.

He was a worker where music was concerned. When the Rolling Stones formed, it was Brian's band. He was the undisputed leader.

For a while, it worked. Brian was always pressing ahead, pushing the others, picking the songs and providing the template for the Stones' bad-boy image. People consistently referred to the devil when describing him, and Harold Pendleton, owner of the Marquee Club, called him 'an evil genius'. He took more drugs and slept with more women than the others did. For a band that would be riven by sexual one-upmanship, perhaps this was always destined to be part of his downfall.

1 The elements of punk rock that made it so exciting appear to have their clearest origins – in Britain at least – in John Lennon and Brian Jones.

In the early years, Mick and Keith were still not fully formed. When the band appeared on American TV and Mick tried (vainly) to dance like James Brown, Brian outshone him by simply turning his back on the audience – an electrifying, taboo-shattering statement.

In fact, American TV was where Brian made his greatest impact generally. He had many faults, but racism was not among them. In 1965, he smashed another taboo when he introduced his hero, Muddy Waters, to a mainstream US TV audience.

'When we first started playing together,' Jones told Jimmy O'Neill, host of *Shindig!*, 'we started because we wanted to play rhythm and blues, and Howlin' Wolf was one of our greatest idols. It's about time we shut up and had Howlin' Wolf on stage.'

In *Sympathy for the Devil*, Trynka emphasises 'the importance of a handsome English man who described the mountainous, gravel-voiced bluesman as a "hero" and sat smiling at his feet. If any moment epitomized the life work of Brian Jones – in all its sexiness and purity – this was it.'

The rockslide started with the usual minor pebbles: there were the five pounds extra that Brian was paid, and for which (in a band driven by Jagger's financial hunger) he was never forgiven. Then there was Mick and Keith's moving into a flat together. And as Jagger and Richards flowered, Brian began to burn out. As the maker tells his replicants in *Blade Runner*, 'the light that burns twice as bright burns half as long'.

He took too many drugs and drank too much, his vividity blurring into sloppiness. Mick and Keith were more calculating, re-tooling Jones's wild image and turning it into something more sustainable.

When the mercurial, self-promoting Andrew Loog Oldham became manager, Brian's fate was sealed. Oldham wanted to go down in history as the person who created the Stones, not Brian Jones.[2] He sacked pianist and Jones recruit Ian Stewart (see Chapter 22), crucially weakening Brian's powerbase and instantly providing him with a lifelong enemy.

Oldham's PR partner, Tony Calder, told Paul Trynka that Oldham was sexually attracted to Jagger: 'Andrew fancied Mick more than he did everybody else.' And in the lazy manner that still decides much music industry thinking today, Oldham wanted an analogue for the brand 'Lennon–McCartney'. After the Beatles, you needed to write your own hits. Mick and Keith lived together. They would be 'Jagger–Richards'.[3] He forced them into a room and told them not to come out until they had a song.

Brian's contribution to the Stones' writing was in turn written out of history. He played the marimba on 'Under My Thumb', thus providing its melody, and wrote the sitar part on 'Paint It Black'. Perhaps worst of all, the fact that he and Richards wrote 'Ruby Tuesday' was never acknowledged in his lifetime. Only Jones could have contributed its recorder part, or would have experimented with the sitar or marimba. 'That's a wonderful song,' Mick Jagger told *Rolling Stone* co-founder Jann Wenner in 1995. 'It's just a nice melody really. And a lovely lyric. Neither of which I wrote.'

---

2 It's difficult to resist speculating as to what might have happened had the Stones experienced the nurture of someone like Brian Epstein. But on balance, perhaps the mean, dark, rivalrous glamour of the band might never have emerged in those circumstances.

3 Oldham would do this again, with a band signed to his Immediate label, when he had Small Faces' songs credited as Marriott–Lane, despite Steve Marriott being the primary songwriter.

In Trynka's book, he quotes Stan Blackbourne, the Stones' 1960s accountant, on his reaction to Jones not seeking credit for his writing. 'I used to say, "What on earth are you doing? You write some of these songs and you give the name over as if Mick Jagger has done it. Do you understand, you're giving 'em thousands of pounds! You're writing a blank cheque!"'

When Eric Easton, the Stones' first manager, who was close to Jones, was also sacked, the band wasn't really Brian's any more. Nico, the femme fatale of 1960s rock with whom Jones had affairs (and who claimed he was better in bed than Jim Morrison), said he was an 'untameable being who could never become, like Mick, a conventional careerist'.

Brian got into acid, and became interested in witchcraft and the pagan god, Pan. He began to develop a peacocking, dandyish, romantic style that Keith Richards eyed beadily.

Perhaps chief among his faults was his treatment of women. He was a sadist, having avidly read the Marquis de Sade in his youth. As a teenager, the tension at home broke into full-scale conflict when he slapped his mother and told her she'd be sent away 'like his dead sister'. On tour in Florida in 1965, he at least beat and possibly raped a girl – nothing in the Stones' history is ever fully clear. The band were horrified, and had their roadie Mike Dorsey beat him up, cracking a few ribs. 'I held him up by the collar and belt out the hotel window,' Dorsey told Trynka, and said "if you ever do that again, I'll drop you."'

Brian's status within the band would never recover. Mick and Keith began their habit of working without him. When 'Little Red Rooster' was due to be recorded, they told him to come on the wrong day, and left a note instructing him where to play his slide parts. He was absent entirely from '(I Can't Get No)

Satisfaction'.[4] He may have contributed a harmonica part, but it was later wiped. In future, Richards would re-record Brian's parts in the 'sponge jobs' Jones had once had to perform over Keith's.

Jones missed shows occasionally, and his health – never robust – began to worsen. He became resentful and suspicious, and the band began discussing getting rid of him.

Doubtless exasperated but also jealous, Mick and Keith began to bully Brian from the mid-1960s. Jack Nitzsche, the genius arranger who worked with Neil Young and powered much of the musical creativity around Los Angeles in the sixties,[5] thought Brian the best musician in the band.[6] The word he repeatedly used to describe Mick and Keith's behaviour towards him was 'nasty'.

Keith could be physical. Mick was slyer and cold.

Brian's success peaked with the dark, destructive glamour of his relationship with the actress Anita Pallenberg. They took drugs and experimented sexually. Keith – fixated – used Brian's pneumonia to steal her away.

From there, the only way was down. Keith and Anita abandoned Brian in Morocco,[7] an experience that shook him to the

4 Pleasingly, Jones used to play 'Popeye the Sailor Man' when 'Satisfaction' was played live.

5 Nitzsche was a key player in the life of Danny Whitten, too (see Chapter 14).

6 In fact Brian was always the Stones' most popular member in LA, and California more widely. In his hair and clothes, he provided a template for bands from the Byrds to countless garage rock acts. This influence was still being felt in the nineties, not least in the form of the Brian Jonestown Massacre (see Chapters 18 and 30).

7 Jones was obsessed by Moroccan and North African music, and identified the blues' roots within it. He recorded local music and envisioned a post-Stones project based on it. One of the first people to hear some of these recordings, in

core. Half crazed by acid trips, he'd discovered their affair, confronting, and allegedly beating Pallenberg. The final straw came when he roused her in the middle of the night, again high on acid and now in the company of two Berber prostitutes. He wanted Anita to join them in a foursome. Far from submitting to this ugly test of her loyalty, she fled to spend the night with Richards. The next day, she and Keith simply left Brian where he was.

Back in London, he carried on taking a lot of acid, added Quaaludes to the mix, and seemed to lose confidence in his guitar playing. He wanted Anita back, and found a submissive analogue for her in the young, tragic model, Suki Potier. The Quaaludes, booze and other substances rendered him useless in the studio. Mick had his amp turned off when he passed out. Later, before the end, he spent hours staring at a saxophone reed, politely brushing away offers to help change it.

The relentless, well-documented persecution of 1960s musical stars by the forces of law and order hit Brian Jones the hardest.[8] He was oversensitive, frightened, incapable of managing

---

Morocco, was author and junkie William S. Burroughs. He appeared, 'a cadaverous figure in a raincoat and hat' in Marrakesh, where Jones was staying. Burroughs links a number of our rejects: as well as meeting Jones, he was beloved of Kurt Cobain (thus indirectly linking him to Jason Everman, Chapter 12), who recorded with him, and by Tony O'Neill (see Chapter 18), who used Burroughs's writing on late 1960s needles to advise on my chapter on Danny Whitten. Burroughs is viewed as a sort of junkie high priest, which perhaps naturally attracts rock stars, with their predilection for killing pain with the drug. When Burroughs met Kurt Cobain, after they'd recorded 'The "Priest" They Called Him' together, Burroughs told his assistant: 'There's something wrong with that boy; he frowns for no good reason.'

8 Artists such as Donovan, the Beatles (see Chapter 1) and the Rolling Stones were pursued by the police in countless raids for drugs. These were often led by Detective Sergeant Norman Pilcher of the Flying Squad, immortalised (perhaps) as 'semolina pilchard' in 'I Am the Walrus'. The raids appear to have almost

the process. He wasn't in a team like Mick and Keith, and his guilty plea to a possession charge made the rest of the band resentful. They anyway blamed the busts on an ill-advised interview he'd given about drugs.

By the late sixties, the band was reaching its pomp, and Brian was approaching his nadir. Freed from the psychedelic fad they'd never been comfortable with, the Stones emerged with the strutting, raunchy blues-rock that would define them: 'Jumpin' Jack Flash' and 'Sympathy for the Devil'.[9]

In the studio, Brian wandered around, lost, or sat for hours waiting for instructions. Once, he asked Jack Nitzsche what to do.

'Just pick up a guitar,' the producer suggested.

Brian did so, and asked Mick what to play.

'You're a member of the band, Brian, play whatever you want,' Jagger replied.

So he played something, but Mick stopped him and said, 'No, Brian, not that – that's no good.'

At the end of the session, 'Mick walked up to the founder of his band and said, "Just go home, Brian."'

Jones had often thought of leaving, but by now he was too broken, too submissive, too afraid of Mick. He waited instead for the blow to fall.

---

certainly crossed the line into persecution and corruption. Drugs were very likely planted, and charges were trumped up. Even the judges involved broke the law by commenting on active cases. William Rees-Mogg, father of Jacob, wrote a crucial editorial in *The Times* defending Jagger, calling for tolerance, and asking 'who breaks a butterfly on a wheel?'

9 Despite the critical view being fairly clear, that the late 1960s and early 1970s period Stones of *Beggars Banquet*, *Sticky Fingers* and *Exile on Main Street* is the band's finest, their biggest song on Spotify is 'Paint it Black' – a song Brian Jones was instrumental in writing.

In June 1969, it did. Jagger and Richards travelled down to Brian's Sussex home, a country house that had once belonged to A. A. Milne, and took Charlie Watts along, just in case there was trouble. In fact, Jones was something close to relieved. The worst had finally happened.

He was left in his house with the last of his girlfriends and the dregs of the Stones' dodgy hangers on – the band had always had an ugly fascination with criminal types and gangsters.

A month later, he drowned in his overheated swimming pool, drunk and doped on countless downers. His death would give rise to years of murder accusations and conspiracy theories, none of which is close to being as interesting as his life.

When he died, face down in the pool, he was twenty-seven years old.

Mick Jagger was angry that the death threatened to over-shadow the Stones' upcoming concert in Hyde Park. But no matter, the rotting attachment was finally gone.

Brian Jones was dead, which, in Marianne Faithfull's view, left Keith to inherit his dark glamour, and finally 'free to become him'.

We've sucked you dry.

John Cale, the Velvet Underground

He's completely mad – but that's because he's Welsh. – Lou Reed

When Lou Reed met John Cale, he found the perfect partner in his mission to create anti-Beatles, anti-hippie, discordant musical transgressions. If they'd lasted for longer than a flash of white light, Reed and Cale might have been a harder, nihilistic Lennon–McCartney. As with all great pairings, Reed's vision would have been impossible to achieve without Cale.

'Lou and I were that once-in-a-lifetime perfect fit,' Cale said, years later. 'His words were deserving of something far more intriguing than a typical folk rock, blues structure. "Heroin" or "Venus in Furs" didn't work as tidy folk songs – they needed positioning – rapturous sonic adornment that could not be ignored.'

But when Reed decided he'd quite like to try being a rock star in a more traditional mould, he found Cale less of a fit. In one of the more cowardly rejections we'll encounter, Reed despatched the Velvets' guitarist, Sterling Morrison, to fire the viola-playing Welshman.

The band replaced Cale with bassist Doug Yule, who would later take over as guitarist and frontman when Reed himself quit the band.

David Bowie (see Chapter 29), a huge fan of the Velvet Underground, once spent hours talking to Yule backstage, thinking he was Lou Reed. This fruitful incident became central to Bowie's ideas about artifice, persona and fame.

One of our happier rejects, John Cale went on to have a decades-long and highly successful career in experimental music. He's still releasing albums at the time of writing, at the age of eighty-one, and I had the pleasure of working on one during my spell at the Domino Recording Company.

He was philosophical about being fired by Reed, later saying that their relationship was 'a non-sexual love affair that ran its course'.

All the Musicians Kicked Out of Fleetwood Mac

From 1960s blues in swinging London to coked-up LA pop-rock, no major band has evolved more than Fleetwood Mac. And in musical terms, evolution usually means a few firings.

The *Rumours*-era intrigues are notorious – the band's couples and crew sleeping with each other, breaking up, behaving wildly, and writing iconic songs about it all. There are also lots of great stories of people who simply left the band: founder Peter Green, a genius who fried his brain with acid; guitarist Jeremy Spencer, who quit before a gig at the Whisky a Go Go to join the Children of God cult.

And the core members of Fleetwood Mac were no strangers to firings themselves. Both Mick Fleetwood and John McVie had been kicked out of John Mayall and the Bluesbreakers (McVie, twice) for drinking.

But despite their ever-changing line up, it wasn't until the summer of 1972 – after the band had been going for five years – that anyone actually got fired from Fleetwood Mac. Perhaps Mick's experiences and predilections made him a tolerant sort of bandleader.

1. Danny Kirwan – guitar/vocals, 1968–72

It got intolerable for everyone. – Mick Fleetwood

What a journey Danny Kirwan had. From obsessive fan to actually *joining* the band at eighteen years old. From being 'emotionally fragile, so into it that he cried as he played' to finally letting his emotions get the better of him.

Kirwan was a brilliant guitarist, singer and songwriter. He made a bit of a name for himself with his blues band, Boilerhouse, and came to the attention of Fleetwood Mac. Peter Green briefly considered managing Boilerhouse, but he was also looking for someone to help write songs, because Jeremy Spencer wasn't interested in doing so. Danny was a fanboy, standing in the front row at every Fleetwood gig, turning up early to help load in and carry gear. Green was looking to grow the band out of its blues roots, and Mick Fleetwood finally suggested they simply hire Kirwan.

'It was clear that he needed to be with better players. In the end, we just invited him to join us. It was one of those "ah-ha" moments when you realise the answer is right there in front of you.'

Kirwan was slim, with a sensitive, rounded face emphasised by his chin-length hair, which curled in around his jaw and – combined with a fringe – created the impression of a circular frame. In pictures, he looks occasionally innocent and often rather troubled and tired.

Heavily influenced by Django Reinhardt, he was noted for his melodic, gentle playing, characterised by lots of bent notes and vibrato. He made the perfect foil to the fiery improvisational solos of Green and Spencer. And before long, he was enabling the evolution that Green had been planning. The pair wrote Fleetwood Mac's first number-one single, 'Albatross', together.

'Once we got Danny in,' Green said, 'it was plain sailing. I would never have done "Albatross" if it wasn't for Danny. I would never have had a number-one hit record.'

In fact, Kirwan's ideas would extend far beyond his spell in the band. Fleetwood Mac's manager, Clifford Davis, noted that Danny was 'the originator of all the ideas regarding harmonies and the lovely melodies that Fleetwood Mac would eventually encompass'.

But the master should always beware the protégé. Davis had also noted Kirwan's 'high standards' from the outset.

'When we were on the road he was constantly saying "Come on Clifford, we must rehearse, we must rehearse, we've got to rehearse."'

Kirwan had a short temper and lacked a sense of humour. He was the sort of person who wanted to turn up an hour early for everything. The druggy, experimental Peter Green was a very different type. It showed in his playing – he had the sort of improvisational chops that Kirwan could never muster. Their differences made the music better, but also meant that they didn't get along.

If the protégé grew frustrated with the master, he never quite got over the need to impress him. The band's producer/engineer, Martin Birch, 'got the impression that Danny was looking for Peter's approval, whereas Peter wanted Danny to develop by himself'.

'We just didn't get on too well basically,' Kirwan said. 'We played some good stuff together, we played well together, but we didn't get on.'

Eventually, Green, frustrated, damaged and wanting to be free, left the band.

'He suddenly said: "enough is enough",' John McVie said. 'It was in the middle of a European tour – but he worked out all the contracted gigs and left six weeks later. He just didn't want to be a guitar star any more ... All the pressures, possibly coupled with a degree of acid loss, seemed to put him off the rock scene.'

Mick Fleetwood's take, looking back on it later, was more frustrated: 'He finds it difficult to be around people. He couldn't give a shit about anything. He used to be such a super positive, highly intelligent guy. He knew exactly what he wanted to do ... It's as if he thought himself into a corner, and never got out of it.'

Evolution kicked in. John McVie's wife Christine (who died in November 2022) joined the band on vocals and piano, and became 'the glue'. Spencer was terrified of becoming a frontman, and Kirwan was forced to step forward too. He was not cut out to cope with it: 'The pressure on Danny's sensitive temperament was tremendous,' Fleetwood said. 'There was one terrible night when everybody decided they wanted to leave, but one by one, I talked them all back in.'

During a US tour in February 1971, Jeremy Spencer made his dramatic departure. Always a split personality, he'd veered between wild, suggestive stage performances (occasionally so lewd as to have got the band in trouble) and obsessive bible reading.

On the plane down from San Francisco to LA, ahead of the doomed gig at the Whisky a Go Go, Spencer was sitting next to John McVie and staring out of the window.

'He suddenly turned to me and said: "Why do I have to be here if I don't want to be here?"' McVie recalled. 'Well, everyone in the band felt like that at one time or another, so I didn't give it a second thought . . . But that was the last time I spoke to him for two years.'

In LA, Spencer wandered off to a bookshop and met members of the Children of God on the street. They found him ripe for recruitment. Psychedelic drugs, which seem to have been the bane of the band's existence around this time, may well have played a role. Fleetwood later recalled that Kirwan and Spencer had taken mescaline, the powerful natural hallucinogenic, when the band arrived in San Fran: 'It really did a number on them, Jeremy in particular. The effects seemed to last far longer than they should have.'

This left Fleetwood Mac at the start of an American tour with no frontman and only one guitarist. Cancelling the rest of the dates would have been financially ruinous, so in desperation Clifford called Peter Green and asked him to fill in. Green considered himself retired from music and had sold his guitars. In an outstanding display of decency, he nevertheless agreed to come back. There one was condition – the shows must all be improvisational jams.

Green flew out to San Bernadino, part of the vast suburban sprawl as you head out from LA to the desert, the mountains looming up to the north. After half an hour's rehearsal in the dressing room, the show went on.

Pity poor Danny Kirwan: stressed from touring, drugs and line-up changes, in the throes of incipient alcoholism, one minute under pressure to step forward, to write and perform, the next playing second fiddle to his wild musical mentor.

Kirwan liked rehearsing, planning, knowing what he'd be play-ing. Now, in Fleetwood's words, 'not once did we take the stage knowing what the set was going to be'. McVie recalled that 'we were scared stiff. We would go on stage every night, look at the audience and not have a clue what we were going to play.'

Regardless, the shows went down brilliantly, and the tour – and the band – were saved once again.

Fleetwood Mac recruited the Californian guitarist Bob Welch in April 1971.[1] He was laid back, outgoing, well trained and talented. He had curly, blondish hair, a long, strong-jawed face and a beaming smile. At first, he seemed to fit right in: 'I was expecting they'd tell me to learn these songs and sing this way,' Welch said, 'but it was nothing like that. We just jammed and played some blues on the side.'

Fleetwood had a definite style as bandleader: 'Mick ran a loose ship. Most of the time it was jam city. We basically got drunk and had a good time.'

And Welch rated Kirwan's playing, describing him as 'metic-ulous' and 'mature'. 'The notes had to be exactly right,' Welch said. 'He didn't play any twiddly licks just to fill time. Danny's style, which he modelled after Pete Green's, was a "make every note count emotionally" style. I learned a lot from Danny about

1 Bob Welch is part of one of many surprising connections between our rejects. In Chapter 10 on Steven Adler, it was Welch's heroin that Adler first tried. Welch had hospitalised himself with the stuff, and his house sitter invited Adler and his girlfriend over. The lump of sticky brown heroin ended up, finally, with Guns N' Roses' Izzy Stradlin, who came straight over to collect it when Adler told him about it on the phone. After many years of sobriety, Welch shot himself dead in 2012 at the age of sixty-six. He'd had spinal surgery, was in a great deal of pain, and had been told he'd eventually become an invalid. He left a nine-page suicide note declaring his love for his wife, Wendy.

economy of notes, and really trying to say something in a guitar lead.'

This is a strikingly insightful and complimentary way for one musician to talk about another. Welch had identified Kirwan's key ability. He wasn't interested in showing off, noodling in the heart-sinking, masturbatory style that defines the worst type of guitar playing. Kirwan's attitude was that if it wasn't saying something – if it wasn't making the listener feel something – then it shouldn't be there. This economy is a key part of greatness in music.

'When he left,' Welch would recall much later, 'Fleetwood Mac lost a certain lyricism that they wouldn't get back until Stevie Nicks.'

And not only did Welch notice Kirwan's talent, he was also willing to admit that he learned from it.

Despite this, he soon found Kirwan difficult to get along with. Mick Fleetwood saw that a 'personality clash' was developing, with Kirwan picking fights with Welch. 'Danny was a brilliant musician, but he wasn't a very light-hearted person, to say the least. He probably shouldn't have been drinking as much as he did, even at his young age. He was always very intense about his work, as I was, but he didn't seem to ever be able to distance himself from it and laugh about it.'

Kirwan appeared to be increasingly paranoid, even 'disturbed'.

'He would always take things I said wrongly,' Welch said. 'He would take offence at things for no reason.' Welch got the impression that his appreciation for Kirwan's playing wasn't mutual: 'I think Danny thought I was too clever a player . . . too jazzy, too many weird notes. I don't feel he loved my stuff to death.'

By the summer of 1972, it had all got too much. Danny Kirwan didn't have the temperament for the crazed schedule of touring, writing and recording that Fleetwood Mac underwent in that period. Decades before concerns over musicians' health found any sort of place on the agenda, their management kept them going at full tilt.

Things, as they do, came to a head. Kirwan had undergone almost four years of gruelling, continuous work since the age of eighteen. He'd had to take on songwriting duties for a major international band as it went through various ruptures, and then been forced to take front of stage when the band's founder – and his hero – had departed. He coped by drinking heavily, and by that summer was 'living mostly on beer.'

Danny Kirwan had thus become something of a timebomb and, before long, the final explosion took place. It took the form of a violent incident backstage in the US in 1972. Mick Fleetwood recalled it in his biography, *Play on Now*:

We all felt a blow-up was brewing, but we didn't expect what happened. We were sitting backstage waiting to go on. Danny was being odd about tuning his guitar. He went off on a rant about Bob never being in tune ... He got up suddenly, and bashed his head into the wall, splattering blood everywhere. I'd never seen him do anything that violent in all the years I'd known him. The rest of us were paralysed, in complete shock. He grabbed his precious Les Paul guitar and smashed it to bits. Then he set about demolishing everything in the dressing room as we all sat and watched. When there was nothing left to throw at the wall or overturn, he calmed down. Five minutes to show-time and there was blood everywhere. Danny said: 'I'm not going on.' We were already late to the stage and we could hear the crowd chanting for us. We had to go on stage without him.

Welch recalled that Kirwan was 'pissed out of his brain, which he was for most of the time. We couldn't reason with him. I think we told the audience Danny was sick, which I guess he was, in a way.'

Kirwan watched the show from the mixing desk as the band struggled through the set. Afterwards, he offered them an unfavourable review of their performance. Enough was enough.

'Danny was fired,' Mick Fleetwood said. 'He was the first person ever asked to leave. He was desperately unhappy, a nervous wreck, and didn't enjoy being on stage. It got intolerable for everyone.'

Nowadays of course, someone would likely realise that Danny Kirwan's mental health was suffering, and that he needed a break and treatment for alcoholism. As with the case of Danny Whitten (see Chapter 14), however, this simply wasn't a part of the paradigm. Struggling on with Kirwan appeared to the band to be a form of loyalty: 'I would say "the guy doesn't show up to rehearsals, he's embarrassing, he's paranoid",' Welch said. 'But Mick, John and Christine remained loyal to him because he was Peter's protégé.'

Danny Kirwan was out of the band. He made a couple of solo records, and gradually drifted into worsening alcoholism and bouts of homelessness. As ever, perhaps the clues to some of his unhappiness are there in the records: Fleetwood Mac's 'Bare Trees' and 'Child of Mine' refer to the absence of his father during his childhood. Kirwan himself was already divorced by the time he left Fleetwood Mac, and barely saw his own son, born in 1971. Finally receiving treatment in his later years, he died in 2018, at the age of sixty-eight.

Shortly after he left Fleetwood Mac, he met Bob Weston, his replacement, in a bar in London.

'He was aware that I was taking over and rather sarcastically wished me the best of luck – then paused and added, "you're gonna need it."'

2. Dave Walker – vocals, 1972–3

We thought we'd try having a front man/vocalist. It only lasted about eight months. – Mick Fleetwood

This one is uncertain, because it doesn't seem clear that Walker was actually fired. Pete Frame's *Rock Family Trees* has him leaving the band and implies it just didn't work out. On the other hand, both the fleetwoodmac.net fan site and Wikipedia claim that he was sacked. On balance, and in the name of completeness then, I think he makes the cut.

Another character on the UK blues scene, Walker hailed from Walsall and made a name for himself in Birmingham. He played in R & B and rock bands the Redcaps, the Idle Race and, most notably, blues-rock outfit Savoy Brown. Leaving this latter band to join Fleetwood Mac, he apparently took too much of it with him: 'The light finally dawned on us that we were throwing away what Fleetwood Mac had been, that we weren't Savoy Brown,' Bob Welch said.

According to Fleetwoodmac.net, Walker spent more time in the pub than in the studio, and both he and the band were frustrated by his lack of creative contribution and stylistic differences. Before heading back into the studio to record 1973's *Mystery to Me*, the band let Walker go.

Immediately after leaving Fleetwood Mac, Walker formed Hungry Fighter with ex-members of Savoy Brown and Warhorse, and fellow Fleetwood reject Danny Kirwan. They played one gig at the University of Surrey in Guildford before disbanding.[2] Kirwan's mental health was in freefall, and a road accident destroyed much of their gear.

Apparently doomed to short spells in massive bands, he joined Black Sabbath in 1977, and left in 1978 when Ozzy Osbourne returned. Still alive and performing music on YouTube, he lives in the US and speaks with a peculiarly Brummie take on a mid-Atlantic accent. In photographs, he bears a strong resemblance to a much older Jesse Hughes, of Eagles of Death Metal.

3. Bob Weston – guitar/ vocals, 1972–4

He was asked to leave after a strenuous
disagreement. – Mick Fleetwood

If Bob Weston hadn't broken a cardinal rule of being in bands, Fleetwood Mac in its final(-ish) and greatest (arguably) incarnation might never have existed.

Weston was from the West Country, and moved up to London in the mid-1960s. As per other members of Fleetwood Mac, he was initially into the blues, listening to Muddy Waters and John

2 The town in which, incidentally – and much to my wife's chagrin – the bulk of this book was written.

Lee Hooker as a youth. In 1967 he joined a mod band called the Kinetic – a name one might choose if inventing a satirical mod band – who based themselves in Paris. They got signed to a French label, released an EP or two, and disbanded.

Weston's return to London coincided with the explosion of British blues of which Fleetwood Mac were a part. He played as a session guitarist for Graham Bond and Long John Baldry, who'd performed on the same bills as Fleetwood. In September 1972, shortly after the firing of Danny Kirwan, Weston was invited to join the band to play co-lead guitar with Bob Welch.

Fleetwood were about to record *Penguin*,[3] and Weston contributed slide guitar on 'Remember Me' and harmonica and banjo on 'The Derelict'. He performed a vocal duo with Christine McVie for 'Did You Ever Love Me', and contributed the album's instrumental closer, 'Caught in the Rain'.

Later that same year, the band recorded another album, *Mystery to Me*, on which Weston again made significant contributions in writing and playing.[4]

All in all, things seemed to be going brilliantly. The new line up was apparently gelling, and live performances, which now featured the vocals of Christine McVie and Bob Welch, with Weston's bluesy guitar front and centre, were working brilliantly. Weston was very good looking – with his square jaw, perfect

3 This album derived its name from an obsession of John McVie's: 'I used to live near London Zoo, and was an associate member of the Zoological Society . . . I could go in free at any time. Well, I used to photograph animals, and penguins in particular really fascinated me . . . I didn't sit there and talk to them or anything like that, but I used to spend hours watching them and reading books about them.'
4 As with other titans of the sixties and seventies (Beatles, Stones, Bowie), the productivity rate of Fleetwood Mac in this period is astonishing.

wavy hair and piercing eyes, he looked a bit like a seventies-rock Michael Fassbender. At first, these looks presumably seemed an upside. Mick Fleetwood was relieved and happy, and the band embarked on yet another US tour.

And then Mick discovered that Weston was sleeping with his wife.

Jenny Fleetwood had insisted on coming clean to Mick in person, before leaving with the children and heading to LA.[5] For a little while, the group gamely attempted to carry on. But it was never going to work, and after a gig in Lincoln, Nebraska, Fleetwood told the McVies and Welch that Weston would have to go. He was fired unceremoniously the next morning.

'I got a phone call early, about eight,' Weston said. 'I hadn't even had a cup of tea. Next thing, there's a knock at the door and the entire road crew was standing there. They were all looking daggers at me, very menacing, all broken noses and scars . . . It was horrible seeing all those lads with whom I'd worked so happily emanating such a lot of hostility towards me. I think I was a scapegoat. There were all these other affairs going on within the band, but I wasn't good at boxing.'

Once again, Fleetwood Mac seemed on the verge of dissolution. 'I thought the band was on its last legs anyhow,' Weston said. 'John and Christine were saying, "You leave the band and I'll stay; no, you leave and I'll stay." And they were the kingpins of Fleetwood Mac! Christine's affair with Martin [Birch, the producer] was rattling on. It was all in tatters!'

5 Jenny Fleetwood – now Jenny Boyd – is the sister of Pattie Boyd, who was married to George Harrison, then had an affair with and later married Eric Clapton. Both sisters were models in the 1960s. Jenny underwent two four-year bouts of marriage to Mick Fleetwood.

Ultimately, though, sleeping with the bandleader's wife is a sure-fire way to get fired: 'It was the most expensive affair I've ever had in my life,' Weston said. 'Cost me a career, that did!'

Bob Weston was in the band for a little more than one year.[6] Despite the brevity of this spell, it would have far-reaching implications. Disheartened once again at the loss of a member, and suffering under the strain of the affairs, drink and drugs, the rest of the band pulled out of the tour. There would be severe financial penalties for a cancellation, so Clifford Davis and Mick Fleetwood attempted to assemble a 'Bogus Fleetwood Mac' to play the remaining dates. This became an infamous saga in itself, and led to the exit of Bob Welch, and finally Clifford Davis, and to a lengthy legal drama.

But in the main, it eventually meant that Fleetwood Mac found themselves looking for a singer and a guitarist, and thus paved the way for the entrance of Lindsey Buckingham and Stevie Nicks.

4. Billy Burnette – guitar/vocals, 1987–95

It didn't take two guitarists to replace Lindsey.
Fleetwood Mac has had as many as three guitarists,
even four, in its long history. – Stevie Nicks

By 1987, Lindsey Buckingham was ready for a break. He and Stevie Nicks had become a couple in the early seventies, when

6 Weston never had much of a career after Fleetwood. He played with blues veteran Alexis Korner (who thus links Fleetwood to another subject of this book – Brian Jones, Chapter 6) and had an intermittent solo career. In 2012, at the age of sixty-four, he was found dead in his flat in London. The cause was gastrointestinal haemorrhage caused by cirrhosis. Presumably, alcohol played its part. This means that Kirwan, Welch and Weston all died in their sixties.

they began performing as Buckingham Nicks, and had still been one when they joined Fleetwood Mac in 1974. They broke up in 1977, during the maelstrom of sex, drink and drugs that provided the backdrop to *Rumours*. 'I needed to get some separation from Stevie especially, because I don't think I'd ever quite gotten closure on our relationship,' Buckingham said. 'When you break up with someone and then for the next ten years you have to be around them and watch them move away from you, it's not easy.'

Mick Fleetwood called in two replacements: Rick Vito and Billy Burnette.

Burnette had been a professional musician since the age of seven, when he recorded 'Hey Daddy (I'm Gonna Tell Santa on You)' with Ricky Nelson. This early start was in large part due to his father, Dorsey, a rockabilly musician and founder of the Rock 'n Roll Trio.

Billy grew up in Los Angeles, surrounded by famous musicians and, occasionally, infamous cultists: 'I snuck into concerts for years,' he told *Rolling Stone* in 2022. 'I asked Jimi Hendrix how I could get into his concert at the Forum. He goes, "Carry this." And I carried his guitar alongside him and got in.'

He also visited Charles Manson's Spahn Ranch as a teenager – the setting memorably re-created in Quentin Tarantino's *Once Upon a Time in Hollywood*.

'God, that was scary. We had no idea what was happening there. There was nothing in the press about it yet. They put me on a horse and went, "This is Tex Watson's horse."[7] The horse

---

7 Watson led the group of Manson Family members who murdered Sharon Tate, and several others, in 1969.

ran up to the hills and I got all scratched up from the tree branches. I've been scared of horses ever since then.'

In a terrifying foreshadowing of what would happen on the night of Sharon Tate's murder, the Manson Family wrote 'Pig' in the dust on his dad's Lotus Europa, which he'd driven to the ranch. 'They were telling me to get out of the machine and come join their group. The whole thing was just really scary.'

He also met Manson himself, on more than one occasion: 'I used to hitchhike to the beach all the time with my guitar. He picked us up one day and gave us a ride with him from Topanga Beach. Also, my dad knew Terry Melcher' – the producer whom Manson became fixated on, and whose house Sharon Tate and Roman Polanski had fatefully moved into.

By the time Burnette joined Fleetwood Mac, at the age of thirty-four, he had an illustrious career behind him. He'd met Elvis Presley, released solo albums on major labels, toured with Bob Dylan and John Fogarty, and penned songs for Ray Charles, the Everly Brothers, Greg Allman, Jerry Lee Lewis, Loretta Lynn and Ringo Starr.

This being the eighties, he had a voluminous mullet, and with his dark hair and eyes, looked a little like a young Billy Joel. He'd been a huge fan of Fleetwood Mac, imitating Peter Green's guitar licks, hearing Buckingham Nicks through a wall and obsessing over *Rumours* and *Tusk*.

In fact, it was Buckingham who first invited him to play with the band. In the early 1980s, Nicks was focusing on her solo career, and Fleetwood put together a band called the Cholos, and later the Zoo. When Lindsey performed on *Saturday Night Live*, the Zoo were the backing band, and Burnette was invited to join. He became great friends with Lindsey and Mick, working hard and partying all night.

By the time 'things got weird' between Buckingham and Nicks – 'something happened' at a band meeting – Burnette's solo career was just starting to take off. And then Buckingham departed, and Mick asked Billy to join Fleetwood Mac.

'I'd just been nominated for Best New Country Artist. Things were starting to go somewhere.' But he couldn't say no: 'How can you? It was Fleetwood Mac.'

And anyhow, he already felt like 'part of the family'.

He and Vito split the parts up, Burnette singing Buckingham's parts and Vito playing lead. Best of all, Buckingham had given them his blessing. In fact, Burnette felt like an 'equal' member of the band: 'It just felt natural. I sort of became the spokesperson for the band.'

When the band settled down to record 1990's *Behind the Mask*, Burnette contributed several songs. No wonder he felt himself to be a full member of one of his very favourite bands. To Fleetwood Mac's credit, they were unusually generous over the finances too, splitting everything equally between the six current members: 'Concerts and everything, from then on. It was very generous. It was so nice of Stevie. They were all so free with their money. They were a great band to be with.'

By the beginning of the nineties, though, the omens were not auspicious. When the band was asked to play Bill Clinton's presidential inauguration in January 1993, Stevie Nicks asked if Burnette would mind if Buckingham played instead of him.

A brief hiatus was followed by a new line up, featuring Burnette, Dave Mason from Traffic, and Bekka Bramlett, daughter of the duo Delaney & Bonnie and member of the Zoo.

Mick and John were the only original members in this line up, and Mick would later express regret at giving it the Fleetwood Mac name.

This permutation gave its final performance on New Year's Eve in 1995, in Las Vegas. Behind the scenes, a reunion of the 'real' line up was being plotted. Burnette had intuited this, and tried to warn Dave and Bekka, who didn't believe him.

At first, he felt 'used' when the news broke that he was no longer in the band. Worse, Bekka, with whom he was having a relationship, had just committed to buying an expensive house that she'd no longer be able to afford. In later years, though, Burnette has become more philosophical.

'I don't feel like I'm poor little Billy that got treated bad. I made a lot of money with them.'

Despite being upset that he wasn't invited to re-join Fleetwood in 2018 (see below) he's remained friends with Mick, and the pair still record together. He has no regrets, and his time in the band marked the pinnacle of his career. 'It was the biggest ever. God, it's a hard one to top.'

5. Lindsey Buckingham – guitar/vocals, 1975–2018

> *Stevie never wants to be on a stage with you again.*
> – Irving Azoff, Fleetwood Mac's manager

Ouch – this one must have hurt. It seems Mick Fleetwood waited as long as possible before making the call.

It was sheer dumb luck that Mick Fleetwood walked into Sound City Studios in Van Nuys, LA, in late 1974. When he did, he struck gold.

'Mick Fleetwood had happened to bump into a guy called Thomas Christian,' Buckingham recalled, 'in a supermarket somewhere, I think – and they'd got to discussing recording studios, because Fleetwood Mac were looking for a new studio to record their next album. This guy suggested that Mick check out Sound City in Van Nuys.'

A little over ten miles from Hollywood into the fabled San Fernando Valley, Van Nuys is where Brad Pitt's character, Cliff, lives in *Once Upon a Time in Hollywood*. I know from bitter experience that a modern-day drive to the place is not like Cliff's propulsive blast in the film. Now, you're likely to sit in a lot of traffic on the freeway and surface streets, giving you time to observe LA's scruffy, endless spread. This is Los Angeles drained of glamour – a working place of low-rise office blocks, studios and nondescript apartment buildings.

For anyone working in music or film in LA, though, a trip to the San Fernando Valley is just a normal part of life: it's where there's space for the big studios, the industry stuff, the behind-the-scenes world where things get made. Sound City Studios was where Buckingham Nicks had recorded their eponymous album in 1973. Unfortunately, it had 'stiffed out', in Buckingham's words.

Lindsey Buckingham grew up in Palo Alto, thirty miles south of San Francisco and now best known as a key site in Silicon Valley. Initially learning to play guitar along to his older brother's extensive collection of rock 'n' roll 45s, he then 'fell under the spell of folk music in the mid '60s. I was a good folk picker,' he said, 'but I couldn't master a raunchy rock 'n' roll style.'

When he joined his first group, Fritz, he thus played bass as well as singing. The group's primary vocalist was Stevie (Stephanie) Nicks.

The group 'went nowhere fast'. A move to LA failed: 'We couldn't relate to Los Angeles, and Los Angeles couldn't relate to us,' and they split up in 1971. If the band had broken up, Buckingham and Nicks had got together. 'Stevie and I became romantically involved, and we decided to strike out as a duo, calling ourselves Buckingham Nicks.'

A second attempt to move to LA failed once more, but it did provide time to write.

'We were set to move down to LA, but I was ill and was laid up for eight or nine months, during which time Stevie and I sat around working on songs and ideas . . . I got hold of an electric guitar and started to work up my lead playing.'

They finally made it down to LA, and eventually released their album on Polydor. It failed to make an impact, and the pair did session work where they could find it while Nicks waitressed and Buckingham did telesales.

As it turned out, they did have some success in a very specific place: Birmingham, Alabama.[8] 'Of the few gigs we'd done, two were in Birmingham. For some reason, we really caught fire in that town. Some DJs had picked up on the album, and it was a huge success there.'

One day in Van Nuys, Buckingham and Nicks were back at Sound City, working on some demos. Buckingham went out to

8 Birmingham is infamous for the racist bombing of a black church in 1963, in which four young girls were murdered. The city also features in Lynyrd Skynyrd's 'Sweet Home Alabama', in part a riposte to Neil Young's 'Southern Man'. 'In Birmingham they love the governor (boo boo boo!)' goes the Skynyrd lyric. This is a reference to Alabama's segregationist governor George Wallace, elected the same year as the Klan's terror attack on the 16th Street Baptist Church. After agreeing to join Fleetwood Mac, Buckingham Nicks had one final gig, a headline appearance in Birmingham. They played to seven thousand people, thus going out on a huge high.

get coffee, and heard their song 'Frozen Love' 'leaking out from somewhere.' He went to investigate, and 'Mick Fleetwood was standing there, stamping his foot to the rhythm.'

Keith Olsen, Sound City's engineer, had been using the song to show the studio's qualities. A week later, Bob Welch left Fleetwood Mac, and Mick called Olsen to ask if Buckingham might join.

'At the time, we were having a New Year's party at our house, wondering if 1975 would be a better year for us, and Keith walked in and said "hey, I've got some news . . . Fleetwood Mac want you to join them." You could have knocked me down with a feather.'

A great deal of ink has been spilled on the pomp of Fleetwood Mac, and I suspect it might be condescending to you, dear reader, to run through it all again. Suffice to say that the alchemy the band needed had taken place – in more ways than one. Buckingham was the perfect partner for Mick Fleetwood, a musical soulmate of the kind that Danny Whitten once made for Neil Young. This was poured into the mix along with the huge songwriting and performing abilities of each member, and with the deluge of personal problems they had – sex, drink, drugs, break-ups, fall outs, firings and inter-band affairs.

They made two great albums: 1977's *Rumours*, which captured all of the above, and the recording of which became a respite and a release from everything that inspired it; and 1979's *Tusk*, which required years to earn its critical place, an album that could only be made because Mick Fleetwood trusted Lindsey Buckingham to direct it, and a record that formed a precursor to the cool, cocaine minimalism of the early 1980s. Buckingham's very appearance exemplified this transition, from the hirsute, seventies rocker to the very thin, clean-shaven look he adopted around *Tusk*.

But it seems that Buckingham never really got over his break-up with Nicks. He appears to have borne a grudge against her – though not against Mick, with whom she had a liaison in 1977, the same year she and Buckingham broke up. This may speak of the misogyny as inherent in music as it has been in society more widely: 'The guys in the business were "supposed" to do drugs,' Nicks said. 'They were "supposed" to sleep with a different chick every night, that was the romantic idea.' Not so for the women: 'We almost always had boyfriends, but they weren't on the road because they'd just get stomped on. For me to have a guy out on the road with us, and have Lindsey glaring at him the whole time? Or for Christine to have a guy out and John just walk past and flip him off? No, we both learned very early on that we would never bring boyfriends on the road because it created arguments.'

But if the McVies' marriage unravelled with a degree of politeness, Buckingham and Nicks's dissolution was tempestuous: 'John and I used to be civil – "What key is this in? What do you want me to do on this song?"' McVie said. 'But Stevie and Lindsey were fighting all the time. Very volatile. Their relationship still is an ongoing battle.'

And Buckingham's grudge seems to have hardened and soured over the years, as these things do – particularly when you have the ego required to be a performer, and you're rich and powerful enough that it's difficult for anyone to correct you.

Their relationship appears to have been fractious for years. 'Gold Dust Woman', a biography of Nicks by Stephen Davis, contained allegations that Buckingham was abusive towards her.

Nicks apparently told her mother in 1977 that Buckingham had thrown her to the floor. The book also claimed that Buckingham tried to trip and kick her while performing onstage in 1980, and slapped and choked her during a fight in 1987, in front of the band. For his part, Buckingham has remained silent regarding these allegations, or said he can't recall them.

After this, and all the other high dramas, the end when it came was oddly bathetic. It was a smirk that did it. In 2018, Stevie Nicks was awarded the MusiCares Person of the Year Award. She gave an eight-minute speech, during which the rest of the band stood behind her. In the recording, they all appear to goof around, and Christine McVie looks at her watch – possibly a reference to the joke Nicks makes at the outset about talking for too long. Buckingham doesn't seem any more pointed in any of this than the other bandmates.

Around the same time, he'd asked for time off from the band to carry out some solo dates, and the request had apparently not been granted.

In the spring of 2018, he was informed that Nicks was angry with him for 'smirking' during her speech, and that she couldn't go on performing with him. Buckingham assumed she'd leave, but when everything went silent for a few days, he contacted Irving Azoff, the band's manager, and was told he was being fired. Billy Burnette, Buckingham's former stand in, had let the cat out of the bag on Twitter: 'Breaking news: Lindsey Buckingham is out! New line up to be announced soon and I'm not in it????? A little pissed off but I'll get over it.'

The band released a short statement: 'Lindsey Buckingham will not be performing with the band on this tour. The band wishes Lindsey all the best.'

'Ironically,' Buckingham said, 'nothing went down that night that was as contentious as the stuff we'd been through for forty-three years.'

'It was the straw that broke the camel's back,' Nicks said.

She has claimed that the perceived smirk was nothing to do with it, and that Buckingham's request for time away was the reason for his dismissal. She has spoken of dreams in which her dead parents (her father, apparently, liked Buckingham) told her that 'it was time to get divorced from him'.

Buckingham was disappointed that no one stood up for him, and has made clear that he'd like to re-join someday, if Nicks would allow it. But he understood what had happened, because he understands the rules.

Ultimately, Buckingham proves that even a titan of a band – a key creative force – is still subject to the group's internal logic: 'It would be like a scenario where Mick Jagger says, "Either Keith goes or I go,"' he said. 'No, neither one of you can go. But I guess the singer has to stay. The figurehead has to stay.'

Bob Stinson, the Replacements

Come on, fucker. – Paul Westerberg

The Replacements are one of those bands. Beloved by a certain stratum of serious fan, and largely unknown by a more casual audience, they matter almost *because* they never fulfilled their potential.

But without them, there'd be no alternative rock. It was the Replacements coming to Seattle that inspired the formation of Mudhoney and Pearl Jam. Their slanted, classic rock hooks, played with an insouciant punk attitude, can be detected in every band from Pavement (see Chapter 21) to Wolf Alice.

The bulk of US punk and hardcore that formed the proto-alternative scene of the eighties was highly politicised and deliberately abrasive. By contrast, the Replacements' lyricist and singer, Paul Westerberg, sang witty lyrics about thwarted love and dead-end angst. The band wrote great songs and played them in their loose, punk style, almost like a spiky, nihilistic Springsteen. Alongside REM, they created fertile territory for underground bands that the mainstream listener could get into.

So the Replacements have a very special place in their fans' hearts. And their guitarist, Bob Stinson, is another member of that elite group of rejects: he has the dubious honour of having been kicked out of the very band he founded. If each group is like a family, in the Replacements' case they actually *were* family – Stinson's younger half-brother, Tommy, was the bass player. After what was essentially a battle between Bob Stinson and Westerberg, Tommy became the right-hand man to the band's victorious singer. The agony and injustice of all this must have been close to unbearable.

In images of the Replacements from their early to mid-1980s heyday, Bob Stinson looks like the tough, troubled Minneapolis bad boy that he was. He's a little taller and heavier set than the rest of the band – who all had a skinny, post-punk look – and in the early pictures he's got the physical presence of someone who looks like they can fight. He had a large head, fine blondish hair that receded early, and there's frequently a dopey, mischievous expression on his face. His eyes – heavy-lidded and a little downturned – often appear slightly glazed. Later images show him looking pale and pained. We have no idea what he looked like in middle life, let alone old age, because he was dead at thirty-five.

As is so often the case, Stinson's eventual destruction was encoded in the band's DNA. Raised in part by an alcoholic[1] mother, he spent many years in the juvenile care system, where he learned 'to drink, get good drugs, and play guitar'. Back at home aged nineteen with his mother and a twelve-year-old Tommy, his half-brother seemed to be heading the same way he

1 In 1993, a long article on Stinson in *SPIN* claimed that his mother was an 'alcoholic throughout his childhood', but had got sober around 1986. According to *SPIN*, Bob's father, with whom he had no contact from the age of two, was an alcoholic too.

had. 'He was throwing stones through gas station windows and shit like that, and my mom said, "something's got to be done."'

Bob decided to start a band to keep him out of trouble.

The group was called Dogbreath, and its drummer was Bob's fellow high-school dropout, Chris Mars. Westerberg in turn was acquainted with Mars but had no idea he was a drummer. He had accidentally overheard Dogbreath, though, jamming in the Stinsons' basement on his way home. He liked the sound so much that he began hiding in the bushes outside to listen. After being introduced through Mars and deploying a little persuasion (Westerberg lied to the band's preceding vocalist that the other members hated him), he became the group's vocalist, contributing what the writer Michael Azerrad called his 'raw-throated adolescent howl'. He also introduced the other members to punk.

Initially, like fellow Minneapolis punks Hüsker Dü, the Replacements played fast, hardcore style, but replacing the politics with tales of youthful misadventure. Classic rock was in their bloodstream, though, and they quickly began welding riffs and choruses to a punk contrariness. This sound and attitude would define them: they were against playing the game, against the 'industry' and its manifestations, such as music videos. They showed all of this by getting wasted a lot.

From the outset, the band was formed around an archetypal rock 'n' roll conflict – that between lead guitarist and vocalist. Stinson believed in getting loose and not giving a fuck. Westerberg, no saint himself when it came to intoxicants, was torn between ambition and punk integrity. As with other bands, this began as a fruitful creative tension and ended as a battle that broke the project apart. Westerberg won the power struggle, but after the albums *Let It Be* and *Tim* in 1984–5, the Replacements' best days were behind them.

But the battleground itself was image versus reality. For Stinson, getting wasted was core to the band's credo. For Westerberg, increasingly, it was just a style the Replacements used to distinguish themselves. *Actually* not giving a fuck was hampering their success. Speaking to *Musician* magazine in 1989, Westerberg said 'Bob believed the image we played with onstage. He thought that was the Replacements. He didn't understand, "Oh, we gotta play some music, too. We gotta do something."'

Westerberg might not have wanted to make music videos, but he was certainly ambitious. You can hear it in the piano ballads he wrote, such as 'Androgynous'. Here, the howling vocal isn't of existential abandon – it's the sound of Westerberg showing his chops. By the time they'd got to their last album as the original unit, *Tim*, and the song 'Swingin Party', Westerberg's lyrics had the iconic, anthemic feel of mainstream rock. He sings of solidarity with those who feel afraid, of how the fearful – him included – will 'hang side by side' at the final 'swingin party'.

Things came to a head on an infamous appearance on *Saturday Night Live*. In the era following John Belushi's louche regime, the show had cleaned itself up. No booze in the dressing rooms, strict prohibitions over swearing. The Replacements broke both these rules. They smuggled in alcohol and drugs, and steadily consumed them. As ever, Stinson, a burgeoning addict, went further. He was 'getting high in the bathroom' when costume changes were suddenly decided on, and appears clearly intoxicated during the performance.

When the band play their single, 'Bastards of Young', Stinson charges around drunkenly in a strange outfit of matching bell-bottomed trousers and skimpy waistcoat in lurid blue and pink stripes. (Stinson claimed that 'Lori, ah, Mrs Westerberg' – Lori Bizer, who married Westerberg in 1987 – gave him the outfit.) He fluffs his solo, at which point Westerberg steps back from the mic and says: 'Come on, fucker.' He hadn't moved back far enough – the words were clearly discernible to the live TV audience. Whether it was in anger or encouragement is a matter of debate. Either way, Stinson was not long for the band. *Saturday Night Live* executive Lorne Michaels was furious and banned the Replacements from the programme.

The end, when it came, was toxic. In that shocking and upsetting *SPIN* article – published the year before he died – Stinson was interviewed extensively. Those closest to him (if 'close' is an apt term for an estranged wife) made a defence of him, but the only other band member to speak to the reporter was Mars. Westerberg and Tommy Stinson refused.

Stinson's wife, Carleen, and Mars both suggest that the band had been told to clean up its act if its members wanted to be successful, and that Stinson was simply the scapegoat. Worse, Carleen claims that Stinson was deliberately knocked off track from a brief spell of sobriety, after completing a court-ordered rehab programme. He'd been sober for three weeks when the band played a series of gigs at the Entry in Minneapolis. Before one of them, Westerberg allegedly took a bottle of champagne over to Stinson and said: 'Either take a drink, motherfucker, or get off my stage.' Stinson began drinking again, and never stopped. 'Bob felt that no one liked him unless he was drunk,' Carleen told *SPIN*.

A few weeks later, still in Carleen's telling, a (drunk) Westerberg called Stinson and explained that he'd been 'getting lectured by record executives in New York who were fed up with Bob's behaviour. "I don't think I can play with you anymore," Westerberg finally blurted. Bob murmured okay and hung up.'

'It was never the same after he left,' Mars told *SPIN*. 'I remember in Detroit, somebody got together like 1000 cardboard cut-outs of Bob's face for the show and passed them around for everyone to put on. It's like they were protesting. They wanted Bob back.'

The Replacements are one of those bands in which the singer's lyrics could be about the guitarist. On 'Here Comes a Regular', for example, Westerberg sings of a hard-drinking barfly. The lyrics had to be sympathetic in order to work in the songs, so Westerberg must have understood Stinson, must have empathised with him too.

The Replacements' core aesthetic was about being beat, broken – second best, as their name implies. They set the template for the romanticised loser that would become the nineties alternative archetype. They had lived it, and their fans believed in it and were drawn to them because of it. On some level, Westerberg believed in it too. But without the embodiment of this pathos that Stinson supplied, without his authenticity, the band was never the same again.

In a *New Yorker* review of Bob Mehr's *Trouble Boys: The True Story of the Replacements*, David Cantwell says that it's 'Bob who emerges as [the band's] heart and soul'. He carried on working as a cook during his years in the band, and never quite got over listening to Yes. He was eventually diagnosed as bipolar, and *Trouble Boys* claimed he'd been physically and sexually abused by a boyfriend of his mother.

I think Westerberg's behaviour is interesting and contains clues to what he wanted from the outset. He hid in the bushes to listen to a band Stinson started to try and help his half-brother. He lied to the band's singer to get him to leave, and the trajectory of his writing is clearly in the direction of popular success. The Replacements' final album, *All Shook Down,* in 1991 is essentially Westerberg's first solo album. He really wanted it, but he never truly got it – not even after firing Stinson. The band had lost its heart.

But in the heat and madness of touring and TV appearances and drink and drugs, perhaps no one is finally to blame. Mehr's book opens with Stinson's funeral. 'We were just kids,' Westerberg whispers to Carleen. 'We didn't know shit.'

After he'd been fired, Stinson worked as a cook and janitor and played in various part-time bands around Minneapolis, his drinking and drug abuse worsening. He had a disabled son, with Carleen, to whom he had no access. He was found in his apartment, dead from organ failure, in 1995.

Interlude:

Big Bands and Arch Enemies, Inspiration and Original Sin

In 1990, at the age of ten, I received some terrible news. I was walking down a hilly street in the suburb of Leeds in which I grew up, accompanied by my best friend Andy. Andy was a couple of years older and my mentor in music – happily we're still friends today. It was Andy who'd introduced me to Aerosmith, Bon Jovi, Def Leppard, Skid Row and the heavier stuff he liked but I wasn't sure I did – Metallica, Megadeth, those two unholy Ms – and Sepultura, Pantera and a band of apparent Satanists called Deicide. But any such differences fell by the wayside in the face of our shared love of Guns N' Roses. They were the best: the wildest, the toughest and tenderest, hardest, ugliest and most beautiful band in the world. They transcended genres and united rock's tribes, from thrash to hair metallers and from hard to classic rockers – anyone who loved a great song. Quite simply, they were the greatest band out there.

And that day, walking down the hill on that suburban street, probably coming back from the video rental place on the short parade of shops where we'd go to borrow 15-certificate horrors, or hardboiled films featuring Arnie or Sly, Andy told me that Steven Adler had been kicked out of the band (see Chapter 10).

I found it difficult to believe. Adler, the drummer, was one of the cornerstones of Guns N' Roses. His shaggy blond mane was atop one of the five skulls on the cross that formed the cover of *Appetite for Destruction*, their masterpiece of a debut album. He was thus immortalised, fixed – the same cross was even tattooed on vocalist and band leader Axl Rose's arm. How could he just be gone? He *couldn't* just be gone, surely? And why?

'He's a druggie,' Andy said, rather sternly. He's never been very keen on drugs or the people that take them.

In my optimism, I was sure it could only be temporary, the sort of falling out we might have in the playground and could last at most a few days. Surely they'd make friends and Steve would soon be back in the band? Perhaps I also felt some first, inarticulate stirring of my own defects as Andy told me about immoderate Steve Adler being erased from the picture.

Andy didn't seem bothered, and I seem to remember he didn't rate Adler as a drummer anyway. Years later, I like to think it became clear that Andy was wrong in this. GNR's rhythm guitarist, Izzy Stradlin – himself once partial to a gargantuan intake of hard drugs – said that the band was never the same after they lost Adler's swing. I think he's right – just listen to the demented third act of 'Paradise City', a piece of music deploying the funk that's a key if underrated weapon in the GNR arsenal, with Slash darting around Adler's drums to produce a fluidly percussive solo. Swing is the magic, infectious ingredient that grips the ear and moves the body. You either got it or you ain't, and GNR had it, at least at first.

Andy went on to be a very talented musician who formed several bands but never quite made it. Over the years I'd go and watch him play, and gradually I watched him give up on the bands and produce music by himself at home. I tried to make music, too, in my youth and again in my early twenties. I knew quite clearly that I didn't have talent, but I also knew I loved music and wanted to be involved. Some dumb, lucky instinct led me to decide, early on, that I should thus try to help the people who could play music. That in turn led me to a career in the music industry.

'I'd give my right arm to be down in London, working for a record label,' Andy told me one day early in my career, via email. He'd stayed in Leeds, working jobs he didn't like to fund his bands. Like any job, I was realising even back then, working for a label is not always all it's cracked up to be. But the good days usually feature interesting characters – and the music industry has a surfeit of those.

If the rejection of Steven Adler is the original sin, then the story of Jason Everman (see Chapter 12) of Nirvana's second act is the inspiration. These two bands have been central to my own musical life, and in some ways they're the lodestars for this book.

There are people out there who think the two *Use Your Illusion* albums, released simultaneously in 1991, represent GNR's best work, but for me their star was waning by the early nineties. The band was too bloated, inflated by success but poisoned by ego and addiction. I remember sitting on a wall in that same Leeds suburb, describing to Andy a sound I'd been imagining, something I thought must be out there somewhere and desperately wanted to hear. It was thrashy, heavy and hard but it wasn't macho or metal.

'Faith No More?' Andy tried. Good, but not quite right. More a mix of metal, funk and pop. Then one day, watching

Top of the Pops together, the video for a song called 'Smells Like Teen Spirit' came on. I was transfixed. 'That's it!' I told him. 'That's what I was looking for.' It was raw, pure, poppy, perfect. I fell deeply in love with Nirvana and never really fell out of it again. Because of that band and their origins on an indie record company, I fell in love too with the idea of these labels.

I was growing up. I didn't like that Axl Rose had been in the news for attacking a girlfriend. I didn't like it when he called Courtney Love 'bitch' backstage at the MTV Awards. I liked that Kurt Cobain represented the bullied kids, the sensitive people. He hated homophobia and macho behaviour and 'jocks', and this spoke to me – I was unpopular at school, and our equivalent, the rugby lads, made my life a misery. I loved Kurt's thrift-store cardigans, scuffed Chuck Taylors and Fender Jaguar; I loved his home-cut hair and handmade T-shirts; I loved lanky Krist Novoselic on bass and hard-hitting Dave Grohl on drums. I loved the anger and hurt and seriousness without pretension, the beautiful catchy hooks that shone out of the swathes of feedback and snarling guitars.

I fell for Kurt's vision of life: the mainstream is full of hypocrites and bigots, and Guns N' Roses epitomise this in music. I loved the photo of Kurt standing before a disused Los Angeles cinema where the artist Jenny Holzer had taken over the signage with one of her slogans: MEN DON'T PROTECT YOU ANYMORE.

It all spoke to me very deeply. I too was from a northern, regional city. I too disliked the macho behaviour of the popular kids at school, with their relentless gay slurs and ugly talk about girls.

I burned my GNR CDs and didn't look back for about ten years.

By then, of course, I'd grown up properly. Enough to see this childish fanaticism for what it was, and to understand that Guns N' Roses and Nirvana were simply the two best bands of their generations. The transcendent artists of respective musical scenes that, like any others, couldn't last for ever. It was natural for them to hate each other: one was old, the other was new – in the brief window in which they crossed over and this mattered.[1]

---

1 Not that this diminishes what Nirvana stood for, of course, or excuses the bigotry that Axl repented of, but to which Izzy is apparently still subject.

10

Steven Adler, Guns N' Roses

I'm tired of too many people in this organization dancing
with Mr Goddamn Brownstone . . . – Axl Rose

One day in summer 2016, I found myself standing in what would once have been the mosh pit at a Guns N' Roses concert. The show was at Dodger Stadium in Los Angeles, and thus a homecoming. The tour was entitled *Not in This Lifetime*, and the industry was still reeling from the idea that Axl Rose had finally come around to the reunion. The area a friend and I were standing in was now a sort of corporate compound for ultra-VIPs and people who could afford tens of thousands of dollars for a ticket. A little way ahead of me stood Charlie Sheen, smoking a large joint. Behind us was a tall, haughty man in a plunging V-neck T-shirt and baseball cap who would shortly tell us off for dancing. I was ecstatic – standing maybe thirty feet from Axl, Slash and Duff – no longer needing to watch them on the big screens.

I should explain that this is not the typical level of access for me. My jobs in the music business have given me a lot of privilege, but it hasn't often extended to exclusive areas at shows of this scale. Rather, I'd bought regular person tickets for myself and a friend, and he, being the sort of magical, irresponsible, often frustrating character who thinks things could always be a little bit more fun, had led us on a bid to illicitly access the 'mosh pit'. During a song we didn't know from *Chinese Democracy*, we'd taken a break from our average, distant seats to go to the bar. There, ordering shots of tequila and pints of IPA, we'd met two friendly older women, consumed more shots, and discovered they were in the standing area closer to the front of the stage. My friend – a charming, boyish Australian with the energy of Tigger – accepted their invitation to try and get us in.

In my Englishness, I was reluctant to say the least. What about our seats? What if someone came and took them? What about the *rules*?

We reached the outer ring of security. My friend flounced through with the two women, and a large security guard placed a hand on my chest and shook his head. 'Nuh-uh,' he said. Inspired by witnessing a man bypass a nightclub queue a few weeks earlier, an idea struck me. I pulled twenty bucks out of my jeans pocket and offered it. The guard said, 'Hmm-mmm, okaaaay,' shifted his eyes right and left, placed the note into his own pocket and let me go through. *Wow*, I thought.

For five minutes we danced and yelled with the band on top form and the lofty, skinny palms rearing up above the stadium's edges into the mild, glowing LA night. Then my friend decided things could be better still. 'Let's go to the mosh pit!' he said.

We repeated the ritual of my reluctance being overwhelmed by a tsunami of drunken, positive energy and tried the trick again. Once more, my friend and the women managed to slip through the cordon with smiles and flashed tickets. Once more I was stopped, this time by a more professional-looking guard.

Forlornly, I tried the twenty bucks trick again. He shook his head in shame and dismay. 'Are you crazy?' he said.

Just then, the women came back. In a whirlwind of persuasion, begging, smiles and unsolicited physical contact, they found the harassed, overworked guard's weak spot: he wanted rid of us all, and the quickest way to achieve this was to give us what we wanted.

And that's how we ended up in the twenty-first century's idea of a mosh pit – cynical, money driven, a high-value 'experience' in which a gym-fit man in a plunging V-neck T-shirt tells you off for dancing. (After the second telling off, my friend flicked the man's baseball hat off, revealing the advanced, male-pattern baldness he presumably wanted to hide.) But never mind, because we were standing directly before Guns N' Roses. And then Steve Adler was brought out to play drums, and I felt a surge of the sort of pure, innocent joy that's largely lost with one's youth.

If this was my own little rock 'n' roll story, it pales into insignificance compared to that of Steven Adler. I'll pause here to admit that I was nervous to come to him. As I said previously, Guns N' Roses are a lodestar for this book, and Adler is the reject's emblem for our purposes. I didn't actually know a great deal about him, though, and quite a lot depended on him.

In the pictures of Adler I remembered from my childhood, he was always fresh faced and smiling, a great big beam that lit out from within the shaggy blond hair and among the moody, unabashed pouts of the rest of the band. That smile seemed to make the tragedy that befell him worse, as if it was his boyishness that had somehow made him ill-prepared to resist the pitfalls.

I'd seen clips of Adler over the years as I'd idly clicked through YouTube videos: sitting backstage in the early days, grinning, bashing a single drum and wearing a hat with beer holders and a straw. One from years later of him on some dreadful celebrity rehab TV series. I'd noted that his drug use had resulted in his speaking with a bad, permanent slur, and for some reason this put the fear of God into me.

I knew little more than the headlines about him – the sacking, the drugs, the terrible descent into addiction. I'd heard the notorious story about the sex noises on 'Rocket Queen'. That Axl, annoyed with Adler, had brought a woman the drummer was seeing into the vocal booth and had loud sex with her, the resultant sounds becoming a prominent feature of the song. Adler, according to both his and Slash's books, was the only member of Guns N' Roses willing to confront Axl over his increasingly problematic and egotistical behaviour. This, too, appears related to his essential boyishness – he didn't have the social skills to realise that it spelled his doom. Perhaps, more generously, it also implies a degree of spine that the others lacked.

I assumed the ending of the story might be relatively happy. If he was able to perform with the re-formed GNR, even for a song, I guessed that meant he was now clean. I'd heard rumours of strict controls being in place backstage, in 2016. Of smartly timed arrivals in separate black SUVs with police motorcycle escorts. Surely Adler in his chaotic form would not be allowed within a mile of this next-generation backstage?

But more than anything, I was nervous to get to Adler because, in only knowing the headlines, I didn't really know if he was any good. I worried that a key inspiration for this book was just a minor figure, a piece of eighties Sunset Strip flotsam – or worse, something that did need excising by a band on their way to greatness.

If this was the case, it would undermine one of the central underlying suspicions I'd had when setting out on *The Rejects*: that bands are best when they're together in their original form. That every kicking out is a tragedy, if sometimes a necessary one.

Adler's rejection was the original sin that formed the way I looked at things. If Guns were best without him, then perhaps the entire project of examining the rejects was diminished. I feared that his story would prove that the cold professionalism I've come to so dislike was in fact the only route to greatness.

So it was with some trepidation that I began my research with Adler's autobiography. The spirits had seemed to align: on my wife's insistence, we'd taken a family holiday back to LA. Having left the city for the dull safety of the Home Counties of England a year earlier, she now missed it terribly, and I did so more than I cared to admit. Sitting in the baking SoCal sunshine by some friends' pool in Ojai – the fortunes of these friends doing little to soothe our regret – it felt right to engage with Adler properly.

The opening of the book was not reassuring. I hesitate to say this, but Steven Adler does at times come off as a younger and slightly more likeable Donald Trump. The whiff of the unreconstructed 1980s has not been scoured from him by his brutal years as a drug addict. Early in the book, he tells his readers, 'I love the ladies. Primo poon: accept no substitutes.' He seems to select a wife based on the fact that her buttocks were no wider than his palm. Happily, she turns out to be one of the better people in his life, until she is necessarily forced to leave him.

There's an alarming passage that made me realise that the Trump comparison would have to be made. It comes after Adler recalls an episode from when he was eleven years old. He and his two friends, Ricardo and Jackie, had already become heavy weed smokers. One day while high, the conversation turns to their futures. His two friends want to be a mechanic and a builder. Adler, picturing Steve Tyler of Aerosmith singing 'Dream On', says: 'Well, I'm gonna be a rock star!'

Here, he pauses the narrative to tell the reader a secret. 'Whether you want to be a rock star, play in the Super Bowl or go to Harvard, you just got to say it out loud and believe it. That's it. But you got to have 100% unwavering faith in what you're saying. I did it, the guy who's helping me write this book did it. Believe it and you will be it.'

This philosophy, in which all you have to do is believe it and it comes true, and from which springs the idea that reality is simply what you say it is, is rumoured to be Trump's too. The power of positive thinking, and all that. Sinisterly simplistic, both childlike and childish – a plastic Florida realtor's take on the American dream – this view is endemic in a certain strata of Los Angeles life.

The writer David Foster Wallace referred to the city's 'odd ambient blend of New Age gooeyness and right-wing financial acumen'. I wouldn't describe Adler as having any sort of financial acumen, but he strongly reminds me of the human products of this ambience. They are like children stuck in adult bodies, with all the potential for havoc and darkness that implies. I met a wannabe rock star in my LA years who told me, wide-eyed with a type of fanaticism, that 'the gold is right there at our feet, and all we have to do is lean down to pick it up!'

Indeed, before we reassure ourselves that this idea is confined to the Trumps of the world, we should bear in mind its other guises; Gen Z Instagram 'manifesters' and militant identitarians, for example, for whom reality is at best a hindrance and at worst an enemy.

Like so much Los Angeles culture, this idea has sprouted widely into the West at large. Adler's philosophy lives on. And in his case, at least, who's to say he wasn't right?

In LA, I often encountered people who seemed to be doing an impression of being grown up but were just waiting to find someone they could be naughty with – to play with among the adult toys of drugs and drink. At one stage in his book, Adler describes almost getting a deal in place for a post-GNR outfit formed with members of a band called Vain. After a successful showcase for three execs from a major label, he's asked by one about his drug habit.

'Without blinking an eye, I reassured her: "That's behind me. I'm clean."' He suggests that the band and executives go 'back to my house, where we could relax more comfortably and sign off on the details of our deal'. This line struck me, because it's the sort of unconsciously sleazy thing you hear from this LA type all the time. As the band and execs arrive at Adler's Studio City home (in the infamous 'valley' of vapid, heat-dumbed California cliché), a strung-out woman in a beaten-up car arrives to deliver some smack in a cigarette packet. He claims to have been furious – though he presumably made the arrangement. Either way, the deal is off, the execs go home and the project, like everything else in Adler's life, falls to pieces.

You suspect that, even had the dealer not shown up, Adler would have invited the execs in and given them more to drink. Before long, out of sheer enthusiasm, he'd have suggested they enjoy a small pipe of primo-grade crack together. After that, he'd have bounded out on to the driveway to beamingly wave the hurriedly departing execs off, before turning to his band-mates for a kick-ass high five, everything having gone so well.

'Really, emotionally Steven wasn't much older than a third grader, a sixth grader tops,' Slash says in his own autobiography. (I got more of the answers I was looking for there – but, as Slash himself likes to say, we'll get to that.)

I'd always been fascinated by the sheer levels of self-destructive, unrestrained behaviour of Adler's generation of hard rockers. Guns N' Roses seemed some sort of nadir of this: Slash shooting speedballs and getting into gunfights with imaginary beings; Duff loading an alcoholic drink with ice to put on his night-stand, so that it would be chilled when he began drinking on waking the following morning; Izzy taking so many sleeping pills while flying that he had to be carried unconscious through an airport. The treating cocaine like others might coffee. The endless unprotected sex with groupies and ensuing visits to STD clinics.

All of this is the well-documented behaviour of rock stars, but the sheer amount of it in the 1980s always struck me as remarkable. In part, I just couldn't understand why these artists thought it was going to be OK, behaving like this. Did they not realise the huge cost they'd soon be facing? Slash had a pace-maker fitted at age thirty-five. Duff McKagan's pancreas almost exploded when he was thirty. Adler, of course, was the worst of the bunch: a man who found himself wandering barefoot in the streets, begging for money, not knowing who he was, covered in foul pustules before waking up in hospital having had a stroke. For all the wildness of the sixties and seventies, there was nothing quite so extreme. What made them like this?

A few months before I read Adler's book, I'd held my nose and read *The Dirt*, the book about Mötley Crüe by Neil Strauss. The friend I'd seen Guns with at Dodger Stadium had tirelessly recommended it. But I hated Mötley Crüe. They might have been a progenitor of Guns N' Roses, but they were a progenitor of its bad bits. I had heard very little of their music outside 'Girls, Girls, Girls' and 'Kickstart My Heart', and I never wanted to hear any more. Further to this, Neil Strauss is also the author of *The Game*, the notorious book that proposes to teach men how to sleep with women by 'negging' them. A book-length treatise on 'treat 'em mean to keep 'em keen', and something of which several unpleasant men I met in the 2000s were disciples. This, too, might have been a progenitor of something, but if so it's the Incel movement.

'It's just a really good book,' the friend said. 'And he's a really good writer.'

Annoyingly, he was right. *The Dirt* documents the sleaze and madness of 1980s LA hard rock in a way that's undeniably compelling. There's a lot of group sex, violence, heroin, coke, death in car crashes, unhinged drinking, guitar necks up girls' bottoms, overdoses, egotism and chaos. Nikki Sixx, the group's architect, overdoses on heroin and is hospitalised, only to wake up, tear the IV out and discharge himself to go home and do more smack. Not so incidentally, he's saved from this OD by Steven Adler.

The relevance here is that these bands were formed of a certain type of person from a certain type of background. With the exception of Slash's bohemian roots, they were people from the troubled, white American working class; poorly educated, from broken homes. Very much 'white trash' in the American vernacular. From a very young age – pre-teens in some cases – these kids were given shocking levels of freedom, even by the lax standards of the 1970s. They skipped school, fought, took drugs and had sex. They hung out in abandoned houses and with people they shouldn't have.

I don't mean to tell a sob story on their behalf, merely to suggest that this sort of background left them ill-prepared to resist the temptations of rock 'n' roll excess. In fact, it was the very excess of their heroes – bands from the Stones to Aerosmith – that they wanted to emulate in their own, immature way. In the end, they far exceeded all of it. All except perhaps Axl, who it appears is or was too much of a control freak to ever descend into a drug hell.

The key elements of Adler's biography are as follows. He was born in Cleveland in 1965 to an Italian-American father and Jewish mother, Deanna. His father was a violent gambling addict and 'wannabe gangster' who beat his mother in front of Steven and his older brother. Eventually Deanna left him and, influenced by the enthusiasm of her older sister, took her children to California. There they lived the hardscrabble existence of a single mother with two kids in a small apartment in the San Fernando Valley – Adler is very much a valley boy at heart.

Steven had a strong bond with his maternal grandmother, a Jewish matriarch who eventually came out to California with his grandfather and lived in Hollywood. Adler would live with them from time to time after his bad behaviour got him kicked out of his mother's home at age eleven. Deanna had remarried to a man Adler portrays as decent and straightlaced, and whose surname he still bears. He gained a beloved half-brother, Jamie, when the couple had a son of their own.

Steven appears to have an alarmingly potent love/hate relationship with his mother. Early in the book he tells us, 'I continue to harbor a hatred for her that is out of all proportion with reason. Yet I've never . . . loved anyone so deeply.' Later, he pauses the narrative – when describing one of the many times she joined an effort to save him – to say 'right now I *hate* the fucking bitch. I am furious with the way she's treated me.' Nevertheless, she comes across as loving him deeply enough to try everything to help him. In one vivid episode, she tries to drive him from Vegas to a rehab in LA, begging him to put out the crack pipe he keeps pretending not to be smoking while leaning around the seat, getting dizzy and ill herself from the fumes.

In California, Adler skipped school, skateboarded, smoked pot and drank. He had sex aged eleven, and throughout his and Slash's books, episodes are related in which he slept with women as old as thirty when he was in his early teens. He met Slash when the future guitarist asked him if he was OK after a skateboarding accident. The two became best friends, and it was Adler that gave Slash a guitar for the first time, and whose dream it was to start a rock band. 'I owe it all to Steven Adler,' Slash writes. 'He did it. He is the reason that I play guitar.'

The pair began to listen to music together – Aerosmith and the Stones loom large – and explore the Sunset Strip in the age of hair metal. They came to hate the bands that defined this era – Poison being the archetype – sowing the seeds for what Guns N' Roses would set themselves against. They snuck into clubs, memorably pulling back a curtain to see a tall, pale, stick-thin Nikki Sixx with a matching black and white outfit and bass guitar.

Adler seems to have been able to sleep with women almost at will, and never lacks girlfriends. One of them drives him to a house on Laurel Canyon belonging to Bob Welch, sometime member of Fleetwood Mac (see Chapter 8). He isn't there, because he's been hospitalised after OD'ing on smack, but his houseguest invites them in and offers Adler crack for the first time. Adler is instantly spellbound, in the way a different kid might become hooked on a videogame, telling his protesting girlfriend: 'Look, I'm having fun. If you wanna go, go.' He never saw the girlfriend again.

Later, the houseguest shows him the dark, sticky rock of heroin (Mr Brownstone) that had sent Welch to the hospital. They smoke some together, but Adler just vomits and claims not to enjoy it. By this stage he's met Izzy Stradlin, who comes to the studio to collect the heroin when he hears about it and instantly leaves when he has.

Izzy, Slash, Steven, Axl and Duff meet, begin to dance in and out of each other's lives, have several false starts on the way to forming a band.

In a striking, brief interlude, Adler refers to multiple instances of being sexually assaulted by men in these years. The managers of a club that he and Slash attended gave Adler Quaaludes and 'had their way' with him. 'I just wanted to hang out,' he says, but

'I ended up doing a lot of things I didn't understand or really have any control over.'

He's lured into cars and homes with the promise of drugs, where he says men touched him 'all over . . . All you know is an orgasm feels good. I was used, abused, whatever. Let's get high. Let's party.' Two 'clean cut' guys lure him into an apartment, where another man in his forties, a 'completely scruffy looking loser', locks the door behind him. 'I'll spare you the ugly details,' Adler writes, 'but they hurt me pretty badly. Part of my mind just kind of shut down. They didn't beat me up, but they did everything else.'

He gives very little time and import to these incidents, though the implication is he was assaulted and even raped multiple times. Adler's book was written in 2009, and I wonder if in the age contemporary to my own writing, these incidents might rightly have been given more significance.

Even before Guns formed, Slash found Adler frustrating. 'He never kept up the dedicated work ethic that Duff and I shared; though he maintained twice the social schedule,' Slash writes. Worryingly for my own purposes, Slash initially seems sceptical of Adler's drumming, though he was obviously willing to go along with it.

By 1985, Guns N' Roses had taken form. They lived in a rehearsal-cum-storage unit, the legendary Hell House in which nightly debauchery took place. Crowds of hangers on would gather. Smack, crack and coke would be consumed alongside huge quantities of alcohol. There was a lot of sex, including the occasion that led to Izzy, sharing a woman with Slash, ejaculating on to the lead guitarist's leg. 'That definitely stopped me in my tracks,' Slash writes. 'I said, "Hey! Izzy . . . man. We've *got* to get a bigger place."'

These are the brief, inspired, incendiary years that produced *Appetite for Destruction*. Interestingly, Slash and Adler seem to concur on almost everything, including most of what went into Adler's eventual sacking. The band worked hard and practised every day. They won fans quickly, and importantly won enemies too. Enemies and hatred are often good signs that a band, or in fact any kind of artist, are doing something right – that they're striking enough to inspire passion on either side.

In his telling, Slash's descriptions of Adler's drumming become warmer: 'Steven would watch my left foot to determine the tempo, and he'd look to Duff to cue every drum and bass fill. Those two had a really cohesive relationship – they would communicate the changes and subtleties of every single song through eye contact.'

One incident in particular stands out from this time, relating to the band's writing splits and the publishing royalties that depended on them. In Adler's version, Axl had a tantrum over them, and claimed he should get more than his bandmates. Eager to keep the peace, Adler volunteered to take 5 per cent less than an even split, expecting the other bandmates to follow suit. He was met instead with stony faces and blunt acceptance. The deal worked out at 15 per cent for Adler, 25 for Axl and 20 each for Izzy, Slash and Duff.

Slash recalls the incident differently, claiming that Axl was specifically focused on reducing Adler's royalties. He quotes Rose as saying, 'There's no *way* Steven gets twenty percent, the same as I do. I want twenty-five percent and Steven gets fifteen. He's a drummer. He doesn't contribute the same as the rest of us.'

Either way, this seems to have been the cause of Adler's soon to be burgeoning fear that the band didn't think he was a good enough player. 'I think Steven was permanently scarred by that,' Slash writes.

For a while, though, they were the tightest of units. Adler describes how hard they worked on *Appetite*, how the death of a friend of Slash's from a heroin overdose drove them to make the best record they could. *Appetite* was released in 1987, and for almost a year, no one cared. Success was not overnight, but hard won through touring and a lucky break with 'Sweet Child o' Mine' being added for rotation on MTV.

In 1988 the band supported their heroes, Aerosmith, who had recently spent something in the region of a million dollars getting clean. Guns N' Roses were issued strict instructions – no drugs around Steven Tyler, Joe Perry and co, and all alcoholic drinks in unmarked cups.

Tyler's one remaining vice appears to have been sex. One evening, he deploys the ever puppy-ish Adler in an orchestrated group-sex session on the tour bus.

'Now you three, suck his dick,' Tyler says. 'You, sit on his face while he eats your pussy. You two, make out.'

During these years, Adler says he always made a point to smile on stage and in pictures and videos. Before he'd joined GNR, he'd admired the obvious enthusiasm of Mötley Crüe's Tommy Lee. 'He was always beaming. I got chills. That was gonna be me. I couldn't stand musicians who looked so serious up on the stage. Like they were constipated. Playing music is a pleasure and a privilege.'

The breakthrough takes place. A *Rolling Stone* writer, dispatched to cover Aerosmith, is called by his editor to tell him that GNR are now the main story. They support the Rolling Stones. They travel around the world. In Germany, Adler reflects about the Holocaust and his grandmother in a profound mode that doesn't quite suit him: 'As we were crossing the English Channel, all I could think about was World War II and the invasion that was staged from those frigid waters. Because of their sacrifice, I could play my music in a free world.'

He does the same thing later, shooting the video for 'Patience' in LA's Ambassador Hotel and standing on the spot where Bobby Kennedy was assassinated. 'I was smoking weed in the kitchen, tripping out on the tragedy that happened within these very walls. I had the same feeling of loss and doom when I was in Germany.'

After the rise, the fall. Adler breaks a hand punching a bar door when a tour with Alice Cooper goes on hiatus. He takes more and more heroin and cocaine and begins to worry: 'Now . . . maybe it was the recurring shitty self-esteem, but I began to harbor this growing dread that Duff and Slash didn't think I could play the drums that well . . . I could tell they didn't think I was a good drummer, and I started to think they didn't think I was so cool either.'

'Steven could get very emotional at the drop of a hat, and his way of showing it was complete and utter defiance,' Slash says.

A post-tour spell in tiny apartments in Hermosa Beach began Adler's terminal downward spiral, according to the lead guitarist. 'He was doing shit tons of blow and always had one girl or another keeping him company.'

The band is at a pinnacle, but Adler is already in descent.

By 1990, Guns N' Roses were huge. They had a debut album and a follow up of B-sides and live songs that had both gone platinum. But after the tours were over, the rot set in. Axl's ego was already ballooning, and communication between the members had been damaged by drugs, distance and differing approaches. Music was already changing, in its ever-revolutionary cycles. Nine Inch Nails and Faith No More were coming through, and a few young bands in Seattle were already setting themselves in opposition to what GNR represented.

Axl insisted the band go to Chicago to write together. They all stayed in apartments in the same building, but Axl seems to have been almost entirely absent from the sessions. Izzy had recently experienced something so frightening and unspeakable that he'd called his dad, gone home to Indiana and got permanently clean. He arrived in Chicago to see Axl flinging the entire contents of a kitchen out of a window, and turned back immediately. Slash eventually left for LA when Axl blew his top because two groupies refused to have full sex with the band and would only offer to 'blow' them.

Adler kept a butter tray full of cocaine in his fridge. Slash began to see him as 'irretrievable'. Back in LA, Steven became isolated, spending all of his time doing heroin, coke and crack. His friendship with Slash appears to have become permanently broken at this point, because his behaviour – no worse, but more relentless than Slash's – had begun to menace the band.

More incidents occur and seal Adler's fate. He falls over a drum riser when leaping on to stage. He continues to fearlessly attack Axl's own terrible behaviour – his contemptuous lateness on to stages, his failure to ever show up at rehearsals and writing sessions. Crucially, Adler struggles to play drums on the band's new song, 'Civil War' – the last on which he would. In his telling, this is because he's detoxing and on strong prescription medication. In Slash's, it's because he's too wasted on smack.

'At this point I could see that his mental and physical health had become questionable,' Slash says. 'I think somewhere along the line we'd forgotten that Steven was the type who needed someone to look out for him. He was like a curious kid you couldn't leave alone in the house.' The band's internal ethic kicked in: 'You could do whatever you wanted to yourself, but you had to deal with the repercussions. That's the way it worked with us.'

Adler went into rehab – and escaped – twenty-two times in this brief period. The rest of the band began to rebuild their relationships and work together again, but Adler was now firmly an outsider. When he did show up, he'd lose the time signature halfway through songs or forget where he was entirely.

Eventually, the sword of Axl Rose descended. Adler was forced to sign a sobriety contract, which stated that he'd be fined, then kicked out, if he failed to turn up to rehearsals sober. The contract also stripped him of his royalties if he lost his place in the band.

Adler signed it, but – as the band presumably knew he would – failed to stick to the agreement. In July 1990 he was finally kicked out.

He subsequently and successfully sued Guns N' Roses for a great deal of money. The sobriety contract was based on Adler's having an attorney present when he signed it, and he hadn't. His mother rode to the rescue. 'Mom really went to bat for me. She contacted a top entertainment lawyer and proceeded to sue the band.' During the court case, Adler kept a stash of drugs on him and went to the bathroom to take them as often as possible.

All the band members were summoned for questioning at the court case. Adler describes Slash and Axl's arrogant demeanours as having helped him win: 'You stupid fucks. Thanks, boys. Your condescending attitude was one sweet gift to me.' He was awarded $2.5 million and regained his 15 per cent in royalties.

Given the nightmarish descent into the very worst type of addiction that would ensue over the next twenty years, it seems possible that he'd have been better off without the money to enable him.

In the endless horror show that Adler describes, grimly luminous moments stand out. The time, years later, he runs into his ex (she of the narrow buttocks) who had obviously loved him deeply. She takes one look at his ravaged face and body and bursts into tears. The time he breaks out of his own house, demented and hallucinating, to try and buy a Slurpee (that childlike aspect again) and even the cops don't want to pick him up, he's so filthy. The times that Slash, years later and cleaned up, obviously regretful, makes multiple attempts to get Adler to rehab and save him. The most memorable of these is a group intervention alongside his family.

'I nodded to each hopeful shiny face,' Adler says. 'I saw the love in their eyes. God only knows I owed them. But the only thing I owed them was the truth. So . . . I promised them that I would go straight out and do more drugs than I'd ever done before. Then I saw the light go out in their eyes.'

There's the stroke that left the slur. The huge, swollen pustules all over his body that a doctor lances on a couch in a house his desperate half-brother has rented for the latest attempt to save

him. The smell so bad that everyone else leaves the room, retch-
ing, only Jamie being able to remain present. The love that this
implies, and which is endlessly thwarted and abused.

Eventually, decades later, the miracle of sobriety – or so it
seems for now. Adler back on stage at Dodger Stadium, my own
heart swelling with childlike joy.

So that's the story of Steven Adler. But what of the critical
questions: was he right to doubt his talents? Were Guns N'
Roses at their best when he was their drummer? Were they
right to reject him? After reading Adler's book, I wasn't sure. He
clearly needed to go from the band – of that there seemed no
doubt. Even his own protestation that he was trying to get clean
and was under the influence of opiate blockers appears under-
mined by everything that came before and afterwards.

But what about when things were, however briefly, good?
Was Adler *ever* the right drummer? He doubted himself, after
all, and he describes becoming a drummer almost by default.

It was Slash's book that gave me the answers. They are
emphatic, and I felt genuine relief on discovering them.

'To Steven's credit, and unbeknownst to most, the feel and
energy of *Appetite* was largely due to him. He had an inimitable
style of drumming that couldn't really be replaced, an almost
adolescent levity that gave the band its spark.'

Izzy Stradlin agrees. 'Our songs were written with Steve playing the drums and his sense of swing was the push and pull that
gives the songs their feel. When that was gone . . . nothing
worked.'

But even if the wider story vindicates Adler as a creative force,
his own one genuinely is a tragedy. He didn't have to doubt his
playing. The rest of the band didn't think he was no good. He

didn't have to be so afraid. If he'd known that, might his drug intake have become slightly less destructive? I think not. In fact, I think it more likely he began to doubt himself because of the drugs. After all, that's what they do – make the user paranoid, make the world around them darker. Every surge of druggy joy is a using up of its natural counterpart.

Adler's permanent adolescence was his true tragic flaw. His enthusiasm, openness, lack of restraint or adult social tools. All of these proved both his greatest strengths and the weaknesses that meant he was always doomed.

Guns N' Roses were at their best around *Appetite for Destruction*, and Adler *was* a cornerstone: a true, pivotal part of the band at their zenith. (Plus, it was him that insisted the group stop wearing make-up.) The raw, punk, gutter-rat rock 'n' roll energy of *Appetite*-era Guns N' Roses was their greatest work. It turns out that even the best songs from the *Use Your Illusion* albums were written during the *Appetite* sessions: 'You Could Be Mine', 'November Rain', 'Don't Cry' – even 'Estranged' had been gestating way back then.

I'd finished Adler's book in a hotel in Buellton, California, and started work on Slash's. But I also wanted to hear from my friend Andy, who'd told me about Adler's sacking all those years ago. Was it true he hadn't rated him? How did he remember the moment on that suburban hill as he broke the news to me?

Andy replied to the email I sent him a few days later. Since it seems I misquoted him at the beginning of this book, I'd like to give the last words of this chapter to him:

I'm not sure that I didn't rate his drumming generally when he was on form. I know that I've always been very wary of harder drugs from a young age . . . they showed us a really basic film at school about a kid who took drugs for the first time and immediately died and it properly shook me . . . I can still vividly picture it to this day!

I know I'd heard reports that when they were in the studio for *Use Your Illusion* his drumming had massively contributed to the length of time it took for them to record as they faffed about for ages with him messing his parts up before eventually replacing him . . . I imagine I was on my high horse about how you shouldn't take drugs and ranting about how unprofessional it must be to have one band member slowing everything down.

Possibly also part of the whole thing for me back then was that Matt Sorum replaced him and at that time I was massively getting into heavier music such as Metallica, Slayer, Pantera, Sepultura etc. So Sorum's style which was a lot heavier and flashier would have been right on brand for me at the time. Looking back I'd probably prefer Adler's drumming if I was choosing with my music tastes now.

If you listen to *Appetite* it's got that quintessential GNR sound that we all fell in love with. Sorum was technically the better drummer but Adler had more 'feel' and the band as a whole with him in it is, looking back, what I remember fondly of GNR.

I watched those VHS tapes of their performances on the *Use Your Illusion* tour over and over as a kid, with Axl running around in white cycling shorts and a plaid shirt and the long solo from Slash (where he did the theme from *Godfather* as part of the solo) and the ridiculous drum solo from Sorum with his little leather gloves! But there was a performance I had taped from TV which I think was the one of them playing at the Ritz NY in 1988. Again looking back at that, they had so much more natural swagger and less bullshit going on . . .

Lots more than Adler's absence contributing to that though I'm sure (Izzy leaving of course was massive). As we've seen so often, many bands struggle to keep it together after they breakthrough in such an insane manner. GNR definitely disappeared fully up their assholes (and particularly Axl's).

11

Alan Lancaster, Status Quo

Early on we got [our manager] Pat Barlow
to sack him, but took him back again on
a three-month trial. Unfortunately that
lasted until 1984! – Francis Rossi

From an interview with Michael Hann, author of *Denim and Leather: The Rise and Fall of the New Wave of British Heavy Metal*:

My absolute favourite sacking! Alan Lancaster was the bassist in the classic line up. In 1984 they did their *End of the Road* tour, their last ever shows, culminating in fifty thousand people at Milton Keynes Bowl. And I was there, I only went because it was Status Quo's last ever show and I thought: 'Well, y'know, let's go and see Quo.'

A year later they were back for *Live Aid*. It was like, OK, fair enough, it's *Live Aid*, they're Status Quo. Then a couple of months after that they were back for good, except without Alan Lancaster. And it turned out that the whole splitting up for good thing was because they were sick of Alan Lancaster, and he'd said that if the band ever broke up, he'd emigrate to Australia. So they did split up, and he did emigrate, and once he was safely in Australia, it was: 'Right, we can get the band back together now.'

As a teenager I felt genuinely betrayed when they re-formed.[1] I only went cos you were packing it in, and you lied to me!

1 On the idea of a reunion with Lancaster, Francis Rossi memorably commented: 'It would be like trying to get your dick up your own arse . . . impossible.' For his part, Lancaster described seeing Quo go on without him as 'like having your child abducted'. In 2013, though, the original line up got back together for a *Frantic Four* tour.

12

Jason Everman, Nirvana

Some moody metalhead. – Kurt Cobain

If I were, somewhat childishly, to invent a perfect hero – a sort of personal *Übermensch* – the chances are he'd look a lot like Jason Everman. If you've ever seen the front cover of Nirvana's debut album, *Bleach*, then you've seen him: He's the guitarist on the right, playing a Fender Telecaster, his head obscured by a thrashing mass of long, curly hair.

The cover image gives him as much prominence as Kurt himself. This is surprising because he only spent a brief spell in Nirvana, and he didn't play a note on *Bleach*. But he did pay for the album's recording. He'd spent the previous summer doing brutal work on his father's fishing boat in Alaska, and he used some of the money to pay the $600 studio bill that Sub Pop, Nirvana's label, either couldn't or wouldn't.

The band credited him because 'we wanted to make him feel more at home,' Krist Novoselic, Nirvana's bassist and founding member, told the band's biographer, Michael Azerrad.

Everman was kicked out of Nirvana after a few short months. He'd struggled to bond with the band, and his long periods of silence on the tour van had become unbearable. Never mind, things were shortly to look up when he was invited to play bass for Soundgarden, a band he preferred. But the same problems dogged him. A black cloud would appear, and his mood would turn. He spent the time on the tour bus with his headphones on, unspeaking. Soundgarden called a meeting, and they kicked him out too.

This meant Everman had been thrown out by not one, but two of the biggest bands of the 1990s – a unique level of achievement in the field of rejection. But it's what he did next that really counts.

Novoselic recounted a moment on the tour van with Everman to the *New York Times*. 'He was just pondering. He asked me, "Do you ever think about what it'd be like to be in the military and go through that experience?" And I was just like . . . *no*.'

I'd been aware of Jason Everman since I was twelve or thirteen, but mostly as a piece of trivia related to the band I was obsessed with – something I might deploy to demonstrate my superior knowledge. I remembered his face in the *Bleach*-era images – serious, expressionless, his stare direct; his nose ring and the long, very light brown, curly hair.

As the years went on, I'd forgotten most of what I'd once read: that he'd also played in Soundgarden, what Nirvana had said about him. I'd also been too young to read between the lines and understand the role Everman had played in Nirvana, which was more important than it might appear.

I wanted to have a career in indie record labels because of Sub Pop, the company that signed Nirvana. To my youthful mind, it was the indie label that put out the unadulterated, underground stuff, and everything went wrong when the majors got involved. Looking into Everman's story again, with years of experience under my belt, I saw that he'd been taken advantage of – not least by the label.

But I only had cause to look at Everman again because of the thrilling shock I got when I came across an article about him written many years later.

Jason Everman was born on a remote Alaskan island, where his father had set the family up to live close to nature. 'My birth certificate says Kodiak,' Everman told the *New York Times* in 2013, 'but I'm pretty sure it was Ouzinkie, where my parents lived in a two-room cabin with a pet ocelot called Kia.'

Sadly, the marriage didn't last. Everman's mother, Diane, disliked the lifestyle and left with Jason when he was a toddler. She remarried, to an ex-US Navy man, and the family lived across Puget Sound from Seattle. Coming from a broken home – 'that legendary divorce' in Cobain's lyrics for 'Serve the Servants' – would later be one of the few things that united Jason and Kurt.

Everman's upbringing was tough. His mother never talked to him about their time in Alaska. His half-sister, Mimi, told the *New York Times* that Jason didn't know about his real father until his early teens. She also claimed that their mother was 'extremely depressed, an artistic genius who was also a pill-popping alcoholic. Jason and I really learned to take care of ourselves.' Jason developed a stutter. 'My mom joked that this is how she cured Jason, by telling him, "Either spit it out or shut up." I became really adept at finishing his sentences for him.'

Clay Tarver, who wrote the *New York Times* article, knew Everman from when they'd both played in Seattle bands, before and around the time grunge exploded into the world's consciousness. Interestingly, Tarver describes Everman's stutter and his mother's approach to it as leading to 'silence'. It was Everman's silence that bothered the bands he joined later. Perhaps he learned early on to 'shut up'.

'The silence evolved into acting out,' Tarver wrote. At school, Everman and a friend 'blew up a toilet with an M-80'. An M-80 is a powerful firecracker, originally used by the US military to simulate artillery fire, and later sold as a firework.

Like Steven Adler (see Chapter 10), one of the key figures in Everman's life was his grandmother, Gigi. She now intervened, enlisting a therapist who was also the sports psychiatrist to the Seattle SuperSonics, a now defunct basketball team.

The therapist happened to have a collection of vintage guitars. One day Everman picked one up, and the therapist began to play along with him, leaping at the chance to make some progress. It was the first time Everman played a guitar.

'It was a big family joke that those were the most expensive guitar lessons ever,' Mimi told Tarver.

Then Jason discovered punk, and everything changed.

'The collision of fifteen-year-old me and punk rock was a causal event in my life,' Everman said at a talk he gave in 2014. Behind where he stood on the stage, a screen showed him as an adolescent, standing skinny and smiling in a Black Flag T-shirt against a rural Washington background. 'Punk rock was the one thing I truly loved and truly brought me joy.'

His only conduit to the music was a Sunday night, one-hour hardcore show on the local college station KCMU. Punk was hard to come by in the far-flung Pacific Northwest. Everman's experience reminds me of Kurt Cobain having read about the

Sex Pistols but never having heard them, or any other punk music, and desperately seeking out some way to do so in Aberdeen – his own tiny Washington town.[1]

I know this feeling. At fifteen, I too was seeking out punk and indie rock, saving up pocket money to take the bus into Leeds and brave the record stores. I had it easier, of course, and a bigger challenge for me was deciding which CD or LP of the several I wanted I'd risk spending my money on. I'd dig out names I'd read about in the *NME* and *Melody Maker*, or in Azerrad's book about Nirvana. Occasionally, I'd pluck up the courage to ask a question of one of the pale, imperious young men – riddled with music knowledge – who stood behind the counter.

In those days records could be actively frightening. There were Dwarves LPs with naked women covered in blood and gore. Sonic Youth's *Confusion Is Sex*, a record I bought in a second-hand shop, both looked and sounded utterly alien. I tried hard to track down scary-sounding bands like MDC (Millions of Dead Cops) and even Dinosaur Jr's goblin-like figures and dismembered bodies seemed thrillingly sinister.

These days, of course, you can demystify a band – or even a whole genre – in a mere few minutes online.

Everman savoured every second of that hardcore radio show. 'I'd have access to these bands in LA or New York, these exotic places I'd never been to. And this music that really spoke to me on this visceral level. It was essentially a sonic middle finger, and

1 Eventually, Kurt found a copy of the Clash's *Sandinista*. Getting home to play it and hoping to finally hear the visceral, raw punk rock he'd previously only imagined, he was appalled to encounter a three-disc album of funk, reggae, disco and 'rap'.

since I was a fifteen-year-old, gawky, walking middle finger, we complemented each other.'

Punk rock inspired him to learn guitar. The earlier music he loved, like Black Sabbath, seemed like something he'd never be able to play. Black Flag made him think: *Oh, I could probably play that.*

But punk also gave him a philosophy. 'This loose doctrine of individuality, question authority, think critically, think for yourself.'

This ethos chimed with his self-reliance and taught him to think and do for himself.

Before long, Everman began playing in high-school bands, 'all in' for his love of punk rock. He also reconnected with his father, spending several summers in Alaska working on his fishing boat. Eventually he managed to save $20,000 – a huge sum for a high-school graduate in the late 1980s.

It's here that grunge's family tree kicks in. Everman had been a childhood friend of Chad Channing, Nirvana's original drummer, who would himself be kicked out before they hit the big time. But the person originally to introduce Kurt and Jason was Dylan Carlson, bandleader of Earth, and a key figure in the annals of grunge.

It was Carlson who bought Kurt the shotgun with which he killed himself. Domestic incidents had led to Kurt's firearms being confiscated by police twice in the previous ten months, so he asked Carlson to purchase the shotgun on his behalf. Later, rumours would spread that Courtney Love had hired Dylan to kill Kurt. The rumours were as idiotic as they sound – Dylan and Kurt were firm friends and junkie brothers-in-arms. For a while Carlson lived with Mark Lanegan, singer of Screaming Trees, a close friend of Kurt's and another heroin addict.[2] In his book *Sing Backwards and Weep*, Lanegan recalls Carlson saying: 'Fuck, man, if anyone was gonna have me kill somebody, it would have been Kurt having me do Courtney.'

I met Carlson myself, briefly, when he played Ninja Tune's twenty-fifth anniversary event at the Masonic Lodge in Los Angeles. Diminutive, quiet and polite, he had a face tattoo, long hair and a beard. He looked younger than I'd expected, given the life he'd led. I remember that payment for the show was apparently quite urgent. I briefly wished I could sit down and ask him about everything – the early years, Sub Pop, Seattle, Kurt – but these were the anxious moments before a performance, and it wouldn't have been appropriate.

Everman joined Nirvana in the period just before the release of *Bleach*, which had already been recorded by Jack Endino. When Kurt mentioned wanting to find a second guitarist, Chad Channing suggested his childhood friend. Jason loved the demos that the band had made with the Melvins' exceptional drummer, Dale Crover,[3] and leapt at the chance. The heavier sound that the band had around *Bleach* seems to have been part of the appeal. While Everman always refers to punk rock in the interviews he's given, Kurt and Kris were convinced that his true passion was metal.

2 Mark Lanegan was one of the last people Kurt Cobain tried to call before killing himself. In his junkie seclusion, Lanegan didn't pick up.
3 Even Chad Channing didn't play on every song on *Bleach*. Nirvana had originally borrowed Dale Crover to play on the demos. He was the drummer Kurt would have really liked to have for Nirvana at the time, and his versions of 'Floyd the Barber' and 'Negative Creep' were considered so much stronger than Channing's that they were used on the final album.

'Early on, they began to realize what they'd gotten into with Jason,' writes Azerrad. 'Although he said he'd been into punk for years, Kurt's inspection of his record collection revealed, to his horror, little more than speed metal records.'

Later, on the trip to New York that would seal Everman's fate, he would decide to go and see the speed metal band Prong at CBGB, rather than watch Sonic Youth with the rest of Nirvana.

'We basically were ready to take anybody if they could play good guitar,' Kurt told Azerrad. 'He seemed like a nice enough guy, and he had long Sub Pop hair.'

Sub Pop's aesthetic at the time revolved around the unique, kinetic live photography of Charles Peterson – a label finding someone like this, in its early days, is part of the essential luck and alchemy needed to make an impact. In many of his photos, the bands – Mudhoney, Soundgarden, Tad – are flinging their hair around wildly, the perfect visual representation of grunge's wild abandon.

It seems Sub Pop did indeed take to Jason, and not only because he'd paid the bill they owed for *Bleach*'s recording. They liked him so much that they wanted to include a Peterson photograph of him swinging his long, curly, strawberry-blond locks on the back cover. Predictably, Kurt nixed this, and the photograph was used on a limited run of posters in the album's second pressing instead.

Unfortunately, his deployment of the hair on stage was less effective. Steve Fisk, producer for Soundgarden, Beat Happening and Screaming Trees, saw Nirvana at an early show.

'I hated them,' he told Azerrad. 'Jason kept moving his hair, but it wasn't in time with the music at all. I'm sorry – I've seen

Black Flag and you move your hair in time with the music or you don't move it at all.'

Fisk would become a convert on hearing *Bleach*, but his tone here is revealing. Nirvana seem to have been treated as at best a fledgling and at worst a joke by grunge's emergent gatekeepers – not least by Sub Pop themselves. In his book, Mark Lanegan recalls turning up to see Nirvana support label-mates Tad. Sub Pop's Bruce Pavitt assumed Lanegan must be there to see the main act. Lanegan told him, presciently, that 'Nirvana are the best band you have. By far. They're one of the best bands I've ever seen.' The Sub Pop label owners looked 'puzzled'. Lanegan's was a minority view at the time, showing how difficult it can be even for dedicated, passionate people to spot the early stages of genius in their midst.

From the beginning of his time in the band, Everman's role was crucial, if indirectly so: 'Kurt didn't have much experience with playing guitar and singing and remembering words at the same time,' Azerrad wrote. 'He wanted a second guitar to thicken up the sound. With another player on stage, Kurt didn't have to try as hard; consequently, he became a much better player.'

And a much better performer too. After seeing a Nirvana show, Mudhoney's guitarist, Steve Turner, was heard 'raving that Kurt Cobain played guitar on his head!'[4]

The band stayed at Jason's house on the eve of the *Bleach* sessions. He was there to sign the contract with Sub Pop (the

---

4 The evidence for this unlikely skill is readily available in one of Charles Peterson's most famous photographs. In it, Kurt indeed appears casually inverted, playing guitar in a Soundgarden T-shirt, his legs daintily crossed as they point to the venue's ceiling.

label's first long-term one) that would change everything for the imprint. Later, when Geffen bought Nirvana out of it, Sub Pop would find themselves abruptly in funds, and with their logo included on millions of copies of *Nevermind*.

But it's where money is involved that a pattern emerges. Not only did Everman pay for *Bleach*'s recording, but an anecdote from the tour he joined reveals his financial support went further.

Somewhere along the line, Nirvana had started smashing their equipment at the end of their shows. This was a time-honoured tradition that harked back to sixties bands such as the Who, but Nirvana harnessed its visceral thrill for a new generation. The problem in the early days was paying for it.

'The band played a great show in Pittsburgh,' Azerrad wrote. 'So great that Kurt smashed one of his favourite guitars, a sunburst Fender Mustang. Jason got really mad about that. "We said, 'What? It's rock and roll!'" says Krist, who concedes that "we were broke and he was kind of financing the show."'

I think it's unlikely that Everman was paying for a single show on a long run of them – I think it's far more likely he was financing the entire tour. This was his big chance, his moment to take part in the thing that had changed his life and become his 'joy'. The money he'd made must have been precious to him, given the manner of its earning. This is how he spent it.

I think a question of character comes into play here, too. Regardless of cost, I don't think Everman would ever have been into smashing up guitars. His subsequent career would mean holding equipment in deep respect, taking care of it as a matter of instinctive discipline and routine. His life would depend on doing so.

In 2014, I went to Seattle and attended a Nirvana exhibition at the Experience Music Project (EMP) – the music museum set up in part by Microsoft's Paul Allen.

The city goes some way to explaining the angsty sound it produced in the early 1990s. It glowers and glimmers with weather, surrounded by steep hills and mountains and deep-green, rain-swollen forest. To my British mind, it was like finding a massive American city transplanted to the Scottish Highlands, with vast concrete freeways running across the sea lochs.

Designed by Frank Gehry, the EMP consists of three brightly coloured metallic shapes with a monorail running through them. They hunker beneath the cloud like a bright, possibly damaged, overly optimistic child's toy.

The exhibition was called *Nirvana: Taking Punk to the Masses*. Inside, I gave myself over to my fandom and quietly, reverently studied the handwritten tapes, early T-shirts, photographs and contracts. In the background, Nirvana's amp stacks played ambient, ominous low feedback, which I thought was a nice touch. At the end of the exhibition, I even bought the book.

In pride of place in a glass cabinet, they had Kurt's famous black Fender Stratocaster, with a sticker reading VANDALISM, BEAUTIFUL AS A ROCK IN A COP'S FACE.

I can't imagine Jason Everman ever quite getting with that.

The financial stuff with Everman isn't exactly unusual. As bands claw their way into survival or success, money is begged, stolen or borrowed. Other bands have taken on well-financed members in more explicit transactions. Perhaps that's a more honourable way to do things. It's still unpleasant though. In an interview on YouTube, Sub Pop's Bruce Pavitt makes light of the money Everman spent on *Bleach*'s studio fees, though rightly acknowledges that it is 'a little ridiculous and kind of embarrassing. The record label is supposed to come up with the cash.'

His manner segues from embarrassment to one approaching pride, which is difficult to admire. 'We actually spent zero . . . and sold two million copies, so that might be the most profitable record in the history of the music business.'

But Everman wasn't stupid. When Krist and Kurt came up with their notorious early T-shirts, which read NIRVANA: FUDGE PACKIN CRACK SMOKIN SATAN WORSHIPIN MOTHER-FUCKERS, Jason had them printed up for sale.

'Jason probably made a mint,' Azerrad writes. Much deserved, I'd say.

But if Jason Everman had financed the tour, he also caused it to be cut short. Working their way up the east coast towards Canada, the band never made it beyond a long stop-off in NYC. Everman's moody silence was driving everyone mad.

'We were totally poor,' Kurt told Azerrad. 'But, God, we were seeing the United States for the first time. And we were in a band. It was just great. And if Jason wasn't such a prick, it would've been even better.'

Krist and Kurt, Nirvana's only true core members, had taken to going on long walks in the places they stopped off on tour.

'Do you think the band is kind of weird ever since Jason joined?' Krist asked Kurt.

'Jason's stage style was more show-biz than the rest of the band,' Azerrad wrote. 'He posed, swinging his hair in the classic Sub Pop style, doing a rockets rooster strut. "He was like a peacock on amphetamines," says Kurt. "He was so posey . . . it was embarrassing. It was so contrived and sexual. It was gross."'

Everman wanted to contribute to the band fully and write songs, but of course that was never on the cards. Novoselic claimed that Everman never wanted to jam together, but Everman told Azerrad that their 'time was completely occupied by learning songs that Kurt had already written'.

Also, Novoselic didn't like that Everman brought girls to a rehearsal. While the other band members clearly noted and struggled with Everman's introspection on tour, Krist seems to have been particularly focused on removing him, and on the idea that he was 'rock' and Nirvana was punk.

Things came to a head in New York City. 'He wouldn't even talk to us any more,' Novoselic said. 'The Mudhoney guys were in New York: "Why is this Jason so quiet?" We played a good show. Still, Jason was quiet.'

Kurt, Chad and Krist spent time together, going out to eat and bonding: 'Without Jason. He would not hang around with us.'

One night, staying at the apartment of a music industry contact, Kurt and Krist made the call. They'd bought some cocaine on the street and were drinking together. 'They decided they were going home and that Jason was out of the band,' writes Azerrad. ' "We were happy," said Krist. "It was a relief."'

'I always felt kind of peripheral,' Jason told Azerrad. His own view was that he'd quit the band due to his lack of input, something borne out by the other members, who admitted they never actually told him he was out. Chad Channing recalled that Kurt didn't like confrontation, and the band simply drove back to Seattle in one long, gruelling, presumably very frosty journey.

It took fifty hours, Azerrad wrote. 'Not stopping for anything except to get gas, eat a doughnut or go to the bathroom. The whole time, nobody said a word. Nobody even told Jason he was out of the band.'

'I don't recall ever being asked for input on songs, which is ultimately why I left,' Everman said. 'I probably wanted to do things that were not simple enough for them, ideas that were mine as opposed to Kurt's. There wasn't a tremendous musical difference – maybe it was just a control thing.

'Basically, anyone besides Kurt or Krist is kind of disposable. Kurt could get in front of any bass player and any drummer and play his songs and it's not going to sound that much different.'

I think Everman misread this. Actually, Kurt was looking for the right musicians for the sound he envisioned. He wanted a drummer with the sort of explosive power that Chad Channing didn't have, and he found him in Dave Grohl. Later, Kurt threatened to kick Dave out too. But these threats appear to have been idle. Nirvana's sound *did* depend on Grohl's drumming.

Everman played a useful role in the band, but the brutal truth is that Nirvana's success as a project depended on him leaving after he'd performed it.

He never did get his $600 back. Kurt laughed it off as 'mental damages'.

Kurt certainly had that 'splinter of ice' seemingly necessary for a visionary and a bandleader. There's a video on YouTube titled

Nirvana Discuss Jason Everman's Departure For Soundgarden. In it, Kurt, Chad and Krist sit smoking on a bench, lit brightly but with darkness behind them. Music plays in the background. They might be outside on a warmish night, somewhere a show will or has taken place, but it's hard to tell as the video's quality is poor; it would have been filmed in 1989 or 1990.

The video is fascinating and a little excruciating. Fascinating because the group's dynamics are on full, if unconscious display. Excruciating because the primary impression it leaves is how young these people are – Kurt would've been twenty-two or -three, Krist only two years older. The camera focuses mostly on Kurt – so obviously the band's leader. He's by turns sardonic, silly and self-conscious, in the way that many twenty-two-year-olds are.

The fact that the band will be asked about Jason Everman's departure has obviously been made clear, because halfway through the video, when Chad makes a joke, Kurt makes one in return. 'Yeah, Chad. You're the next to go,' he says, grinning and airily moving his face closer to Channing's. Channing would indeed be next to go, which gives this moment a sinister poignance.

Then Kurt looks back at the camera. 'Are we gonna ask the Jason question now?' he asks in friendly but pronounced defiance.

'Oh yeah,' says the interviewer. 'What's it like playing as a three-piece?'

''Cause we were a three-piece for two years before,' Kurt says, 'so it's no big deal. We wanted another guitar player because I'm such a shitty guitar player that I couldn't really be that great of a frontman.'

This is a remarkably honest and clear-eyed answer – if told in the form of a joke – and I think reveals how much of a plan Kurt, like all great bandleaders, had.

The band then go on to joke about studying guitar, unconsciously grouping up to take the potential heat out of the question. After a moment of this, Krist reveals the strength of his own position in the group and the dominance his extra years allow him.

Continuing the riff on Kurt's becoming a better frontman, he says: 'I straightened his fucking ass out. Let me tell you one thing – he steps one fucking hair out of line and I'll fuckin' . . .' He raises a broad forearm as if to backhand Kurt across the face. Kurt smiles at him – in a natural way he never does at Channing – and flinches laconically.

Channing continues goofing off – he does this throughout, apparently slightly nervous.

'So what happened to Jason?' the interviewer asks.

Novoselic's edge reveals itself further. He fake smiles at the camera and says: 'He's a bass player for Soundgarden, that's what happened.' His tone is mild, but to my mind there's a discouraging venom in his demeanour at this stage.

'He just up and left?' the interviewer asks.

Channing tries to politely fudge the nature of his childhood friend's departure from the band. Kurt, whose eyes take on a harder look as this progresses, abruptly leans forward to interrupt. His bandmates go immediately quiet, and Channing looks at the floor.

'During the week we kicked him out,' Kurt says, 'he tried out for Soundgarden. It worked out awesome.'

'We're very happy for him,' Krist says with evident sarcasm.

'We like the guy and stuff still . . .' Channing says, without any.

'We *love* him,' Kurt says, his manner very much in line with Krist.

'He's a good friend of ours and all that,' Channing says, before reverting to goofing off.

Kurt goes on to explain the band's new melodic direction, and how Jason hadn't liked it.

'We had a few songs we hadn't recorded that he really liked, and we didn't wanna do 'em, meaning I didn't wanna do 'em, 'cause I'm such a dictator.'

Everman told Azerrad that he had no hard feelings regarding his departure: 'I think that the most objective way to sum it up is that it was implicitly mutual.' What he remembered most clearly was that 'when they dropped me off in the alley behind my house, I didn't believe I would see any of those guys again – even Chad – and I was at peace with that. I was free.'

Everman was aware of the narrative around his departure, that he was 'this knuckle-dragging heavy metal guy who just didn't get it.' But in his view, 'at the end of the day I just wasn't a good fit for Nirvana.'

Everman, for whom philosophy went on to play a crucial role, appears to be telling the truth here. He's reflected on what happened and come to terms with it. And he's right that he was never a fit. Black Flag's aggressive, heavy, masculine punk was the template for him, and viewed with the distance time provides, Nirvana had little in common with it. There's another YouTube video of an instore performance in LA that's one of the few times Everman was filmed playing in the band.

He does indeed toss his hair badly and out of time with the music. His demeanour is not of the insouciant, irreverent, unpretentious style that defined Nirvana and captured my heart.

Everman is right. He was never supposed to *be* in Nirvana.

And there was a fundamental personality clash between Kurt and Jason. Cobain admitted he might have alienated Everman with his alcohol-fuelled 'volatile personality'.

'I was just trying to be "punk rock" or something,' Kurt told Azerrad. 'I had this terrible Johnny Rotten complex.'

There's something called a 'Sex Pistols moment', originating from two gigs the Pistols played at Manchester's Lesser Free Trade Hall in 1976. Watching those performances were Morrissey, Ian Curtis, Tony Wilson, the Buzzcocks and Mark E. Smith, and each of them went home alight with inspiration. A Sex Pistols moment is when you find the thing you love and realise anything is possible.

In his book *I Swear I Was There: Sex Pistols, Manchester and the Gig that Changed the World*, author David Nolan wrote that without this gig, there would 'be no Buzzcocks, Magazine, Joy Division, New Order, Factory Records, "indie" scene, no The Fall, The Smiths, Haçienda, Madchester, Happy Mondays or Oasis . . . Maybe there would be no Nirvana.'

I've referred to my own Sex Pistols moment already. It came when I first encountered *Smells Like Teen Spirit* as a twelve-year-old. Finding Nirvana – listening to their music and their influences and reading everything I could about them – changed my life. My choice of career sprang from the indie record company they started out on – the one that left it to Jason Everman to pay for *Bleach*'s recording. In a way that's as true as it is ridiculous, I owe everything to that moment.

But I had a second, more minor Sex Pistols moment around the same time, one to which I'm reluctant to admit. It came when I first saw footage of the SAS storming the Iranian Embassy in 1979. Bear with me here – I'm aware that a fascination with Special Forces is often the hallmark of unwholesome far-right types.[5] But to me it seemed astonishing that human beings could be trained to achieve these things. They were like endurance athletes who used their abilities in the most dangerous situations imaginable.

So, as I deep dived into punk and indie rock, working backwards from the bands on Kurt Cobain's T-shirts and poring over Michael Azerrad's book, I also read countless SAS memoirs. I was struck as much by the intelligence that characterised these men as I was by their preternatural hardness. One of the writers had dragged himself to the top of Pen y Fan for the umpteenth time on the notorious selection course, only for an instructor to materialise from the mist and ask: 'What's the square root of 1764?'

As boys do, I asked my dad about these soldiers.

'I wouldn't want to meet one,' he said.

'Why not?' I asked.

'Very hard men,' he replied.

In the documentaries I watched, a chorus of baffled Scottish prison guards described what had happened after the 1987

5 The potential unhealthiness of this interest is perhaps best expressed by John le Carré in *A Perfect Spy*. Towards the end of the book, Special Forces-type troops are stealing across rooftops to apprehend the novel's antihero. His wife, watching in anguish, recalls her husband's attitude to the fetishisation of such soldiers: 'A society that admires its shock troops had better be bloody careful about where it's going Magnus liked to say.'

Petersfield riot had gone on for four days. A guard had been captured and tortured by prisoners, and Margaret Thatcher had seen enough.

'Middle of one night, the prison bus appeared through the back gate, and all these strangers disembarked carrying large rucksacks.'

'They all wore balaclavas, and just looked exactly the same.'

'Nothing was said, it was just men in black.'

'If you asked their name, they were called John. Everyone was called John.'

It took the faceless men a mere five minutes to storm the prison and rescue the guard before further harm came to him.

I was transfixed by the grainy footage of Northern Irish streets and desert expanses. Cerebral types described how they were taught to 'attack an ambush', or pointed at pictures of their friends in secret, dirty 1970s wars, and said, 'Look at him. He's in the middle of enemy territory, and he's just happy to be there.'

And that's what Jason Everman did next.

I can't remember exactly how I came across Clay Tarver's 2013 article, but I remember where I was. It was mid-afternoon in Los Angeles, and I was sitting at my desk in an office in Echo Park. Days in LA start and end early, but I was probably being lazy, surfing the internet idly as the day wore down, the sun deepening to orange and dying across the jungly hillsides.

Beyond these, through the windows of the loft-style office, you could just see the Hollywood sign, peeking through the stained metal framework of a large billboard hoarding above Sunset.

The article was titled 'The Rock and Roll Casualty Who Became a War Hero'. I recognised the name, and then the face of Jason Everman. A little electric thrill ran through me: a sometime member of my favourite band had gone on to become a decorated Green Beret. After that, he'd graduated in philosophy from Columbia University, becoming a real-life warrior poet.

I tumbled into the rabbit hole, and over the next few years read and watched everything I could about Everman, feeding the mild but growing obsession that would lead to the writing of this book. I was hoping for my own second act in life; dreaming that it might be in some way as successful and fulfilling as his.

In the recording of a talk he gave to a veterans' group in 2014, Everman appears a man transformed. He seems humble, relaxed, keen to relay a story that might be interesting to hear, but without any of the smugness that can creep into this modern, TED-style endeavour. His longish hair is tied into a ponytail, and he has a thick, greying beard. He's tanned, his eyes bright blue and clear, and his forearms heavily tattooed. He illustrates his points with constantly moving fingers and hands, the precision of which echo that of his diction. If you were forced to choose a single word to describe him, it might be 'fulfilled'. Certainly, he is a million miles away from 'a moody metalhead'.

He shows the picture of himself as a skinny teenager in the Black Flag T-shirt, and then another from 2004. In this second, he's standing against a background of desert and arid mountains, slimmer and with his hair shorter but still unruly. In his hands is what looks like a machine gun, rather than an assault rifle. He's got lightweight boots on, and the easy demeanour that defines the Special Forces.[6]

'That's Afghanistan I think . . . oh-four?' he says. 'Just off a target there, I think it's about five in the morning.'

Just off a target would mean back from raiding the home of a suspected terrorist. These raids always took place in the middle of the night, which gave both cover and maximum psychological impact.

In order to explain how he got from the first picture to the second, he talks about his life after he was kicked out of Soundgarden.

'I'm living in San Francisco. I'm a professional rock musician. It was the year of sex, drugs and rock 'n' roll.[7] But underneath this surface of kind of living the dream, I was profoundly dissatisfied.'

Segueing into language presumably derived from his philosophy degree, he says he began 'examining what was going on', and why he 'had a constant weight on [his] shoulders, and this sublime malaise'.

He finally put his finger on it. He wasn't happy doing what he was doing. He had a filmmaker friend who was a former

6 Members of Special Forces units are known for wearing their hair longer, choosing their own gear and weapons, calling each other by first names and generally getting preferable treatment. This is very much at odds with the relentless discipline and uniformity of the regular army, and can be a source of resentment.

7 As I was finishing writing *The Rejects*, Everman turned up as a guest on Joe Rogan's Spotify podcast. During the conversation, he revealed that after he'd left Nirvana and Soundgarden and joined the dreadfully named Mindfunk, he'd had a dalliance with heroin – first smoking it, and then injecting. 'I'm a completist, I guess, I don't wanna do it halfway,' he said. It seems the sense of adventure he obviously craves could easily have found darker outlets.

Navy SEAL – the US Navy's Special Forces unit and now arguably the most famous in the world.[8] Everman asked the friend about his experience.

'It was hands down the best decision I ever made in my life,' his friend said. 'It challenged me in ways I'd never been challenged before. Complete job satisfaction. And when I left and did other things, that's still the part of my life I'm most proud of.'

Everman went away and mulled it over. He played festivals, set off on a US tour. He kept examining; wondering why he was sticking with 'the rock thing'. He concluded that he was doing it for external validation, not internal. 'Was I a musician because other people thought it was cool, or was I doing it because I thought it was cool? The conclusion I came to was "well I'm definitely not doing it because I think it's cool, because I don't think it is any more."

'By turning my back on this world of cool . . . Basically I sloughed off these shackles of cool, I felt this weight lift off my shoulders. I felt free.'

That phrase 'sloughed off these shackles of cool' haunts me. Over the years, at the low points, when the music industry has seemed most shallow, fickle and stupid, I've yearned to escape from its tyrannical cool. Almost everyone in the industry is trapped in it. The music industry revolves around youth culture, and thus its workers must signify their understanding of youth, of cool.

But for most people, cool seems naturally less important as you age. As you exit your twenties – your youth – and then your

---

8 It was the elite-within-an-elite SEAL Team Six that killed Osama bin Laden, and rescued Captain Richard Phillips.

thirties, and your friends in finance pay off mortgages and buy cars with their bonuses and contemplate retirement, the compensatory power of cool is much diminished. It just seems a bit silly.

Two months later Everman was at Fort Benning, Georgia, getting his head shaved. He joined the US Army Rangers, an elite, airborne light infantry unit. Becoming a Ranger is an established route to making it into the Special Forces – they're the soldiers who secure the perimeter while the Special Forces raid the building. If you've seen *Black Hawk Down*, you'll have seen them do exactly that.[9]

It's worth noting that Everman's interest in the military seems to go a lot further back than this period of disillusion with the music scene. There was the time on Nirvana's tour bus he asked Krist Novoselic whether he'd ever considered the military. His stepfather had been ex-Navy, and both grandfathers ex-military. Like suicide, the armed services run deep in families.[10]

In 2008, Everman turned up in a *New Yorker* article about the play *Black Watch*. He'd attended it with other veterans, and he wasn't thrilled with its anti-war themes nor its suggestion that soldiers only join up due to a lack of alternatives.

'I didn't join the Army because I didn't want to work the deli counter at a convenience store,' he said. 'I joined because I had a specific agenda: to develop the warrior aspect of my persona.'

9 In this sense, the US Army Rangers are directly comparable to the British Army's Parachute Regiment. The latter provide the greatest number of graduates to the SAS, and often perform a similar special operations support function in battle.

10 There were several suicides in Kurt Cobain's ancestry, which apparently makes the same outcome in a descendant far more statistically likely.

Curiously, this is a slightly more strident and pretentious manner of speaking than Everman has in footage of him or other interviews.

He went on to tell the writer, Rebecca Mead, that as a teenager he'd been 'inspired by the autobiography of Benvenuto Cellini. He was the quintessential Renaissance man: an accomplished warrior, an artist, a philosopher.'

This was during Everman's period at Columbia University, which might explain his having apparently reached peak philosophy: 'It's the Platonic ideal of the tripartite soul,' he said. 'Wisdom, courage and temperance. Those are Plato's words, not mine.'

As to the play's anti-war message: 'War sucks,' Everman said. 'I can say that with empirical knowledge – but there are alternatives that are worse in the world.' Mead goes on to report that he'd 'done nothing as a soldier that compromised his ethics'.[11]

Like Kurt with Nirvana, it seems Everman had a vision too.

Everman was twenty-six when he signed up and started basic training to join the Rangers. Relatively old, but utterly determined.

It was when he was in the middle of this hellish selection process that Kurt Cobain killed himself with the shotgun he'd had Dylan Carlson buy.

11 Interestingly, Benvenuto Cellini doesn't appear to have been big on ethics. A sixteenth-century goldsmith and sculptor best known for the autobiography to which Everman refers, he appears to have gleefully murdered several people. (He also had a titillating penchant for sodomy, regarding the ethics of which I of course make no judgement.)

According to Tarver's article, Everman had three drill sergeants, two of whom were sadists. Luckily, it was the easy-going one who saw an article.

'He was reading a magazine, when he slowly looked up and stared, then walked over. "Is this you?" It was a photo of the biggest band in the world, Nirvana. Kurt had just killed himself. Next to Cobain was the band's onetime second guitarist. A guy with long, strawberry-blond curls.

'Is this *you*?'

'There was a lot of, "OK rockstar, give me 50",' Everman said.

The hell of basic training out of the way, Everman entered the next phase of his life as a US Army Ranger. He told Clay Tarver that his first action was somewhere in Latin America, in the covert war on drugs. Now he experienced genuine combat: 'The bond of locking shields with each other, working together to defeat a common enemy. It's a heightened state. Kind of like being in a band onstage, only more so. Everyone looks around, and you *know* something cool is going on here. I knew this was it. This is living.'

He served around three years as a Ranger, then left the army and returned to the US. In Columbia University's *Owl* magazine, an article on him claims that he worked as a bike courier in New York City. He wanted to save money for a trip to Nepal, where he hiked the Himalayas and stayed in a monastery 'in the Everest region' for a few weeks. While there, he divided his time between meditating and doing chores.

From the start of his military life, he'd wanted to make it into the Special Forces. He'd re-enlisted in 2000, and was beginning the final phase of doing so when 11 September 2001 unfolded.

'I saw the video and kind of innately knew we were going to war. I don't believe in fate, but I did feel a strange sense of kismet.'

Fate or not, Everman's enlistment into the 3rd Special Forces Group, better known as the Green Berets, coincided with a massive surge in intensity of battle for Special Forces soldiers.

In Afghanistan, the Green Berets came under the command of General Stanley McChrystal. Known as the 'warrior monk', McChrystal was an obsessive, ambitious soldier who believed wholeheartedly in the efficacy of Special Forces (many generals and military high brass generally remain more sceptical). He took a radical approach based on the philosophy that 'it takes a network to defeat a network'. This meant building an internal special operations intranet, to which soldiers of every rank had access. Basically, they built their own intelligence network, one which everyone could both contribute to and make use of.

McChrystal's modus operandi was sheer, relentless aggression. He was the architect of the helicopter-borne night raids, where Special Forces soldiers stormed the homes of suspected terrorists, then used the intel gathered to immediately storm more. This took place night after endless night, and represented the sort of high-intensity combat of which many Special Forces operatives had hitherto only dreamed.

Everman was a part of these raids. He told Clay Tarver that he'd ridden horseback with the Pashtun, which means that he was there in the war's opening years, training and supporting the Northern Alliance of fighters against the Taliban and fomenting the overthrow of their regime.

'Fighting isn't like the movies,' he told the *New York Times*. 'It's slow, deliberate.'

Later, he fought in Iraq, where Special Forces were deployed at the tip of the spear in more conventional warfare. He rode in a Humvee with the 'full might of the US forces' behind him in the column. He fired grenades as Iraqi tanks exploded, their turrets 'shooting off into the desert'.

'I saw stuff I never thought I'd see. Buildings blew up in front of me.'

At the veterans' group, he told the audience that his experience was everything his Navy SEAL friend had suggested.

'The experience of war and combat – there's no substitute for that. It's a unique and rarefied event.'

The bit-part guitar player had blossomed into his leading role. Tarver recalls Everson's half-sister Mimi meeting a pair of Special Forces soldiers. 'They didn't approach like the usual fanboys who asked: "your brother was in Nirvana?" No, they came to me like: "Jason Everman is your brother?" One turned to the other and said, "dude, do you know what that guy's done?"'

The moodiness that destroyed his relationships with the two huge bands he was briefly a part of didn't go away entirely, it just didn't matter any more.

'He'd get moody sometimes,' an unnamed Special Forces vet told Tarver. 'But it didn't interfere with the task at hand. I'd rather work with somebody who's quiet than ran their suck constantly.'

And the bonds he formed in the military were much stronger than they'd been in music: 'The deepest, most meaningful human relationships I have are with men I served with,' he said during his speech to the veterans' group. 'Guys I call brother, without irony. Much as I liked them, I never called guys I played music with brother.'

Soldiers, especially the elite ones, pride themselves on never leaving a man behind. Bands, in their obsessive pursuit of their own missions, have no such qualms.

Everman left the military as a seasoned and highly decorated veteran. Among his medals is the Combat Infantryman Badge, awarded to Special Forces soldiers who have fought in ground wars.

Without his service, he says he'd never have had the courage to apply to Columbia. Along with the courage, it must have helped that he had a letter of recommendation from General Stanley McChrystal. Everman graduated with a bachelor's degree at the age of forty-five.

Why does any of this matter? Well, without wishing to veer towards the realms of self-help, it's because of what it tells us about fulfilment. Most of us – me especially – can't live through what Everman did (more's the pity, as far as I'm concerned). But we can learn from what he got out of it. And fulfilment, after all, is what we'd wish for all our rejects.

'Challenge leads to achievement, and achievement leads to joy,' Everman said in his speech. 'Seems kind of obvious, but it took me a long time to figure it out.' He equivocates over whether joy is really the word, and whether life satisfaction might be what he really means.

He certainly seems satisfied, judging from the filmed interviews he's given in recent years. There's an ease about his features and posture that wasn't there in the stiff pout of his rock period. There's a light behind the eyes and he's quick to smile.

When I came across that article in 2014, I was wilting from the lack of a challenge, and chained to my desk by those shackles of cool. I can't claim to have made the sort of escape that Everman did, but I wouldn't be writing this book if that moment hadn't taken place.

Everman's story is inspirational – it shows that rejection can be the best thing that ever happens to you, and that every life has several acts. Our former selves stay with us, of course: 'When I listen to Black Flag today,' Everman says, 'I still get goose bumps on my arms.'

It makes me wonder about archetypes, too, and the fact that Everman has perceived and even designed his life through them. That idea of the tripartite soul: 'Throughout my adult life,' he's quoted as saying in the *Owl*, 'I have made the conscious effort to develop three aspects of who I am: the artist, the soldier and the philosopher.'

These are old-fashioned ideas, to put it mildly. Amid the ironic detachment of Gen X – of which grunge is the defining musical movement – they'd have seemed antithetical, overly earnest, childlike if not childish. It would be a laughable idea if Everman hadn't carried it out. Even his name, one letter away from 'everyman', has a sense of the archetype about it.

We don't tend to view our lives in these terms, or types, any more. Might something have been lost?

The story also says a great deal about the arc of a life and its fruition. To think that while Kurt Cobain was blossoming, reaching his tragically early peak in only his mid-twenties, Everman was fledgling – tossing his hair, badly, in a band he shouldn't have been in. The image of him in the desert with the machine gun is the one he was always destined for.

In this case, at least, the reject's life was more natural, more fulfilling, and less dark than their bandleader's. Kurt died at the moment when the full, dreadful weight of adult life was becoming evident. Everman figured out how to throw that weight off. He became a rock star of a different kind and earned a formula for happiness.

Whose life would you choose? It's a stupid question, I know. But is the answer clear for you?

Everman deployed a quote from Ernst Jünger to close his veterans' talk, and I'll now steal from his example:

'Time only strengthened my conviction that it was a good and strenuous life.'

The Lodestars Cross Paths in the Sky

On 1 April 1994, Duff McKagan of Guns N' Roses (see Chapter 10) and Kurt Cobain of Nirvana (see Chapter 12) were both in the first-class cabin of a flight from LA to Seattle.

A few days later, Kurt killed himself. Four weeks after that, Duff almost died when his pancreas swelled and ruptured.

Duff's alcoholism was in its final stages on the flight and was outwardly visible: 'My hair had started to fall out. My body was starting to show it, like huge boils.'

Because of this coincidental crossing of paths, he was one of the last people to speak to Kurt Cobain.

'It was, like eighty-seven words. I was really fucked up. We were both fucked up. I was in my hell, and he in his, and this we both seemed to understand.'

Kurt's misery was pronounced enough for Duff to sense it even through his own. 'The thought crossed my mind to invite him over to my house then and there. I had a real sense that he was lonely and alone that night.'

We know this urge to help was genuine because of something Duff would do a few years later, and that we'll come to shortly. Sadly, he didn't act on it that night with Kurt.

The two rock stars standing together at a baggage claim had begun to draw attention, and Duff got distracted. 'There was a mad rush of people. Lots of them stopped to gawk. I lost my train of thought for a minute and Kurt said goodbye. I received a call two days later that he'd died.'

As you'll remember, Mark Lanegan of Screaming Trees should also have been one of the last people to speak to Kurt, but he was already too far down the road into his own junkie hell to pick up the phone. He did go to Kurt's house a few days after that unanswered call, with Dylan Carlson, to try to find him. Just before they departed, Lanegan, smoking a cigarette and waiting for Carlson, was standing at the bottom of a staircase leading to a small room above the garage. In that moment he had a 'terrible premonition'.

Kurt had killed himself in the room above the garage the same day that Lanegan went looking for him.

Many years later, Duff McKagan would play a large part in saving Lanegan's life. He turned up uninvited at the treatment home Lanegan was due to be kicked out of, put him up in Los Angeles, loaned him cars and clothes, employed him and helped him stay sober.

'He took me under his wing like a guardian angel,' Lanegan said.

Dave Mustaine, Metallica

It's difficult for me to comprehend that the only thing
you feel when you look back on the last twenty years
is rooted in the Metallica thing. – Lars Ulrich, in a
filmed therapy session with Dave Mustaine

IMPOVERISHED, TRANSIENT CHILDHOOD?
CHECK.
ABUSIVE, ALCOHOLIC PARENT? CHECK.
MIND-FUCKING RELIGIOUS WEIRDNESS?[1]
CHECK.
ALCOHOLISM, DRUG ADDICTION,
HOMELESSNESS?
CHECK CHECK CHECK.

D ave Mustaine's autobiography makes his tribulations clear
from the very first page. Like Steven Adler (see Chapter
10), he entered his teens in the 1970s, and led the wild, unsu-
pervised life that characterised his generation of white trash,
hard-rock musicians. But Mustaine is a very different kettle of

---

1 Dave Mustaine spent a period of his childhood as a Jehovah's Witness. Later
in life, despite reading The Satanic Bible, he 'never became an actual Satanist . . .
but certainly did dabble in the dark arts.'

fish to Adler: sharper, more – even monumentally – driven, angrier and meaner.

I didn't like Megadeth, in their eighties and early nineties heyday when I was a kid. Heavy metal wasn't my thing – I didn't like the macho posturing, the endless moshing and the silly leather wristbands.

My friend Andy was into them, of course. I remember 'Symphony of Destruction' playing in his house. Once, his older brother, who loved more melodic music – primarily Depeche Mode – came into the living room where Megadeth were on the stereo, and said: 'What's this? The GRRRR RAAARGGH band?' Much to Andy's annoyance, I laughed in delight.

But coming back to Megadeth now, and looking into his notorious firing, I find Dave Mustaine a lot more interesting.

It's that drive that really stands out. This is a man who was kicked out of Metallica and started a new band that also became one of the 'Big Four' thrash-metal groups, alongside his former bandmates, Slayer and Anthrax. Far from being satisfied at having avenged himself, he never seems to have truly got over his firing. Perhaps that's because Metallica have always been bigger, and are generally considered better. As Lars Ulrich, Metallica's drummer and founder perfectly expresses above, though, I find it amazing that Mustaine didn't move on.

'James Hetfield,' Mustaine writes in his book, 'who used to be one of my best friends, as close as a brother, once observed that I must have been born with a horseshoe up my ass. That's how lucky I've been.

'But the thing about having a horseshoe lodged in your rectum: it also hurts like hell. And you never forget it's there.'

★   ★   ★

Mustaine was born in La Mesa, San Diego County, in 1961. He had two much older sisters and one born three years before him. His father John, who seems to once have had a promising career, had sunk into alcoholism and become abusive. Mustaine recalls his father dragging him home by using channel locks (like large pliers) on his ear. He was four years old at the time.

This unhappy start in life quickly spiralled into his parents divorcing, and a succession of different towns and schools.

'For the most part we were a family on the run, always trying to stay one step ahead of my father, who supposedly was devoting himself to two things: drinking and stalking his estranged wife and children.'

Just when Mustaine got settled, his mother would inform the family that his father had found them, and the moving van would turn up in the middle of the night.

There were food stamps, Medicare, a long, damaging bout of Jehovah's Witnessing with an aunt. The young Mustaine became a 'pariah, always getting picked on, always getting smacked around, which really hardened me'.

He found solace in imaginary worlds populated by his toy figurines, and later in baseball.

And then came music. An uncle who played Frankie Valli and the Righteous Brothers; a sister who had records by the Beatles (see Chapter 1) and Cat Stevens. Mustaine was given a cheap guitar on graduating elementary school and began playing in bands with other kids.

Perhaps the seeds of his rage at being ejected from Metallica are there from the start, because he seemed to be looking for companionship as much as anything else: 'I loved having that bond – where you sit down with another musician. Joining a band was about camaraderie as much as anything else, I suppose. I wanted to *belong*.'

But as for Adler, Mötley Crüe, Aerosmith and, before them all, Lemmy (see Chapter 19) – it was also about sex. The minute Mustaine started playing guitar in bands, he found himself able to attract women.

He discovered drugs and harder rock – Led Zeppelin, and particularly KISS. A symbolic break from healthier pursuits came when his brother-in-law Bob – a beloved figure who had encouraged Mustaine in sports – punched him in the face for listening to Judas Priest.

Marijuana led to alcohol and harder drugs, and before long Mustaine was selling pot to buy more of it, and deliberately flouting his mother's Jehovah's Witness faith. He wanted something like 'normalcy', not endless moves and being considered a freak.

He began asking his mother to hand over packages to visiting buyers when he was out. 'Remarkably enough, she went along with it. At least for a while.' Before long, she fled their apartment, and at fifteen he found himself living on his own. Now, it was either 'sell dope, or peddle my ass. And there was no fucking way I was going to let that happen.' On the other hand, he didn't mind trading dope for sex with girls, especially if they threw in AC/DC records as part of the deal.

A move to Idaho to live with his sister Michelle didn't bring the calm he hoped for. According to Mustaine, Michelle was 'heavily into witchcraft and black magic'. Perhaps she, too, had needed to rebel against her mother's religion. 'This was the beginning of a very long and disturbing flirtation with the occult,' Mustaine writes. 'The effects of which haunted me for years.'

He placed a hex on a boy who'd physically attacked him, making a voodoo doll and breaking its leg. 'A short time later, Wilbur was involved in a car accident; his leg was broken.'

Mustaine eventually moved back to Orange County, California, to set about the 'pursuit of a rock 'n' roll lifestyle'. He practised his guitar, attended parties, fought, fucked and smoked weed.

Before long, inspired by watching local players picking up girls, he was making serious attempts to start a band. An array of odd teenaged characters of various musical abilities was recruited, lost, dropped and even killed in car crashes. Mustaine began selling harder drugs – cocaine, LSD and Quaaludes – alongside the pot, and making more money. But while marijuana calmed him down, when he drank, he 'tended to get really violent'. Initially, he spurned cocaine on the basis that it was linked to disco and house music – for 'Village People and Donna Summers crowds, or the pussies you'd see at a Flock of Seagulls concert'.

A reconciliation with his father was thwarted when John Mustaine fell off a barstool, banged his head and suffered a cerebral haemorrhage. After a brief spell in a coma, he died. Despite his large extended family living in the area, there'd been no one the doctors could ask for permission to crack his skull and relieve the pressure.

In the hospital, Mustaine arrived with a bottle of whisky, and was told by his sister Suzanne that he'd end up just like his father.

'I was a rock 'n' roll rebel. I had my guitar strung across my back, I had a knife in my belt, and I had a sneer on my face.'

Even before he met his fellow members of Metallica, Mustaine had realised he liked to be the boss. 'I had no desire to be a hired gun in someone else's band. I liked to be in charge. I was not good at taking direction.'

Mustaine came across an ad in a local paper from a band looking for a guitarist. The ad referenced Iron Maiden, Motörhead and Budgie, the Welsh band and heavy-metal pioneers. These groups represented something of an unholy trinity for Mustaine, and he called the number provided that same day.

On the phone, Lars Ulrich had 'a strange accent . . . and sounded very young. The pair instantly bonded over Budgie – a band that only a true metal aficionado would know. The pair met up at Ulrich's parents' house, in a rich part of Southern California close to that in which Mustaine's mother had worked as a cleaner. Mustaine was twenty, Ulrich not yet eighteen.

He was introduced to James Hetfield and the other members of the fledgling band when he auditioned for them. From the beginning, he was wary and a little resentful of their differing backgrounds. Ron McGovney, the bass player, drew particular suspicion for his photos of Mötley Crüe and his 'yuppie metal' look.

Mustaine had never been on an audition before. 'Fuck that! I was a leader, not a follower. Playing backseat to someone else really didn't sit well with me and indeed had put me in a bit of a foul mood.'

He found the band odd and comical: 'Lars was as foreign looking as the day we met. James was rail thin, with black spandex tights and a cheetah-print shirt . . .' and, of course, 'a wide leather bracelet. He was trying really hard to be a rock star.'

Lars Ulrich might have seemed foreign, young and laid back, but he had a drive just as great as Mustaine's, and he was already the bandleader. In retrospect, it was never going to work.

Mustaine joined the band, and battle immediately commenced. As ever in music, hair and clothes provided a proxy war. Lars had strong opinions on the footwear. Mustaine wore 'shiny white leather Converse All-Stars. Lars was of the opinion that rock stars wore traditional Chuck Taylors. Fuck that!'

Ulrich liked bands with glammed-up hair. 'You were either like Page and Plant,' Mustaine says, 'hair down, and thus cool. Or you were like KISS, Mötley Crüe and so many imitators (hair up, and thus not so cool). My hair went down. Always did, always will.'

Looking back, Mustaine can perceive the problem clearly: 'I was a band leader. So was Lars.' Ulrich's 'heart was in the right place . . . his taste was misguided'.

But on the most important element, Lars got it right. He came up with Metallica's name.

The band began gigging and recording. Despite his clarity in diagnosing the problem, Mustaine can't help scoring points. He was 'struck by Ulrich's mediocrity' as a drummer. Most of the new material was 'written by me. I point this out simply as a way of illustrating that my role in Metallica was actually quite prominent. I was the lead guitar player and one of the primary songwriters. A band member's role doesn't get more vital than that.'

There were the usual teething problems. Hetfield was anxious on stage and didn't do banter, so Mustaine leapt in. Metallica got better, played more shows, recorded demos, supported bigger bands and built some buzz.

'I'm not sure how we managed to accomplish as much as we did, given the lifestyle we were leading – all that fucking and fighting, drugging and drinking and vomiting. But we did.'

As the band developed a fanbase, experiencing the thrill of having their audience know the words to their songs, Mustaine became increasingly 'aggressive, driven, and unpredictable, and I drank way too much'.

The whole band drank heavily – they were nicknamed 'alcoholica' – but the others were 'different types of drunk'. Mustaine was the 'angry, hostile' kind, as opposed to Lars and James being 'happy drunks'.

When Hetfield kicked one of Mustaine's dogs to prevent it from scratching Ron McGovney's expensive sports car, things boiled over. Rehearsing the same day, a fight broke out and Mustaine punched Hetfield, 'turning his mouth into a pile of bloody Chiclets'.

Ron, a lifelong friend of Hetfield, jumped on Mustaine's back, only to be thrown into an entertainment centre, smashing it to pieces.

'The fight might have gone on longer if not for the presence of my friend and martial arts training partner Rick Solis. I was enraged, ready to kill both Ron and James, when Rick came up from behind and grabbed my elbow, pinching the ulnar nerve and rendering me incapacitated.'

'You're out of the band!' Hetfield screamed.

'Come on, man,' Ulrich said, 'I don't want it to end this way.'

'Fuck you! I quit!' Mustaine responded.

This initial break-up lasted a mere twenty-four hours, but in fact the damage was never repaired. Mustaine and McGovney disliked each other intensely. Acquaintances of Mustaine's broke into Ron's house, and in response to being accused, Mustaine poured a can of beer into the pick-ups of Ron's expensive bass.

Never mind – Ron wasn't long for the band. They'd discovered a brilliant new bass player in San Francisco – Cliff Burton – and soon they were moving the whole band to the city as a condition of his joining.

There were moments of brotherhood yet to come, when Mustaine leapt to Ulrich's defence in fights or bonded with Cliff over music. The bad omens were already appearing though. Mustaine wasn't in the loop over trips to New York, and his name was missing from recording contracts. On stage on the east coast, his higher quality amps suddenly appeared on Hetfield's side of the stage, and he was given 'lousy' ones.

The night before the trip east, Mustaine slept with the girl-friend of another guitarist. His name was Kirk Hammett, then a member of Exodus. Lars Ulrich and James Hetfield had already decided they wanted him to replace Mustaine.

Things fell apart on the trip. During a spell driving the band's U-Haul – drunk and exhausted – Mustaine lost control on a patch of ice, and the truck crashed. Later, rust from the vehicle's ceiling fell into his eyes, and the rest of the band refused to take him to hospital. The self-styled impresario who'd invited them out to New Jersey turned out to be less impressive than expected, and the band's frantic partying took a darker turn. One evening 'took a twist, and alcohol and cocaine gave way to crystal meth. It was evil shit.'

Metallica were taking a lot of drugs, but also gaining a lot of fans. Groupies were there for the taking, and 'everyone wanted to hang with us'.

'You're a bad motherfucker!' the fans shouted at Mustaine when he was on stage. 'I'd nod approvingly. I *was* a bad motherfucker.'

But in the background, plans for Mustaine's sacking were now afoot.

The death blow arrived at the worst of all possible times – a Monday morning. The band had spent the preceding weekend drinking heavily, as usual. Mustaine recalls the moment with cinematic horror:

'When I awoke, they were standing above me, all four of them, grim resignation etched on their faces. My bags were already behind them, packed and ready to go.'

Lars and Mark – the band's road manager – took the lead.

' "You're out of the band," Lars said, without a trace of emotion. "Get your stuff. You're leaving right now." '

It's impossible not to pity the young Mustaine, the full nightmare of rejection descending on him – the destruction of the comradeship he'd craved: 'I felt like I was back in grade school, when I had no control and every day was a vertiginous nightmare.'

On the long, gruesome bus ride back to California, dead broke and withdrawing from alcohol, Mustaine spotted a pamphlet on the floor. It was a handbill on the dangers of nuclear proliferation: *The arsenal of megadeath can't be rid no matter what the peace treaties come to.*

Despite this damascene moment on the highway, and all the good that it inspired,[2] Mustaine never really got over his firing.

---

2 As part of researching *The Rejects*, I interviewed the music writer David Hepworth (see Chapter 22). He made the point that 'Generally speaking, it's a good thing when they [band members] are asked to leave. It's like anything in life, actually – people leaving jobs is more often a good thing than people starting jobs.' A musician like Lemmy (see Chapter 19) seems to have understood this far more instinctively than Mustaine – for whom, perhaps ironically, Lemmy was a hero.

Through all the subsequent years – the towering successes (never quite as towering as Metallica's), the addictions to coke, booze and heroin, the black magic and the born-again Christianity, the injuries and recoveries and platinum records – his departure from Metallica remained an open wound.

Like other rejects in this book (Pete Best springs to mind; see Chapter 1), the ambition that took Mustaine to the heights now meant he couldn't recover. That drive was a blessing and a curse. He did it all over again, in his own way, with his own band. But as well as powering him, his ambition tortured him. He'd been fired. His friends had turned on him. He could never seem to heal.

That, it seems, is one of the pacts that a musician must make. *This band ain't big enough for the two of us.*

14

Danny Whitten, Crazy Horse

The following is a work of fiction by the author. Names, characters, places, and events are either the product of the author's imagination or are used fictitiously. Any resemblance to actual persons, living or dead, events, or locales is entirely coincidental.

Every musician has one guy on the planet that he can
play with better than anyone else. You only get one guy.
My guy was Danny Whitten. – Neil Young

1. 2 October 1972

I've seen the needle and the damage done . . .
but every junkie's like a setting sun.

Oh boy. This ain't working like it used to.

I wake up shivering and pull the comforter tight. The sheets are wet – almost like I pissed the bed but there's too much of it to be that. It's sweat. The shivering means I keep finding the cold patches and that makes the whole thing worse. My knees have started up again too. Those motherfuckers.

Sitting up is difficult, but I get there. The air is dusty, and everything is dirty – the sheets, the floor, the top of the nightstand. And damn – it's hot. It's not just me, or the need. The blinds are thin and fall ain't really arrived in LA. I got big windows, the biggest room in this place – the penthouse suite in a mid-city flophouse.

There's a quart of Don Julio on the nightstand, about half full. I reach for it and try to still the trembling in my arm. Relax. Take it easy. I bring the bottle up and feel the vapour rise and burn my eyeballs. I take a slug, pull a face, put the bottle back. My stomach is raw and for a moment I think I'll puke. Deep breaths. Maybe if there'd been ice in the box I'd have gone and got some. Used a glass, made a real drink. I laugh. Who am I kidding?

Alrighty then. Stick to the plan, Danny boy. In the nightstand are my works and a thin glass tube with what I've got left inside it. The needle has come away from the eyedropper. Damn it. I pop it back in, but my fingers are trembling, and it takes a long time to get the cuff back on. I used to have a real hypo, but I threw it out when I tried to kick. You need to be in good with a doc or a vet to get yourself one of those, and yours truly ain't.

I need water to shoot up. I take another slug of tequila and stand up. The pain sparks out of my knees into my shins and thighs. 'Goddammit,' I say out loud. Which ain't helpful because I don't wanna draw attention to myself. But the house is quiet. No one appears when I make it to the kitchen. I breathe deep and relax a little.

The kitchen is tiled pale yellow and red, Spanish style. The ceramic in the taps is chipped and cracked. There are dirty pots from more days than I can remember, and the flies are havin' a fiesta. These things wear me down. Still, it could be worse. Where I grew up, you could see the dirt through the kitchen floor. That makes me think of Brenda. I miss you, big sister. Maybe I'll see you on this goddamn tour. I get a little beat of excitement when I think of that.

I half fill a glass, then decide to fill it up and drink it. The cold hurts me inside but I know I need it. I grip the sink and let it pass, half fill the glass again and head back to my room.

I go through the ritual. For a little while, this was what I loved. The candle, music playing. The smell of the hit heating and bubbling. The plump vein ready and waiting. Not any more. It takes a lot of looking for it. I miss a couple times – 'come on baby' – then I find it and draw blood into the dropper, and I squeeze the nipple. There's that warm, distant sun. A weak edge of bliss I can't fully move into. The shivering edges off and my knees feel a little better. It's not enough to catch a nod, but I don't want that – no sir. It's just enough to get straight. I've got a plan. I've got a plane to catch.

I've gotta get off of this shit.

I take a shower. Afterwards, when the mirror clears up, I see my big dumb head looking back at me. My blond hair's gone dark with the water. They used to tell me I looked like a surfer or a farm boy, but you'd have to say I look a little less good than that right now. Neil's roadie, Willie B. Hinds, calls me the Golden Lizard. Maybe I'm finally living up to that shit. I take another slug of tequila and smoke a couple cigarettes and feel better.

In my jeans and boots I stand a little stronger. When I left the Navy, they told me I'd be in a wheelchair by forty. So that gives me eleven more years upright. But hey, like I keep telling folks – at this rate I ain't gonna make thirty, so the least of my worries is a goddamn chair.

There's a cleanish shirt in the wardrobe. I feel cooler now I'm well, so I put on my suede jacket with the fur collar, too. I love this fuckin' coat, man. It's like my suit of armour. Out in the brightness I try not to think too much. The dope is good for that. It silences those little asshole voices.

There's a diner on Western, and I find one of the corner booths I like and slide into it. It's quiet at this between time. The booths are bright red and the cream tables are clean. The sun floods the place through the big old plate glass windows. It's good, this happy, healthy stuff. The waitress is a grizzled old bird – she must be seventy at least. I order scrambled eggs and coffee and she eyes me all suspicious when I say I don't want toast. That shit'll scratch up my insides, I want to tell her. But I just give her my best country-boy smile, like I'm a charming disgrace.

When I'm finished eating, I smoke two more cigarettes and contemplate the tasks that lie ahead. The waitress comes back to take my plate and gives me the stinkeye. I laugh.

'Somethin' funny?' she asks.

'Almost everything, when you think about it long enough.'

'Oh yeah,' she says, standing over me with the plate in her hand, like she might break it over my head. 'Like what?'

'Oh, you servin' a bum like me at a grand old age like yours.'

And – hallelujah – there you go – she knows how to smile after all.

There's a phone booth in the corner and I go to it and slide in a dime. 'Come on, baby,' I say as it rings. 'Don't do it to me.' My old heart feels like it'll blow when someone picks it up.

'Yeah?' says a voice.

'It's Danny.'

'Danny who?'

159

'Whitten. Come on now.'

'What up, pumpkin head?'

'I was thinkin' I'd swing by. In maybe a half hour.'

'Do your thing, baby,' the voice says, real cool, and hangs up.

Winnie is my man. He lives near the Peppermint West, which brings back the good memories. Dancing competitions, Marie Janisse. A real hot number on the scene – her words, not mine. I can't see her any more. I don't want her to see me like this.

Winnie lives in a low rise behind a strip mall. Dingy yellow paint and shady motherfuckers sitting in the walkways. I buzz, and like always he doesn't open for a good couple minutes. When he does, he stands in the crack of the doorway where he can peek out left and right.

'What up, blond boy,' he says.

His hair is a big unruly 'fro, and he's got a kaftan with some cool cosmic shit on it. He's a jazz man. The music is playing from behind him, saxes and trumpets in a beautiful squall. Man, I love black music. I know it's dumb, but it makes me feel better that he's a music guy.

I grin, slip him twenty, and he palms across another little glass tube.

'You still dancin', pumpkin head?' he asks.

'Like a bull in a china shop.'

He laughs – a wheezy smoky sound and a smile that's all big yellow teeth.

'That's good,' he says, 'I remember that shit.'

In my dance-contest days, me and Marie had a routine. She'd pull a red scarf out of her sleeve and I'd charge her down like a bull. We won with it every time.

160

'You take it easy,' Winnie says. He begins to close the door.

'I won't see you for a while,' I can't help saying.

'Oh yeah? Why not?'

'I'm leaving town. Me and the band are back with ol' Neil.'

Winnie's eyes go a little distant. I don't know if he's jealous or if he just doesn't care.

'All right,' he says. 'Well, stay cool, baby.' And then the door's closed and he's gone, and I better hightail because the cats in the shadows are looking at me all hungry.

I take a cab to LAX. I'm late – I'm always late. I feel cool, though. I took another shot. Three a day, is the plan. Weaker doses each time. I got my guitar and a grip with a change of clothes, a fresh bottle of top-shelf tequila and enough Valium to last for weeks. Frisco, here I come. The city where the drugs found me in the first place.

On the plane I think of Rochelle. There's a letter in my wallet but I don't need to read it. She's asking when we'll be together, if we'll ever be together. When she's older, I wrote back. When I'm good.

I wrote my best ever song for her. 'I Don't Want to Talk About It'.

I think of Brenda too. I don't want either of them to see me like this. I wanna get straight. Sweet lord, I'm gonna.

2.

They send Willie to pick me up from San Fran airport. He's a friendly little wise-faced guy with a Buick.

'You don't look so good,' he tells me.

'On the other hand, you look fuckin' great.'

'I try my best,' he says, watching the road. He wears glasses and I don't think he can see too well in the dark.

'Come on, Willie,' I tell him. 'You drive like a little old lady.'

He chuckles, and I feel him relax a little. 'All right, golden boy,' he says. 'Let's get you to the palace.'

It feels good to break out of the city, the traffic, the stop signs. Every time we hit one I feel like I'm gonna scream. Then we're winding up old Bear Gulch and into the forest. Neil lives at the end of it. The pines press in on the headlights and the car bucks and drifts on the dirt road. Big old forest bugs swirl in the white cones of light and patter against the hood. I can feel the need coming on. Sweat is pouring off me and I need to find a bathroom.

'You all right?' Willie asks me.

'Ready to get where I'm going.'

'Remember how you used to drive around the speed bumps?' he says. 'Scaring the hell out of us on the wrong side of the highway?'

I laugh. Good old Willie. 'I sure do.'

We reach the ranch. There are hippie girls sitting by a fire. I can hear music coming from the big cabin. And there's Jack Nitzsche, walking on over to the car. Dearly beloved sometime bandmate. A skinny little guy with his sideburns and long thin hair and sharp eyes behind the spectacles.

'Howdy,' he says as I get out.

I think perhaps I've got away with delaying the big hello with old Neil, but then I see Jack's eyes flick over my shoulder and stay there. I turn and see the main man himself, loping down the track from the house. Carrie Snodgress is with him. Now that he's a star, he left his wife. He picks his way carefully, lanky in his jeans, plaid shirt and boots. He's bearded and wears a soft-looking hat. Carrie's got on calfskin boots and a leather coat over her dress. It's cold up here. I'm shivering a little, that's for sure.

'Danny,' Neil says. That soft voice that comes from his nose as well as his throat. He looks at me all warm. There's a light in his eyes like he's on a mission from God. 'How you doing?'

'I'm good,' I tell him, and give him the full-beam smile.

'That's great,' he says. 'Welcome.'

I look at Carrie. She's beautiful. Soft and slim, and you can picture how good it would be to kiss her, to feel her limbs wrapping around yours. She's got these big old eyes that turn down a little at the sides and make her look serious and kinda sad.

'Hi,' she says, smiling at me.

'It's good to have you back, Danny,' Neil says. 'This is gonna be fun.'

Neil doesn't know what's wrong with me. He's a little naive, for someone so smart. He sniffs a little coke, smokes a little weed, but he's never been near no needle.

'I'm excited,' I say. Please God, make Willie show me to my goddamn place.

'Well,' Neil says, giving me his cockeyed, goofy type of grin. 'Settle in, I'll see you tomorrow.'

'See you then.'

Willie is carrying my bag and guitar. He's heading towards the buildings beyond the fire as Neil turns and leads Carrie up the hill again.

Jack gives me a look I don't like.

163

'Jesus Christ, man,' he hisses. 'You're fucked up.'

'I'm just on Valium, man,' I say, 'take it easy.'

'Bull*shit*,' Jack says.

His eyes flick after Neil and Carrie. And even as fucked up as I am I see the desire in them. Jack wants Carrie. Ambitious, for this Phil Spector-lookin' motherfucker.

'Keep on dreamin', Jackie boy,' I tell him.

'Ah come off it, Danny,' he says, embarrassed.

'G'night, Jack.'

I set off after Willie, who's turned around, waiting for me.

When I reach the firepit I pause, a little out of breath, and take in the hippie girls. They don't look back at me in the way girls used to. I glance over my shoulder. Jack is heading up the hill. He's gonna go tell Neil. Shit.

Still. I got more pressing matters to attend to.

Willie is leading me toward the White House.

'Aww,' I say, coming to a stop.

'What is it?'

'You putting me in there?'

'Yeah. The whole band's in there. What's up?'

'Ain't there nowhere else?'

'No, there ain't.'

'What about that old Airstream?'

'Seriously?'

'Goddamn it, Willie, yes.'

'Neil ain't gonna like it.'

I don't know what to say to that, so I say nothing. I grab my stuff and head to the trailer.

3. 11 October 1972

My God, I love Neil. I hate him too, but that's just my own sickness talking. Neil likes playing in groups, but basically he's a solo artist. Deep down he knows he has to do the gig by himself. Sometimes I wish it was me standing in the middle of that stage, but I know it ain't my place. Danny the sideman, *that's* me.

No, I been more than that, I try to remind myself. It was me and Neil that made 'Cinnamon Girl'. Man, I remember letting out that 'whoo' as Neil's second solo kicked in. The truest sound I ever made. I was the happiest man alive, and you can hear it.

David Briggs, Neil's producer, told me I'm world class. He told me it was good for Neil to have a guy up in his face who could sing his fuckin' ass off *and* play the best guitar of anyone who ever played with him.

'That's how you get good,' he told me. 'By being with people who are good.'

He said I just gotta wait. 'You can't pick your own time – that's picked by other people for you – you just gotta keep being yourself.'

It sure reassured me at the time.

According to Jack Nitzsche, I give Neil the blackness he lacks. He likes to make clear that Billy and Ralph don't impress him. He says I'm the only black man in the band. I don't know about that, but like I said, I love black music.

I gotta hang on to some of this, remember these good things, or I'll go crazy. Please believe me. I should be up there in the fuckin' stars and instead I'm way down here in the dirt.

Neil forgives. He comes to take a look at me and he says: 'Maybe tomorrow.'

And after all, this has been going on for too damn long. I remember a night on stage with the Horse, at the Fillmore East. It was the early days with me and the big H. I was blissed out so hard on the drug and the beautiful heavy groove that I just stopped playing and shut my eyes and smiled and suddenly Neil was shouting, 'Danny! SING!'

After the show, Neil tore the band a new one.

Jack told me about it later. He was yellin' at 'em like it was their fault.

'All right – who scored for Danny?'

'I wanted to tell him "Danny did!"' Jack said. He gave me one of his little angry-man frowns when I laughed. 'It wasn't funny. Like anybody else in this band knows how to score smack in the middle of the night in Manhattan.'

That first tour was the best time of my life. I got this bad feeling it'll never be that good again. It was the time we all realised what a big star Neil was gonna be – we felt like we would be too. But he was different. He was friendly and talkative backstage, like we all were. But before each show he'd walk off outside on his own for ten minutes, like this preparation thing. On stage he had this real stoned, quiet persona. I saw that he was different, that he saw everything differently.

He played that demon dog Old Black, and I played his orange Gretsch 6120 from the Buffalo Springfield days. Man, the sound of those twin guitars. Raw and real deep, always on the edge of control. Heavy and howling like weather, beautiful and wild. Behind us, Ralph and Billy's rhythm section drove us on like war drums. We'd improvise around the songs like Coltrane or Davis. It was just what we all wanted.

Neil would open up with acoustic songs some nights, and then we'd tune up and play 'Everybody Knows'. He'd speak to the audience.

'This is Danny Whitten on guitar. He wrote this song and I thought it was so good I better get in on a good thing and co-write it.'

Then we'd tear into 'Downtown'. If anybody wrote a better song about scoring drugs, I ain't heard it. The Velvet Underground can kiss my ass.

'Hey, I can tell you guys want to play, don't you?' Neil would say at the end of the sets. 'What do you want to play?'

Me, Ralph and Billy, in unison: ' "Down by the River".'

Stephen Stills would show up, and sometimes Neil would bring him out to play. Man, we'd get $250 a night in the spring. It was just before everything blew. You could feel it coming. By the summer, Neil was playing shows with Crosby, Stills, Nash and Young and people were calling 'em the American Beatles.

And then Neil fired us. It turned out it *had* been coming – just not for us. Neil likes to keep on movin' on.

Being at Broken Arrow is a little like the Laurel Canyon days, back when we were the Rockets and everybody wanted to stop by and play. But this is more organised, professional. We're here to learn Neil's new songs.

Now Neil directs. He's got this cool, hard focus, this vision that's almost like a fuckin' mountain face. You can't conceive how it got made or how anything could conquer it.

I had a vision, I know that. When I was the frontman and we were Danny and the Memories. I made everyone dress real smooth – green velvet pullovers, black pants and boots. 'Make sure those shoes are shined, boys.' Back then it was me everyone looked to for direction. 'Sixty-five – there's me at the front, clean cut and smooth as hell, even though that was the crazy year . . . Acid, pot, the girls.

Then we saw the Byrds, and knew we had to learn to play as well as sing. We all moved back to LA, and I grew my hair long and shut myself in a basement for six months, and when I came out, I played guitar. We renamed ourselves the Psyrcle – you gotta laugh – and we started over again.

But all the time I was just a sideman in waiting. Just pretending . . .

Shit.

4. 25 October 1972

I keep being late. They let me use a car and I drive into the city to score. It takes a long time, up and down that track from the ranch and back. I try to keep the doses low, but I've overdone it a couple of times and couldn't play.

Now I'm here and I'm failing it's harder to hold the darkness back. There's something rotten in me, I know it. I'm shit and I come from shit. My daddy was the devil and he made me. Those three years with him ain't never really ended. Brenda, I wish we could talk about it sometimes. Why are we so afraid? We left him, didn't we? I thought we'd escaped.

Even the good bits of us ain't right. Grandma and Mamma tried, but they were both goddamn drunks like me. Brenda, at least it didn't get you. You're so good and I love you so much.

Remember how we used to sit on that dirty floor and make up stories? We used to take it in turns to go look through that smeared-up old window and see if Mamma was coming home? Two jobs, three. Never knew what sort of mood she'd be in.

The bottles in the cabinet. The good times when she danced. Boy – she could dance. Slinkin' around the living room, lost in the music, drink in her hand. If we were lucky, she'd dance with us.

Later, Grandma in the armchair with the worn through arms. Picking at the stuffing in her sleep. Drunk and drooling. Waiting on her to wake up and maybe make us dinner.

Why am I so fuckin' sad?

Neil comes to the trailer. He sees how I am, and he says: 'It's OK, Danny, maybe tomorrow.'

5. 27 October 1972

I'm working on a new song. It's called 'Oh Boy'.

I think about the times I was happier than now
Oh boy

6. 31 October 1972

I can't play. It's like I'm sleeping standing upright.

We try to rehearse.

'Danny, ya gotta play,' Neil says. 'Ya gotta learn these songs.'

'Hey, Jack,' I say, 'play "Be My Baby".'

No one laughs. There's a lot of silence now, whenever I'm around.

7. 7 November 1972

We're sitting around the table in the big room. Neil likes us to eat together. There's a community forming up here but I ain't part of it. These people gotta live together, sleep together, eat together for a year.

Neil doesn't like me being in the Airstream. He knows there's something up with that. He took me aside earlier.

'It's gonna be hard, Danny,' he told me. He speaks softly. He always did but now everybody listens to him, falls silent when he speaks so he can keep it real soft. 'It's gonna be a real tough tour. The biggest we've ever done. Ice hockey arenas.'

He's telling me to get straight, that he can't forgive for ever.

So I made it to dinner. I feel pretty good. I got the dose right. I'm sweating a little but I'm not falling into my own plate. The tequila helps. I got a big old tumbler filled almost to the brim. I must've drunk the best part of a bottle today but it ain't really touched the sides.

Around the table are Jack, Neil, Carrie. David Briggs is here. He looks tired, serious. Everyone is working hard, except me I guess.

Ralph and Billy are drinking beer and talking about Billy's mom, Velma. She's Crazy Horse's witch-mother, and she's got flu. Ralph and Billy are dark little guys. People used to joke that we looked like a surfer backed up by two mobsters. I love 'em, but I can't seem to know what to say to 'em.

There are two hippie girls in calico dresses cooking some sort of stew. Neil's on a health kick, at least with what he eats. There are joints going around. It's only me drinking hard liquor. I finish off my glass and pour another.

We're halfway through eating and no one is speaking. I feel this urge to say something, that this is some sort of opportunity I shouldn't miss. I wanna be the Danny of old, to hold the floor.

'I ever tell y'all how my knees got fucked up in the first place?' I ask. I look around the table, the faces blurring into each other. I take another drink.

'Tell us, Danny,' Neil says. He puts his fork down, leans back in his chair with one hand on the table.

'It was when I was in the Navy, back in Ohio. I had this CO, man, a sick son of a bitch. Most sadistic man I ever met.'

Everyone's quiet, but Jack – good old Jack – he can't help wanting to help me. 'Like a big guy?' he asks.

'Not really. Just mean. He had these eyes like little fuckin' stones. One night it got real cold, like fifteen degrees. Everything froze over. He put me on guard duty for the whole night.'

'Shit,' somebody says.

'I did it, eight hours. I tried to keep warm, pacin' and hoppin' and all that. In the morning I had frostbite in my knees. They swelled up like two fuckin' balloons, man. I was in bed for four months.'

'My God,' Carrie says.

'It gave me rheumatoid arthritis. They said I'd be in a chair by the time I'm forty.'

No one says anything, but I got their attention. It occurs to me I can still hold a fuckin' room. Danny the frontman.

I finish the drink, pour another. I can feel the heat of the stares. The two hippie girls are blurry, awkward figures at the end of the room.

'Did you ever feel like killing somebody?' I ask the table.

171

Jack – God bless you, Jack, you might be a little snitch but I know you love me – laughs.

No one else does.

8. 11 November 1972

I spend more time in the trailer on my own. Sometimes whole days disappear. I got some coke on my last run to Frisco, and more smack than I ever bought in one go. I'm a rich man, baby. I did speedballs for a couple of days until the coke ran out. After that, between hits I drank a lot of tequila and swallowed Valium. How long's it been, a week?

It's easier to come out at night when everyone's asleep. I walk around the ranch in the moonlight that slashes through the pines. It's cold but I got my coat. There are coyotes howling, sometimes they sound close. I look up at the low, rolling hills around the ranch like I might see one silhouetted against the sky.

In the afternoons Carrie brings me sandwiches. I can see it's hard for her to sit in the trailer with me. It's bad in here. She's like this beautiful, clean thing, visiting my hell.

'How about we go outside, Danny?' she asks. She has her hands crossed in her lap.

'I'm sorry,' I say. 'I guess I'm feeling pretty rough.'

'It's OK.' She's pale – from the stink in here perhaps.

'You know,' she says. 'Neil has so much faith in you. He just knows you're gonna be great again.'

Oh boy.

'Come on, try to eat,' Carrie says, and gestures to the sandwiches. They sit on the plate – layers of cheese and turkey and some healthy lookin' bread. They're big and impossible. The idea I could put one in my mouth . . . I been living on milk and Magic Puffs.

I laugh. 'I guess it's hard to teach an old dog new tricks,' I tell her.

'I guess so,' she smiles back at me.

And this smile just breaks me. I wasn't ready for it and suddenly I'm crying.

'I can't do it, I can't do it,' I tell her. 'I don't belong here.'

And I cry while she strokes my hair and tells me it's OK. But of course, both of us know it ain't.

9. 16 November 1972

Neil comes to visit me between rehearsals. He brings an old Martin acoustic with him and tries to teach me songs one on one. I try, I do. The speedball run scared me so now I'm shooting more smack. I nod out a couple of times.

'Maybe tomorrow,' Neil says.

10. 18 November 1972

There's a knock at the door. Shit. What time is it? It's bright outside the windows. The door opens before I can say anything, and Willie is standing framed in it.

'Danny,' he says. He ain't smiling.

'Good morning, Willie.'

'It's a little later than that, Danny.'

'All right. What's up?'

'Why don't you come on up to the house?' Willie says.

'I'm gonna need a little time.'

'Twenty minutes,' Willie says. 'Don't keep Neil waiting now.'

'Sure.'

The door closes. I find my works and some water and cook up. I'm frightened and I keep missing the vein. Eventually I get there.

I'm already in my clothes, so I just take a drink, smoke a cigarette and head outside.

'Come on, buddy,' Willie says.

It's weird, man, walking up to that big old house. That fairy-book place with its towers and turrets. It's like a wizard's house. I guess it sort of *is*. I'm up above the stands of pines in the ranch now. I can see the white house, the cabins, my trailer. Neil's cars are lined up beside 'em. Fifties Caddies and Buicks. He pays a guy full time to take care of 'em.

I gotta stop halfway up because I'm out of breath and sweatin' again.

'You all right?' Willie asks.

'Nope,' I say, and laugh.

'Take your time.'

I squint up at the house, but I can't see anyone behind the glass in the dozens of windows.

'All right,' I tell Willie, and we set off again.

Neil answers the door. He don't smile. I can hear someone in the kitchen and guess that's where Carrie is.

We walk through to the living room. Whenever I been up here before, that's where Neil is. In the corner of the room, Old Black is leaning in a guitar stand. That old demon dog Les Paul. Only Neil had the patience to retune the motherfucker every five minutes because of that dumb-ass Bigsby vibrato.

I stand in the centre of the room. Neil looks at me. Willie has slipped out. It's like the world is rushing towards me, tearing into me so I don't feel steady on my feet. It's at odds with the psychic cool of the smack. It's like my body knows what's happening despite it and is acting accordingly.

'Sit down, Danny,' Neil says.

By the window there's a big old armchair, an upturned barrel for a table and a smaller wooden chair. I take that one. Neil sits down softly in the armchair. He's got the sleeves of his plaid shirt rolled up. When he's serious his jaw takes on this kinda tight look, and there's no smile to take the sting outta those hawk eyes.

'I'm sorry, Danny,' he says. 'It ain't working. I've gotta let you go.'

I realise I'm smiling, this weird-feeling grin that's locked over my mouth.

'I'm sorry,' he says again.

'I get it,' I tell him. 'Ain't your fault.'

'We'll get you back to LA. Give you a few bucks.'

'Thanks, man.'

'Maybe you can get some help with this shit.'

'Maybe.'

'Get straight. Then we can play together again. It's just I need you to play.'

'Shit,' I say. 'Please, Neil. Please don't do this.' The smile's gone now and I can feel the tears coming.

'I have to, Danny. It's not happening, man. You're not together enough.'

'I've got nowhere else to go, man . . . What am I gonna tell my friends?'

'Go back home to LA. You tell 'em you're not well and you need to get better.' He glances at the door.

'I know I can get it together. Please, Neil.'

'Not this time, Danny. We're too far into it all now. I'm sorry. I tried.'

'. . . Well all right,' I say.

Neil stands up. 'Goodbye, Danny,' he says. 'Take care of yourself.'

'Sure thing, Neil,' I say.

We shake hands, and then Willie is back in the room and we're headed out and Carrie appears and kisses me and she's crying and I'm out the door. I can hear Carrie talking to Neil and she's saying: 'I'm scared, I'm scared, this doesn't feel right,' but then the door closes behind me with a slam. Before I know it, we're at the bottom of the hill.

'You wanna say any goodbyes?' Willie asks.

'Nope,' I tell him. 'Just let me get my shit.'

11.

Fifty bucks and plane ride back to LA. Goddammit.

I'm in the toilets at San Francisco airport. I'm getting my shit together to shoot up but then this rage just surges up in me. I throw the smack into the bowl and flush. Then I'm stomping my works under my boot with little pieces of glass shooting off all over the place. I hear voices outside sounding surprised. I realise I'm shouting, and then I'm smashing my head into the door over and over.

'What the hell?' someone yells.

'What's going on in there, sir?' someone else says.

I wrench open the door and clatter out with my guitar case cracking into the frame and storm past them. There's a man in a suit and another in slacks and a shirt, both of them staring.

'Get a fuckin' grip,' I tell myself. I find a seat and wash down a Valium with a slug of tequila. The bottle is almost empty. It was full when I left the ranch. I can feel myself trembling, people lookin' at me. I wanna scream and shout and smack myself in the head.

'You asshole,' I tell myself, keeping my voice low. 'Stupid fucking asshole.'

The two women at the gate look at me real funny when I board but I make it on to the plane. I've finished the bottle before we even take off. Things start to get blurry. Time breaks up into little segments with lost bits in between. I got that same feeling that the world is rushing towards me like wind. Then I come to, and I can't remember what happened.

I push the button in the plane's ceiling, and a woman appears beside me.

'Sir?'

'Tequila,' I say.

She looks at me doubtfully, but she goes and gets the drink.

'Would you like soda?' she asks.

I shake my head, focus on trying to take the cup off of her without spilling it.

I can feel the need coming on, the fuckin' pill wasn't enough to hold it back – never is. I scrabble in my bag for the bottle, then drop the lid and almost spill the pills. 'Motherfucker,' I say.

The man next to me tuts and says: 'For God's sakes.'

I wash the pill down with the drink.

This ain't gonna be enough. I need more alcohol. I panic and hit the button again. This time two women come and they're telling me I've had enough and they're not gonna give me no more. I'm standing and telling them they don't understand, then I try to push past 'em to get to the drinks and they're pushing back and looking afraid. And then I feel hands on me from behind, gripping my arms and crossing 'em and whoever it is turns me around so I can't see 'em and they push me down the gangway to the back and into an empty row.

'Settle down or I'll cuff you,' says a voice.

I'm in the window seat, and he sits down next to me. A big guy in a sports jacket with a Marine-type haircut.

'You a cop?' I ask him.

'Yup,' he says. 'Now shut up and sit still.'

The fear and the anger and the shock and the pills and drink are too much. I pass out.

Outside LAX the sun beats down on me. Two cabs refuse to take me but the third does, thank God. There's traffic on the 405 and I'm shivering in the backseat and all I can think of is home. The sun is setting when I get off on Manhattan Blvd. I need to walk back to Western to the liquor store, where I buy two more bottles of Jose. Then I'm walking to the house, crying.

No more smack, I keep telling myself. It's a strict diet of Valium and booze. It's funny, when I became the guy who knew about drugs, I told 'em never to take depressants when you're drinkin'. Well, I can't take my own advice now. This is the only way through.

My new song keeps running through my head in this broken little loop and already I hate it. I keep thinking about Jack. I feel like I need to know if he loves me like I think he does. I get up and make it downstairs to the phone.

When I call the White House, Jack answers, thank God.

'Danny?' he says.

'Would you be there for me, no matter what?' I ask him.

'Sure,' he says.

'That's all I wanna know.' I hang up and go back to my room.

The night is upon me now, and I know I can't face it. I take another Valium and drink a whole shitload of tequila. Fuck you, Danny boy.

I stand, and limp across the room again. I need to make it to the bathroom. I ain't sure why.

The world has stopped rushing towards me now. It's almost silent. I take a few more steps. Then one more – into the black.

Interlude:

The Elephant in the Room

Whooooo!

It's the happiest sound imaginable. It comes at two minutes and ten seconds into Neil Young and Crazy Horse's 'Cinnamon Girl', a little way into Young's oddly brilliant, one-note guitar solo. It's the sound of Danny Whitten, losing himself in the music he was making. 'It feels so good, you have to laugh,' says Jimmy McDonough in his definitive biography of Young, *Shakey*.

It's also the sound of two musicians perfectly in tune with each other. They've hit upon a new kind of music; heavy and raw but urgent, bright and beautiful too. It's been called 'proto-grunge', which is a bit silly, but in its own way quite accurate. The unadorned, unpretentious style, the rawness (that word again — it's really the only one) in the recording but also the playing. The looseness and 'realness' that Young says he's always strived for.[1]

But it's another song that I became obsessed with while writing this book. It's called 'Come on Baby Let's Go Downtown', which was first released by Crazy Horse, without Young, shortly

---

1 And of course it's there in the aesthetics too — Young in 1969 and 1970 was fond of a plaid shirt and well-worn jeans.

before Whitten died.[2] The live version which features Young is a surging shot of pure, druggy euphoria, with the weird alchemy that all great songs have – that indefinable thing that makes it magical. Having discovered it embarrassingly late, with the fervour of the convert I quickly decided it was one of my favourite rock songs ever recorded. The song is about scoring heroin, the drug that would indirectly kill Whitten (he died of acute diazepam and alcohol poisoning, desperate to get off heroin) and destroy his place in Young's band.

It appears on *Tonight's the Night*, Young's loose, druggy 1975 album mourning the deaths of Whitten and Bruce Barry, his friend and roadie. The album sounds like the later stages of a really good party – raucous and rough – made bittersweet by the undertow of sadness. It's amazing that an artist in his pomp put out such an unpolished record – but, ever the contrarian, that's exactly why Young did it.

Despite the co-write credit on the album, 'Downtown' is a Whitten song. He presumably wrote it in 1968 or early 1969, because Young and Crazy Horse were playing it on the tour around the *Everybody Knows This Is Nowhere* album. The 'main' version on *Tonight's the Night* was recorded live in 1970. Curiously, though this recording is generally considered to have taken place at the Fillmore East in Manhattan, it's not the same

---

2 In his book *Deep 70s*, the aforementioned David Hepworth included 'Downtown' in a list of deep cuts from the decade. I asked if he had any thoughts on Whitten: 'I don't know an awful lot about him at all, I just know his music. But clearly, the people who make it . . . they just have a kind of commitment to survival that a lot of people who don't make it don't have. They've just got something inside them that keeps them going. Neil Young, Keith Richards, you've got loads of people who've been near the edge but have come away from it and survived.'

version that appears on *Crazy Horse at the Fillmore 1970*. On the version on that album, Whitten and Young sing the original lyrics:

Come on baby let's go downtown
Let's go let's go let's go downtown
Come on baby let's turn you around
I'll turn you turn you turn you around

On the main version from *Tonight's*, the lines about turning around have been replaced by a repeat of the main chorus refrain. Presumably, 'turn you around' was slang for getting well again when withdrawing from the drug. Perhaps it was this that Neil suggested they cut, thus turning the song into a co-write.[3]

For me, 'Downtown' is the perfect drug song. It captures the illicit excitement, the mission and the sense of promise implicit in scoring. One element of its genius is the framing of the song as an attempt to persuade a lover or friend to join the narrator. Anyone who's ever scored drugs will recognise this. No one really wants to go off and get them on their own. They want accomplices, to share the fun but also the guilt.

Whitten conjures this perfectly, selling the victim on the plan with talk of food stoops, a full tank of gas and a 'jumpin' tune'.

3 Despite the lines Young uttered onstage regarding 'Downtown' – that he thought it was so good he better make it a co-write – I somehow don't believe this was a cynical act. Generally, though, 'change a word, take a third' is an established method for a canny musician to make money from another. While we're on the subject, I find it hard to believe that Whitten didn't have a hand in some lines from 'Cinnamon Girl': 'Pa send me money right now / I'm gonna make it somehow / I need another chance / you see, your baby loves to dance.' Whitten occasionally asked his mother to send him money when his primary source of income came from dance contests.

A full moon has risen, and the dealers will soon be out and 'sellin' stuff'.

It must be downtown LA the narrator wants to go to score,[4] but it could be anywhere in America. It could be some smaller town or city, back in Ohio or Georgia: full moons and pick-up trucks, a quick bite, nervous excitement and music, alcohol and cigarettes. The dark promise of pleasure that comes with the night.

This is an experienced user talking:

Pretty bad when you're dealin' with the man,
And the light shines in your eyes

I imagine this to be a reference to encountering the police, and their shining a torch into the narrator's eyes to check his pupils.

One line in the song is harder to gauge:

Don't you be caught with a tear in your eye

Clearly addressed to the friend or lover the narrator wants to persuade, this is more ambiguous. Are they afraid, or are they already sad for Whitten/the narrator, because everybody knows this only goes one way?

The music is perfect – driving, country-tinged rock 'n' roll. The twin guitars of Whitten and Young playing a surging, euphoric riff before each chorus. A little run of notes jetting forward – very much like the rush of a drug.

★   ★   ★

4 In this, it foreshadows 'Under the Bridge' by Red Hot Chili Peppers, which recalls Anthony Kiedis's drug scoring in downtown LA.

I find Young's role in the song fascinating, because he essentially sings backing vocals for Whitten. Whitten's voice is pleasant enough – middle register, laid back, a country boy. Young's acid tone regularly cuts through it, slicing up to the song's surface and then down again. It's a perfect example of what separates a great, unmistakeable voice from a merely good one.

But Young also sounds rather animated, performing the song with an almost angry urgency. It's as though he passionately wants to get across the song's meaning, particularly when the lines about dealing with the man are repeated at the end. 'Come on now,' he ad libs, towards the song's end.

I wonder what Young thought and knew about the song's content. Is there a certain horror in singing so passionately about something that would go on to destroy your friend? If so, perhaps it just shows the complexity of life and the love of music. Young was, well, *young* at the time, twenty-four or -five. He'd have had no idea what was coming. The rest of the songs on *Tonight's the Night* are the sound of someone who knew all too well.

All of which brings us to the elephant in the room – drugs. As I've been writing, I've become more and more conscious that a lot of these stories end in addiction and sometimes death. I think it's important to acknowledge it. There are other, inspirational stories and characters along the way, but it's impossible to ignore the fact that a key cause of musical rejection is substance abuse.

Danny Whitten reminds me strongly of other characters in this book. His drug use was about as out of control as Steven Adler's of Guns N' Roses (see Chapter 10). Apparently, Whitten spent weeks at a time lying in his bathtub and shooting speed-balls, the notorious mixture of cocaine and heroin. He began to tell people that his hero was Bela Lugosi, the horror-movie actor and fellow junkie. That love of junkie culture – the dark romance of it – is common to other characters we meet along the way, Slash, Tony O'Neill (see Chapter 18) and Mark Lanegan being examples.

Like many of these other musicians, Whitten came from a broken home. Military service didn't offer him the redemption that it did for another key character in the book, Jason Everman (see Chapter 12).

Like Kurt Cobain, Whitten suffered chronic pain, for which heroin offered the ultimate, most efficacious relief. When Kurt killed himself, he used a phrase from Neil Young's 'My My, Hey Hey (Out of the Blue)' in his suicide note: 'Better to burn out than to fade away'. The comparison between Cobain and Whitten wasn't lost on Young, who was deeply shocked by this. Kurt's death inspired 'Sleeps With Angels', Young's 1994 song from the album of the same name, which he dedicated to Cobain.

What is it about drugs and music?

I think in some ways it's pretty simple. Music performances take place at night – they're a part of *nightlife*, where everybody wants to kick loose, unwind and have a few drinks. Once you've had a few drinks, a little bit of something else can seem a very good idea.

Musicians have to perform in this setting. Night after night in different places when on tour. The nerves backstage are palpa-ble. Most musicians I've known have liked to have a drink before going on stage. A friend of Danny Whitten's related a story about his being unable to perform when coming off heroin.

That must have been terrifying – and was certainly insurmountable in his case.

There's relentless socialising in music. Playing together, recording together. Going on tour. Dinners with local label staff or radio people. Interviews and journalists. Other bands, friends of friends and one-night stands. On tour, there's no anchor. You're always on the road and fun is always on offer. It might be the hundredth night for the band, but for fans and friends at the show it's the first, and they want to celebrate and have fun.

I've lost count of the times, out with musicians for dinners or drinks, when someone has suggested taking things further, and before I've known it the maelstrom of fun and abandon has been upon me. 'You want to get weird?' Sometimes you can feel it coming. It only takes one person to suggest it, another to waver, somebody else to shrug, and suddenly there's next to no chance of resisting the shivering wave of anticipation running through the group.

Music is visceral. It acts on the emotions, and players and audience want to lose themselves in it. This can easily be enhanced with substances. House music and ecstasy, hip-hop and weed, rock music with uppers, jazz with smack. Danny Whitten was already using heroin in 1969, so was that 'whooo' on 'Cinnamon Girl' chemically induced?

Performing music isn't like sitting behind a desk, typing as the sun comes up.

A lot of people involved in music will try drugs at some stage. At that point, there's an element of lottery as to how addictive your personality is. The good news is that things are getting better. Musicians and the industry are more aware of the dangers. I've only ever met one player who was a regular user of heroin.

Cocaine is treated more disdainfully than once it was. You're as likely to find bands practising wellness sessions together on tour as you are hunched over a table with rolled up notes. The drug use that remains is often a bit more organised. Early nights for six days and then we all take ecstasy after the show on Saturday – that sort of thing.

There's a greater emphasis on safety in all aspects of culture these days, and it's happening in music too. Everyone is more aware of the dangers.

But way back in the wilds of the 1970s, Danny Whitten didn't have much of a chance of getting off the nightmarish track he was on.

Neil Young: 'We knew what we had. We all knew it was really good. Then to see it get fucked up was really depressing. Seeing drugs come in and fuck it up, seeing the whole thing just go downhill. The inexperience of not knowing how to deal with heroin use, not knowing what it was, being too young for certain kinds of decisions. But that was the hand I was dealt with at the time. The destruction of Danny's life . . .'

Jimmy Chamberlin, Smashing Pumpkins

It would take a lot of tea in China. – Billy Corgan
on ever taking Jimmy Chamberlin back

I t wasn't exactly murder, but the drummer had to go.

By 1996, grunge was past its sell by date, and heroin had done its worst among a new generation of musicians. Smashing Pumpkins' drummer Jimmy Chamberlin had long been struggling with the drug. In fact, the Chicago band had relocated to Georgia to record their breakthrough, *Siamese Dream*, largely to keep him away from his dealers.

The band released their follow up – the sprawling, overwrought *Mellon Collie and the Infinite Sadness* – in autumn 1995. By the summer of 1996, they were still touring it, and keyboardist Jonathan Melvoin had been recruited for the shows. Melvoin came from a musical family: his sister Wendy was a member of the Revolution, Prince's backing band; his father was Mike Melvoin, a prolific jazz drummer who played on hits by Frank Sinatra, the Beach Boys and John Lennon, and eventually became president of the Grammys.[1]

---

1 In this role, Mike Melvoin was heavily involved with the Recording Academy's MusiCares programme, which gives aid to musicians struggling with addiction.

Somewhere along the *Melon Collie* tour, Chamberlin and Melvoin began using heroin together. The pair survived an overdose in Spain in May 1996, but in New York City two months later, Melvoin's luck ran out.

A very pure strain of heroin had appeared on the streets of New York that year. Emanating from the Lower East Side, it was branded as 'Redrum', i.e. 'murder' spelled backwards – a reference to Stephen King's *The Shining*. Redrum was pure enough to be intended for snorting, not injecting. Nevertheless, on Friday 12 July, around 11 p.m., Chamberlin and Melvoin returned to the upscale Regency Hotel in Manhattan and shot some up.

What happened next was reported in a *New York Times* article, which quoted NYPD spokesman Capt Michael Collins.[2] The pair had passed out, and 'when Chamberlin awoke at 3.30 a.m., he found he could not rouse Mr Melvoin and summoned the band's security manager for help.[3] The two men made several attempts to revive Mr Melvoin, including putting him under a shower, the captain said, and called 911 at 4.02 a.m.'

Paramedics arrived shortly afterwards, but Melvoin was already dead. Chamberlin was arrested for possession, though cleared fairly quickly of negligence for not calling 911 sooner. The police and paramedics believed that doing so would not

2 Interestingly, this article was written by Neil Strauss, he of pick-up bible *The Game* and *The Dirt*, the book on Mötley Crüe mentioned in Chapter 10 on Steven Adler.

3 Later reports, and Melvoin's Wikipedia page, claim that the pair had in fact retreated to their separate rooms to inject the heroin. It was Chamberlin who found Melvoin dead, though, which would perhaps have been tricky if they were indeed in separate, presumably locked, hotel rooms.

have saved Melvoin's life. He'd been drinking before injecting the heroin, and that might have made him more vulnerable.

Two days after Melvoin's death, another NYPD captain, Dennis McCarthy, spoke to the media about Redrum. 'Now they know that the purity's pretty good,' he said, referring to Melvoin's death, users were more actively seeking it out. People were asking for it by name at a 'drug supermarket' on the Lower East Side, which McCarthy described as 'the heroin capital of New York City, maybe the world'.

'People have gone from shooting heroin, primarily from fear of the AIDS epidemic and needles, to snorting,' McCarthy said. 'And in order to snort heroin you have to use a higher proof to get the desired high. Were you to shoot that level of heroin, you would certainly OD, which is what happened in this particular case.'

McCarthy explained that heroin designed for injecting is typically 40 per cent pure, while Redrum was 70 or 80 per cent. Asked why Melvoin died, and Chamberlin didn't, he said: 'every individual has a different capacity to absorb whatever they throw into their body, and I guess he wasn't able to deal with it as well as the other individual'.

Strauss's *New York Times* article went on to describe the backdrop of both the band and the wider music scene. 'The members of the Smashing Pumpkins have had a history of personal problems,' it said. 'Mr Chamberlin has been treated for addictions to alcohol and heroin, and Billy Corgan had a nervous breakdown in 1992.'

The article perfectly summarises *Mellon Collie* as 'a two-CD set in which lyrics of depression, self-pity and nihilism are augmented by heavy, distorted guitars and mock-classical string arrangements'.

Alternative rock fans 'like their heroes to be melancholy instead of macho', Strauss claimed. Heroin went hand in hand. Its use had 'long plagued musicians, but music-industry executives said they could not remember a time in the last two decades when heroin use had been more rampant'.

Strauss goes on to survey the wreckage: 'Jerry Garcia of the Grateful Dead and Kurt Cobain of Nirvana [see Chapter 12] were struggling with heroin addiction when they died; Kristen Pfaff[4] of Hole and Dwayne Goettel of Skinny Puppy died of overdoses; Shannon Hoon of Blind Melon, after being treated for heroin addiction, died of an overdose of cocaine. And Scott Weiland of the Stone Temple Pilots, Kelley Deal of the Breeders and Al Jourgensen of Ministry have all been arrested for heroin possession in the last year and a half.'

As for Chamberlin, he was rapidly fired. In a statement released on Wednesday, 17 July 1996, the band said: 'For nine years, we have battled with Jimmy's struggles with the insidious disease of drug and alcohol addiction. It has destroyed everything we stand for.'

Hurting yourself with drugs is one thing, but being involved in the death of someone else is a sure-fire way to get kicked out. Looked at in a certain light, the drummer had killed the keyboard player.

Despite Corgan's strong words regarding a potential return for Chamberlin, he did in fact re-join the band. In the spring of 1999, Smashing Pumpkins were set to go on tour with the newly formed Queens of the Stone Age. That band's founder, Josh Homme, who played a key role in the lives of Nick Oliveri

4 Mark Lanegan, whose spectre is beginning to haunt this book, was looking forward to a first date with the very beautiful Kristen Pfaff when her untimely death took place.

(see Chapters 23 and 26) and Mark Lanegan, broke the news of Chamberlin's return.

Speaking to MTV, he said Corgan had told him ' "Dude, Jimmy's back in the band." To me that says they're gonna rock again, because that's when they kick ass, when they have Jimmy. He's not the only key to it, but that team between Jimmy and Billy is a cool little thing.'

Chamberlin was too good to be left out for long. A serious drummer whose style was described as 'kinetic', and drove the band's sound, he and Corgan were arguably the creative core of Smashing Pumpkins. Corgan famously overdubbed some of guitarist James Iha and bassist D'arcy Wretzky's parts on *Siamese Dream*, something he'd never have done to Chamberlin.

And what of Jonathan Melvoin? Like other characters in this book (such as Steve Mann, Chapter 2), he's been immortalised in song. Before joining Smashing Pumpkins as a touring keyboardist, he'd played with Prince for a number of years, along with his sister Wendy. Prince wrote the song 'The Love We Make', from 1996's *Emancipation*, about Melvoin. Alongside its overtly anti-drug themes, it reflects Prince's religiosity. He sings of believers cleansing and purifying themselves. 'Put down the needle', he implores. 'Put down the spoon.'

Almost twenty years after Melvoin's death, Prince himself would die from an accidental overdose of fentanyl, the notoriously potent opioid.

A year after Prince's tribute to Melvoin, Canadian singer-songwriter Sarah McLachlan released 'Angel', which would go on to become her most successful song. It was inspired by a *Rolling Stone* article about heroin deaths among musicians, and more specifically by that of Jonathan Melvoin. Its lyrics address a spirit, leaving its body in a 'cold hotel room', flying away to be in the 'arms of the angel'.

'I've never done heroin,' McLachlan said, 'but I've done plenty of other things to escape.'

Finally, in 1998, Wendy Melvoin and Lisa Coleman – the Wendy & Lisa of Prince's backing band – released an album under the name Girl Bros. It contained a song called 'Jonathan'. The broken end of the song's chorus is as perfect a musical evocation of grief as is likely to exist anywhere:

How I love you
Oh I . . .

16

Glen Matlock, the Sex Pistols

*YES DEREK GLEN MATLOCK WAS THROWN OUT OF
THE SEX PISTOLS SO IM TOLD BECAUSE HE WENT ON
TOO LONG ABOUT PAUL MCCARTNEY STOP EMI WAS
ENOUGH STOP THE BEATLES WAS TOO MUCH STOP
SID VICIOUS THEIR BEST FRIEND AND ALWAYS A
MEMBER OF THE GROUP BUT UNHEARD AS YET WAS
ENLISTED STOP HIS BEST CREDENTIAL WAS HE GAVE
NICK KENT WHAT HE DESERVED MANY MONTHS
AGO AT THE HUNDRED CLUB LOVE AND PEACE
MALCOLM MCLAREN* – Telegram from Malcolm McLaren
to Derek Johnson, *New Musical Express*, February 1977[1]

And so Glen Matlock, the original bassist in the Sex Pistols,
became the subject of one of the greatest legends of a
musical firing.[2]

1 The telegram refers to an incident in which Sid Vicious lashed *NME* journalist
Nick Kent with a bike chain at the 100 Club. Apparently, Kent had been
disparaging about John Lydon's abilities as frontman. Vivienne Westwood,
McLaren's wife at the time, approached Kent after the violence and said of
Vicious, 'Oh God, that guy's a psychopath. He'll never be at one of our concerts
again, I promise that!' Shortly afterwards, he was in the band.
2 There was a second, weirder claim that became a rumoured reason for his
departure: that he was 'always washing his feet'. This was also untrue (the reason,
rather than the washing – Matlock has an admirably fastidious air).

The problem is it isn't true.

Certainly, the band's style had morphed. 'Originally it was brothel creepers and Teds,' Matlock told *The Times* in 2023. 'Anything to not be a hippy with long hair. Malcolm had rock 'n' roll on the shop[3] jukebox, and when I met Steve and Paul it turned out we all liked the Faces. That's where it started, long before John joined the band.'

The fledgling group went to see the Faces play, and supporting them were US proto-punks the New York Dolls. The flash of inspiration took place, and the band cooked up the songs that would become *Never Mind the Bollocks* in drummer Paul Cook and Glen Matlock's Denmark Street digs.

Lydon, as Johnny Rotten, started out modestly as a frontman.

'In our little rehearsal room, we all had Fender amps turned up to ten, so we never heard a word of what John was singing. He probably never heard himself singing. But he had a plastic bag filled with scraps of paper and when we were playing what became "Anarchy in the UK" he was pleased because he had something that fitted. He never thought he'd be a singer in a band.'

Everything changed after the band's infamous TV appearance on Bill Grundy's primetime *Today* programme. Lydon and Cook swore while the Bromley Contingent – including Siouxsie Sioux – giggled in the background. Interestingly, Matlock, with his feet up on the table, a smirk on his face and sarcastic answers at the ready, seems very much a part of the pack. Lydon makes a bit of a fool of himself, and it's Grundy's 'we'll meet afterwards, shall we?' to Sioux that's perhaps least

---

3 The notorious SEX – the shop that McLaren owned and ran with Westwood, and which pioneered much of the uniform for the punk look.

well-judged on his part. The appearance effectively ended the presenter's career.

Afterwards, McLaren didn't need to call the newspapers – they were calling him.

'John got lead singer disease the moment he got his boat race in the papers,' Matlock said. And the bassist soon found himself not enjoying things.

'I'm getting all this shit from John and Malcolm, Steve [Jones, guitarist] and Paul weren't backing me up.'

Worse, he'd heard they'd tried Sid Vicious out on bass.

Mike Thorne, the Pistols' A & R at EMI, had taken Matlock out for a curry and told him that if he left the band the label would be interested in what he did next. So leave was what he did. A week later, the master publicist McLaren sent his telegram to the *NME*.

'Two weeks after that,' Matlock said, 'I'm in the Blue Posts [pub] and Malcolm comes in and says: "It's not working out with Sid, can you come back?"'

'The way you treated me, are you fucking joking?' Matlock replied.

The Sex Pistols would burn out only one year later, and Matlock is philosophical about things: 'It reminded me of what John Entwistle once said of the Who: that if he was jumping around like Daltrey, Townshend and Moon, the band would fall apart. There was a balance when I was in the Pistols. Sid Vicious wanted to be the lead guy, and the equilibrium went.'

He was happy to take part in the reunions, years later. There was money involved, and he didn't have to be crammed into a van: 'We didn't even have to get on the same flight.'

Despite a long career, he'll always be best known as a Sex Pistol, and as the subject of that 'sacking'.

'It reminds me of what Keith Richards said when a journalist asked him the price of milk: "I don't know, man, I've been a rock star all my life." I've been an ex-Sex Pistol all my life. No matter how much you try and do other things, it is always there.'

Your face doesn't fit.

Adam Ant

And with Adam of Adam and the Ants, it was the image of piracy
that I gave him to relaunch his career – Malcolm McLaren

Malcolm McLaren was always someone I admired as a pioneer of punk, of iconoclasm, of DIY, of blowing something up to epic cultural proportions by sheer force of will. That said, in writing this book I've realised he does occasionally appear to have been a bit of a bastard (see previous chapter).

In 1980, budding New Wave bandleader Adam Ant hired McLaren as manager. Only a month later, instead of doing what a good manager should – apply vision and strategy, exercise a duty of care, develop income streams and organise his artist – McLaren decided to steal members of Adam's backing band (the Ants) to form Bow Wow Wow.

Maybe this had something to do with the fact that Ant had hired McLaren for a flat fee – a very unusual arrangement, given managers work on a percentage basis. McLaren's unrepentant view was that his 'job had come to an end after four weeks, and really at the time, I wasn't that interested'.

But perhaps we mustn't be too hasty to judge. Ant credited this move on McLaren's part with giving him the kick up the arse he needed: 'He already had the idea for Bow Wow Wow, and he had to get rid of me. He didn't do it particularly nicely, but he did it, and I'm glad he did do it, because it set us both free, if you like.' And anyway, Ant said rather sweetly in an interview, 'I didn't understand all the anarchist stuff.'

'He [McLaren] likes to do things, and give it all this [chat], and then afterwards he smashes it all to bits, he just destroys it.'

Ant related this destructive urge to something in McLaren's unhappy childhood.[1] 'He's whacky, he likes to take things and really upset things, y'know? He likes to turn them upside down.'

Prior to being cast aside, Ant knew that McLaren had been fostering the idea for Bow Wow Wow, because the manager had subjected him to 'hours and hours of philosophy' on what a band should be. With Bow Wow Wow, he was putting this philosophy into practice, and ditched Ant in the process.

The singer forgave McLaren, not least because the experience gave him the impetus to form a new band and achieve mainstream success. In 2013, he included a tribute to McLaren on his album, *Adam Ant is the Blueblack Hussar in Marrying the Gunner's Daughter*.[2]

'Malcolm was a sort of mentor in my life,' he said at the time of the album's announcement. 'As close as you can get to a surrogate father.'

Nevertheless, of course the incident hurt.

'At the time it was devastating. There's one thing a band splitting up, but we were buddies and there was a camaraderie. He

1 The marriage of McLaren's parents collapsed when he was very young, ostensibly due to his mother's multiple infidelities. He was raised, and in part home-schooled, by a picaresque grandmother who braided his pubic hair and taught him that 'to be bad is good because to be good is simply boring'.
2 The song is called 'Who's a Goofy Bunny?' – a reference to McLaren's slightly goofy teeth.

talked about taking rock 'n' roll back to its basics. He played us all kinds of records from Django Reinhardt to Charlie Parker. He'd talk to you for an hour, and if you were lucky, you'd understand a minute of it. I just sat there and listened, and it sparked off certain directions for me.

'What he was talking about in those meetings is pretty much what you hear when you hear the Bow Wow Wow sound.

'It was devastating on a personal level. On a professional level, it turned out to be pretty good for both parties.'

In fact, McLaren made Ant a compilation tape that crucially included Burundi Black's 'Burundi Black', giving Ant the inspiration to add 'ethnic beats' to his striking new pirate aesthetic.

What lessons can we take from this? That there's creativity buried in destruction – the new growth can't take place until the older has burned away. That sometimes we need a good hard kick, a reason to do something.

One conclusion might be that a musician should always pay their manager on a percentage basis, giving them reason to stick around. But looked at in a certain light, one would have to conclude that McLaren did the perfect job for Adam Ant. And all in only four weeks, and for the price of a thousand quid – and a band.

18

Tony O'Neill, the Brian Jonestown Massacre

Where's my FUCKING ORANGE JUICE? – Anton
Newcombe, the Brian Jonestown Massacre

'So, Tony – were you ever actually thrown out of a band?'
The boyish, bequiffed head on the screen in front of me pauses briefly, and then nods emphatically and says: 'Yes!'

I can't help but be relieved. I knew that Tony O'Neill's stints in Kenickie and the Brian Jonestown Massacre had ended abruptly, but I wasn't actually sure he qualified as a fully fledged reject. In fact, it turns out that his kicking out story is one of the best we'll encounter. But we'll get to that.

O'Neill is a brilliant novelist. I came across his debut, *Digging the Vein*, via the underground literary magazine site *3:AM*. Billed as a dark, brutal, funny book about a descent into drug addiction in LA, it sounded like my kind of thing, and it didn't disappoint. A few years later, I read his breakthrough *Sick City* after Bret Easton Ellis included it in a 'currently reading' tweet.

Digging the Vein is told in the first person, and O'Neill is frank about its highly autobiographical nature. A young musician in a Britpop band goes on tour to LA and doesn't come back. Falling in with a druggie crew of friends, he takes a lot of coke, meth and pills. He gets married on a whim, and it doesn't go well. Funded by writing music videos, he tries to keep playing music, and is introduced to smoking heroin by a bandmate. And then he brings a sex-worker friend back to his apartment, and she shows him how to shoot up. So begins a nightmare of full-blown heroin and cocaine addiction, played out amid the streets, motels and junkie bands of late nineties LA.

The novel is inspired and highly compulsive, relentless in the best of ways, capturing the underbelly of LA in all its sleazy glory. It's a very funny book, with a voice and consciousness that the reader finds alluring. O'Neill admirably refrains from spending too much time on his narrator's feelings, instinctively understanding the novelist's well-worn credo, show don't tell.

He followed *Digging the Vein* with *Down and Out on Murder Mile*, a sequel detailing his anti-hero's return to London with a wife and fellow junkie in tow. They live in pre-gentrification Hackney, transposing the grim daily life of addicts to the streets of London. Again, the book is very funny, and the reader wants to spend time in the narrator's company.

But it's LA that O'Neill always returns to in his work. He broadened out the canvas with *Sick City* and *Black Neon*, showing he was just as comfortable inventing characters and setting them loose in thrilling plots.

O'Neill was born in Blackburn in 1978. Looking at him today, you'd never suspect he'd spent years living the gruelling life of a heroin and cocaine addict. When we speak on a video call, he's friendly and enthusiastic, laughing a lot and talking rapidly about the work and his history. He's of Irish descent, and has greying black hair, large bushy eyebrows and the elegantly

202

downturned eyes of a silent film star. His accent has become a blend of Blackburn, Irish and New York, his conversation punctuated by 'y'knows' as he happily digresses into entertaining tales. His forearms are tattooed, and he has the appearance of someone who could still be in one of those smart, stylish 1990s indie bands. As we talk, I wonder if he survived his worst years partly due to his charm and smarts.

He moved to London at eighteen to join Marc Almond's band, and then drunkenly talked his way into Kenickie at one of their shows. When they went to the US, he married a girl he'd only just met and returned to LA as Kenickie were breaking up.

In writing novels, he seems to have found his true calling, but I wonder if he ever misses being in bands.

'I don't miss it really. I was very aware that you have a window in music. For me, I grew up a working-class kid in Blackburn in the northwest of England watching *Top of the Pops* every week. And in a weird way I kind of made it as far as my mind could conceive of it. I did *Top of the Pops*, which was wild, and I spent those years of my life touring and got to see a lot of the world. My time in the music industry was a fork point in my life, and it made it lead off somewhere more interesting. That it didn't end up being music for ever didn't bother me.'

His main plan had been simply to escape Blackburn, and the prospect of a life on the grind.

'My biggest fear growing up was . . . My dad was a bus driver, my mum was a home help. She did shopping for old ladies, nursing – she worked in a nursing home until she was almost eighty, she was looking after people younger than her. They worked their whole lives. Nothing like that interested me and all I really wanted was to do something in the arts.

'I was the weird kid at fifteen that was reading Burroughs. I didn't know whether I wanted to be William Burroughs or Iggy Pop. I didn't want to stay in the north of England and work a job I hated and end up with 2.4 kids and a semi-detached. I was so scared of that I ran a little hard in the other direction, and probably right off the edge of a cliff.'

Where he actually ran was LA, and full-scale drug addiction. *Digging the Vein* is full of terrifying stories and black comedy: the job he gets interviewing a dreadful Stones covers band, which requires travelling to Vegas with them in a tiny van, jonesing for heroin; the overdosed sex worker in his apartment; the two Venice gangsters he spends a couple of days with, and whom he shocks by injecting crack. He invites them to the place a friend of a friend has lent him to detox in, and they take him out on jobs, returning bloody from beating a rival as he sits in their SUV.

On the third night, they leave him in the car again while apparently going off on another such job. He sees a street character appear on a sidewalk and begin doing push ups, staring at the vehicle. After a moment, he realises he's being watched. He runs back to the guesthouse, but it's too late. The gangsters have burgled the place. The narrator sees a set of tools they've left behind, and decides he might as well pawn them for drugs. From there, things only get worse.

'Thankfully I survived. I did put my family through hell. I joke about the drug stuff but now, at forty-three, I've got an eighteen-year-old daughter, and that's the age I was doing all this stuff. She's very on the straight and narrow, and I'm like "man . . ." – it really hits me now, what I put my parents through. When I was my daughter's age they didn't know where I was.

The first they heard from me in months was a call from a treatment centre asking for three grand cos I was in detox. And they never disowned me or hated me for it. Thank goodness I didn't die; there's a few instances where I came very close. What a horrible thing to do to your parents.'

When he'd recovered, he realised his time in the music industry was up.

'By the time I got clean I was still only in my mid-twenties. It felt like it was ever-decreasing circles. My first real proper bands were with Marc Almond, then Kenickie. Then with the Jonestown it was good but smaller, then I had this other band that almost made it, we were signed to various big labels, but it never really did anything. Then the last band when I came back to England, I played with Kelli Ali from Sneaker Pimps. We got to play decent-sized venues, but it just never really happened. And then when Nico [his daughter] was born, I didn't want to go off on tour in the hope that maybe this next thing will be the one that breaks. I'd just gotten clean and felt like being off on the road wasn't a good place for me.'

That said, his passion for music remains undimmed. In our correspondence he constantly refers to new bands and gigs he's planning to attend in NYC.

'I'm a massive music lover,' he says. 'You don't ever lose that bug. I look back on the time fondly and I remember the feeling of playing a great show . . . but a lot of the other stuff I didn't like. It's such a hard industry, and the winners and the losers, the gulf between their experiences is so great.

'Bands that when I was a fan, I thought were big . . . you find out they all had to do regular jobs afterwards. I had the same view about writers, I thought they all lived in big houses, and then I reached out to them and they're all, like, teaching.

'If I'm gonna struggle at something in the arts, I prefer writing because I get to do it by myself and I'm completely responsible for the work of art that's done. I don't have to do it with a committee, and I don't have to rely on a label. I guess there's publishers . . .'

As for those musicians that still carry on?

'I respect people that can still be on the road, but I don't think I'd have the stamina. There's very rarely a good second act for a musician.'

The loss of that first taste of success is clearly painful to O'Neill's narrator, as it was to him. He says that, in some ways, it was easier to become an addict than to re-join the real world.

'In that first flush of fame you get so disconnected from the real world it's hard to adjust. And I think that's why when I got to LA I found it so hard that I became a heroin addict. I assumed I was gonna walk into another band situation. And the thought of getting a job . . . I ended up working at the Virgin Megastore on Sunset Boulevard. I can't tell you how depressing it is to go from the person on the CD cover to the person selling the CD. And it was the Sunset Strip, so musicians would be coming in, you know like Marilyn Manson. And you're like "No, no, no, I shouldn't be doing this."'

Like a photograph's negative, drug addiction offered a dark inversion of the life of a successful musician.

'It was much easier to fall into that twilight world of drug addiction, because you're used to not getting up at nine a.m. or having someone telling you what to do. That made more sense on a kind of muscle-memory level than getting a day job.'

I wonder how he explains his escape from the trap into which he'd fallen.

'A lot of it is dumb luck. To quote Nick Cave, I don't believe in an interventionist God, but I do sometimes think I had something looking out for me. It could have ended very badly many, many times, and probably should've done.'

In *Down and Out on Murder Mile*, the sequel to *Digging the Vein*, the narrator describes eventually meeting a woman in London and falling in love. In fact, he's encountered her before. High one day in the back of a tour van, he takes the tour manager's mobile and randomly calls a female name. The voice at the other end is American, and appealing, and the pair embark on sex talk. Later, backstage at a show, the narrator is stunned by a woman who walks in. 'Oh, finally you two meet,' the tour manager says. It's the woman from the phone, Vanessa, and they pick up where they left off. The narrator describes a lot of very good sex with her, and eventually she inspires him to get clean.

In the book's acknowledgements, O'Neill thanks his wife – Vanessa – who doesn't mind him writing about her. There's the old cliché that 'happiness writes white', and is boring to read. In O'Neill's work, though, as in life, this falling into love is just as exciting to encounter as the dark rush of the drug scenes.

'For me the biggest thing that happened to me and saved me was probably meeting Vanessa,' O'Neill says now. 'I don't mean to put all of this on her, like she's this *deus ex machina* that came in and saved my life, but in a way she was. Just being in a relationship with someone that wasn't an addict and wasn't hardwired that way, that was the biggest thing for me in reprogramming my own mind. If you ask my parents, they think she's a saint because if we hadn't got together, I'd probably be dead.'

The novels conjure up a very strong sense of Vanessa. She's mixed race – half Hispanic, beautiful; bold and brave enough to handle the narrator.

'Growing up in NYC, she'd been around addicts and wasn't so scared. When we were first seeing each other, I was still using needles – most people would run a mile from that.'

At the time, O'Neill was into a 'whole, like, "junkie pride" thing – unapologetic. "Some people like a drink, I like to shoot heroin, that's just my thing." Full-blown addict denial.'

But addicts and non-addicts don't mix.

'Surprise surprise, we fell for each other really hard. You quickly come up against the fact that it's unsustainable for one person to be in the throes of opiate addiction and the other not to be. Either the non-addicted person has to become an addict, or the addicted person has to stop, because your lives become completely incompatible.'

One choice was obviously the better one.

'I've been in relationships with two addicts, and they always end up in complete hell. And when Vanessa got pregnant, I knew I couldn't be an addict and a father. And being an addict is a full-time job.'

Being with a non-addicted person he loved revealed the true nature of the trap he was in.

'If we wanted to go away somewhere, I had to get permission from my doctor to get takeaway doses of methadone, and Vanessa would be like "You wanna live like this? You have to ask permission?"

'And it's true, you start doing drugs because you have this cockeyed idea that it's some kind of freedom, and in the end it wasn't, I had to ask permission to do everything. I couldn't go somewhere if I knew I didn't have drugs set up there . . . Your world just becomes incredibly small. And suddenly here was this chance, there was a baby on the way, and she was like: "What are we gonna do? I can't stay with you; we can't have the baby if you're gonna be like this."

'If I hadn't met Vanessa, I'm not saying I wouldn't have got clean eventually, but it wouldn't have happened when it did. And who knows if it would have happened. It would have taken some other outside intervention because I was so wrapped up in my own addiction at that point that I couldn't even see it.

'Fate or whatever threw me a bone in a way that sometimes it doesn't do for people. And I get it, some people might look at my story and say: "Why you? It's so unfair, so many other good people died the first time they did it or couldn't get clean."

'I don't know why me. All I know is ever since I got clean I've tried to live my life in a way to make it worthwhile and make it count. And to make up for the harm I did to my parents. I want to do whatever I can to be the son that I wasn't. I had a great relationship with my parents, I love my parents, it wasn't a rejection of them. Always in the rehab places it's like "there's something in your childhood, just think", but in my case it really wasn't. We weren't rich, but I had a pretty idyllic child-hood. I just liked getting high, I was just hardwired that way. There's certain drugs I know that I enjoy so much that I can't do 'em. Because I'm not very good on moderation – to say the least!'

An autobiographical approach to writing fiction is sometimes sneered at, particularly now that a recent fad for 'autofiction' has faded. Years ago, I interviewed Alan Warner – a favourite novelist of mine – and he told me that novelists 'should write what they *don't* know. It's called fiction, you're supposed to make it up.' This advice set me on a rocky path in terms of my own attempts at writing, and I came to realise the idea was questionable anyway.

The more I encounter fiction and the people who write it, the more I've realised autobiographical work is more common than we might think. The British novelist Rachel Cusk has even said that it's 'increasingly the only form in all the arts'.

In O'Neill's case, this is what makes *Digging the Vein* and *Down and Out* so vivid and compulsive. His writing beats with the living pulse of experience.

The narrator of *Digging the Vein* describes bouts of writing throughout the novel. Like everything else, it falls prey to his addiction. But when getting clean, O'Neill began writing more regularly.

'It wasn't really a conscious effort to switch into writing. I mean, *Digging the Vein* I wrote because I was detoxing, and I was at home and I needed something to do. I wrote it all back to front, it was never going to be a novel. I just wrote it like a long series of diary entries or essays. It was something to do with my time while I was home. I didn't want to be out, I wasn't feeling good, it took me six months to feel normal. It was the period when Vanessa was pregnant with Nico. By the time she was ready to give birth I realised what I had was novel length.'

He and Vanessa moved to New York City, her hometown, and O'Neill stumbled across a publisher.

'It was very random. I didn't really know how to go about getting a book published. When we first moved back to New York I didn't have work papers or anything, so I was trying to either work off the books or do interning just to meet people. This was when people were still using Craigslist for everything, and I saw a publisher looking for interns. So I answered it and it ended up being Contemporary Press, who are now no more.

'It was basically a press started by four or five friends. Their office was a bar on the Lower East Side, and they wanted someone to show up at the meetings and take notes. All they'd really published up until then was each other's books. It was before it got really easy to do self-publishing, they still had to work with printing factories and all that, and they kinda had a thing, they were into neo noirs, which wasn't what I was doing. But I ended up getting friendly enough with them that I just slipped my MS on the submissions pile – they didn't really know I wrote. And when they read it, they really liked it, and they were like "Listen, this isn't really what we do but we'd like to publish it anyway."'

'It got into a few indie bookstores in NYC, and I basically parlayed that into getting it out, getting it reviewed. It was also when literary sites were just starting online, and you could really self-promote. There was a lot of hustling about!'

He had a spell with a major publisher, Harper Perennial, but has largely worked with indie presses – the book world's equivalent of indie record labels.

'The indie publishing scene is very much like the indie record scene; it's got the same problems too. As the means of production become completely democratised, you get a glut of material.

'There was a period when people who were really serious about writing could start to self-publish and get noticed, but now everybody is publishing anything and it's really hard to get noticed cos there's so many self-published things.

'I'm the sort of writer that probably shouldn't have ended up on a major press, but I did. It was a quirk of the times and who happened to be running Perennial. They were just taking risks. When I got signed, they also ended up signing Dan Fante, Jerry Stahl. I was basically on a press with all my favourite writers. Sebastian Horsley,[1] who I knew from AA meetings in London. I mean, someone did an article about it, and they called it "Harper Perennial's club house for losers". In a nice way, because we were all fuck ups. We were all the sort of people that major presses shouldn't touch.'

In the music business, the departure of a senior A & R person usually denotes a change in direction. It seems the same applies to publishing.

'When Carrie Kania who was running Perennial moved on, they went in a more commercial direction and a lot of the writers went back to the indie world. But just having some books on a major press to point to transforms your fortunes.

'I'm not a famous writer or a writer that's sold a lot, but if you like a specific area of writing you've probably heard my name. I'm the very definition of cult, in that some people know me but I really don't have a pot to piss in. To be honest, in the writing game that's pretty good, because there's so many voices, it's so easy to get drowned out.'

O'Neill has some notable fans though. James Frey wrote an intro for one of his books, and Irvine Welsh and Bret Easton Ellis have both championed him. Most of these connections

---

1 Dan Fante was a writer and the son of John Fante, another novelist famed for his LA-set work. Jerry Stahl is a novelist and non-fiction writer perhaps best known for his chronicle of addiction, *Permanent Midnight*. Sebastian Horsley was a British artist, writer and 'dandy' provocateur.

were apparently made through word of mouth, rather than the skilled networking often deployed by writers and musicians alike.

'Writers who like each other tend to find each other,' he says. But he 'doesn't move in writers' circles, believe me'. He lives in a small town in New Jersey, twenty minutes' train ride from Manhattan. His books are simply the sort that people press on each other.

Ellis read *Sick City* and reached out to say, ' "Hey, I like your book." We struck up an email correspondence. There's actually a pilot for *Sick City* written by Bret Easton Ellis out there in the world. He's great, super supportive, someone who doesn't mind reaching down and helping pull writers up a couple of rungs.'

In my experience, writers can be more jealous and hostile to each other than musicians.

'Yeah, they can be, and I think it's probably cos they think if someone else is doing well that's one less seat at the table or something, it's really stupid. When people reach out to me, I always make an effort to reach back, because I always remember how important that was.'

In previous interviews, O'Neill has talked about how he goes for a musical feel in his prose, in the way that another writer might go for a Hemingway feel in theirs. I wonder how that works, exactly?

'I never studied writing – for me studying writing was reading a lot. I never did any further education because at eighteen I got the gig with Marc and chose to do that instead of college. So my writing is very untrained in a way, but what I do know a lot about is music, so I just tend to think in those terms.

'For example, writing *Digging the Vein* I was thinking of early Tom Waits stuff, that way he had of describing a type, that neo-Beaty noir. It had a bit of Bukowski in it, but it had its own thing and had a rhythm to it. Especially in *Digging the Vein*, I was writing descriptions trying to get a rhythm to them, almost like they made more sense if you read them out loud, they had a bit of a flow to them.

'I just tend to think of other arts in terms of music. They're not crossed off from one another. It's the same brain muscle you use if you're writing a piece of prose or a piece of music, and for me my frame of reference is just so much bigger with music.

'There's a lot of writers where I can tell what their music influences are, not because of references but just because of the way they write.'

I wonder if writing so much about drugs ever makes him want to take them again, but he says the process is therapeutic.

'In the beginning it was very much a therapy: I was trying to get some perspective on it all. I realised I was going to start forgetting things and I wanted to write it down.

'One of the things they say in Twelve Steps is that addicts have a built-in forgetter. And it's like as soon as you have a bit of distance you start forgetting about the bad stuff. All you really remember is the fun and romanticised stuff and that's what leads you back to it again. I can swap funny stories about scoring all day long; nobody wants to hear the story about the time you were sat in the bathroom for three hours trying to find a working vein and you pricked yourself with a needle four hundred times. So writing it down was a way to set everything in paper so it couldn't be forgotten and I couldn't go back and revise the history later.

'I tried to describe a lot of the boredom and waiting around of addiction as well the highs. The highs are a pretty small part of *Digging the Vein*. The rest of it's just mechanics of what life as an addict is like. I think to non-addicts it's interesting, because you don't really know what the mechanism is; what do addicts do with their day, where do they get their money, where do they go? That's all a bit of a hidden culture unless you're in it. I sometimes think of my books as like travelogues of junk life.

'It's almost like the Scientologists have that thing where if you have a trauma you keep repeating it until the e-meter lies flat. A lot of things that had happened I didn't wanna think about, because they immediately made me react in a horrible way. By working them through on paper I could get a bit of remove from them. Certain things that happened were just horrible, thinking about them provoked strong feelings, like nausea. That fight-or-flight reaction. That sort of stuff is unhealthy to be carrying around, and writing it down almost puts it in a third-person perspective where it doesn't have that immediate hold on you.

'So no, it's not like being on a diet and writing about some fantastic dinner you wish you could have!'

I also want to know what he thinks about LA now. The city's odd, contradictory ambience is well-established; both paradisical and nightmarish all at once. There's an underlying dread to the place at times, even a spookiness. David Bowie (see Chapter 29), on leaving the city, said, 'the fucking place should be wiped from the face of the earth'.

'I've always had a big love–hate relationship with it,' O'Neill says. 'I mean I fell in love with LA when I first went there, when I was touring with Kenickie. Growing up in a town like

Blackburn in the northwest, you know, a mill town, you step off the plane in LA and everything is just technicolour. It's bright, it's warm, there's palm trees, everything is larger than life. It's like stepping onto another planet.

'Some people in the band didn't like it – they thought it was too fucking weird and outside their realm of experience, but I was always trying to get outside my realm of experience.

'But with everything that happened to me it did start to have negative connotations. When I left, I thought I'd never go back. All I could associate it with were the worst times possible. Complete darkness. I mean the last six months I was in LA my experience was crack houses and short-let motels and street corners. I've since gone back, and going back not enmeshed in the drug culture I've experienced it more like an outsider, and I now have a view on it that's a little more in the middle. I still like going back there, it formed such an important part of my early years.

'It feels a bit like being back in London, like going home. I'm a bit of a weird case. I grew up in England but my family's all Irish, I always considered myself Irish. Both my parents have strong Irish accents and, when I was younger, I had a bit of an accent from growing up in an Irish house. I never felt English. Especially because it was the eighties, the IRA stuff was going on, there a was a bit of [he clashes his fists together] between the Irish and the English then. So I always felt a bit Irish and not quite at home in England. But then I'd go to Ireland for my summer holiday and having more of an English accent, the kids there'd be like,' he grimaces, 'argh . . .

'I remember one time I was hanging out with my cousins and there was this really pretty girl there, I was about ten. And I thought this girl was so pretty and wanted to talk to her, and I was a bit nervous and finally worked up the courage and said something to her. And she just looked at me and said: "You fucking English are always coming over here causing trouble."

'I never really felt strongly one thing or another. I've always been an expat. You spend so long in other places you end up essentially stateless. There's a lot of places I have a nostalgic pull towards – I feel it towards London, I feel it towards LA, I even feel it towards Blackburn these days when I go back.

'My wife laughs at me now, she's like, "Your accent's horrible, it's like this Blackburn, American thing, you just sound like you're from nowhere." And when I go to Blackburn people think I'm American. Unfortunately, I've spent so much time in different places it's just become a nothing accent.

'I'll always have a soft spot for LA. It's the weirdest city I've ever been to. It's very much like a David Lynch film. It can seem so nice and obliging on the surface, but you walk through the wrong door and you can be in the seventh circle of hell immediately. There were always these undertows that unless you're clued into them you might miss them. There was a weird seediness to LA that NYC doesn't have – maybe it had in the seventies but it doesn't any more. There's a very particularly LA brand of seediness that I'm always entranced by.'

I recognise this vision of LA. Unlike a traditional city, in which you might walk around and spot the sort of places you like, in LA you need somebody to lift the veil for you. A great restaurant might be in an unassuming adobe building or a strip mall. Events take place in private houses high up in the hills, where the privacy can be enabling.

On a visit to LA around the launch of *Down and Out on Murder Mile*, O'Neill and Vanessa went to the book expo party at the Warner Bros. lot. Afterwards, they hung out with Ron Jeremy all night.

'He took us to this porn party in the hills where people were fucking everywhere. I have all these amazing pictures, me in a three-piece suit getting spanked by a deaf porn star. It was so weird! The best thing was after we'd left: our minds were blown, we thought this was the craziest thing ever. We're in the car and we're like "Wow, Ron, that was wild," and he's like "That was lame, it was so quiet," and his friends are like "Yeah, that was a total sausage party, there were no chicks." That to me was like Sodom and Gomorrah, and it was just a boring party to him. There's a lot of things like that that'll happen to you in LA, you just have to hit the right thing at the right moment, and you'll get access to these weird hidden worlds.'

While he's been steadily working on screenplays and ghost-writing memoirs – O'Neill co-wrote *Hero of the Underground* for Jason Peter, an American football player who became a heroin addict, and at the time of writing he's working on a memoir by the punk musician and artist Judy Nylon – there hasn't been a new novel since 2014's *Black Neon*. It turns out that around its publication, O'Neill hit a bump.

'It was just a really weird time in my life because I relapsed. I'd been clean for ten years and I got hit by a car – me and my daughter got run over while crossing the road. And she's OK but it freaked me out. I got injured, she got injured worse actually. She made a full recovery, but it was a combination of me blaming myself for it . . . I mean we were on a zebra crossing and the driver was in the wrong but still, you know what it's like, she was ten. And I blamed myself for it and I was also in pain, and the doctors were giving me painkillers and I fell off the wagon. And it was a short relapse, but it completely disrupted my writing for years. I got writer's block then, which I never believed was a real thing. Even though the relapse was short it triggered a really depressive bout in me.

'I had to get my confidence back, I spent a lot of years just writing screenplays and stuff like that. It was weird, the longer I got away from writing long-form stuff, it started becoming like a kind of phobia, like can I do it any more? You sort of forget what a marathon it is writing a book. And I was doing a book a year, and suddenly every time I sat down to write, I started doubting myself a chapter in and scrapping it. I've got so many unfinished books.

'Quitting booze a year and a half ago really helped me focus my mind in. The Judy [Nylon] thing came along, and I was like "OK, I've done that." For a writer it's a bit like being a sports person, but instead of your body you've just gotta keep your mind in tip-top shape, and my mind wasn't in tip-top shape. I'm somebody who's prone to depression and addiction, and I know that, and I kind of succumbed to it a little bit. Whatever the balance was that was right that allowed me to write at such a clip, it threw it off and everything ground to a halt for a good while.

'There was a point where I was just doing courier stuff and I really felt like I'm not a writer any more – I'm a fucking courier – and that would feed into me being depressed about my situation. But I got myself out of it again, you've got to – what are you gonna do, you can't roll over.

'So I started going along to a Zen Buddhist place around here and meditating and really just started looking at my life, and that's when I decided to quit drinking and the writing started coming back. So that's why the next novel feels important.'

Does he fear another relapse in the future?

'I would never be so smug as to say never. You can't ever say that, you know. I never thought I'd get hit by a car, but sometimes life fucking deals you weird cards. I feel at this stage in my life I'm a bit better equipped to deal with it.

'When that happened, I was gliding, things had been going right for me for a long time. Really the test is when life throws you a shit sandwich. I wasn't prepared for that, but I feel like now I am.

'Like they say in Buddhism – they always make you recite this thing where it's like "I'm human, so I am going to get old, I am going to die, and people are going to change." And it's getting comfortable with that, and I was never comfortable with that.'

It seems that the pluck that helped O'Neill get through the bad years had a flipside – it led to overconfidence.

'I think I was still in that mentality of "It's not going to happen to me, I'm too quick." And I think even being able to quit dope made me a bit cocky in a way. It was like "I quit junk, I wrote the book, I've got the family, I'm . . . yeah!" And then all it took was this little thing and I was back at the bottom of the ladder again. And I think that's why the depression was so big afterwards; it was such a shock to my ego. I was very consumed in the egotistical thing of having beaten it. Almost like I'd gotten away with a bank robbery. You have to come to terms with the fact that not every day's gonna be a good day and not every year's gonna be a good year. And at this point in my life, I'm familiar with that feeling a bit more now. It won't come as quite as big a shock.'

I wonder how he feels about the changing landscape of fiction. *The Times* and the *Guardian* have both run long articles in recent years, examining the idea that it's becoming harder for men to compete. O'Neill baulks at the idea that a writer should even think about this. In fact, thinking about the audience too much has led him astray before. After *Sick City*'s success, he focused too much on second guessing his new readership.

'The people that liked *Sick City*, what are they going to expect from the next thing? You can't think about any of that stuff, cos it'll kill you. That stuff is poison, thinking about how people will react to it.

'The best, purest experience I ever had of writing a book was the very first one, because I wrote it not even thinking it was a book, I just wrote it for myself. And for me, tapping into that feeling is how I'm working my way back into being able to write again, because that's the only way to do it. I might think about all that other stuff later. If I think about it while I'm writing it, it'll kill it dead.'

The face on the screen breaks out into a trademark grin.

'Anyway, I can always pull the junkie card – that's my marginalised card, right?'

The defiance of junkie culture is something O'Neill still identifies with.

'I got told off on Twitter for using the phrase "junkie", and someone said: "no, it's 'drug addicted person'" and I was like "Listen, I was the one putting needles in, I'll call myself what I want." And again, it wasn't a pejorative term to me, we used it among ourselves because we disdained non-junkies. It's that kind of attitude. No addict refers to themselves as a drug-addicted person, it's just not realistic. I get using it in a clinical sense, but I'm not gonna have a non-drug user lecturing a drug user on what the proper term to use is because they're marginalising themselves. If you want to improve the life of drug users, end the drug war, and we can worry about the language later.'

There's an element of O'Neill that, if not quite unrepentant, hasn't lost all sense of the dark romance of the junkie culture he was once steeped in. His daughter, Nico, is named after the singer and heroin addict.

'We were listening to a lot of *Chelsea Girl* when Vanessa was expecting. She [Nico] is lucky she's a girl, cos if she was a boy her first name was gonna be Burroughs. She's like "you can't call somebody Burroughs – that's a horrible name."'

And what of musical rejections – does O'Neill have any favourite stories, other than his own?

'There's quite an art to getting kicked out of a band,' he says. 'The best reason I've ever heard – even though I know it's an urban myth – is kicking Glen Matlock out of the Pistols because he liked the Beatles. To me, crimes of taste, stuff like that is kind of good. Believe me, when I was in Kenickie, the stick I used to get for liking Morrissey. One of the most painful memories I have . . . We were all super young and the most rock 'n' roll it got was drinking too much. It was very innocent. It was almost like being in the Monkees, being in Kenickie.

'I remember we'd all make tapes to play on the bus and everyone would try and one-up each other about how cool their mixtape was. And I finally plucked up the nerve to do a mixtape, and it started off OK, but I put some band on there that everyone hated, and it was a long song too. Four minutes into it I realised that the van had got very quiet, and finally somebody said: "Is this song ever gonna fucking end?" And somebody ejected the tape and threw it out.

'And I've got to admit I still think about that day on the tour bus and cringe a little bit. I can't remember what it was now, but for eighteen-year-olds they had really good taste in music. They were all into the Fall and the Stooges and really cool stuff, and me being young and just come down from Blackburn my taste was probably a bit more parochial. I got a baptism in cool very quickly when I went down to London. I remember Marc gave me a bunch of albums – Wire, Johnny Thunders, the Cramps. But up until then my musical taste had been dictated by what cassette tapes I could get out of Blackburn Library. So I'd say crimes of taste are legitimate.

'Also, there'd always be bands where there was one guy who was ten years older than everyone else and was bald. They obviously had to be the best musician in the band because otherwise they'd have got rid of them a long time ago.'

I remind him that in *Digging the Vein*, Atom, the character based on Anton Newcombe of the Brian Jonestown Massacre (see Chapter 30), kicks a bandmate out for describing the production on a Zombies album as 'faggy'.

O'Neill laughs. 'We'd argue about that stuff all day long. I always remember Anton had this big Arthur C. Clarke book of short stories that he'd hollowed out. And inside he had this big veterinarian syringe and a spoon. And when the Arthur C. Clarke book came out, you knew you were in for a long debate on this or that Byrds B-side.'

It's time to get on to his own firing. There's a scene in *Digging the Vein* in which Atom/Anton kicks out the final two musicians in his band, one of whom is the narrator. The scene is hilarious and terrifying, and it turns out it was taken directly from life.

'LA had quite a small scene,' O'Neill says. 'My band Southpaw shared quite a lot of members with Brian Jonestown Massacre.

There was a period where we used to go see them gigging all the time. I had the same heroin dealer as Anton. So a lot of time we'd be hanging out at the same house waiting for the guy to show up, and Anton would be there. He was a trip, because he'd be wearing Jesus robes and all this stuff. He was always like that, twenty-four/seven.

'There was a point where the rest of the BJM were pissed off with Anton because of his drug use. So he fired them all and decided to replace them with people he could trust, which was people he knew used as well. If everybody was on the same drugs, there wouldn't be so many arguments.

'He had me, our guitarist Stephen, and this guy Tommy[2] on drums, who was a speed freak but also a junkie as well. So Tommy was a bit up and down – literally. We had a gig booked at the Troubadour – it was meant to be this big "the Jonestown's back" show of strength. We had six months leading up to it to get a whole new set, but we never practised anything. We learned one new song in six months.

'We'd get to the studio and all the equipment would be gone because Anton pawned it for junk money. So the first thing we'd have to do is rustle up money to get the musical equipment out of the pawn shop.

'Anton was one of those people who when they use heroin get really hyper – he had a weird anti-reaction. The rest of us'd be nodding out and he'd be bouncing off the walls.

'And so as soon as we got to the pawn shop, instead of getting the guitar out, he'd want to buy some vintage gun he found. So it was endless – one bit of equipment out, one in, and all the

---

2 The names of these players have been changed to protect identities.

hassle of trying to get drugs delivered. We never learned anything.

'Eventually, someone would say, "Anton, maybe it's time you cooled it on the drugs," so Anton would fire them.

'At the end, we had two weeks left and the last men standing were Anton, myself on keyboards and Tommy the drummer. We were like: "How are we gonna do it?" And Anton's like: "I'll get you a Hammond organ and we'll do it like the fuckin' Doors, man. Just play everything on the organ and it'll be fine."

'Anton called for one more rehearsal at his house, but when Tommy and I arrived, he was getting something delivered, and he didn't want us to be there because he didn't want to share. So he sent us out to get orange juice for him, and the car broke down. Tommy had this shitty old VW Bug that he was always putting five dollars of gas in, and he ran out of gas. Anton lived way up in the Hollywood Hills, and we had to go and fill a Gatorade bottle up with a couple of bucks of gas to get there. It took us hours to get back.

'And yeah, Anton had this big thing with the Masons. He was obsessed by the Masons, and he had this ornamental Masonic sword that he really believed . . . This is the thing – he was out of his mind at this stage. He thought the FBI was watching the house – you never knew what you were going to get with him. He actually believed this sword had mystical, supernatural powers and, if you pissed him off, he'd get it out and point it at you. And yeah, we came back hours later, drenched in sweat, baking in the desert heat. We're dopesick and we had to get this car up the hill with a little bit of gas. We finally get back and Anton's like "Where were you guys? This is meant to be a rehearsal. We've got a gig in two days."

'So Tommy's telling the whole story, how the car ran out of gas. And Anton's like. 'Oh yeah? . . . Where's my FUCKING ORANGE JUICE?' And then he starts swinging the sword and chasing us.

'Thankfully, from Anton's house out it's downhill, and we ended up rolling the car down until we could get the engine to turn, and that's it.

'And the show that happened afterward is the one in the documentary [*Dig!*].[3] He stopped the woman [Ondi Timoner, *Dig!*'s director] coming in to film because there were so many drugs, so there's a period where he fires the band and then it says: "six months later", and he's doing a gig at the Troubadour and people are throwing fruit at him. That was the gig we were meant to be doing, but he'd literally fired everyone. But, oh man, he wanted to take our heads off with that sword . . .'

There may be more famous rejects among these stories, but I'm not sure there's a kicking out to top that.

It's notable that for all the darkness of his years as an addict, O'Neill appears to be on friendly terms with most of the people he worked with.

'The only times I ever got fired from bands was when I was completely at the worst of it. I was normally very reliable. With Kenickie, I was so young I wasn't really doing drugs.

---

3 The feature-length *Dig!* documents the friendship and then fall out between the Brian Jonestown Massacre and the Dandy Warhols. In the film, Anton is seen becoming increasingly erratic and ill looking. Shortly before the six-month gap, he's filmed attempting to shoot a video on a Hollywood hilltop. He makes everyone wear white and tells the cameraperson to broadcast a message to his fans: 'Tell them to wear white, and be ready when I call.' The whole thing has a deranged, cultish vibe.

Honestly everybody just drank. When I joined Marc's band, he'd stopped doing drugs at that point, he wasn't drinking or anything. I was just a young kid who wanted to get into trouble, but I was too naive to find it. It was only when I got to LA and I got into hard, serious drugs that I became unreliable.'

It turns out that even Anton reached out to O'Neill a while ago.

'He'd read *Digging the Vein* and I'd heard he'd made a snarky comment to someone, and he wasn't happy I'd told the story. But he then reached out and was like, "Hey sorry we didn't get anything together, it would have been fun."'

'Weirdly enough, everyone survived. One person in particular I thought was probably gonna die, Stephen, is now a big property developer, and is rich and selling houses in Topanga Canyon or someplace . . .'

Another second life after music, but one for another time.

Bonus Track: The second rejection of Tony O'Neill

Hey Jamie –

Random thought – but our conversation got me thinking a bit and I remembered something that happened right after the Jonestown that wasn't in any of the books, because it didn't really fit in. But it was another instance of me getting fired from a band, that happened within a couple of months of Anton chasing me out of his house with the sword. I know this because I was at the peak of my addiction, at least the peak before I pawned all of my musical instruments and stopped playing altogether (until I returned to London a few years later and tried to get myself together).

I joined an LA band called the Push Kings, who were . . . a kind of indie/power-pop outfit from MA originally but had moved to LA to try and make it big after a few well reviewed but not massive-selling albums. They hired me right after I left the Jonestown on the recommendation of a producer who was working with them who had also recorded some demos for my band, Southpaw.

Anyway, they were really nice lads but definitely night and day from the Jonestown. No drugs, just booze and weed — they seemed quite polite and sweet, really. It's the only reason I can think of why they didn't suss that I was totally strung out on heroin at the time, because it was getting impossible to hide. You know what the weather is like in LA, yet I wore long sleeves year round because my arms were such a mess. I'd started shooting cocaine as well as heroin, and when you're on a coke run you can inject up to 20–30 times in the space of a few hours, so my arms were always a bloody mess.

Anyway, rehearsals were going well and we were about to do some shows on the west coast but I could tell that they were getting a bit suspicious of me. Like how I'd go to the bath-room at rehearsal and not emerge for 20 minutes or so, because I'd be in there trying to hit a vein. I'm sure I nodded out around them a few times and had to act like I was super tired from a heavy night.

Anyway, it all came to head, weirdly enough, at a Momus gig at the Troubadour on Sunset. They were friends of his and big fans. I like him too, I was really into that album of his *The Little Red Songbook* at the time. So I went along with them to check out the gig, and we were hanging out backstage when – as per – I needed to get high. I was on a real tear that evening, had just scored a lot of cocaine so was on a terrible cocaine run. I went on a wander from the backstage area to find a quiet bathroom away from the backstage . . . I found a bathroom, it had no lock so I barricaded myself in with a bin, and I was in there for ages trying to shoot up while vaguely aware of people trying the door once in a while and me telling them to fuck off, I was busy.

Right as I get the business done, the door crashes open. Turns out I'd wandered into the greenroom bathroom, and poor old Momus himself had been trying to get in there to spend a penny before going on stage. I must have been in there for AGES. The way I remember it, the needle was still in my arm and was covered in blood from trying (and failing) to find a vein. I look up and there's the Troubadour's (massive) security guys, Momus, and a few members of my band all gawping at this awful image of utter junkie degradation. They didn't call the police, but I was ejected from the venue and the Push Kings all in one fell swoop! So that one was quite dramatic.

That said, they were the exceptions not the rule. Every other band I left on good terms. Addiction made me into a different person, and one that I barely recognise these days. All of my fun memories from being in bands come from the times when I wasn't strung out – playing the Royal Albert Hall with Marc Almond in the late 90s, that first American tour and *TOTP* with Kenickie, sharing a bill with Garbage in my Kelli Ali days. I'm always open about my heroin days, but that was a point in my life when I was stumbling from one disaster to the next, somehow staying alive (and out of prison) through sheer dumb luck. Funny, but definitely black comedy.

Anyway, I just wanted to share that in case it might be useful to you.

Interlude:

God Smack

I sometimes think this book is *about* heroin. It seems to loom over everything, or curse our characters like the albatross in *The Rime of the Ancient Mariner* by Coleridge (a junkie).

I tried the drug once myself. A friend – now the straightest of arrows – introduced me to it. He'd also given me cocaine for the first time at university. On New Year's Eve 2004 I was twenty-four, and this friend had come to Shoreditch in London to spend the night with me. We'd bought a couple of grams of cocaine, and in his shoe was a tiny ball of foil that contained heroin. He'd bought it off a likely looking homeless person, having sought him out by his pinprick eyes. For a few months, my friend had smoked the drug regularly, hiding it from his girlfriend and enduring bouts of withdrawal, then seeking out this homeless person and accompanying him to an Islington squat for more.

That night, I watched in fascination as he smoked a hit before we went out to a party at a bar. He held a lighter beneath the brown powder on a piece of foil, and it transformed into an oily liquid, then thick smoke that swirled into the foil cone he used to inhale it. He 'chased' the running, burning liquid as it slid over the foil, the process which gives smoking heroin its infamous name.

He asked if I wanted to try it, and I said no.

Later, back at home, anxious from the coke and the usual disappointments of a New Year's Eve, I finally cracked. He helped me by holding the lighter and foil. The first hit instantly removed all of my anxiety, like the sun burning away cloud.

'It silences the inner monologue,' my friend said.

We were in my sparse room, dimly lit, in a basement flat. Submerged below the quiet streets at the edge of the City. In my flatmate's bigger room, my friends were partying.

The second hit gave me a blissful, ecstatic, bodily high that lingered softly in an hours-long afterglow.

Two female friends burst in, shocked at what we were doing, chastising the friend for giving me heroin. I was too blissed out to care or to worry.

I decided there and then that I'd never take the drug again.

Lemmy, Hawkwind

It fell to me to break the bad news. He was really
upset, there were hugs and tears and he went back to
England. Apparently he slept with several of the band's
girlfriends . . . – Dave Brock, Hawkwind

I think I remember the first time I encountered Lemmy. I say
think, because it doesn't quite seem to add up. As I recall it,
I was sitting in my friend Andy's living room, and as usual we
were watching music videos, probably on MTV. Amid the slew
of grunge, alternative rock and crossover rap, something unusual
came on. It was Motörhead performing 'Ace of Spades'.

As I remember, they were in a small space lit in bright neon
colours, surrounded by amp stacks. I could tell straight away
that this wasn't exactly the kind of music I loved, but that it bore
some connection to it. It wasn't like the glossy American hard
rock that was falling out of fashion. And though the look of the
band was closer to heavy metal, it didn't have the sleek high
fidelity of Metallica.

Whatever this was, it didn't have any of that glamour. It was
raw, but not in a grungy way. It made me think of rough men
in roadside cafés, or the threatening-looking Hells Angels I'd
seen at a town fair in Halifax. I used to make my pocket money

beating on pheasant shoots, and the lead singer looked like a menacing character from the decrepit, smelly old Transit we were ferried around in. Rock stars were usually handsome, and Lemmy definitely wasn't. He was playing a bass, which seemed unusual for a frontman. He also appeared to be straining to sing the song, his voice as rough as his looks. The whole thing had an off-putting element, as well as being hard to turn away from.[1]

This must have been 1993, because 'Ace of Spades' re-entered the charts that year on the back of a dance remix. The problem is that, by then, I'd moved away from the suburb where Andy lived, and I can't find the video anywhere. It might be the band's appearance on *The Young Ones* I'm remembering – something Andy and I loved watching – but in my memory there was more neon. Perhaps the whole thing seemed so lurid that it became even more so in my mind.

Lemmy is the happiest type of reject – the kind for whom being sacked simply opened a path to their true destiny. When he was kicked out of the space-rock group, Hawkwind, it was the best thing that could happen to him. He was never meant to be a second-tier member of a group of hippies – he was born to be a hard-rock pioneer.

Lemmy was born Ian Kilmister in Stoke-on-Trent in 1945. His youth was a very British, post-war version of that lived by the US hard rockers whom he'd eventually inspire. His father abandoned the family, and Lemmy was a truant who had problems with authority. It wasn't exactly a troubled childhood, because he appears to have carried it off with a certain irascible,

---

1 An initially repellent aspect is an under-recognised quality in music, and in art generally.

unflappable panache. These characteristics, along with a resistance to heroin and needles, appear to have contributed to his relative longevity. Unlike the US hard rockers, he never ended up having to get clean. In fact, he appeared never to repent nor regret his lifestyle of daily hard drinking.

In Lemmy's ghost-written book, he comes across as upbeat, good-humoured and highly unreconstructed. He preaches the virtues of the corporal punishment he received at school, and decries sissies.

He was obviously well loved by the rockers he inspired. Lars Ulrich describes how, at eighteen years old and as an 'awkward, snot-nosed kid', Lemmy embraced him with open arms. As the future drummer for Metallica (see Chapter 13) followed the band around Europe and the US, he was invited into their 'inner sanctum'.

'I felt like these guys cared about me. Lemmy was so fuckin' hospitable, like the original party host and caregiver. He took me under his wing and made me feel I belonged to something bigger than myself.'

In 1982, in Lemmy's LA hotel room, Ulrich threw up all over himself. Motörhead included a photo of the incident in the artwork for their 1986 album, *Orgasmatron*.

Lemmy appears unfazed by responsibilities or what most of us would consider the real stuff of life. He brushes aside the reappearance of a child he'd fathered and had given up for adoption, but largely for his son's privacy. Early in his life, he became self-reliant and happy in solitude: 'I don't really mind being alone now. People think it's weird, but I think it's great.'

Lemmy's year of birth puts him in a particularly interesting position in musical history. He was present for the early years of

British rock, and saw the Beatles, the Stones and the Hollies play live, but he was active in every key era that came afterwards: 1970s hard rock, 1980s metal, the alternative scene of the 1990s and 2000s that in many respects still defines US guitar music.[2]

This bridging is neatly summed up by Lemmy himself. Merseybeat-era Liverpool 'was like Seattle became in the early nineties – the record labels came up and signed everything that moved.'[3]

He loved the Beatles (see Chapter 1). 'They were the best band in the world. There will never be anything like the Beatles.' He remembers that the *Daily Mirror* ran 'a page every day about what they were doing. Imagine: a big fucking newspaper devoting a page each day to a band?'

The Beatles were 'anything but sissies'. They were 'hard men. Ringo's from the Dingle, which is like the fucking Bronx.' The Rolling Stones, on the other hand, 'were mummy's boys. I did like them, but they were never anywhere near the Beatles – not for humour, originality, songs or presentation'. Go tell 'em, Lemmy.

He was there at the Cavern one night, when John Lennon was called 'a fucking queer', put his guitar down, walked into the crowd, found the culprit and 'gave him the Liverpool kiss, sticking the nut on him – twice! Then John got back on stage.'

---

2 A band I'm working with at the time of writing – March 2023 – is in the US alternative chart. Around them are Weezer, Linkin Park, Red Hot Chili Peppers and Blink-182.

3 In 2010, Lemmy, Slash and Dave Grohl performed 'Ace of Spades' at an awards show in LA, linking Guns N' Roses (see Chapter 10) and Nirvana (see Chapter 12) – the two biggest bands of their generations, and key subjects for this book.

The Cavern, the Sunset Strip and the formative years of alternative rock – all in one lifetime.

Lemmy stumbled his way into Hawkwind. He'd been playing in bands and roadie-ing for Jimi Hendrix. By this time he was a 'speedfreak', loving amphetamines best among the quantities of LSD, cocaine and Quaaludes he happily consumed. Outside heroin,[4] Lemmy retained a rosy view of most drugs. 'Orgasms on acid, by the way, are fucking excellent.' Drugs were essential to his trade.

'I don't give a fuck what they say – keep fit, eat your greens, drink juice – fuck off! It's not true! I don't care if you eat two hundred artichokes, you still won't last through a three-month tour.'

He'd tasted success in the Rocking Vicars, falling prey to the Beatles-inspired trend of women snatching clothing, jewellery and even hair from musicians. 'Sounds like fun, doesn't it? Ha! Have you ever had a pair of jeans *ripped* off you? It's fucking agony, believe me.' As for the hair snipping: 'If you've never seen forty serious, grim-lipped birds, all holding scissors, rushing at you . . .'

A move to London hadn't brought the immediate solo success he'd envisioned, somewhat uniquely: 'Everything was going to

4 Lemmy really hated heroin. He once saw someone inject some, only to emerge from the toilet with his face black and his tongue sticking out. 'Somebody had sold him rat poison – took his money, smiled at him and sold him certain death. I thought, "Hell, if that's the kind of people who are hanging around with heroin, you can fucking have it."' Heroin also killed 'the girl I was most in love with in my life' – a fifteen-year-old black girl, Sue, his relationship with whom exposed the racism within the supposed 'era of peace and love'. Sue also slept with Mick Jagger, and quipped of the singer's reputation: 'Well he was good, but he wasn't as good as Jagger, you know?'

be wonderful and huge women would get a hold of me and do things to me with raw carrots. You know – shit like that.'

But through his love of speed, Lemmy befriended the only other user in Hawkwind, DikMik (Michael Davies), who 'played' a ring modulator. This audio generator could create frequencies that went 'out of human hearing', but could make audience members 'flop about'. Lemmy wanted to join the band as their guitarist but wound up on bass instead. 'The day I joined Hawkwind was when I first started playing bass.' It was August 1971, and the previous bassist hadn't shown up, but had foolishly left behind his instrument.

The band was into playing unpaid benefit shows for people who'd 'been put in jail for some fucking thing and we thought it wasn't fair because we were freaks and everything wasn't fair because of the pigs – you know, all that crap you talked in those days.'

Despite joining the band, no one ever actually told Lemmy he was in it.

Lemmy observed Hawkwind's leader, Dave Brock: 'I learned a lot from him, really, about vision and tenacity.' Though perhaps not about his 'spanking fantasies'.

'He used to pass schoolgirls on the road and lean out of his car, yelling, "Spank! Spank! Spank! Hello girls, spanky-spanky!"'

Lemmy was less enamoured with Nik Turner, the band's older frontman, a 'moral, self-righteous asshole, as only Virgos can be'. Lemmy brought in an old bandmate from a previous gig, drummer Simon King, unaware that he was sowing the seeds of his own downfall.

For a few years, he seems to have been blissfully happy in the band. He liked Michael Moorcock, the British novelist who wrote texts for Hawkwind and occasionally appeared with them, and from whom they got their name.

'We used to go round his house for free food now and again, he would have these notices on his door: "If I don't answer the first ring of the bell, don't ring it again or I'll come out and kill you . . . I'm writing. Leave me a-fucking-lone.'

He recalls Robert Calvert, the performance poet, who turned up 'half the time for the gigs, and the other half he didn't'. When he did appear, he'd read his poetry, or that of Moorcock. But he was 'falling apart mentally' and not 'as brilliant as people make out now. Of course, when you die, you become more brilliant by about fifty-eight per cent.'

'It was magical,' Lemmy says, 'the time I spent with Hawkwind.' He describes how the whole band and 'about ten chicks' would climb into a deserted estate around a burned-out house and trip on acid. 'That was a great time, the summer of '71 – I can't remember it, but I'll never forget it!'

America, where he'd end up living from the 1990s onwards,[5] made even more of an impression: 'I took to it from the start – unlimited whoopee! You've got to understand how drab and awful England was back then. The first time I was in Boulder, I looked out the window and there was this range of mountains that looked like they were right on top of the hotel, but they were fifty miles away!'

---

5 As I write this, in March 2023, my wife has won the strange tug of war of the last two years, and we're moving back to LA. I'm surrounded by boxes once again. I wish I could ask Lemmy what it was about LA that kept him there, because I'm sure he'd have had a positive take on the place, about which I have mixed feelings.

From paradise, the fall. It boiled down to drugs, but in Lemmy's case only that they were the wrong kind. It wasn't as though everyone else wasn't on them, after all.

'It was okay in those days to do shit like that. It really isn't now – everyone's into health and being politically correct, anti-drug and all that. But drugs were our common denominator. It was the only way we freaks could tell if somebody was one of us.'

And it wasn't just drugs. As ever, power dynamics had shifted too. In 1974 a second drummer, Alan Powell, had joined Hawkwind. The two drummers' pompous, centre-stage set up annoyed Lemmy from the start: 'Things started to go downhill when the drum empire took over.'

Lemmy 'gave those two fuckers no peace. I'd be standing by the side of them, urging "hurry up you cunts!"'

And Lemmy was by now 'too forward'.

'During my years with Hawkwind, I really came out of any shell I might have been in, stagewise. I was always at the front of the stage and showing off, and since I wasn't the leader of the band, it was considered most presumptuous. And I'd started to write songs, which I think pissed everybody off as well.' That and also, since DikMik had left in 1973, Lemmy was 'the only speed freak left in the band'.

In 1975, Lemmy got busted for cocaine possession while going over the Canadian border. The thing was, he didn't have any cocaine: the rudimentary test the cops did couldn't discern between coke and amphetamines. That would only become clear later, when the charges were dropped. In the meantime, it was jail.

'I'd been locked up in cells overnight, but never in a serious jail like this one. I remember I was in the delousing room, ready for the spray when this wonderful voice behind me said, "You're bailed."

'Well, as I found out later, the only reason the band got me out was because my replacement wasn't going to get to Canada in time. Otherwise, they would have just let me rot.'

The band flew Lemmy on to Toronto. 'We did the gig to tremendous applause, then at four o'clock in the morning, I was fired.'

The band had held a vote. Dave Brock wanted to keep Lemmy, but he couldn't conjure a majority. Simon King, one half of the 'drum empire,' and someone Lemmy had invited into the band, voted against him.

One of the things I like most about Lemmy is his dislike of hippies, for whose hypocrisy I share his distaste.

'If I'd been caught with acid, those guys would have rallied around me. I think even if I'd been doing heroin, it would have been better for them. That whole hippie subculture was so fucking two-faced, when you get down to it.'

The band was left critically injured. On the verge of success in America, a mediocre new bassist joined, and the drum empire's pomposity took over.

'There was no nuts in 'em,' Lemmy concludes. 'When I left Hawkwind, the cojones came with me.'

But no matter. Onwards to the future, to form Motörhead, 'the dirtiest rock 'n' roll band in the world – if we moved in next door your lawn would die.'

Lemmy is perhaps the only person to turn the cause of his throwing out – being a 'motorhead'/speed freak – into a band name and a trademark.

Under that new banner, he would shape an entire genre.

I'm too good for you anyway.

Postscript

A year after Lemmy's death in 2015, Dave Brock gave an interview to *Classic Rock*. It struck me for being the most positive take I'd come across from a bandleader regarding a sacking.

Lemmy played bass like a guitarist and it gave him a style that was all his own. It was the same with those gruff vocals of his. Nobody sang like him. And as he came up with [Hawkwind songs] 'The Watcher' and 'Motorhead' pretty soon we realised that he was also a really good songwriter.

I used to share a room with Lemmy on tour, which was quite an experience because he would be up for days on end.

[After the bust at the Canadian border] there was a big band meeting. He was voted out by two to four. Simon House and I had wanted to keep him but the rest disagreed. Nik Turner even said that either Lemmy left or he would.

But even after the sacking I never fell out with Lemmy. It was the other members of Hawkwind that he hated. He was going to be the best man at my wedding in 2007 until problems with his heart hospitalised him. That makes you realise he'd been ill for quite a while.

It's great that he made it to 70. I never thought he'd make it to 50. The old cunt had said he wanted to die on stage, and that's very nearly what he did. But there was always magic between us, and I'm so grateful that he was in my life.

LaTavia Roberson and LeToya Luckett, Destiny's Child

You thought I wouldn't sell without you, sold
nine million. – Beyoncé Knowles et al.

In 1999, two members of Destiny's Child discovered that they'd been fired in one of the cruellest examples of rejection we'll encounter: a video had been premiered for a new single, 'Say My Name', and neither of them were in it.

The group had already released two albums together: their eponymous debut and the far more successful *The Writing's On the Wall*. Things had apparently started to go wrong during the recording of this breakthrough record. Beyoncé's father, Matthew Knowles, had taken over management duties several years previously, and Roberson and Luckett accused him of not paying them fairly, and of setting up Beyoncé for solo success. They had attempted to get their own, separate manager. In music, when things get to this stage, it's very unlikely they'll improve.

When the video for 'Say My Name' appeared, it featured two new members – Michelle Williams and Farrah Franklin – in their places. Things worsened for Roberson and Luckett a year later, when Destiny's Child released 'Survivor', a huge global hit. It contained the lyric about sales, above, which seemed a taunt specifically aimed at them.

Luckett had met Beyoncé all the way back in grade (primary) school and claimed to have been her 'protector'.

'I came into class and she's sitting in my seat,' she told *TheGrio* in 2014. 'And I was like, "Mrs Wester, get your girl, because she's definitely in my seat right now." We became the best of friends. I was like her low-key bodyguard. Nobody knows that though.'

Interestingly, there are other lyrics in 'Survivor' that could well relate to this. Beyonce sings of being better off with an unnamed individual out of her life. She claims this person thought that she'd be helpless and 'weak without you', but that in fact she's stronger.

If so, hearing the song would have been particularly painful for LeToya Luckett.

Either way, the rejected pair tried to sue Destiny's Child, claiming that the line about sales was a 'deliberate, disparaging, defamatory factual misrepresentation'. In an approach typical in the American industry, they also sued Sony, the group's label, for breach of contract, defamation and fraud. This type of aggressive, widespread suit is designed to cause the maximum panic in as many parties as possible, and thus increase the chance of a settlement.

In this instance, it didn't work – the pair lost on all counts.

'It's ridiculous,' Destiny's Child's attorney said in a statement. 'It's unfortunate that the plaintiffs have nothing better to do with their time than to draw up new lawsuits to file.'

★   ★   ★

Eventually, the two fired members would indeed find other ways to fill their time. They formed their own group, Anjel, but this soon fractured and they went their separate ways. Luckett had a modest solo career before appearing to transition smoothly into acting. She's married with a child and lives in Atlanta, where she appeared on VH1's reality TV show, *T.I. & Tiny: Friends & Family Hustle*.

Things were harder for LaTavia Roberson. She'd been in a girl group with Beyoncé since before Luckett was involved. Perhaps she wanted it all even more and took the rejection commensurately harder. After it happened, she suffered from depression and alcoholism. In 2016 she told *People* that: 'It was very difficult because of the way that I found out about it. I hate even talking about it, and it's been 20 years – but it is what it is. We saw the "Say My Name" video on TV, and that's how I found out I was no longer in the group.'

In a testament to her character, though, she seems to have recovered, and is now a motivational speaker and mother of two.

In fact, despite the brutal nature of the rejection, the hard feelings seem to have been put behind everyone involved. Roberson posted images of herself with Beyoncé on Instagram, and Luckett has spoken positively about the group and its leader too.

For her part, Beyoncé thanked them both during an acceptance speech for a 2014 MTV award. Perhaps some wounds can heal after all.

21

Gary Young, Pavement

*From his perspective, the Pavement part of his life
was quite . . . baffling.* – Stephen Malkmus

There was a song a kid played me on the back of a bus once, on a school trip. It was low slung, low-fi indie rock; insouciant and slacker but driving, arch but strikingly purposeful. It was catchy, almost sing-song, but it was *cool*. This was rock with anything macho or overly earnest stripped away. It was self-evidently intelligent and felt utterly modern. It was by Pavement, and though I became a fan of the band I didn't hear the song again until very recently. Despite that, its melody was crystal clear in my head for the thirty interceding years.

There are some bands I've listened to in a way that strikes me as odd. There can't be many records I've played more than *Crooked Rain, Crooked Rain*, Pavement's second album. And yet I'm ashamed to say I've hardly bothered with any of the others. Sure, I've listened to *Slanted and Enchanted*, the debut album whose title perfectly describes the band's sound, but only a handful of times. How can you love a record as much as I do *Crooked Rain* and not be compelled to listen to the others? Especially when, with other bands I've loved, I've obsessively listened to every note they ever recorded?

Maybe the timing was off. *Crooked Rain* was one of the last guitar records I really loved before drifting into trip-hop and hip-hop. And I seem to remember Pavement's third album, *Wowee Zowee*, got mixed reviews on release. But even so, I listened to *Crooked Rain* obsessively all over again in my early twenties, driving around Leeds doing a lowly summer job. I was able to understand it slightly better by then. As I said to my daughter in the car recently, revisiting the album yet again, I'm never *completely* sure what Stephen Malkmus is singing about.[1]

Perhaps this concentration on certain works in the oeuvre is somehow related to the enigmatic Malkmus, Pavement's towering talent of a bandleader. I've also obsessed over two of Malkmus's later records (with the Jicks), *Real Emotional Trash* and *Pig Lib*, both of them brilliant, without really exploring further. Perhaps, as so often in my musical life, there are treasures out there I'll come across later.

All of which is to say that it was due to my strange approach to listening to Pavement that I'd never heard about Gary Young, their first drummer.

Through my day job in music, I became friendly with Chris Cunningham, the genius video artist and musician perhaps best known for Aphex Twin's 'Come to Daddy' and 'Windowlicker' videos, and the one he made for Björk's 'All Is Full of Love'. Over a drink one night, we got talking about Pavement, and he

1 I've never been a Springsteen fan, but a recent podcast on *Nebraska* had led me to that album. It's the first time I've ever liked his music, and I'd encouraged my daughter to listen carefully to the story told in 'Highway Patrolman'. Shortly afterwards, I put *Crooked Rain* on, and she began asking me what the songs were about. The contrast was striking. That said, on his solo records Malkmus does relate stories himself, if usually slightly obliquely.

told me he strongly preferred the early stuff – *Slanted and Enchanted* and the singles and EPs around it – not least because he preferred Gary Young's drumming.

I'd always liked Steve West's drumming on *Crooked Rain*, which as I remembered it was light but kinetic, with a skipping, near-breakbeat quality that seemed ideal for the band: non-macho, very indie rock.

So who the hell was Gary Young, I wondered?

I went away, read a bit, discovered he'd been fired from Pavement, decided to write about him. Then, on the very morning I was writing these words, it was announced that he'd died.

Chris texted me a link to a Pitchfork article: 'Gary Young, Pavement's First Drummer, Dies at 70'.

'Ugh,' he said.

The way Chris described Young, he was older than the rest of the band, about forty when they were starting out at the beginning of their twenties. He'd ended up as their drummer partly because he had a studio space they wanted to use.

Chris sent me a link to his playlist of Pavement favourites, and there, at the top, was the song that had been in my head for thirty years. 'Texas Never Whispers'. My heart thudded with excitement as that sing-song melody burst from the speakers. I also felt like a fool. It would've been easy enough to find the song if I'd really looked. It just hadn't been on an album, which was where I'd tried searching over the years. Instead, it had appeared on *Watery, Domestic*, the band's 1992 EP that also featured another favourite Pavement song, 'Frontwards'. Embarrassingly, I only knew the latter song because of *Quarantine the Past*, the sort-of-best-of they released in 2010.

The *Watery, Domestic* EP was the final Pavement release to feature Gary Young. And the drums on 'Texas', I realised, were superb.

By coincidence, a film about Young, aka The Rotting Man, had been premiered at South by Southwest in 2023. It's called *Louder than You Think* and was directed by Jed I. Rosenberg. I tracked Jed down on LinkedIn and messaged him, and he quickly sent a friendly reply. Before long, I had a link to the film.

I was completely gripped by it, conjuring as it did the early 1990s, and the indie rock that I loved and changed my life. Among the archival footage were new interviews with Young, Malkmus,[2] Pavement co-founder Scott Kannberg, bassist Mark Ibold and vocalist and percussionist Bob Nastanovich. In order to tell the stories for which no footage existed, Rosenberg had enlisted the puppeteer Adrian Rose Leonard[3] and her team. Uncannily recognisable marionettes of Young, Malkmus and co acted out the wild stories from the band's early years, amid re-created cityscapes or bright graphics.

Despite quite a lot of very bad behaviour, it seems that there was something eternally innocent about Gary Young, which is neatly captured by his puppet-self. In his prime, he had long

2 Malkmus was interviewed by video call for the film. He's reflective, shyly charming and likeable. It's easy to see why he's so beloved in indie-rock and leftfield circles. Late on in the film, he raises his left hand and is revealed to be wearing a strange, pale glove. Why, I asked Jed, the director? 'I wish I had a better answer,' he wrote. 'But one moment it suddenly appeared on his hand and we just had to roll with it . . .'

3 Leonard worked on the revival of *Crank Yankers*, a very funny prank calls and puppets show that originally ran in the US in the early noughties. I watched quite a lot of this, alone and slightly lonely on Mike Ladd's couch-cum-bed in the North Bronx in 2003.

black hair in a ponytail, and a wiry frame with the look of upper-body strength associated with a drummer (and, in his case, a gymnast – but more on that shortly). His really striking feature was his eyes. They were very large and an arresting blue, their sockets turned slightly downward at the sides. They look a bit like Gollum's in the *Lord of the Rings* films when he's being nice, or one of those sad goblin garden ornaments. That said, he usually looked happy. There was either a glint of mischief in the eyes or a distance. In photos he sometimes looks as though he's gazing at something wondrous that no one else can see. Perhaps he was – in 1969 he apparently took acid 375 times.

Gary's puppet in the film has exactly his eyes. At the end of the documentary, after it's acted out his antics, the older, stooped, clearly very ill Gary shakes it by the hand.

Young was born in Mamaroneck, New York, in 1953. He appears to have had a difficult-to-control energy from the outset. His brother Rory, interviewed in the film, says that today he'd be diagnosed as hyperactive. He broke his mother's ribs twice – once inside the womb and once bouncing on her as an infant. When they were kids, Rory was kept awake at night in their shared room by Gary endlessly thudding his head on to his pillow.

'We were always astounded that we managed to keep him alive,' his mother says in the film.

His brother thinks Gary had some kind of chemical imbalance, as though adrenalin was always charging through his system. He began to take drugs – weed and later heroin – to calm himself down. The latter drug is only mentioned once in the documentary, by Rory, and it's clear that the real demon in Gary's life was alcohol. The latter-day Gary in the film walks with a painful stoop, speaks slowly, and has clammy-looking, wasted skin and wispy hair. He's clearly in the terminal stages of alcoholism, a glass of Sunkist and vodka rarely out of shot.

'Hit the drums as hard as you can every time.' – Gary Young's advice to Bob Nastanovich.

Young and his wife Geri originally came to California when they fled Gary's marijuana charges. Gary stole his mum's credit card to book the flights. They wound up in Stockton, a small city in the Central Valley, south of Sacramento.

'You can't escape,' Gary says in the documentary, indicating on a map how Stockton is locked in amid hills on all sides.

Inspired by the revelation of the Beatles (see Chapter 1) on *The Ed Sullivan Show*, he'd always wanted to be a musician. He began playing in local punk bands, most notably the Fall of Christianity, and made a small fortune selling weed. He invested the money in a house and recording studio – the one he and Geri still occupy in the film.

He met Stephen Malkmus and Scott Kannberg when they booked the studio. The pair were schoolfriends who, finding themselves back in Stockton after college, had decided to start a band. Kannberg had recently completed an urban planning degree: 'So, Pavement,' he says laughing in the film.

When the two twenty-year-olds turned up at Gary's, they smelled pot, and noted that Young was 'cooking a chicken in his fireplace'. He and Geri seemed like 'brash New Yorkers', and Young had a strange penchant for acrobatics.

'He liked to do handstands off the roof,' Malkmus says. 'He had this sort of routine, in a great way. Dangerous weird stuff that he could do. He sort of was like a cat, or if there is a superhero that, like, gets hit by bullets and smashed and is just fine . . .'

Before long, Gary was playing drum lines for the pair in the studio.

From the outset, the key question of style arose. Pavement were the perfect iteration of the indie band. In their own way, they were ambitious. They really wanted to do it, to make great records and have success, but they wanted to do it their way. They may have played their songs with slacker stylings, but that didn't mean they didn't take them seriously.[4] It was about tone, the way the songs sounded and presented – so important in music.

In indie rock – in its widest sense, the tradition of music that takes in the Replacements (see Chapter 9), Sonic Youth, Nirvana (see Chapter 12) – that fuzz and bleed on the guitars is part of the music's transcendent quality. You know it when you hear it – in the way jazz fans recognise the tone of a Coltrane or a Davis.

Pavement were setting themselves up as the anti-rock stars, but their drummer thought differently. He might have played in punk bands, but he also loved Yes – the muscular, maximal drumming of Bill Bruford. As well as a great drummer, Young wanted to be a showman. And he didn't buy into 'lo-fi'.

'Why would I make it shitty, on purpose?' he asks in the film.

---

4 Many years ago, Kim Gordon of Sonic Youth expressed this perfectly in a quote. I've been unable to find it, so I'll paraphrase. 'It's not as if we write these perfect pop songs and then deliberately play them with our left hands.' The loose, lo-fi tone was key to the way the songs were envisioned. It was what made the music so new and so arresting.

Malkmus disagrees. 'We were into roughing it up, and ambient sounds.'

Nevertheless, Young's studio environment was crucial in capturing the band's sonic vision.

'How loose it was at Gary's definitely helped the sound,' Kannberg says. 'The instruments he had, the equipment he had.'

When the fledgling band had begun touring, they gradually enlisted Bob Nastanovich on percussion and (largely) backing vocals, and Ben Ibold on bass. These latter pair were very much beginners with their instruments.

For these electric, early shows, Gary was very clear on his brief, even if no one else was.

'You see, my job, in a sense, was to: Wreak. Fucking. Havoc,' he says in the film, pointing to a picture of Stephen Malkmus on stage. In the background, Young is standing on his head.[5] 'And I think I did a real good job of it,' he concludes.

In early Pavement live footage, it's clear they had a great drummer – totally natural, propulsive, playing freely and without watching himself.

'He loved to do rolls,' Kannberg says. 'Very, very frenetic. You're like, man, he's never gonna come back and get on time. Which was great for our songs because it kind of added this . . .

---

5 Obviously, in many ways Young fits into the wild drummer mould/cliché. Kannberg even says in the film that he's from the Keith Moon school. I once worked with a great band called Paris Suit Yourself. The three primary members were French and looked at things from an experimental and art-driven perspective. Somehow, they had found a crazy American drummer. He seemed to spend most of his time in only a pair of bright, tight Y-fronts, beat the hell out of the drums, and liked to do handstands. The band never felt entirely at home with him, but by God he added something.

weird element to it. You're like: "Is it gonna fall apart, or is it gonna get back there?"'

Cue lots of footage of a bare-chested Young, lost in the music, beating the hell out of his drums.

Nastanovich, another good friend of Malkmus's, had originally joined as tour manager. His segue into 'percussion' was designed as a backstop. Before the tour, Malkmus told him: 'Get a couple of drums just to keep time. Gary's a bit shaky, sometimes he's just too drunk to play.'

'I got hired to be in the band,' Nastanovich says, 'from a musical perspective, sort of as an insurance policy to make sure that time was being kept.'

As brilliant as he could be on stage, Young kept getting cripplingly drunk. Malkmus was amazed by his powers of recovery.

'Again, going back to surviving the apocalypse . . . He was back again from death's door.' Getting back up and carrying on after he 'seemingly could not even move'.

More bluntly, Kannberg recalls that 'the first time I've ever seen what an alcoholic really looks like was that tour'.

Gary kept breaking up performances to go and get a drink, then dancing around instead of playing. But it was exciting, they were young, Gary's behaviour just seemed part of the vibe. They didn't think it would really go anywhere anyway.

'These kids,' Gary says. 'I was forty and they were twenty, and no one believed I was the drummer in the band.'

In some of the pictures – the earlier ones, and on a good day – Gary doesn't actually look that much older, that out of place in the band. In a way, he was blossoming, finally realising a long-held dream.

★　　★　　★

Ah, the early 1990s: the underground bands, the thrill of discovery; older brothers with record collections, tapes on the back of the bus. The fanzines and thrift-store sweaters, the blissful lack of mobile phones. The long-since-peaked powers of the music press. The heady mixture of anti-rock star stylings with enigmatic lyrics and lo-fi guitars. The full bands doing lots and lots of filmed interviews – no one does this any more – often, for no apparent reason, shot outdoors and through a fisheye lens. The members faintly awkward, shy and ironic.

How strikingly handsome Stephen Malkmus was, and still is. The perfect indie-boy pin up.[6]

Pavement might not have thought much would happen with their career, but as Geri says: 'One thing led to another.'

At first, Young didn't take the band seriously, but as they progressed towards *Slanted and Enchanted*, he became a 'huge artistic contributor to Pavement,' Nastanovich says. 'Not only was he a brilliant drummer, but he was kind of different than the other drummers from the genre. The drum tracks weren't made by a guy my age, they were made by someone from a totally different generation of music.'

Malkmus says that the *Slanted* songs usually started with him and Gary playing first, Malkmus 'talking him through the songs. And sometimes there'd be a free part where I'd say . . . "rock!" and so that's when he could do his triplets or weird stuff on these pretty simple four/four songs.'

---

6 I've always remembered reading, as a young teenager, that Courtney Love had asked of Stephen Malkmus and Lou Barlow of Sebadoh: 'Which one do you marry, and which one do you fuck on the side?' The many implications of this were somehow profoundly stirring.

In an interview from 1993, the band are seated (outdoors). Asked to list their influences, Malkmus says that it's easier to list similarities, and does so. Young chimes in: 'We're also really influenced by a song called "I'm Telling You Now" by Herman's Hermits.'

'Oh man,' Malkmus says, lowering his head to his knees.

When Mark Ibold joined the band in 1991, he was 'prepped' about Young, and how he'd done 'acid three hundred and sixty-five times in 1969, when he was sixteen. Hearing something like that makes you go "Jesus Christ, what's this guy gonna be like?" The nice thing is that he's like a completely normal, gentle person.'

Before long, the band were playing bigger shows and festivals, including Reading in 1992 – the same year Nirvana played their iconic set. People began to say that Pavement might be the new Nirvana.

Gary was in heaven: 'Y'know, he was famous!' Geri says, still looking surprised. 'We were on the street in Scotland and these people would come up to him. I mean, it kind of blew me away.'

Malkmus takes a more reflective view. 'By that point Gary would've become more of a, like, WTF factor in our band. Y'know, he's an old, like, hippie, playing with these seemingly clean-cut kids. So, it was quite a contrast.'

And Gary's sense of stagecraft started to contrast, too: 'No one at that time would, y'know, throw a stick up in the air and catch it,' Ibold says, 'and then stand up. We were all trying to get away from the metal bands that we listened to in the eighties or whatever.'

Sure enough, the footage shows the bare-chested Young flipping sticks into the air as Malkmus stands, head cocked and serious in the shoe-gazey tradition, a few feet away.

'It was classic progressive-rock extravagance in how a band should be presented,' Malkmus says.

Nevertheless, Pavement began to like to thrash about and rock out on stage too. 'I think some of the looseness of Gary's life probably translated into our live shows,' says Kannberg. That's a key insight, because it seems that like many of our rejects, Gary Young gave Pavement something crucial.

Gary's style was mixed with 'some unconfident dudes that were worried about being cool or something,' Malkmus says, 'or just were so nervous that they couldn't move, or had to look down at their instruments 'cause they couldn't play, or had never had a PA wedge [monitor speaker] in front of them.'

But as Pavement became a seasoned live act, they did begin to move, to lose themselves. Gary Young gave them that.

In the present, Young, clammy and pale, his bottle of vodka beside him, asks: 'Did you ever see the movie *Rollerball*? That's what I want. Whatever I could do to make the fucking shambles out of the whole thing.'

Young wanted tension, Nastanovich says. And the rest of the band eventually didn't. The drummer would regularly halt shows to come to the front of stage and speak on the mic, joking about the band's clothes, or his Yes T-shirt. 'Fuck you, hippie!' someone yells on seeing this. One night in Atlanta, he fell backwards eight feet off the stage, but managed to clamber back up, visibly hurt, and somehow finish the show.

'It might have been entertaining for people to see that, but it wasn't a good show,' Ibold says. 'And we were worried about it.'

Behind much of Young's behaviour there appears to have been a craving for fame. In a band of anti-rock stars, Gary wanted to *be* one.

The frequency of his coming to front of stage and taking the mic grew, and his clothing became louder.

'He'd wear, like, bright shirts, or shorts with a tie. He wore topsiders a lot, which was kind of funny,' Malkmus says, laughing.

He was beginning to make a name for himself, but of a kind that wasn't sustainable.

'All fame and no fortune,' Geri says in the film's present.

The fun and the chaos quickly became exhausting.

'He would introduce himself to every single person that came to Pavement shows. Sometimes that got pretty extraneous and exhausting – sometimes there'd be twelve-hundred people,' Nastanovich says.

'At first, he would just kind of stand outside the shows welcoming people to the show,' Kannberg says, 'and everybody was just like "I didn't realise the homeless guy outside was the drummer."'

Then Gary began to hand something out to the crowd, usually vegetables, but sometimes pennies. Supporting Sonic Youth, Thurston Moore helped Young make and distribute mashed potatoes and gravy.

The show became 'Gary Young and Pavement', jokes Nastanovich in an interview from the time.

The word everyone keeps coming back to is 'tension'.

When it worked, it worked. 'He was one of the funniest guys you ever met,' says Kannberg. 'And when he was on fire on drums there was nobody better, and those shows were just incredible.' Cue footage of Young thrashing his drums like Dave Grohl. On his best nights, Nastanovich says, he may have been the best rock 'n' roll drummer in the world.

Improbably, Young had been a trophy-winning gymnast in his childhood. He chose to deploy this skill by doing his head-stands at the front of the stage during Malkmus's emotive solo moments. 'Boy, did that piss him off,' Gary says. For his part, Malkmus appears philosophical and magnanimous.

But the drinking got worse, and often Young was too wasted to drum properly. He went from 'ninety percent there to fifty cent there', according to Kannberg.

At the same time, he began to think the show was about him, and not the band. As far as he was concerned, he was becoming a rock star in the seventies mould he'd been raised on. He was Robert Plant, and Pavement was just a side show.

If Guns N' Roses (see Chapter 10) and Nirvana represented the tectonic shift in music writ large, then Gary Young's story is a far more personal example.

'Gary wanted to sell out,' his brother says, 'whereas Malkmus seemed to be doing everything he could to stop that from happening.' Young's brother is a perceptive man. 'That turned out to be the optimal strategy, because once the people in the record companies realised that this was the forbidden fruit, that just made them want it all the more.'

Their father, a businessman, began asking what Gary's percentages were. His brother began pushing him to get the band to sign to a major.

There was very little money from their recordings – what they made came from touring, and they split it equally. Gary and his family didn't seem to get it.

Then came the clumsy betrayal that pushed things over the edge. One night in New Jersey, Gary didn't show up for sound-check. Chris Lombardi, the head of Pavement's label, Matador, called the band up with news: Gary had passed out in the head of Columbia Records' office.

'He'd gone there and said: "I'm Gary from Pavement, let's do a deal. I want a million dollars,"' Kannberg says, bursting into laughter at the memory.

When caught out, he tried an equally clumsy cover story, claiming Columbia had shown him a briefcase with a million dollars inside it.

By this stage, Nastanovich says, 'He was so far away from the way the band thought philosophically that it was disconcerting.'

'I was like: "You don't speak for the band, Gary,"' Malkmus says. But even when discussing this vexed memory, he does his best to see both sides: 'But y'know, Gary was right, there was certainly potential of that avenue to explore. But at that time, I would've thought that they [major labels] wouldn't have been the right place for the band.'

'Gary decided that he would make a bunch of demands,' Nastanovich says. 'He wanted health insurance, and he wanted a hell of a lot of money.'

His family thought he should have a contract. 'I pushed and I pushed and I pushed,' he says, looking back.

'It got ugly,' Geri summarises.

The time had come. According to Pavement lore, Gary Young agreed to leave after a meeting. As ever, the truth is more complex.

'So, he just said: "Well, then I quit,"' Kannberg recalls. 'And I knew he didn't want to quit, but I think Steve was relieved.'

'It was nice in a way that he was just done with us. He was probably just sick of dealing with me. It was a good time to part ways,' Malkmus says.

Young tried to retract his resignation, but Kannberg wasn't having it. 'You've become a liability to us,' he told the drummer.

Geri understood, but Gary 'took it hard'.

Steve West, a friend of friends, and a 'super nice guy', was invited in.

'Although nowhere near as flamboyant a drummer or performer as Gary, he was very, very solid.' Nastanovich says.

So, Chris Cunningham was right, they replaced flair with solidity.

'It was a completely different band,' Nastanovich reflects.

When did you notice Pavement was a big deal? Young is asked in the film.

'After I left,' he replies.

Harking back to that infamous sacking of Pete Best (see Chapter 1), when Pavement toured England fans began shouting 'Gary! Where's Gary?' Which was 'a bit humiliating for Steve West', Remko Schouten, the band's live engineer says. 'People didn't forget Gary, because he was quite a character.'

Meanwhile, Gary did his best to recover, but 'it took years', Geri says. He focused on gardening, jumped on his trampoline, and spent time with old musical friends in Stockton.

A year after leaving Pavement, and inspired by his gardening, he had a brief resurgence as leader of his own act, Plantman. Their eponymous single became a sort of indie-rock novelty hit in 1994. His old friend Thurston Moore appeared as a tree in the video, Michael Stipe announced it on MTV and, in an odd way, Young's dream came true: 'Huh-huh, is that Robert Plant?' sniggered Beavis, when the song appeared on *Beavis and Butt-Head*.

Plantman peaked when they joined the Lollapalooza tour in 1995, members of Pavement looking on happily from the crowd. It must have felt as though Gary had found his place. But things fizzled out, collapsing into disastrous, drunken gigs. Gary's drinking was now completely out of control.

'Gary's just Gary,' Eric Westphal, Plantman's bassist, reflects on a meeting that went disastrously wrong. He neatly summarises the terrible contradiction at the heart of rock 'n' roll charisma: 'If he would've been more serious about who he was, I probably wouldn't have been as serious about him. I'd probably have never known him.'

There were surreal twists to come for Young – most notably, writing an agony aunt column for a Japanese music magazine – but the glory days were over. Gary and Geri were left to live out their years quietly, as he sank further into alcoholism. His wasn't the violent kind. He seemed slow, good-humoured and warm-hearted, loving to his wife. If his brother's hyperactivity diagnosis was correct, then his medicating himself with booze kept him calmer.

The film, completed well before Gary's death, already feels elegiac. You feel that everyone in it knows he's soon going to die.

Young came across as defiant about his drinking, but a poem-cum-song that he declaims in the film rather gives his true feelings away.

By the refrigerator light
In the middle of the night
I get up to take my pills
Don't wanna turn on the regular light

For fear I won't get back to sleep
When I finally fall asleep
It's not for very long
And I always wake up in a sweat
I'm a man full of dreams
And I wish I could have them
But nightmares is all I'm gonna get
When morning arrives, I'm barely alive
But I pull on my pants anyway
Time to face a new day, it's gonna take me a while
Be noon before I can smile

The couple seem to have accepted the situation, with the healthier-looking Geri taking a pragmatic view.

'It's no secret,' she says. 'We did a lot along the way to try and stop it.'

'I stopped counting the rehabs at about fifteen,' Gary says.

As in other cases in this book, young people in bands are not well equipped to deal with addiction in their bandmates. In the Pavement years, Nastanovich became Gary's handler, which was 'arduous' at twenty-five.

'I loved him, but I also felt like – is it the right thing to have this guy out on the road? You just sort of hope for the best every day.'

Pavement always did right by him, paying him royalties right up to the end. After the band got back together in 2010,[7]

7 This reunion was particularly welcome for Bob Nastanovich, the member of the band closest to Gary, who had recently endured a hair-raising few years. After Pavement broke up in 1999, he pursued his passion for horseracing and became a jockey's agent. Initially very successful, he fell in love with champion jockey Greta Kuntzweiler. Things took a turn for the worse when she had a bad fall, lost her confidence, and got addicted to crystal meth. Nastanovich developed

he began appearing live to play drums on the songs from his era.

'The real truth,' he told fans filming him in the crowd before a reunion show from that year, 'is I didn't get *Slanted and Enchanted* until years afterwards. I didn't get it. Now I realise what it is. This guy Steve West, who took my place, he's the shittiest drummer in the whole world, but he's the greatest guy.'

Louder than You Think is rounded out by a new Pavement song featuring Gary on vocals. It's called 'Please Be Happy (For Us)'. There can't be many rejects for whom this honour has been extended. The band's love for Young is genuine, and rather heart-breaking in the circumstances.

Pavement are a beautiful thing. They really meant it. They stuck to their guns and lived by their ethos. Unlike Nirvana, they resisted the lure of the majors and were left pure and unspoiled, and – despite the break ups – still intact. Stephen Malkmus has been free to pursue his vision. Perhaps that shows what can happen when you forsake taking over the world.

I wanted to be clear on what Chris Cunningham had heard in Gary Young-era Pavement.

'It's probably pretty obvious that what people like about them is something more general, right?' he told me. 'Hierarchically, Stephen Malkmus's songs, the tone, the style of the music and everything. And yet I only like Pavement when Gary Young was drumming.'

---

a gambling habit and was in 'a pretty big hole' in 2010, he told the *Guardian*. He and his new wife would 'like to buy a house', he said. 'Doing this will help. Probably the last time I can play the Pavement card to get me out of trouble! I appreciate the opportunity.'

'*Crooked Rain* onwards, the songwriting did change, but I wonder if they had that same, really specific chemistry. You think of a band like Jesus and Mary Chain or whatever, they've definitely got songs later that I like as much as songs on *Psychocandy*, but I just don't like the way they sound. It's just weird to me how much personality Pavement had around *Slanted and Enchanted* and *Watery, Domestic*.

'That era of indie guitar bands – the absolute pinnacle to me was their sound when Gary Young was in it. I fucking loved his drumming. If you like musicality in drumming, when you listen to indie bands, you're not necessarily looking for that. So Pavement are an anomaly of that era because he was like a prog drummer drumming in an indie band that Steve Malkmus was specifically trying to make sound indie, sound sloppy. And yet they had this old prog drummer – well not old, it's so weird now, saying he was old, he was forty and they were in their twenties!

'It was almost like he was a prog/jazz drummer in a band that didn't really want those kind of fills in their music, but he was doing it anyway. I remember when I first really got into making music myself, especially into drumming. I was really, really interested in trying to figure out – if you isolated those drums – where do they fit, what are they comparable to?

'The drumming in Nirvana just sounds so punchy and hard and minimal. It's almost like John Bonham but more minimal. Whereas the drumming in Pavement is not heavy sounding at all, they almost make the snares sound like jazz snares or something, compared to rock snares.'

And what about the Steve West era?

'More straight up. To me, especially when you get into playing around with sequencers and stuff, Gary Young's drumming definitely sounded off the grid, whereas from *Crooked Rain* onwards it sounded very much like they had a more technical drummer. I guess it depends what you mean by technical, because he wasn't playing jazzy stuff or doing fills or whatever, but he was tighter and it sounded more cleanly recorded. Whereas Gary Young's drumming to me sounded off the grid, it sounded looser but more technical, in the sense it was more jazz than rock.'

Looseness, tone and swing. Those magical ingredients.

Listening back to *Crooked Rain* for the umpteenth time, I found my love for the album was undiminished.

Somehow, though, the drums had lost their zest.

22

Ian Stewart, the Rolling Stones

I don't think the Rolling Stones would ever have got
going if it hadn't been for him. – Mick Jagger

From an interview with David Hepworth, author of
Uncommon People: The Rise and Fall of the Rock Stars:
I'll tell you the one I spend a lot of time thinking about: Ian
Stewart, who was an early member of the Rolling Stones. And
was the kind of glue of the Rolling Stones, in that he was slightly
older than the rest of them – or slightly older than Mick, Keith
and Brian anyway. And he had a proper job, which means he
had a phone, which in 1962 or whatever, you just desperately
needed if you were trying to arrange to play shows or do
anything at all. The rest of them couldn't do it.

So, they utterly relied on Ian Stewart. And Ian Stewart played
the piano and was very professional and had a van and all this
kind of stuff. And then when they signed a management deal
with Andrew Oldham [in 1963] and they were signed to Decca
Records, Andrew Oldham told the rest of them – told Mick
and Keith – that Ian would have to go.

And the reasons were twofold. One, he thought a six-piece
was too many members – which I think he was probably right
about, because already a five-piece was one too many members.

But the other thing was that, if you ever look at a picture of Ian Stewart, he's got a very definite look to him. He kind of looks like a legendary forties film actor called William Bendix, in that he's got a very craggy face with a very pronounced chin. And he looks like a person from an earlier generation, and so he was moved out of the group because literally his face didn't fit, which I think is really interesting.

I'm not saying it was wrong in any way, because Ian Stewart stayed as part of their organisation for years. He died in the mid eighties of a heart attack. But he worked with the Rolling Stones all throughout their career, played on loads of their records.[1] In the early days, he used to play from behind a curtain so he couldn't be seen. He could imagine not being a rock star, whereas the others couldn't.

But I do think that is the most extraordinary but utterly understandable reason why somebody is asked to leave the group. And it's because their face doesn't fit. *They just don't fit the picture.*

It's like Brian Epstein said, after Ringo joined the Beatles [see Chapter 1], it's only after Ringo joined that the picture made sense. And I think there's a lot to be said for that.

---

1 Stewart became the Stones' road manager. Knowing them as well as he did, he used to call them 'my little three-chord wonders' when he came to tell them it was stage time. Once, in front of Truman Capote, he said: 'Alright my little shower of shit – you're on.'

Nick Oliveri, Queens of the Stone Age – Part One

If I ever find out this is true, I can't know
you, man. – Josh Homme

I first heard Queens of the Stone Age – QOTSA – when I was working for a commercial dance label in Barnes, London, and I didn't like them at all. During my three years in the capital, a complete change in my sensibility had taken place. I listened almost exclusively to hip-hop, had moved on from rock to the extent that I'd become unable to enjoy it. It sounded alien and bad.

After Nirvana (see Chapter 12) and grunge, I'd fallen under the spell of Britpop. I listened avidly to Suede, Blur, Oasis, Manic Street Preachers, the Verve and lesser bands such as Echobelly, These Animal Men, S.M.A.S.H and Compulsion. And then, when this scene like all others began to fade away, the pioneers giving way to the imitators who clogged up the culture, I discovered trip-hop. In the mid-nineties, the cool shit, the innovative, cutting edge, underground creative scene revolved around labels such as Mo' Wax and Ninja Tune.

Paul Weller had said in the *NME* that the real contemporary equivalent to a mod 'would be the vinyl junkies buying 12" singles'. I took this to heart – I didn't want to be retro, I wanted the new. One day in my teens, in a little indie record store down by the Corn Exchange in Leeds, uncertainly browsing the 12-inches, I'd listened as a customer had rung up to ask what trip-hop actually was.

'Trip-hop is a white British thing,' the man behind the counter said, haughtily. 'Hip-hop is a black American thing.' It didn't take me long to figure out that hip-hop was the real deal and trip-hop just the gateway drug. I believed rock to be dead, creatively. I thought it had nothing more to offer.

Queens of the Stone Age's 'No One Knows' was a radio hit. In 2002, Radio 1 was at the peak of its powers. It mattered – it was the main target of a British music marketing campaign, the primary route to selling a lot of records. As such, Radio 1, and thus 'No One Knows', was played constantly in the reception at Multiply Records, the dance division of Telstar.

Throughout my college years I'd worked on and off, paid and unpaid at Ninja Tune, but on graduating there were no full-time jobs available. I found a position as production assistant, a posh name for a dogsbody, at Multiply. The label was known for its huge pop-dance hits by Sash! and Phats and Small. This was one of my least favourite forms of music. It would be a staging post, as far as I was concerned. I'd done a first bout of work experience at Ozone Management in New York – the company that represented the cream of NYC underground hip-hop; El-P, Mike Ladd and Anti-Pop Consortium – and I desperately wanted to save up more money and go back.

The Multiply boss was called Mike – a London boy made good, with sharp, clever eyes and a winning smile. He worked hard and played hard, drove a large black Range Rover and had a glassy office at the front of the building. During the day, Bela, his prize-winning South African boxer dog, would curl up at the far end of this large room, beneath the rows of gold and silver discs.

Mike was generous and good hearted. He'd occasionally bounce out of his office and announce we were downing tools to go for a long lunch at the curry house, where we'd all drink several pints. On one of these occasions, he initiated a game in which everyone had to guess the price of an ostrich-skin chair in the window of the upscale furniture shop opposite. If Mike was closest in his estimate, he had to buy it. We watched as he crossed the road, entered the shop, examined the price ticket and did an elaborate double take, waving his credit card at us through the window.

Eventually I saved the money to go back to New York and do another short internship with the newly formed Def Jux, the label set up by El-P and home to Aesop Rock and Cannibal Ox. I'd booked the trip as holiday from Multiply. It was late summer 2001, and I'd been out for a pub lunch with a colleague, Lara. When we returned to the office, Mike was leaning over the reception counter, both he and the receptionist behind it rapt by the two big TV screens mounted on the wall, which normally played MTV. Planes appeared to be crashing into the Twin Towers in New York City.

Mike turned, his eyes gleaming. 'Well, you ain't going to New York now, are ya?' he said.[1]

---

1 I did make it out to NYC when the flights started up again a week or so later. Downtown was still sealed off by police, and a fellow intern and I stopped at the barrier to watch the smoke still rising into the air in the distance. There were a lot of helicopters in the sky and soldiers on the streets, and the city felt utterly transformed.

Among my many lowly tasks was walking Bela the Boxer. This was much more fun than attempting to clear out and reorganise the garage-cum-storage unit, which was stacked to the rafters with dangerously piled, dusty old vinyl and promotional CDs. Walking Bela meant I could wander around for half an hour or so, making plans for the future, smoking cigarettes and daydreaming.

Barnes was a sleepy place, with its village green and duck pond, its expensive clothes shops and well-kept, ornate terraced houses. It was a magnet for rich rock stars too. On my wanders I saw both Simon Le Bon and Richard Ashcroft drive past. I walked past Kylie, who stood outside a recording studio looking happy and relaxed and very small. Once, walking to East Sheen with Lara on the way to her mum's house, we passed Chesney Hawkes. He was moving along the pavement, bare-chested, with a sort of challenging menace in his eyes that was a little frightening.

When I returned to the office after my walks with Bela, I'd stop to chat briefly with the northern, blonde indie girl who'd been hired as receptionist. We were simultaneously united and divided by the fact that we both loved a genre that wasn't the one we worked in, but her passion was just as pure as mine. The indie girl usually styled her hair into two bunches and wore blue or black denim pinafore dresses with tights and Doc Martens. I wore huge baggy jeans, Nike Dunks and a Jazz Fudge T-shirt with a silly slogan on the back.

I associate these conversations with another, older Queens song, 'The Lost Art of Keeping a Secret', because the indie girl loved it – turning up the radio when it came on – and I barely gave it a chance. For me, it was just crappy American rock, detritus in the wake of the greats. I associated it with Blink-182 and frat boys. I hated the idea of the band partly because of Nick Oliveri. I'd seen a picture of them in a magazine, and the bass player wore a T-shirt with 'Cocaine' emblazoned across the chest in the Coca-Cola typeface, and had a bald head and a very long, slim beard – a sure signifier of macho, middle-American cock rock, I was sure.

'No,' the indie girl told me, eyes alight and her voice quiet but certain – absolutely sure of herself. 'They're the real deal.'

As so often in my opinions about music, I was wrong. A few years later my lack of knowledge of rock, even ability to listen to it – this thing I'd once loved – had begun to feel like a sadness. I didn't know how to talk about it when others did. I began to suspect I was missing out. I turned thirty and broke up with a woman I loved, and everything that I'd once been so sure of began to seem free floating and uncertain. 'A heart that is broken is a heart that is open,' Bono would sing a few years later. Much as I hate to quote him, it was true in my case.

On a trip back to Leeds I met up with my old friend Andy. He drove us across the Chevin, the high ridge above Otley that had loomed over our shared youth. I told him about the break-up, and he played *Era Vulgaris* by QOTSA. I quite liked it. 'It's just a really good, solid rock album,' Andy said.

Back in London I found myself googling articles about the greatest rock albums of the last decade. QOTSA's *Songs for the Deaf* was always on it. Dave Grohl had played drums on the album, and his work on it was supposed to be in the purer vein of serious music, rather than the pop-rock of Foo Fighters. I decided I was ready to try to listen to rock again. I ordered a CD copy of *Songs for the Deaf*, and one day in the office I shared with my assistant – now working once again at Ninja Tune/Big Dada – I slid it into the player.

Some samples of the-car-door-is-open-while-ignition-on beeps rang out, then some more of what sounded like mock American radio stations. Then at about forty seconds, rolling drums kicked in. So far so good. A grinding guitar announced itself. Everything sounded as though it was being played through a cheap AM radio. Then at one minute in, this strange filter was turned off and a screaming voice kicked in and everything went very heavy metal. Gah! I thought in disgust and embarrassment. I pressed stop.

My assistant chortled. 'What the fuck was that?' he said. This wasn't the sort of music you played at Ninja Tune. I apologised, slid the disc out, put it back in its jewel case and on to a stack at the back of my desk, where it would remain for several months.

What was I thinking? I wondered. I was sure this was just another sign of my losing the plot in the wake of the break-up and turning thirty, the sense of a rupture having taken place in my life.

But the album was out there now. The purity of my love of hip-hop was waning and my ears were open to other sounds. I began to gradually retune myself and try *Songs for the Deaf* out. I got past the opening track, 'You Think I Ain't Worth a Dollar, But I Feel Like a Millionaire', that had put me off so. I began to understand that this demented opener, revelling in hard-rock riffs and playing with metal cliché, was deliberately designed to set the tone, to lay out the stable, to make clear that Queens were hard rock, that as accessible as they could be they *were* always the real deal. The song was designed to weed out people like me, or the me I'd been. The song's vocal was by Nick Oliveri.

By the time I'd begun listening to the band, he'd already long since been kicked out.

By 2015 I was living in Los Angeles and QOTSA had become one of the most important bands of my life. The year previously I'd seen them play Coachella – the American music festival that takes place a few miles from Josh Homme's hometown, Palm Desert – in a dust storm. Homme, towering on stage, his red hair swept back into his trademark near-quiff above his large, pre-Raphaelite face, paused between songs to wipe dust from his guitar. When he speaks it's in a deep, mellifluous voice with cadences reminiscent of Elvis.

'Welcome to my hometown,' he told the audience. 'Man, the dust. I remember growing up out here, it just gets into everything. Into the guitars, the amps, the drums . . . But you just gotta keep on playing.'

A few hours later, the festival would take on a deranged air. The dust was blowing so powerfully that everyone's skin and hair had become the same sandy colour. Scantily clad women ran around screaming; drunk, high boys moved in groups. Seasoned Coachella attendee types, wearing purposeful gasmask-like apparatus, roamed the site more confidently.

I was ecstatic. Queens had been brilliant; charming, tight, thunderous, aching. The music had begun to make even more sense to me on the LA boulevards or the many lanes of the 10 freeway that led east from the city to Palm Springs. There was something intoxicating in the combination of their brutal rhythm section, growling guitars and Homme's bittersweet vocals and hooks, often delivered in a soaring falsetto. The melancholy beauty of these elements beamed out of the heaviness like sunlight through thunder clouds.

I had understood that the clue was in their name, given to them by producer Chris Goss. ' "Kings" would be too macho,' he'd said. 'Rock should be heavy enough for the boys but sweet enough for the girls.'

I had come to understand Queens as the Led Zeppelin of their day – serious, seasoned players who represented the high watermark of their genre.

I'd moved to LA to set up a new North American headquarters for Ninja Tune. Later in 2014, a colleague from this office and I bought tickets to see Queens play a Halloween show at the Forum. It was a less satisfying affair. We were seated a long way back, at the far end of the vast stadium from the stage, which became from our perspective a little floating, distant rectangle of light and sound. It was like watching a band on television or playing in a place where we weren't.

Also, there were slightly distasteful hard-rawk elements around the show. Before the music began there was a performance by SuicideGirls, who stripteased in wrestling rings. From what I remembered, Suicide Girls was a website featuring pictures of topless, heavily tattooed goth-type women – it had been very popular in the early noughties with the rappers I'd spent time with in NYC. Now, like everything, it seemed to have been fully monetised and corporatised, a transition signified by its new, spaceless spelling.

The show itself was still worth seeing, not least because it featured a major surprise in the form of an elongated encore. The band began playing 'You Think I Ain't Worth a Dollar', and midway through the song Homme threw his arm out in a gesture right of stage, the music stopping. From the wings, Nick Oliveri ran into view. He was dressed in black with a glinting chain wallet, trademark long beard in place and a pair of devil's horns atop his clean-shaved head.

'Holy shit,' my colleague said. 'Nick's back.'

Oliveri stayed on stage to play five songs, including those he sang on *Songs for the Deaf*. He appeared to relish the opportunity and to give it his all; moshing, doubling over during his screamed vocals, moving around the stage with the taut, humming energy of an electrified wire.

After the music had ended and we left the show, I asked my colleague what had happened to Oliveri.

'I dunno,' he said, in his west LA drawl. 'He was too crazy or something. Josh had to kick him out.'

What happened to Oliveri was – according to interviews given later by Homme – that he assaulted his girlfriend while on tour in the UK. Speaking to Zane Lowe on Radio 1 in 2005, Homme said that he'd warned Oliveri previously. 'A couple of years ago, I spoke to Nick about a rumour I heard. I said, "If I ever find out this is true, I can't know you, man." Because music and my life are the same thing. There's no rules until something massive happens. Nick was over here [in England] with Lanegan and something happened again, and he almost didn't make it out of the country. That's not music any more.'

These allegations have never been confirmed, and neither Homme nor Oliveri seem to have spoken of them again publicly since. For his part, Oliveri has said 'I would have axed me too.' Speaking to the music site Antiquiet in 2012, he said that he freaked out when Homme didn't show up for soundcheck at a show in Spain. 'When he didn't turn up, I drank a bottle of vodka and the show wasn't good.' When they were supposed to go back out after the set, Homme told him: 'I'm not going out there with you.'

Some sort of descent seemed to have happened, as is so often the case when drink, drugs and abandon are involved. By 2011, things appeared to have worsened still. The *Guardian* reported that Oliveri had been involved in a five-hour stand-off with a SWAT team after barricading himself in his Hollywood apartment. A neighbour had reported an argument between him and his partner.

So, was this Oliveri, on stage with Queens in 2014, a new, rehabilitated man?

A year later, in 2015, the same colleague with whom I'd attended the Halloween show invited me to a secret Queens gig in downtown LA. This colleague, with whom my own relations were worsening, was friends with a woman from John Silva's Silva Artist Management, who managed Queens as well as Foo Fighters, Nine Inch Nails – even Nirvana, historically. The invitation was intended as a peace offering, and the show was one of the best I've ever seen.

Josh Homme had reportedly been offered a million dollars to play a festival in Brazil, and the band wanted to get into shape. There were no signs that night that they weren't already. The venue was a small room with a few hundred people in it. It was heavily soundproofed with a first-rate rig, and the sound was perfect – both crystalline and heavy. We stood twenty feet or so away from the stage and danced throughout.

It was at this gig that I first saw Nick Oliveri close up. He was standing front left, close to the stage. At American shows even a sellout is only ever two-thirds full because of fire permits and the other interminable American bureaucracy that takes a Brit by surprise. This, combined with the VIP-ish, laid-back crowd, meant you could move freely, get close to the stage. I was on the way to the toilets when I saw Oliveri. He was smaller than I'd imagined – so often the way with characters who cultivate big, cartoonish images. He looked older and careworn; someone who'd gone through a lot in life. A few fans were saying hello to him, shaking his hand and smiling. He nodded politely and a little shyly. Beside him was a very thin woman, whom I seem to remember – because of some combination of her hair, tattoos and clothing – was identifiably a rock-type. There's a difference between the borrowed rock stylings of certain hipsters and the tough, hardened look of the real-deal rocker, and this woman was certainly the latter.

Oliveri didn't perform that night, but stood and watched the show avidly. Afterwards we were invited backstage, but we didn't get anywhere near Josh, who I'd half hoped to shake hands with and congratulate. He towered at the other end of the room, looking sharp in a suit jacket, rings gleaming on his fingers, his hair swept back with a forelock hanging loose.

Oliveri was in there too, closer to Josh.

A few years later, Homme would apologise for drunkenly kicking a female photographer's camera into her head at a Christmas show. In interviews he always appears polite, thoughtful, good-humoured and almost tender – a gentleman. He's made reference to problems with his lifestyle, to not living well, to a near-death experience that led to the creation of the band's second masterpiece, . . . *Like Clockwork*. It would be difficult to conceive of this album having been created by someone who hadn't experienced great psychic pain. People in the industry speak highly of him and say that he's kind.

In 2019, his marriage to Brody Dalle, the Australian singer of punk band the Distillers, fell apart. They put their Hollywood house up for sale, and tabloid site TMZ reported mutual restraining orders and accusations of violence and abusive behaviour. In May 2020 the site claimed to have obtained a stipulation the couple had signed. According to the document, Homme had agreed to participate in a Twelve Steps programme and weekly drug and psychological testing. He also had to use a very sinister-sounding thing called a Soberlink device twice a day for six months, and give Dalle the results. Finally, he'd agreed to participate in a 'batterers' intervention program'.

I wondered how all this would make Oliveri feel, given the reasons behind his own departure from the band. And how it would feel generally to stand at the side of the stage and watch this thing you'd been a part of, playing music without you. He was there at the beginning – before the beginning, even. He and Homme met in high school, then played together in Kyuss, the desert-rock pioneers that made their names when they were teenagers. Oliveri was there during the heat and light that forged Queens of the Stone Age. He wrote, played and sang on the first of their two masterpieces. They had grown up together in the hardscrabble desert, the place of dust devils and gas stations and bone-dry biblical mountains and the sense of being in a place that could kill you, geographically close but culturally far from Los Angeles.[2] They'd honed their

2 Kyuss's drummer, Brant Bjork, said that Oliveri 'always had an edge. But growing up as kids in the '80s he was kind of like a Spicoli', referring to Sean Penn's stoner character in *Fast Times at Ridgemont High*. 'He was like a desert

craft together and lived out their dreams. What was it like? What went wrong? How did it feel to get into an armed stand-off with a SWAT team?

Unfortunately, finding out was going to be easier said than done.

---

punk. Heavy metal kid, long hair, smoked a lot of pot.' Josh Homme recalled driving back from a party in the desert and coming across Oliveri 'walking along the side of the road. And we were in Indio. Nick lived in Palm Springs. So I pulled over and I said "where are you going?" He goes "I'm walking home." He lived twenty miles away and it was like two in the morning.' Homme laughs, telling this story. 'To me, that's so beautiful.'

24

Siobhan Donaghy, Sugababes

As young girls do, you have arguments, disagreements, fall-outs, as far as I was always aware, it was just like sisters falling out. And Siobhan and I are really good friends and still work together so even she recognises that we were just kids. – Keisha Buchanan

In 2000, an annoyingly striking single appeared on British radio. With the idiotic certainty of youth, at twenty years old I pretty much loathed all things pop, but even I couldn't help noticing it.

The song was called 'Overload', and it was by a girl band called Sugababes. Musically, it made use of the usual formula for these things – sanitised sonic references to cooler or more underground genres. In this case, the drums gestured in the direction of hip-hop, and their swing contained a hint of the garage music that was blowing up that year.

What initially grabbed the attention was probably the song's minimalism. It was basically just those drums and a simple melody in the bassline. But the vocals stood out too. The voice that kicked in at around twelve seconds wasn't the usual, slick, over-produced one I'd expected. It sounded like a talented teenager singing at home – slightly raw and unfinished, the song's minimalism exposing the vocal's freshness but also its flaws and childlike quality.[1]

I don't think any of this would have been possible without the backdrop of British music at the time. British garage music (sometimes called UKG and 2-Step) was everywhere.

Despite some of its early hits being oversweet – the sugary vocals and melodies of Artful Dodger's 'Movin' Too Fast' and Shanks & Bigfoot's 'Sweet Like Chocolate' being examples – it was impossible not to be excited by it. For anyone interested in hip-hop, it felt as though garage offered the potential for a truly homegrown form of rap music. When the vocals and melodies were stripped away, you were left with crisp, tough drums and rolling basslines. There was a promise of a new, harder sound in songs such as Oxide and Neutrino's 'No Good 4 Me', which featured fellow members of So Solid Crew and a chorus line borrowed from the Prodigy.

In 2000, garage was ruling the airwaves and the charts with a series of hits – MJ Cole's 'Crazy Love', Oxide and Neutrino's 'Bound 4 Da Reload', which sampled the theme from UK TV staple *Casualty*, and the monstrously good Timo Maas remix of Azzido Da Bass's 'Dooms Night'.

Underground 2-Step producers such as El-B were stripping the music back to the bass and drums, laying the ground for the dubstep that would emerge a few years later. In 2001, a year after Sugababes' debut single, the raw, darker side of garage would explode into the public consciousness via So Solid Crew's '21 Seconds'. This in turn would rapidly segue into the thrilling

---

1 It also contained a lyric about a train going to a 'madman destination'. This somehow lodged in my mind, and made me think of a man going crazy, perhaps with a gun, on a city street.

sonic invention of grime,[2] with Dizzee Rascal's masterpiece, *Boy in da Corner* released in 2003.

But back in 2000, when 'Overload' hit the airwaves, garage had already made British music sparser and rawer. British voices were everywhere. A sonic minimalism had emerged, at odds with the multi-layered American slickness of late 1990s R & B.[3] Rhythmic elements were widely used as melodies, something fully evident in the bassline-hook of 'Overload'.

Before long I'd seen the video for 'Overload' too, and understood, consciously or not, what I was being sold on. Three young girls; one white, one black, one Asian. Cynical, yes – in the way that all pop marketing is. But exciting too. It seemed to represent the UK that was emerging at the time – mixed race, streetwise and contemporary.

The wildly entertaining gossip newsletter *Popbitch*, which played a small but notable role in the Sugababes story, described them thus: 'exciting, teenage popstars who refuse to play by teen pop's rules'.

---

2 If anything, British black music is too inventive for its own commercial good. A genre or sub-genre often barely establishes itself before someone, driven by relentless creative competition, comes along and improves upon or evolves it. This often leaves later-arriving artists to consolidate and commercialise the music. This is roughly what happened with dubstep, which smoothed out grime's rawness, removed much of the vocals, and made it palatable for a more mainstream audience. It functioned largely as trip-hop had to hip-hop – becoming something for a coffee-table audience that didn't really want to hear the rapper.

3 That's not to say that America wasn't in the mix. If anything, it was US producers such as the Neptunes and Timbaland who had begun this revolution in music. The latter's deceptively simple production was full of rhythmic hooks that gripped the ear, making use of space, satisfyingly prominent basslines and minimalist melodies. Aaliyah's 'Try Again' was also released in 2000. Produced by Timbaland, it became one of the most powerful influences over the subsequent musical decade.

In the way these things do – are in part designed to do – Sugababes seemed an instant progression from the genre's 1990s archetypes. The minimal vocals of 'Overload' somehow harked back to the arresting opening of All Saints' 'Never Ever', but this song, for all the reasons above, was undeniably cooler.[4] All Saints looked as though they came from a dinner party, while Sugababes looked like girls you might meet at Notting Hill Carnival.

In the video for 'Overload', gone is the dancing, pouting and posing. Mutya Buena, Keisha Buchanan and Siobhan Donaghy are shot close up against a plain white background – all shy smiles, ambivalent looks and blankness. Nevertheless, perhaps its makers judged the country to not be entirely ready for this mixed-race vision of the future. It's notable that the video opens on Siobhan Donaghy, who is white. You might almost think this is a solo performance until, at a full thirty seconds, Keisha Buchanan, the black member of the group, appears.

Knowing what I do about the music business, particularly back in 2000, I wouldn't be surprised if this was deliberate. Don't judge its architects too harshly, though. They were trying to do something new, and perhaps they thought this necessary to get an ever-conservative public to come along with them.

'It's like United Colours of Benetton.'

It turns out that Sugababes and All Saints actually had the same architect and manager. His name is Ron Tom, and this is

4 Revisiting 'Never Ever' while writing, I watched the video on YouTube and was struck by how unbelievably bad the whole thing was. The weakness of the singing – except that of Shaznay Lewis – the bizarre, terrible lyrics ('I'll take a shower, I will scour / I will rub / to find peace of mind') and worst of all the US video. This comes off like a cheap pastiche of 1990s American R & B pomp. There is a horse, and at times the various members appear to be dancing to entirely different songs.

what he told Siobhan Donaghy, according to her version of Sugababes' origin story. Donaghy left the group midway through a tour of Japan in 2001, but later said 'there's no doubt I was pushed out'.

'I met my manager Ron Tom when I was twelve,' Donaghy told *Ponystep Magazine* in 2009. Briefly mulling over the idea that she'd blow the myth of the band having met at a party, she told the interviewer, 'I like this story, it's much more interesting.'

Ron Tom was Donaghy's best friend's brother-in-law. 'He met Mutya's father in a supermarket. Mutya's father told him how much his daughter could sing and Ron drove round to the house. Mutya sang and, of course, she's got an amazing voice. So he signed us two as solo artists.'

Ron Tom – born Ronald Tomlinson – was originally a rare groove and soul DJ on London Weekend Radio, an eighties pirate radio station.[5] In the 1990s he set up his own studio and label, Metamorphosis, producing jungle and hardcore records. He appears to have gradually begun moving in a poppier direction, working with UK soul artist Don-E and the American singer Jocelyn Brown, a legend in dance music for her guest vocals on house records. From here, it was presumably a fairly natural step to start putting together girl bands.

Finding talented twelve-year-olds and driving to houses on the hearsay of a father are exactly the sort of behaviours required of a self-starting music manager. By the time he'd met Siobhan

---

5 In the world before 'digital' took over entirely, pirate radio was the most important breeding ground for British black music. A few years later, it was stations such as Rinse FM and Deja Vu that would become the primary platforms for grime.

and Mutya, Ron Tom already had a major success behind him with All Saints.[6]

At first, the chemistry between Donaghy and Buena was good.

'We met each other when we were doing this acapella gig,' Donaghy said, 'somewhere on All Saints Road, I think. Me and Mutya really liked each other.'

They decided to sing a duet, which apparently involved Don-E. This having gone well, they decided to keep working together. 'And then, I think Keisha had asked Mutya if she could visit the studio with her. So she did, and suddenly we were a band.'

Donaghy's interview draws back the curtain on a textbook example of musical manufacturing: taking a little bit of something natural, adding more ingredients and shaping it for the market.

'It wasn't any of our decision. Ron Tom just said "Right, you're gonna be in a band." We were like "really?"' Ron Tom confirmed the decision with his reference to the Italian fashion brand Benetton, which was a huge success in the eighties and nineties. It was famous for its multiracial adverts and storefront images. Featuring plainly shot close ups of models from different ethnic backgrounds, these felt radical and refreshing at the time.

'It's genius,' Ron Tom told the newly formed trio. 'You're gonna be called Sugababes.'

Once again, the causes of this brand-new project's eventual destruction were encoded in its very formation.

---

6 All Saints were named for All Saints Road in Notting Hill, an important centre for the UK's Afro-Caribbean community and music.

'We hated, hated the name,' Donaghy told *PonyStep*.

But the group decided that with their album not due to come out for another couple of years, they'd have time to change it. 'When they first said "Sugababes", I thought, "Oh my God, they're going to turn us into the naff band."' The late 1990s and early 2000s were the age of Simon Cowell and *Pop Idol*, *The X Factor* and the rise of the boy and girl band. 'Remember,' Donaghy said, 'that was back when A1 were out, all that shit.'[7]

Against this backdrop, Sugababes may have had some justification for regarding themselves as a cut above. There was at least some musical pedigree behind them in Ron Tom's circle. They were signed to London Records, which had become an imprint of the major label subsidiary PolyGram.[8] For a commercial pop label, it had a slightly more credible feel due to having artists such as Happy Mondays, Shakespears Sister and New Order among its stable, as well as Pete Tong's FFRR dance label as one of its own imprints.

Despite the plan to change the name, it stuck.

'Of course, it was nice,' Donaghy said, 'because it was the complete opposite to our album. The Sugababes weren't really sweet. We were a bunch of horrible teenagers. Therefore, it kind of suited us.'

Further pedigree was lent to 'Overload' by the creative team behind it.

---

7 A1 were a late nineties boy band. Trying to judge the quality of these projects is akin to sifting through turds, but they may indeed represent some sort of nadir.
8 Before the great convergence of majors into The Big Three of today – Sony, Universal and Warner – the landscape of ownership was labyrinthine.

The song was co-written and produced by several writers: Paul Simm, Felix Howard, Jony Rockstar and Cameron McVey. This is an interesting array of characters. Simm had worked with 1990s artists such as Carleen Anderson of Young Disciples, and rave outfit Baby D, who had a mega-hit with 'Let Me Be Your Fantasy'. He went on to write for Amy Winehouse and Neneh Cherry, among others.

McVey is married to Neneh Cherry. He was briefly a pop star himself, having a hit with the Scritti Politti-influenced, Stock Aitken Waterman-produced 'Looking Good Diving' by Morgan-McVey.[9] He's worked extensively on his wife's music, as well as with Massive Attack, All Saints and, in her subsequent solo guise, Siobhan Donaghy.

Felix Howard was a child model and dancer in videos for Madonna and Mantronix. He appeared on the front cover of a controversial issue of the *Face* magazine as a boy, scowling and wearing a hat with a feather on it, as well as the word 'Killer', apparently cut out of a newspaper.[10] He too would go on to write for Amy Winehouse, as well as Australian pop singer Sia. He became a publishing A & R, and signed Calvin Harris, Lana Del Rey and the grime artist Tinchy Stryder.

Jony Rockstar, or Johnny Lipsey, would go on to make his name largely through writing for Sugababes, though he also gained some production credits on Amy Winehouse's work.

9 An excellent, rising synth line from this song would be recycled to great effect in Neneh Cherry's hit, 'Buffalo Stance'.
10 Down the rabbit hole: the creative team behind the *Face* came from *Buffalo Magazine*, an influential, cult fashion magazine at which Neneh Cherry and Cameron McVey both worked. This is from where the title of Neneh Cherry's biggest hit derived.

I include all this detail to try and capture some of the fertile, even hip cultural background that went into creating 'Overload'. Perhaps this helps to explain why the song stood out.

Sugababes' debut album, *One Touch*, was released on 27 November 2000. Less than a year later, Donaghy walked out of the band during a tour of Japan. Apparently, she excused herself to go to the toilet, and never came back.

'It was clear that there was someone in the band who never wanted me in it and that's Keisha,' Donaghy said in 2009.

In April 2002, a few months after she'd left, *Popbitch* provided more information. Under the title THE HORRIBLE HOUNDING OF GINGER-BABE, they lamented the fact that only after Donaghy's departure had Sugababes finally topped the charts. They were no longer the 'exciting, teenage popstars who refused to play by teen pop's rules'. Siobhan had left to 'be replaced by a dimwit Scouser whose previous career highlight had been as founding member of Atomic Kitten'.

The year 2002 was part of a more vituperative age, but *Popbitch* has always had a good ear for quality pop music. It could sense that the departure of Donaghy had turned Sugababes into just another, run-of-the-mill commercial project: 'Goodbye, then, Sugababe credibility.'

When it came to why Siobhan left, it had the dirt. 'She was hounded out by Keisha and Mutya. Their technique, as observed on photo-shoots, was to bitch about Siobhan in the secret girl language, Ava-Gab.' They went on to give a hypothetical example of this: 'Sivva-giv ovva-gorn ivva-gis avva-ga fava-gat cavva-gow. Translation: "Siobhan is a fat cow."'

It's important to note that *Popbitch* prides itself on being a home for 'scurrilous gossip,' and this story is just that. However, these claims weren't a million miles away from Donaghy's own.

By 2003, Donaghy had launched a solo career. She spoke to the *Guardian's* Alexis Petridis for a feature interview. The article quoted Mutya Buena as saying: 'I hate her for running away and leaving us. Why couldn't she have had the guts to tell me to my face what her problem was? No guts, that girl.'

For her part, Donaghy appears to have spoken openly about the misery of her time in Sugababes. Petridis referred to 'bad management, manipulation, personality clashes and teenage alienation', all of which left her 'clinically depressed at 17'.

One can only imagine the horror of being discovered at twelve, finding a musical soul mate and getting signed to a record label, only to have it turn into a living hell, and to be hounded out of the project less than a year after releasing an album. And all of this happened in the middle of Donaghy's teens.

Donaghy had always suffered from nerves. 'I'm not good under pressure,' she told the *Guardian*. 'In my room I could belt it out, but then, put me in front of people and I just couldn't.' She told Petridis that her management's solution to this stage fright was to 'inform prospective producers that [I] should not be allowed to sing on any records'.

'I had no self-esteem,' she said. 'I lacked self-confidence already, being a teenager, and they just battered me.'

But it was when Keisha Buchanan joined that Donaghy said her problems really began. 'We had nothing in common at all, and we went on not to get on. She was Mutya's friend, so I ended up being the odd one out. I don't know why they kept me in the band. Perhaps it was cool that it was a white girl, a Filipino girl and a black girl.'

Despite the alleged reservations of her manager, Cameron McVey seems to have had genuine faith in her singing. According to the *Guardian*'s take, he 'insisted she sing lead' on 'Overload'.

This doesn't appear to have been due to the industry cynicism I referred to above. McVey would go on to work with Donaghy on her solo projects, offering some of the nurture that she claimed her manager hadn't.

'McVey's got kids my age and he knew what was going on in the band from way back when,' she says. 'He got me back writing, told me it would be therapeutic, got me in the studio again.'

On the other hand, she told Petridis that all the money she'd made from the Sugababes had been 'swallowed up by a legal battle with her former manager, who was suing her for breach of contract'.

'I don't give a shit,' she said. 'They've got it on their conscience.'

Back in 2003, Buena dismissed the bullying claims as 'rubbish'. Donaghy said that she 'didn't really have to mention anything, because people know what happened'.

After leaving – or being forced out of – Sugababes, she ended up back at her parents' house in Ruislip, a London suburb. She 'didn't want to get out of bed. When I went on anti-depressants, I was really ashamed. I didn't tell my mum at the time.'

In 2009, when she spoke to *Ponystep*, Donaghy was still trying to make it as a solo artist. She was more candid about the bullying than she had been in 2003. She said that she and Mutya were still friends and got on well whenever they saw each other, but specifically named Keisha Buchanan as the problem. 'She made my life a living hell,' she said.

'I'll never forgive her. No one forgives that first bully in their lives, do they? No one does. Even when you're fifty.'

But a mere two years later, she did.

There's a long, strange postscript to the Sugababes story. Mutya Buena left the group in 2005 and was in turn replaced. In 2009, Buchanan, the only remaining original member, also left. She departed amid further accusations of bullying from the three 'new' members. In a 2009 interview with *MailOnline*, Buchanan said: 'I was a bitch to Heidi [Range – Donaghy's replacement] at first because I couldn't get over the fact that we'd worked since we were 12 and this beautiful girl from stage school had it all handed to her on a plate. I made her life hell,' Buchanan said. 'That's when I said to myself, "this is stupid."'

For her part, Range said that life in the group had become unbearable due to Buchanan. 'We never knew from one day to the next what mood or hurtful comments to expect.'

Buchanan implied in a statement that she'd been kicked out: 'Although it was not my choice to leave, it's time to enter a new chapter in my life . . . I would like to state that there were no arguments, bullying or anything of the sort that lead [*sic*] to this. Sometimes a breakdown in communication and lack of trust can result in many different things.'

Unlikely as it might seem, given everything that had preceded, in 2011 the three original members re-formed as Mutya Keisha Siobhan. That same year, the Sugababes project finally ended, but the brand name was apparently still caught up in contractual issues. The three original members have kept working together since, reclaiming the Sugababes name in 2019 and releasing new music.[11] In 2021, they released a twentieth anniversary edition of *One Touch*, which managed to attract remixes from credible, leftfield luminaries such as Blood Orange.

In 2020, amid the race protests after the death of George Floyd in the US, Keisha Buchanan turned up on British television. Appearing on *This Morning*, she claimed that the accusations of bullying she'd faced throughout her career were due to systemic racism. Blaming the press, she said, 'some people had never met me and just decided that I was the instigator of situations, and no one ever gave me the chance to say what actually happened'.

Explaining why she hadn't attributed this to racism previously, she said she 'didn't really recognise it as racism . . . I thought that being racist meant that you actually called someone a racist word.'[12]

She claimed that she was discouraged from raising questions over songwriting splits, having been told 'this person will feel very bullied if you do that'. It was her fans who'd made her realise this was a form of racism, she said: 'Once George Floyd had passed away and this conversation had come up, I guess I felt safer to do it because everyone was coming up and it felt more unified.'

Presumably, everyone involved learned something from this experience. The band got back together, and Donaghy appears to have forgiven both Buchanan and her manager, who posted

11 This includes a new version of DJ Spoony's garage classic, 'Flowers', perhaps cementing their loose affiliation with that genre.
12 There do seem to have been examples of racism towards Sugababes. The *Guardian* reported that the two non-white members of the band had been called 'evil-looking freaks' in the press.

a series of Instagram images hugging the three original members and celebrating their reunion.

What this story seems to show is that in music, the quest for success outweighs almost everything. Tenacity is absolutely key. If you keep on going, something could always happen. The desire, the pure burning ambition, is often what really counts. The history between bandmates pales into insignificance if success is in the offing. In some ways, this is an admirable trait. Haven't we all wished we could simply move on?

'Overload' itself had an afterlife. In 2015, the author John Niven's music industry novel, *Kill Your Friends*, was adapted into a film. For the soundtrack, the English pop-rock band Bastille covered 'Overload', reimagining it in darker, ominous tones.

Coincidentally, *Kill Your Friends* includes a memorable passage about the tenacity and raw desire required to be a pop star. In return for fifteen minutes of fame, Niven writes:

> I guarantee you that Geri Halliwell would have risen at the crack of dawn every morning for a year and swum naked through a river of shark-infested, HIV-positive semen – cutting the throats of children, old age pensioners and cancer patients and throwing them behind her as she went – just to be allowed to do a sixty-second regional radio interview. This is the kind of person you want to sign. You've got a shot with that kind of attitude. Talented? Fuck off. Go and work in a guitar shop with all the other talented losers.[13]

13 Of course, I in no way mean to imply that Siobhan Donaghy was as craven as this in re-joining a group with a member whose bullying she said had made her life hell. That could just as easily be taken as a sign of maturity.

25

Wiley – Part One

It's disgusting there are no words to condone what he saying,
none!!! As I said before I am worried about him and want to
get him help. – John Woolf, Wiley's former manager

In the 2020s, not all rejections are carried out by bandmates. Society has got in on the act too. Now, a musician can have their career ended instantly because of something they've said or done. This didn't used to be the case. In the age before social media, word took longer to spread and outrage longer to grow. Perhaps we were a bit better at forgiveness, too.

One of these stories is very close to my heart, because it involves the most magical, frustrating, exciting and upsetting experience of my career.

I first came across Wiley during a spell doing music PR in 2003. I was at my desk, leafing through a magazine – it might well have been *Jockey Slut*. Earlier that year, I'd returned to London from a spell of travelling to find an issue of the same magazine with Dizzee Rascal on the front cover. It included an interview with Will Ashon, the founder of Big Dada Recordings, Ninja Tune's hip-hop imprint, and the man I saw as my mentor. 'Well,' he'd said. 'This is about as raw as it gets.' He went on to praise

Dizzee's debut album, *Boy in da Corner*, in a tone that suggested he was a little astonished by it. I knew I had to get this record immediately. As I remember it, the *Jockey Slut* article referred to Dizzee having broken out of the garage scene. No one had yet come up with the term 'grime'.

Boy in da Corner didn't disappoint. It was immediately clear that the promise that had lurked within UK garage – that of a truly homegrown form of British rap music – had been fulfilled. The music had stripped garage down to raw, rude bass, lashing drums and ominous digital melody. Dizzee's rapping was incredibly assured – his flow varied and rapid, playing with the edges of control when he got really animated. The lyrics were stark and brutal. In interviews, Dizzee said he didn't want to make a 'conscious' record. This was the term used for more ethically minded hip-hop at the time, records that sought to push back on anything gangsta, to outline the problem but also the solution.

Dizzee wasn't interested in that. As we'll see, life could be brutal and violent for young black men and women in London in 2003. He wanted to tell it how it was, and if he didn't exactly celebrate it, he certainly wasn't going to critique it.

That summer, sitting at my desk at my PR job in Brixton, I paused on a half-page feature with a picture of a young black man, and a headline claiming that he was Dizzee's mentor.

There was a brief interview with Wiley. It described the 'Eskimo' music he was making – cold, glacial synths, icy snare drums and uncompromising rapping. 'Sometimes I just feel cold hearted,' Wiley told the interviewer, describing how he'd come to make it.

I determined to track his music down.

In those days, this wasn't so easy. There was no Spotify, YouTube or TikTok, and music like this wasn't usually on the nascent iTunes.

You had to go to the record shops that sold it. Wiley was famed for selling white label 12-inches out of the back of his car – this was the way it was done in grime. The records would be displayed in racks in E3's Rhythm Division or the West End's Deal Real and Black Market, with black felt-tip writing on the plain white labels detailing the titles; 'Morgue' or 'Sidewinder'. Seeking them out meant physically going to these places and plucking up the courage to ask for them. It would be unfair to say that the raison d'être of all the young men who worked in these shops was to demonstrate their superior knowledge – some of them were very friendly and enthusiastic – but it wasn't uncommon.

The music I was able to track down was often instrumental. Wiley's 'Ice Rink' made use of synth stabs as cold as freezer burn, minimal percussion, and sounds that might have been sampled from a Nintendo platform game. It was experimental in the purposeful, enjoyable and thrilling way that black music often is.

A better source were DVDs featuring grime MCs battling – *Lord of the Mics* and *Conflict*. A notorious scene from the latter of these was shot in the cramped space at the top of a tower block, where the pirate station Deja Vu had a studio. The cream of the grime scene are all there – D Double E, Tynchy Stryder, Wiley, Dizzee Rascal and Crazy Titch, all taking turns on the mic. Wiley has his hair in cornrows and wears an Akademiks T-shirt, and one of the white plastic crucifix chains that was popular at the time. His large eyes are a little bleary, and he looks impassive, lost in the music, moving to the beat.

Crazy Titch and Dizzee take turns on the mic. Titch is bigger, looks older and more confident. Dizzee is further away from the camera and looks very young and skinny, perhaps a little intimidated from the outset, but holding his own.

The physical movements that would come to define grime's style – shoulders and heads bopping in a way that's both jerky and fluid – are on full display. At first, Crazy Titch, whose name was rumoured to be entirely apt, just seems to listen calmly when Dizzee raps, dancing and looking ahead.

Dizzee passes the mic, and Titch launches into his sixteen bars, his gaze lowered so that we see just his mouth below his hat. He too seems to be lost in the music, building up to a crescendo of aggression. And then he turns on Dizzee and pushes him in the chest. For a moment the camera focuses on Crazy Titch, squared up and looming, saying 'What?' in the direction of Dizzee. The music stops and the other MCs in the room – including Wiley – get between them. There's a lot of shouting and the argument spills out on to the roof.

Without awareness of the potential for violence in this argument, it might seem like pistols at dawn. But a few years later, Wiley would be slashed with a knife in a similar situation. When I finally got hold of him to check he was all right, after listening to this take place on air, he said: 'I'm all right J – they only got my back.' For his part, Crazy Titch would soon be jailed for shooting another musician dead.[1]

Throughout the episode between Dizzee and Titch, Wiley plays peacemaker, eventually saying 'Come on, Dyl,' and trying to remove Dizzee from the scene.

★　　★　　★

1 One of the grime scene's early stars, Crazy Titch's career was rapidly cut short in 2006 when he was jailed for life for murder. He was convicted of shooting dead a producer, Richard Holmes, whom he believed had allied himself with a rapper who'd insulted his brother, fellow grime artist Durrty Goodz.

Their relationship was not to last. In 2003, just when Dizzee's success was burgeoning, the pair went to Ayia Napa with Roll Deep, the wider crew they were part of. Napa is to garage what Ibiza is to house, and for grime MCs it offers both a holiday and a chance to earn some money performing.

What exactly happened on the island has remained subject to debate. A persistent rumour, reported by the *Guardian* at the time and often appearing since, was that Dizzee pinched Lisa Maffia of So Solid Crew's bum. Wiley referred to this during an online spat with Dizzee in 2017, tweeting 'If you didn't try and pinch Lisa Maffia's bum we would still be pals you stupid idiot.'

In September 2023, So Solid Crew founder Megaman claimed in a filmed video that 'Lisa Maffia was on stage . . . Dizzee Rascal was his drunk self, went on stage and grabbed Lisa Maffia's bum . . . While she's on stage performing, pinched her arse.'

Regardless of what exactly happened that night, trouble had broken out and resulted in a brawl. The following day, Dizzee was dragged from a rented scooter and stabbed five times. He was lucky to survive, and he seems to have realised it. He cut all ties with Roll Deep and Wiley, and the grime scene more generally. He was rumoured to have moved out of east London and to want to live sensibly and well.

In 2016, Wiley did take some responsibility for what happened. Speaking to *Time Out*, he said 'there was some fighting with another crew' one night – 'I won't say who, but basically everyone knows' – and that he and a friend decided to 'carry it on'. Whoever they'd fought with had come looking for them the next day but found Dizzee instead. 'The thing we done the next morning led them to go looking for us, but see him and stab him,' Wiley said.

Megaman appears to confirm Wiley's story, claiming that after the Lisa Maffia incident something 'happened down the road with Wiley and a couple So Solid Crew members.'

'Now I'm older,' Wiley told *Time Out*, 'I can see: Dizzee in his head will always be thinking . . . "If you had left it, I wouldn't have got stabbed."'

Megaman takes a less forgiving view of the drunken incident that allegedly started it all: 'In this day and age, that is sexual assault.'

The spat between Dizzee and Wiley has occasionally broken out on radio interviews and social media over the years. Wiley has tried to resolve it, but Dizzee has never shown a sign of weakening. Nevertheless, the one-time friendship is immortalised in music, and perhaps best exemplified in a segment of a radio appearance with proto-grime DJ Slimzee. This clip, twenty-seven minutes long and widely available on YouTube, captures everything that was thrilling about grime in 2003.[2]

In April 2004, Wiley's debut album *Treddin' on Thin Ice* was released by XL, and suddenly his music had escaped the specialist stores and was available everywhere. I rushed out to buy it. Wiley's voice was deeper toned than Dizzee's, and had the charm and likeability that's essential for a rapper to win mainstream fans. A lot of listeners don't really care about lyrics, and just want to hear a nice voice.[3] Like Dizzee, he could play with

2 In October 2023, Dizzee and Wiley appeared to finally make up. Wiley briefly appeared on stage at a Dizzee Rascal performance in Dubai, the pair hugging and smiling. This long-impossible moment passed off anti-climactically – it would once have been major news in UK music.

3 This is one of the ways in which Will Ashon explained the success of Roots Manuva, one of the key artists on his Big Dada imprint, implicitly lamenting the fact that Manuva's lyrics were thus overlooked by a certain tier of listener.

the edges of control in his voice, a fieriness lighting within it on the harder tracks.

The album had moments of brilliance, but it wasn't as consistent as *Boy in da Corner*. When we began working together, Wiley would freely admit this, occasionally railing at the fact he hadn't made a classic album like Dizzee's. Even then, it was clear that in some ways it didn't matter. Wiley was the sort of maverick, mercurial artist who would make flawed albums, but had so many great songs and such charisma that he was always worth listening to.

In 2004 he quickly developed a reputation for being elusive. XL paid for a promotional film about him, in which he failed to appear. Other grime artists were interviewed about him, and the only glimpse of Wiley came right at the end, seen through a car window as he briefly pulled up at the shoot.

He quite often didn't show up to things – live dates or interviews. All of this helped to build up the sort of mysterious persona that goes a long way in music.

Almost as soon as his debut album came out, Wiley was rumoured to have fallen out with XL, and soon left the label.

I first met him at the Rhythm Factory in Whitechapel, where Roll Deep MC Riko had been booked to perform. When a friend and I showed up, Wiley was there with Riko, standing behind the decks, passing the mic and looking happy and relaxed. Later, I'd come to know that Wiley was often very happy to turn up to things, just not necessarily the ones he'd been booked for.

Towards the end of the set, Wiley slipped out from behind the decks and began crossing the dancefloor. Heads turned, but no one spoke to him. He was slim, medium height, moving cautiously through the parted crowd. His hair was short, and back then I think he still wore an equally short goatee beard. His eyes were large and watchful – strangely innocent. He had the tangible, electric charisma of a big musical talent.

When he came close, I reached out to shake his hand and say hello. He responded politely – said something like 'You all right?' or 'What's happening?' – and I asked if he ever hosted nights. I'd recently begun to run my own, at 93 Feet East on Brick Lane. He said yes, and I took his number and shook his hand again.

I didn't really think he'd text me back when I contacted him a few days later. It was good enough just to have met him, to have his number. So I was surprised and delighted when he replied. I asked him how much he'd want to host my night. He replied with '200'. This seemed a bargain, so I took the risk and booked him.

I'd got on well with Plastician when he'd played the night previously. He was from Croydon, home of the emergent dubstep scene. I wasn't hugely keen on that genre – it seemed pretentious and exclusive[4] – but Plastician straddled dubstep and grime, and I knew he had connections to the MCs. So, I booked him to DJ the night Wiley would host.

I remember a very nervous few hours – the anxiety peaking when the set was due to begin, and Wiley still hadn't shown.

---

4 When dubstep emerged, it had a purist, po-faced air. Fans would tell you that you couldn't make judgement on the music unless you'd heard it on the right sound system. As I said in Chapter 24, for me it seemed that dubstep was to grime as trip-hop had been to hip-hop – a whiter, more palatable form. The MCs (the 'shoutiness') had been stripped away, leaving the nice beats behind. This is a generalisation, of course, and there were plenty of black dubstep artists. I was once publicly eviscerated on a dubstep internet forum for expressing this view in the *Guardian*.

And then, quite suddenly, he did. Slipping through the crowd with no fanfare, but leaving a ripple of excitement in his wake, he appeared behind the decks, took the mic and began rapping. 'Practice hours,' he said, and I understood that for him this was a chance to hone his craft. I could feel a wave of buzzy energy ripple through the crowd. The small sea of faces was locked in awe on Wiley.

Plastician happily cut between records and flicked them back for occasional reloads.[5] Between bouts of rapping, Wiley told the crowd to 'get some alcohol in your system' and other such encouragement. He stayed for about an hour. A photographer from *I-D* captured a photo of Plastician, Wiley and me behind the decks, Wiley's money in an envelope clasped in my raised hand.

Wiley and I clicked in a way I have with few artists since. It was partly down to my enthusiasm and knowledge regarding grime, but mainly we just liked each other in that immediate way there's no explaining or predicting. I felt warm towards him from the moment we met.

By the time I began working at Big Dada, Wiley had put a second album out, called – inventively – *Da 2nd Phaze*. It felt rushed, and Wiley hadn't yet reached the peak of his powers. In 2006, his manager at the time approached Will Ashon, the Big Dada founder, about doing an album.

Although Will, with his uncanny A & R's ability to discover new music very early, had been interested in grime since its genesis, he was yet to be entirely convinced by it.

5 As per a 'rewind' in garage, a reload referred to a DJ rapidly flicking a record backwards under the needle, the track being so good that it warranted starting all over again.

A lot of the rapping was just plain bad – MCs didn't always pride themselves on hitting the beat like a serious hip-hop rapper would. The line-ending word repetition could be tiresome, and lyrically it was often uninspired and a bit ugly.

I used to think of grime as akin to punk. Every wannabe MC had felt empowered to get up and perform. It had democratised music to an extent that clearly impacted its quality. But there was something thrilling in this – being in a packed room, watching an even more packed stage, twenty or thirty MCs passing the mic, jostling and competing.

It was 90 per cent dross, and 10 per cent utterly inspired.

We tried to meet Wiley to discuss an album. He came to Kennington tube, but his manager was late and he was immediately menaced by local youths. This was my first glimpse of the parallel world in which young black men live in London and other big cities. He turned around, furious with his manager, and went back to east London and his own 'ends'.[6]

There was another abortive meeting, a more fruitful invitation for Wiley and some Roll Deep members to come to a Roots Manuva gig at the Forum in Kentish Town. That night, Wiley was his friendly, casual self again. His large eyes could be made puppyish and contrite when he wanted. But the idea of signing him went cold for a while. I bumped into him one day on Bethnal Green Road when walking down it with my

---

6 A few years later, Big Dada signed grime artist Jammer. He too visited Kennington via tube, and on his own. Immediately recognisable by his dreadlocks, he too was immediately spotted and menaced, and had to hide behind a wheelie bin for safety.

girlfriend. He had a baby-blue tracksuit on and looked elegantly crumpled, as though he'd been out all night. His gold teeth flashed and he shook my hand and asked if I was all right. He liked to deflect from himself by asking other people questions: 'What's happening?' or 'You all right though?'

And then we got hold of some demos that were clearly some of the best work he'd made. I remember standing outside Tottenham Court Road tube, in the rain, texting with Will, realising that we were going to try and sign Wiley; alight with the sense that great things were happening.

26

Nick Oliveri – Part Two

A s I began writing this book, I reached out to Nick Oliveri on social media. Messages went through on Facebook and Instagram, but I could see he hadn't read them. Undeterred, I assumed I'd be able to track him down eventually. It seemed to me – perhaps arrogantly – that since he wasn't at the peak of his success he should be relatively easy to interview. Since being kicked out of Queens of the Stone Age, Oliveri has focused on his projects Mondo Generator,[1] Stöner and Uncontrollable, as well as playing solo shows under his pseudonym, Rex Everything. He'd also frequently played with the punk band Dwarves.[2] I'd

1 Mondo Generator was originally a Kyuss song. The name derives from drummer Brant Bjork having spraypainted the phrase on the side of Oliveri's Sunn amplifier. *Mondo* means 'world' in Italian, which to my ear makes the band/song name better than it might first appear.
2 As mentioned in Chapter 12, Dwarves were one of the first bands to really terrify and excite me when a friend showed me a vinyl copy of their album *Blood, Guts & Pussy*. This features two naked women and a naked male dwarf covered in animal blood. It gave me intimations of a terrifying, adult, transgressive world of which I yearned to know more. This was before the internet – there was no way to find out who these people were, what they looked like, what they thought or said or did. Your parents wouldn't know. They probably weren't going to be written about in the next edition of *Melody Maker* or *NME*. Your only options were older kids or indie record stores, both of which were a bit frightening too. Now, of course, Dwarves seem rather crass, and closer to American frat-boy humour than the punk transgression I dreamed of. But still, you get the point.

seen him out and about in LA, and his email address was even available online. How hard could it be?

In October 2022, I saw that Oliveri was due to tour the UK and Europe. Billed as the *Death Acoustic Tour*, it seemed the performances would be solo. There was no London date – these were small venues and towns. I briefly considered combining a business trip to Europe with one of the shows, but I was flying to Mexico City for my day job in the middle of the tour, which made that option tricky. That left me with Bournemouth, and a venue called the Anvil Bar – the final date of the *Death Acoustic Tour*.

I reached out to Oliveri's current label, Heavy Psych Sounds. Mondo Generator had put out records with the highly regarded avant-metal label Southern Lord, as well as imprints owned by Dave Grohl and Josh Homme, but Oliveri seemed to have found a home with this small booking agency and label. It appears to be based in Europe, and on its site lists a number of related rock sub-genres: stoner, vintage rock, retro rock, acid rock, doom, proto-punk and sludge, among others. I copied the email address I'd found for Nick, and shamelessly referred to my day job, which I believed might imply I was a serious person who knew how to deal with artists.

After a couple of days, I received a friendly reply from a staffer at Heavy Psych. His name was decapitalised in his email address, which I took as an estimably underground sign. The reply seemed promising: when and where would I like to interview Nick?

This led to a brief exchange in which I suggested Bournemouth. I asked for three hours on the basis that this would be a lengthy profile but said I could work with two. I slightly shamelessly offered to buy Nick lunch. This might give the piece some colour, I thought.

The label staffer then copied the man himself in, summarising the request and asking me to explain more directly. This I did, doubling up on the shamelessness and explaining that my day job at a renowned indie-rock record company meant that I understood that promo could be a chore for artists.[3] I also included a link to a profile I'd written on the novelist Ryan Gattis, as an example of the 'positive tone' I'd be going for. Finally, a friend having recently explained a well-established technique for securing interviews for books, I suggested I could write something about the tour for the *Evening Standard* too, if that provided extra motivation. I was going all in here.

Three days later, Nick Oliveri's bolded name dropped into my inbox. His reply was slightly terse but appeared to be a yes. He asked how long the interview would need to be.

We're on! I thought, and wrote back:

Great, thanks Nick.
If you can spare 3 hrs it would be great, but I know you're on tour and can work with less if needs be.

---

3 Artists in general hate doing promo. Or rather, they begin to hate it, especially as they become more successful. This is something that's difficult to understand until one is actually in the artist's position. Most of us would be – or think we'd be – perfectly happy talking to writers and radio presenters about ourselves and our work. But it can become a gruesome, repetitive slog. Worse: in the age of gotcha journalism, a tired, over-stretched artist can be confronted by a canny writer who has prepared a plan to make them say something controversial. Regardless, promo is important for selling a record. For this reason, it's often a contractual requirement between labels and artists. Labels also make a significant investment in media training to make the whole thing less stressful and risky.

I'd be happy to take you for lunch or something if it helps time wise.
I really appreciate this and am looking forward to it.

I heard nothing for six days, so sent a nudge. This time, Oliveri's reply was quicker, but a lot less promising. He seemed to find the request for three hours absurd, and then laughingly asked if I expected him to write the book for me, too.
Fair enough, I thought, and typed out my reply.

Ha, fair enough! How long can you spare? I can work with an hour if time is tight. A little more would be great.

Once again, Nick's reply became more promising. He asked if we could do some of the interview in advance sessions, by email, FaceTime or WhatsApp.
I replied enthusiastically:

Definitely, I'd be well up for that
And still do an in person in Bournemouth, but quicker?
When would suit you to do a FaceTime soon?
Hope Europe is treating you well!

But to no avail. That was the last I'd ever hear from Nick Oliveri. After a few weeks, I chased up my contact at the label, whose reply made me like him even more. He apologised, told me he didn't know what say, and suggested I give it a final try.
As the day of the show approached, I did try Nick one last time. Nothing.

★　　★　　★

And that was how I found myself driving down to Bournemouth on a dark, dank November night, jetlagged from my Mexican adventure and wondering what on earth I was doing. The following night, I would have a work gig to attend in London. I was already exhausted, and, in my early forties, my fear of exhaustion had taken on the proportions of a mystic dread.

In the essay which gave the name to one of his collections, *A Supposedly Fun Thing I'll Never Do Again*, the aforementioned David Foster Wallace takes a voyage on a cruise ship. When the vessel briefly pulls alongside another, he refers to one of his great contemporaries as he briefly considers doing something brave and brilliant:

I calculate by eye the breadth of the gap I'd have to jump or rappel to switch to the *Dreamward*, and I mentally sketch out the paragraphs that would detail such a bold and William T. Vollmannish bit of journalistic derring-do as literally jumping from one 7NC Megaship to another.

I considered this as my eyes strained into the darkness and rain on the A3 southbound. A braver writer, a Vollmannish writer, might stroll into Oliveri's dressing room and introduce himself. He'd get his interview, dammit, or he'd get beaten up trying.[4] But who was I kidding? I was not going to try that.

A month or so earlier, I'd mentioned to my old friend Andy that I planned to interview Oliveri. His face had darkened slightly. This, after all, was a man who'd been kicked out of his band for

---

4 I would later read that an early iteration of Mondo Generator had disbanded after Oliveri attacked a soundman in Germany.

allegedly assaulting a woman – perhaps the worst sin we've encountered in our journey thus far. Perhaps my 'positive tone' was misguided; so too the near-empathy I'd been attempting to extend.

So what *was* I doing? I felt a little stalkerish as I drove. My interview had been declined, hadn't it? What was I going to get out of watching the show? And what would I have found out anyway that Oliveri hadn't already said in public? He'd recently told *Eonmusic* that 'it took some time to heal' after being kicked out of QOTSA. Was he likely to have anything different to say to me?[5] Then I steeled myself. *I'm not going to Bournemouth for you, Nick Oliveri, I thought. I'm going for my book.*

Cruising at about seventy-three on derestricted dual carriageway, I overtook two slower cars in the left lane, then moved over left myself. The front car immediately pulled out, overtook me, pulled across me and briefly braked. This seemed some sort of omen, a symbol of the night's stormy, aggressive tenor. I gave the fucker a good dose of the full beams and overtook him again.

I drove into Bournemouth just before eight o'clock. I had history with this place. My paternal grandmother – a somewhat glamorous, suntanned, southern figure, to my middle-class northern mind – lived in Canford Cliffs in neighbouring Poole. I think it's safe to say that's the posh bit.

During my teens, a girlfriend and I visited her for a holiday. While my grandmother played golf, we made a few bus trips to Bournemouth – any bigger settlement seemed the better option, back then. I seem to remember that the bus was open-topped, its route winding along the coastline atop the airy cliffs.

---

5 As far as I know, no one has asked him to describe in detail his armed stand-off with SWAT.

During that long ago trip, I looked out for skateboarders or skate shops, talked of plans to buy a better board, generally got on my girlfriend's nerves. I bought CD singles of the Charlatans' 'One to Another', DJ Krush's 'Kemuri', and 'Born Slippy' by Underworld. *Trainspotting* had come out the year before and had made a lasting impression.

We'd begun having sex, and one afternoon when my grandma was out, we had a disaster: the tip of the condom came off and briefly became lost inside her. I remember looking for it together, realising the pearly fluid within her was my come. This caused a sickening panic. We managed to get the details of a family planning clinic in Bournemouth, and made a much less relaxed journey to obtain a morning-after pill. The pill induced nausea, and that evening, after my grandma cooked us dinner, she and I tried not to listen as my girlfriend threw up in the bathroom beside the kitchen.

When the drama abated, she told me she felt proud to be the first among her friends to have had 'sperm in my fanny'.

Now, returning to the scene, older though perhaps not much wiser, I parked in a multistorey beside the police station. A man in leathers was sitting on his motorbike, watching television on his phone. Outside, there were teenagers in the streets, laughing and joking. A young woman, walking alone ahead of me, flinched as I came up behind her, trying to give her as much room as I could. As I approached an alley beside a shop, a woman with a can of cider, speaking to someone out of sight, glanced at me. In the alley itself another woman was squatting down, jeans and knickers around her ankles, unleashing a powerful jet of piss. She giggled and said, 'Sorry, mate,' as I passed. 'Oh, that's all right,' I replied.

I briefly considered texting a friend, raised in the area, to needle him over whether the place was a bit rough. But I was approaching the Anvil Bar, so there wasn't time.

At the venue, a few youngish people with a vaguely rock look were standing outside, smoking. I pushed open the door, took in the rectangular bar, and saw that to the left were some stairs and a large, bearded man with a table and a clipboard. He asked my name and put a wristband on me.

'What time is Nick on?' I asked him. I winced inwardly at having stalkerishly referred to Oliveri as 'Nick'.

The man glanced at his watch. 'It'll be ten,' he said.

My spirits fell. It was five past eight. The bands I worked with began headline slots in big London venues at nine. I had naively assumed that, if anything, gigs would start earlier out here in the regions. Forlornly accepting I had two hours of standing around ahead of me, I descended to the basement. It was smaller than the upstairs room, perhaps eight metres by five, windowless and gloomy. A stage at the far end was covered in lots of the skull/skeleton iconography typical of hard rock and heavy metal. A warm-up band was playing, and there was no bar, so I went back upstairs and got myself a pint.

Back downstairs, I put my earplugs in and settled in to watch the support bands, sipping my pint as slowly as possible. I'll never get used to driving to gigs.

The first support were a classic of the type: talented in a workmanlike way, playing deeply unfashionable funk-rock, heart-breaking in the sense it would never go anywhere. I admonished myself: *who am I to be thinking such things? Perhaps they're just having fun.*

The other punters were all regional rocker types. The youngest were probably in their late twenties. There were lots of middle-aged men, but quite a few women in their thirties. Some wore leather trousers or very tight jeans. A squinting, fifty-something man with unruly red hair and bottle-bottom specs came down the stairs, peered about him, bumbled into a few people, and retreated once more.

The second support were much better.[6] The way they moved, set up, wielded their instruments spoke of something more seasoned. They launched into thunderous desert rock cum metal cum grunge, and the crowd – myself included – began to move with them. I was glad of my earplugs but glad of their music too. The singer's vocals were a minor weak point, but they nearly always are. At one stage they covered a Kyuss song, which was pretty obviously their template anyway.

By the time they'd finished, it was 9.55 and I'd ended up near the front of the stage. When a man in front of me went off to the bar or the loo, I took another step forward. Now I was only one row back. Might as well stay here, I decided. The mild need to pee could be contained. I wanted to get a good look at Oliveri, and maybe take a photo. I'd vaguely decided I didn't need to stay for the whole set. Half an hour would do it, despite the effort. I had to be up early in the morning and had a ninety-minute drive ahead of me. Nick Oliveri hadn't done me the honour of an interview, so I hardly owed him my attendance for the full set.

The crowd began to build again. I became aware of a group of men, newly formed around me. They had a beered-up,

6 I initially misheard their name as Dead Letters, which I thought wasn't bad. It turned out they were actually called Dead Lettuce, however, which I suppose is so bad that it must at least be deliberately so.

slightly laddish vibe about them. Bournemouth accents, short hair with shaved sides. They were talking about being knocked about in mosh pits. One of them, turning around and looking about him with vacant eyes, spilled a fifth of a pint of beer over my right foot.

An American voice said, 'Excuse me,' and then Nick Oliveri was working his way through the crowd, a slight figure in a leather jacket, black jeans and black Vans. When he reached the stage and turned, I saw he had on a white Misfits T-shirt beneath the jacket. From recent photographs, he usually seems to be wearing a classic US punk band shirt.

The men around me – of whom I was realising there were a good five or six together – made surprised mutterings that Oliveri was alone, and carrying his own gear.

'How much you reckon he makes from *Songs for the Deaf*?' one of them asked another.

'Not much,' the other replied.

I debated this question in my mind, rather superciliously dismissing the men as being far from expert in the music business. Personally, I'd have thought Oliveri would have done all right.

It was just before he began playing that the group of men became focused on me, instead of Oliveri.

'Fuckin' tall people at the front, eh? What's that all about?' one of them said.

'I know, mate. Shouldn't they be at the back?'

I'm six-foot-three. Adding to the problem, I'd decided to use this incognito excursion to the regions to try out a pair of Paul Smith boots I'd lacked the confidence to wear regularly. They had very thick soles.

'Look at this, Lurch[7] at the front, mate!' one of them said. The other men all laughed.

'He better have a seven-inch cock, mate,' one of them said, bizarrely. I haven't, but it was a nice idea.

I gave no outward sign of having heard them, standing as casually as I could. On stage, Oliveri was testing the level of the mic.

'Check check check,' he said. 'If anything that's a little too much. Check check check. OK, that's good. Lemme tune up and I'll get started.'

I was vaguely amused – proud, even – to be the centre of the group of men's attention. It reminded me of being an outsider at school, at standing out from the rugby lads. They didn't seem menacing, as yet at least. Still, I inwardly termed them knuckleheads.

Presumably, someone a little way back farted, because the men all started to make the noises associated with having encountered one.

'Jesus, mate, who did that?' one of them said.

'It's Lurch, mate,' one of them said. He adopted a low, Lurch-like voice. 'Mggghhhrrr, Lurch eats raw chicken.'

The others guffawed.

I considered what would happen if they did become aggressive. There were too many of them to fight. A perfect quip – one that belittled them all without quite providing the excuse for violence – did not spring to mind. What then? Endure, follow them home and lob a brick through a window? No, that was getting silly. And anyway, I had to be up early.

_____

7 I imagine this doesn't need explaining, but just in case: Lurch is the very tall, Frankenstein's Monster-like butler in *The Addams Family*.

Thankfully, Oliveri began to play. Sure enough, it was just him and an acoustic guitar. He played a Kyuss song, and 'Gonna Leave You' by Queens. He played some horror-punk stuff I didn't recognise. His scream/howl was impressive, and I wondered how he'd delivered that, nightly on tour, without losing his voice. He had the charisma you'd expect of a musician with his pedigree. He had three open bottles of Corona at the side of the stage, and a bottle of tequila with six or seven shot glasses. After a few songs, he asked a woman to come out of the audience and serve shots to those who reached for one.

'I been doing a bottle a night,' he said. He has a western American accent, a deepish voice gravelled from hard living and hard singing. 'I thought I better start sharin' it,' he continued. 'I ain't quite got it like I used to.'

Most people laughed. One of the group of men – who I noticed was very tall – shoved to the front and grabbed a shot. I failed to muster the efforts required. The men powerfully reminded me of a former colleague, who in a pub after work had aggressively argued that there were circumstances in which a woman should be hit. This man had also liked to muscle his way to the front of shows. At a gig or in a fight, I reflected, this type would always be at the front.

Oliveri began playing again. I glanced over my shoulder at the men. They were smirking and looking at each other. For a moment, I worried they might have done something to the back of the large, pale overshirt I was wearing. Memories came back of ink being flicked on to white school shirts from the nibs of fountain pens.

It was nearly half past ten. I took a couple of photos. Oliveri had mean eyes, I decided. Small, like a sadist in an American road movie. I'd seen enough. It was time to zoom back along the dual carriageways — they'd be emptier now — to smash through the rain and reach the warmth of my house and my family. To guzzle a large Scotch, kiss my children and go to bed.

I might be Lurch, I thought to myself as I turned and moved through the men. But you'll always be knuckleheads, and I'm writing a motherfucking book.

Outside, the streets were full of teenagers, laughing and whooping, drunken in the soft rain.

27

Andy Nicholson, Arctic Monkeys

You're gonna have to get a lawyer. – Ian
McAndrew, Arctic Monkeys' manager

Arctic Monkeys' 2006 debut album, *Whatever People Say I Am, That's What I'm Not*, briefly became the fastest selling debut album in UK history.[1] The band exploded out of Sheffield – and the internet – and seemed to emerge fully formed. Their video for debut single, 'I Bet You Look Good on the Dancefloor', was shot live using 1980s cameras to give it a vintage effect. With bandleader Alex Turner's mod-ish haircut and spiky demeanour, it's reminiscent of the Jam, if Paul Weller had worn T-shirts.

The tightness of the band and their overall chops are evident, particularly Turner (who plays lead guitar as well as singing) and drummer Matt Helders. These two would go on to become the band's most prominent members and creative core. In the bridge of 'I Bet You Look Good', Helders sings the response to Turner's call and provides backing vocals generally. Onscreen, the pair

---

1 It was knocked off the top spot for this rather specific record the following year, by *X Factor* winner Leona Lewis.

face each other for a long moment, sparking off each other's playing.

The band appear very young – they'd have been nineteen or twenty when they shot the video. Despite this, they look like an outfit who have been performing for years. The lean, wiry Turner plays aggressively, moving around the set up with a jerky, electrified, amphetamine urgency. He turns to each band member like a punky sergeant, inspecting them and egging them on with his eyes.

Standing on the left of the screen is the band's original bass player, Andy Nicholson. He's what we northerners might call a big lad or, more politely, heavy set. He wears a greenish polo shirt with the collar up – it could be a Lacoste, but any logo is obscured by the strap of his guitar. His head is shaved and, like the rest of the band except for Helders (who at one stage winks and grins at the camera), he's unsmiling.

Again unlike Helders, he doesn't really seem to react when Turner faces him. Certainly, sparks don't fly in the way they do with the drummer. But that doesn't seem unusual, because guitarist Jamie Cook also appears self-contained on the opposite side of the soundstage.

Andy Nicholson was not long for Arctic Monkeys. In May 2006, the band released a statement saying that he would miss their forthcoming North American tour due to 'fatigue'. His temporary replacement would be Nick O'Malley of fellow Sheffield band the Dodgems.[2]

---

2 O'Malley himself almost self-sabotaged the opportunity to go on this tour. A week after he'd agreed to fill in, he broke his hand during drunken high jinks with his Dodgems bandmates. Luckily for him, the injury was to his plectrum hand, and he was still able to play.

In June, the band announced that Nicholson was 'no longer with the band'. O'Malley's replacement of him would now be permanent. 'We have been mates with Andy for a long time and have been through some amazing things together that no one can take away,' the statement read. 'We all wish Andy all the best.'

Initially, it seemed as though the departure might be mutual, or that Nicholson might even have found touring too difficult and left of his own accord. By August, though, the band had given an interview to *NME* in which Alex Turner said: 'we sorta found ourselves in a situation where we wanted to move forward. It weren't like us wanting to carry on like this as punishment for him wanting to opt out.'

Guitarist Jamie Cook said, 'everyone might say we're wankers and we shit on him, but they don't know. We know, Andy knows and that's all that really matters.'

It wasn't until 2019 that Nicholson gave his side of the story in full, and almost accidentally. Speaking to *The Michael Anthony Show*, a comedy podcast, he said that after returning from a European tour he 'had some family stuff go off at home'. After that tour, the band were meant to have 'three days off, go and record, go on a tour in America for a month. And it's like "I can't really do that right now, I've got some stuff I need to take care of." And then they came back off that America tour and they said "We're gonna keep Nick."'

'Was there an element of you that wasn't as into it as you were?' Anthony asks.

'No . . . I felt like I would've died for it. I felt like I wanted to embody everything this is about.'

After his ejection, 'we didn't speak for two years. I didn't speak to them, and they didn't speak to me.'

Anthony manages to draw the story of the sacking out in a striking, visual memory.

'We were supposed to meet in a pub . . .'

'Did you think they might have been telling you?'

'No, no, not at all. I had no idea. I got to the pub, no one's there. The manager's assistant is sat outside in his car saying, "Oh we're not meeting here, we're going to Geoff's[3] office, jump in." Went to Geoff's office, walked in, them three are stood there. I can see exactly where everyone was stood and sat. And we just started talking . . .' Nicholson pauses here. 'I feel like I've never even told anybody any of this before,' he says. 'Scoop.'

'Al did the speaking,' he continues. 'Jamie did a bit of speaking, Matt not so much. I don't think anyone enjoyed any of it. I remember all that happening in that room, I shook all three of their hands and I walked outside . . . Ian [McAndrew], the big manager, was sat in a café next door. Then I just thought, "This is a big, organised plan. We're gonna get him in here, we're gonna do this, then he's gotta sit there."'

3 Geoff Barradale, the band's co-manager at the time and a former member of bands Seafruit and Vitamin Z, who had a hit with 'Burning Flame'. Barradale is from Sheffield and managed the band before Ian McAndrew, a more prominent manager, came on to co-manage. This often happens with bands: they meet a character who they have a creative rapport with, but need more professional management when things get serious. Usually, at some stage, the 'big' manager becomes the *only* manager — and this is what happened in the case of Arctic Monkeys.

'So I've just found this news out, twenty-one years old, and Ian's saying: "Right, you're gonna have to get a lawyer."'[4]

This is a rejection that shows just how traumatic the experience can be. For several years after it happened, Nicholson seems not to be able to remember very much at all.

'It's weird, I don't know what I did. When I think of the years 2007, 2008 and 2009, it's dark . . . With Al and Helders, we'd had a life before we'd even knew how many strings were on a guitar.'

In Nicholson's telling, all contact had broken off with the band, but there were media reports of him meeting them backstage at Reading Festival in 2006. He was apparently seen with his replacement, O'Malley, 'shaking hands and chatting amicably'.

Perhaps these memories were wiped out by the trauma he endured.

'Were you depressed, like staying indoors, like considering suicide?' Anthony asks on the podcast.

'Really depressed, I mean yeah. Considering like "if these people can do this, what else can happen?" Very close to not being here, do you know what I mean?'

Again his memories, when they do come, arrive in striking imagery: 'I remember when they headlined Glastonbury for the first time, I was in my house, on my own, and it's dark. I was just sat at home, on my own . . . just crying.'

More than any other story, this one seems to show how bad being sacked really feels – in Nicholson's words 'soul destroying' – and how much damage it can do.

4 Years after these events, I worked with Ian McAndrew on the Arctic Monkeys' album *The Car*. A highly impressive character, his advice to Nicholson to get a lawyer was exactly right, and notable for its fairness.

For his part, the famously reticent Turner hasn't spoken about the episode since. Perhaps it's safe to assume he didn't consider Nicholson a fit. Turner increasingly appears the archetype of the detached, visionary bandleader, firmly in charge and completely committed to his own creative world. The rejection of Andy Nicholson was simply an early symptom of this.

Wiley – Part Two

The demos Wiley gave us became *Playtime Is Over*, the first record he made for Big Dada. His manager dropped out of the picture, and though a few others would briefly appear over the subsequent years (I even did a brief stint myself) we largely dealt direct. Will Ashon made it clear that I would be the point man for Wiley. He'd already sensed it was going to be something like a full-time job.

The way I remember it is in episodes. An initial visit to a branch of Miloco Studios in Elephant and Castle, hearing the title track for the first time. The call from the studio manager a few days later, saying that Wiley owed them money, and that when they'd withheld his recordings as collateral, he'd threatened to come and burn the place down. I didn't know Wiley very well back then, so I was nervous when I asked him about it. He laughed it off, and it was obvious he hadn't meant it. But I began to learn he could be intemperate when frustrated.

Another visit to a studio in Mile End, where Will came along. He suggested to Wiley that he vary the tempos more, of the drums and also his raps – grime could be rather one-note in tempo. For some reason, Wiley decided that this meant Will wanted to make him into Roots Manuva – an idea from which he could not be dissuaded. This confusion further solidified the idea that I'd be the point man, and would hitherto communicate any A & R ideas on Will's behalf.

The things he'd say over text or call. 'You might be a white man from Leeds J, but you do know your grime.' He unilaterally decided my name was J, and never desisted. The album came out. Throughout, Wiley sounded fired up and inspired, his rapping tight and confident, his patterns playful and pleasingly relentless at once. The record did well, if not as well as Dizzee's third. There were angrier moments, but the ire was usually directed at himself. 'I should be up there in the stars, J, and I'm down here in the dirt.' 'PRICK PRICK PRICK. Not you, J, me. I'm such a fuckin' PRICK.'

There were many magazine covers shot for *Playtime*. At one, in a bar made of ice in central London, his sometime girlfriend Lady Ny came along. After a short while in the bar, Wiley complained of being cold.

'Aren't you meant to be the Eskimo boy?' Ny said.

He told me he'd blown the huge major label advances he'd received as part of his former crew, Pay as U Go Kartel, on nights out for his friends. Club entries, drinks, hotels, taxis for everybody. Hundreds of thousands of pounds.

On arrival in Germany for a promo trip: an immigration official horrified by Wiley's passport, which he'd put through the wash and from which the photograph was peeling out.

The guard became irate, gesturing at the passport and speaking German.

'Eighty pound, bruv,' Wiley told him. 'I ain't paying it.'

Eventually the man gave up and conceded. In those early years, Wiley seemed to lead a charmed life. He was irrepressible.

It seemed then that he might always get away with it, whatever the latest 'it' was.

On the way back, Wiley sailing through customs in sunglasses, loud shorts hanging low. An older woman had been pulled over to have her bag checked. On making it through to the arrival hall, Wiley grinning. 'They pulled over that old lady, J, and I've got a quarter of weed in my balls.'

A planned trip to America never happened. In order to try and sort out his immigration issues, we obtained his criminal record. It was extensive, and bizarre: *Improper use of electricity* – 'We stole it from the next-door flat, J, to set up a sound system.'

Threatening behaviour in a public place – two entries, following some sort of logic: going to HMV's head office to demand his royalties; arguing with a bank manager over the money his long-suffering sister had put into a long-term savings account for him.

A Eurostar journey during which we ended up discussing God. I told Wiley I wasn't a believer, and used the word 'atheist'. It was completely new to him, as was the idea that there was some official, acceptable form of disbelief. His eyes widened as if he was undergoing a revelation. 'So you don't actually have to believe in God?' he said.

On one of these trips, Wiley pulled up his shirt and showed me some of his fourteen stab wounds. Two sets of seven. Both sets had been inflicted by the same group of men, on two separate occasions. Little puncture scars, rough edged and paler against his skin.

Wiley has spoken openly about what happened: A drama over money owed to a friend of his had spiralled out of control. Wiley turned up to an east London rave to be set upon by dozens of other young men. He was stabbed in the torso, back, leg and 'bum', and hospitalised for several weeks.

Once he was out, he went to west London – outside his comfort zone – to buy some new trainers. By terrible co-incidence, the 'boy who stabbed' him was in the shop, accompanied by friends.

'I'm stupid, J,' he told me. 'Because I'm *Wiley*' – as if scorning his own persona – 'and I was like "I ain't backing down."'

A fight immediately broke out, and Wiley was chased out of the shop and down the street. He managed to tear out a For Sale sign outside a house and swing it at them, but they overpowered and stabbed him again.

This time, he 'nearly died'. His lung had collapsed in the first stabbing, and he'd been told to be careful about smoking. Not that this had reduced his intake of weed.

Why does this stuff happen, I asked him?

'Because we're black men, J,' he said.

He didn't feel at all sorry for himself for the stabbings. He considered them entirely his own fault. He was erratic, charming, funny and loveable,

'You're a full-time job,' I told him during one of these trips.

'I know,' he said, widening his eyes and puffing out his cheeks to expel air – he often did this in contrition or stress. 'That's what my mum says.'

He told me of his upbringing. I wish I could tell the story in turn, though propriety and legality both preclude my doing so. Understanding where Wiley comes from is crucial to this story. Suffice to say that he casually reeled off images from his childhood that would qualify for the darkest of misery memoirs. To him it was just stuff that had happened, that he'd got through, that was less important than his life – and musical mission – in the present.

The episodes could darken. In grime, there was always a contest between different crews, played out by the MCs. These could easily spill over into street violence. As one of grime's biggest stars, and one who hadn't left 'the ends' as Dizzee had, Wiley made a tempting target. In 2006 he began 'warring' with the Movement, a crew consisting of MCs Ghetto (nowadays known as Ghetts, and still having some success) and Scorcher.

When I booked grime DJ Logan Sama and the Movement to appear at my club night, Wiley turned up on his own to battle them live. He arrived before Scorcher and Ghetts, and when I asked him why MCs were always late, he said 'because we feel special, J.' That night, outside the lyrics, things seemed quite civilised. Usually, these MCs were friends of his – Scorcher even went on to appear on the album. But I would come to learn that these relationships could turn very quickly.

The lyrical battle became a real one when Wiley bumped into Ghetto on Roman Road in Bow. In Wiley's telling, Ghetto pulled a knife and chased him. Wiley, carrying a bag with his laptop in it, realised he needed to shed this weight in order to escape. He tossed the bag into the doorway of Rhythm Division, the record store that had been pivotal in grime's early success.

Ghetto stopped and picked up the bag, and the laptop disappeared. On it were several demos that Wiley had recorded and didn't have backed up.

I was only to hear about the subsequent drama a few days later. After threats and pleas had done no good, Wiley had turned to a dark figure for help. Someone on the fringes of his life was a serious organised criminal. In one of his runs of major

330

label pop success, Wiley had purchased a Bentley. This man had told him to return it. 'Nah,' he'd said. 'You can't have that. I can't have you in that.' It wouldn't do for Wiley to be seen to outshine him. He told me of some of the brutal ways in which the man made his living. 'You never want to get into debt with him, J,' he told me. But Wiley had – by borrowing a gun.

In Wiley's version, once he had it, he kicked in Ghetto's door. The rival MC's mum was on the other side of it, and Wiley ran into the house and managed to retrieve the laptop. Wiley's searing *Nightbus* – aimed at the Movement and widely considered one of grime's high points – referred to the incident. 'Don't make me run at you waving my gun at you / crying to my mum and your mum 'cos I came and duppied you.'

Ghetto would later refer to the events in his *Darkside Freestyle,* claiming that an unnamed adversary had 'come to my house and kicked in the glass / next day I made him pay for a new door / he ain't a bad boy / I took man to the cashpoint.'

Despite the lyrical bravado, I had the sense that everyone involved (except, presumably, the gangster) had frightened themselves with this incident, and it quickly settled down.

After the album was out, things gradually slowed in intensity. On Christmas Day 2007, I got a series of texts. Wiley was saying he wanted to listen more, that his dad had told him he should, that he was sorry he hadn't always listened.

A few months after *Playtime*'s release, he'd quickly recouped his publishing advance and had a royalty cheque due of a little over £500. When I called to tell him, he insisted he wanted to give it to me.

'I'm already getting paid,' I told him.

'Na-na-na, J,' he said, 'I told you I'd take care of you.'

We argued for fifteen minutes or so, until he made clear that he wouldn't accept any other outcome.

I told Peter Quicke, the Ninja boss, of the predicament, and he told me I'd keep half and Ninja would take the other. Those, looking back, were leaner years for the label.

Eventually Wiley announced on Twitter that he was leaving Big Dada. Will Ashon cleverly released a statement along the lines of 'Wiley is a one, isn't he?'

The door was left open, and a pattern established. Wiley would make a major label pop album, fall out with everyone – sometimes before the project saw the light of day – then return to us to make a grime record. The split nature of his personality – grime MC/pop star, thoughtful/wild, happy/sad – played out on the stage of his very career.

Will made the point that if he'd been born in the US, where a real infrastructure and market existed for rap music, Wiley wouldn't have had to make the distinction between the street and the stars.

He came back to make more records. The A & R credits became single, and in my name, but the process never changed, we just got used to it. There were more episodes. His arrival in the office, a little older and more seasoned, a toddler daughter in tow. He'd had a pop hit in 2008 with 'Wearing My Rolex', but the major label deal had gone sour, and he wanted to make grime again. He had a huge new scar along his jawbone to his chin.

'What happened with that scar?' I asked him when we were alone.

An older man – his dad's age – had wanted Wiley to get his son on the radio. When it had become clear that Wiley was unable to do this, the son having no talent, the man and his friends had ambushed Wiley on the street one night. They pinned him down and slashed his face with a Stanley knife, a deep, deliberate cut several inches long.

'I'm so sorry, mate,' I told him. I was barely able to process the rage and horror of all this.

'It's all right,' he said. But it wasn't. He was self-conscious about the scar in subsequent photoshoots. His face was the part of him he'd been pleased to preserve through these bouts of violence.

One night, sitting in an armchair at home, almost at midnight: a series of texts that were alarmingly self-lacerating. I did my best to reassure him.

'I love you bro,' he texted me eventually.

'I love you too mate,' I told him.

We worked together on four records in total, spread out across seven years. Wiley's persona in the early 2010s was marked by irresponsible humour. He delighted fans by engaging on forums and on Twitter, frequently getting into arguments.

'Both ur parents are experiencing the credit crunch,' he told an anonymous troll on a forum. 'I ain't.'

Arriving at Glastonbury to perform, he was appalled by the rain, and began a Twitter tirade. He demanded to be taken off the bill and escorted away from the mud. One of these demands was made in reply to an Emily Eavis tweet, thanking a friend for the organic apples.

'Fuck them and their farm,' he said eventually.

'We're no longer working with Wiley,' his agent replied to me one day, when I'd asked for a latest list of live dates, 'since he issued a bomb threat against Norway.' Wiley had jokingly threatened to 'blow up' the country.

Wiley's long-suffering manager, John Woolf, was often the target of these Twitter tirades: 'I hate u u tramp' was a classic example.

He was at the height of his profile, had become a bona fide star, and something approaching that dread state: a national treasure. He was awarded an MBE in 2017, and in 2018 an autobiography was published by Random House. I did a long interview for it, in which I told a few of the stories I have here.

And then, in 2020, during the first wave of the global pandemic, everything went wrong for good.

In June 2020, the Black Lives Matter protests had broken out in cities and towns across America. For a brief period in Los Angeles, we were under both lockdown and curfew. The public safety alerts on our phones – announced with a dramatic alarm, and usually deployed to warn of child abductions or flash flooding – now told us to be in our homes by 5 p.m. on pain of arrest. The National Guard were filling their armoured vehicles at the gas station opposite Ninja's office, and rioting had broken out Downtown and on the West Side.

And then, at the end of July, I heard that Wiley had got himself cancelled. He'd published some sort of deranged, antisemitic outburst on social media. I knew instantly that there was no coming back.

As with all bigotry, the details are rather tedious because there's nothing true being said. Writing on Twitter, Wiley had started by claiming that Israel didn't belong to the Jewish community. From here, he made a bizarre comparison between Jews and the Ku

Klux Klan: 'There are 2 sets of people who nobody has really wanted to challenge #Jewish & #KKK but being in business for 20 years you start to undestand [sic] why . . . Red Necks Are the KKK and Jewish people are the Law . . . Work that out.'

He also said: 'I don't care about Hitler, I care about black people', and called Jewish people 'cowards and snakes'.

Reaction was swift, and quickly became a full-blown media storm. Wiley's manager at the time, John Woolf, is himself Jewish. I'd got to know him a little over the years; he was friendly and sharp, good-humoured enough to deal with Wiley's regular public tantrums with him. Woolf initially tried to calm things. 'I'm talking to him privately,' he said in a tweet. He added that, having known Wiley for twelve years, he knew he 'does not truly feel this way'.

For the record, I'm not someone who takes antisemitism more lightly than other forms of racism.[1] If anything, I swing the other way – I fully concur with David Baddiel that this is a growing phenomenon in society. To some extent this is personal – my beloved American family descends from a Holocaust survivor.

But I knew that Wiley was impressionable. I recalled the way he'd reacted to my telling him about atheism, and various other things he'd said over the years that he'd obviously just been told by someone else. I recalled a phrase I'd heard levelled at Donald Trump, that, like a cushion, he would bear the imprint of whoever last sat on him. I wondered whether some untoward figure had been in his ear.

1 As I make the final edits to this book in October 2023, the worst consequences of antisemitism have erupted in Israel, in the biggest mass murder of Jewish civilians since the Holocaust.

By now, media figures, politicians, antisemitism campaigners and rabbis had all, quite reasonably, chimed in. John Woolf quickly announced that 'following Wiley's antisemitic tweets today we @A_ListMGMT have cut all ties with him. There is no place in society for antisemitism.'

Things spiralled. Twitter and Facebook, which owns Instagram, on which Wiley had also posted, were dragged into the mess and forced to apologise for their slowness in responding.

Wiley initially gave a half-arsed apology himself. On an interview with Sky News, for which the channel was strongly criticised, he claimed: 'I'm not racist, I'm a businessman,' and, using a bastardised form of contemporary HR speak: 'I want to apologise for generalising and going outside the . . . workspace and workplace I work in.' He'd simply been falling out with his manager again, he said. 'I want to apologise for comments that were looked at as antisemitic.'

But if I knew Wiley was impressionable, and could be contrite in private, I also knew he'd struggle to back down in public. According to Sky, during the interview, he 'became agitated, yelling directly at the camera and, at one point, jumping up and hitting his chest'.

There were sad, familiar little details: that Wiley's MBE was framed and in the possession of John Woolf, waiting to be collected.

In a flash of awful self-insight, he told the interviewer: 'fans are fickle. Don't wind me up. I'm forty-one years old. It's not like I've got a big bag of fans. Leave it . . . I'm not current. I'm at the end of my career rather than the beginning.'

This was the same old demon that had driven him for the entire time I'd known him. The pop star/not a pop star. The self-knowledge that he'd never really made it, that perhaps he could have done if he hadn't got in his own way. If only he'd had the tools, the ability to be a bit more together. But he didn't have those tools. Had this exhausted self-knowledge led him to burn everything up rather than fade away?

Either way, he was right: it was all over. Wiley had been cancelled and rejected from society. Before long, he was making minor headlines for posting more unpleasantness and provocation. Then, in 2022, for being wanted by the police, having failed to show up to court on charges of burglary and assault (according to reports). At the time of writing, it's not clear if they ever got hold of him.

Every now and again, he and I exchange texts. When we do, he seems very much like the same old Wiley. When people ask me about him, I do my best to explain the good in him, and the sort of life he's led. I would never turn my back on him, because friendship means being there when someone does something wrong, too.

So much of Wiley's life has gone into his lyrics. In '50/50', the first song from the first album we worked on together, he says:

If I want to turn Muslim,
I'll go and see Ibby and Shifty

I asked him about this at the time. He told me that in the black community, there's a form of conversion to Islam that's almost forced. Friends will invite the target – usually a young black man who's going through troubles – over to a house. As I learned in my years working in music – young black men have more than their share of troubles. It gradually becomes clear what's going on, and if the target shows reluctance, the hosts will try to stop them leaving. They'll cut off the exit, use persuasion and temptation, outnumber the youth and ask for just a little while longer. In Wiley's telling, it could almost be a kidnap. He implied that he'd experienced some of this, but that it hadn't really been a danger for him. I got the sense that Wiley would be hard to keep in a house or a flat and persuade.

This chimed with media reports about disaffected, black British men being radicalised. In 2013, Fusilier Lee Rigby was murdered in London. One of his killers, Michael Adebolajo, told the court that he'd been raised a Christian but had become a 'soldier of Allah'.

There's a long, ugly history of antisemitism in black communities. It's there in the early work of poet and writer LeRoi Jones/Amiri Baraka – who later recanted. It's in hip-hop, in the interviews given by rappers such as Public Enemy's Professor Griff, and more recently in the very high-profile self-destruction of Kanye West. For the last few decades, the font of much of this poison has been Louis Farrakhan, the leader of the Nation of Islam. In December 2021, Wiley set up new social media accounts. Displaying his lifelong habit of doubling down under pressure, he made more antisemitic comments and posted a video of Farrakhan speaking.

The official story was that the whole episode had been started by another row between Wiley and John Woolf. But had some unwholesome character been in his ear when it all began, I kept on wondering? Perhaps it didn't matter, since it was certainly no excuse.

When Big Dada released *Evolve or be Extinct* in January 2012, it contained a song called 'Weirdo'. Its chorus line runs:

I'm a weirdo, but I'm not a bipolar
Turn up at the show, I'm not even on the poster

At the time, fans had been speculating that Wiley suffered from the condition. He'd been live streaming himself boiling eggs in his kitchen, and began uploading comedy 'adverts' to YouTube.[2]

'People say I'm bipolar,' he told *Dazed* magazine in 2011. 'What is "a bipolar"? I've grown up around loads of people who are like me really in terms of their mood swings.'

I decided at the outset to avoid amateur psychology in this book. It always seemed clear to me, however, that Wiley was profoundly troubled. I gave him a lot of leeway as a result. Whether these troubles begin with mental health issues or result in them seems beside the point. Wiley has had a life unlike anyone I know outside the London black community. He's been stabbed fourteen times and had a collapsed lung. He's been jumped and pinned to the ground by older men who slashed his face with a Stanley knife. For much of his life, he was unable to move freely around the city of his birth. He was afraid to shoot the cover of *Playtime Is Over* in Victoria Park, his local green space, because of the risk he'd be spotted and attacked. Years later, he *was* spotted, driving in Hackney, and the car was swarmed, and he narrowly escaped being dragged out of it and whatever might have come after that.

Wiley came from a broken home, raised by a mother and father he loved but with severe struggles in the background.

---

2 Often ahead of his time, this would now be recognised as exactly the sort of creative digital marketing that YouTube treats as best-in-class.

There were people in his life he was terrified of, and who carried out some of the worst kind of crimes I've ever had the misfortune of hearing about.

It's hard to imagine all this, for most of us, but I think we should try; as we travel around London or other British cities by foot, car or public transport, the risk to our person is infinitesimally small. There's a parallel world out there that other people have to live in, and many of them weren't blessed with a vast talent like Wiley's. I remember a young producer in the Roll Deep studio, saying that he'd got a girl pregnant. Most of the other young men in the room were already fathers, most of them not partnered with the mother. They greeted this news as though the producer had undergone a rite of passage.

'Can't you guys at least use the pull-out method?' I asked. They shook their heads and rolled their eyes and grinned sheepishly.

'Nah, J,' the young producer said. 'My dad's a Rasta.'

I always knew it would end badly for Wiley – how else could it? – and feared the day it would come. Artists can't be that maverick, madcap, genuinely edgy, and survive. It was always heading for a burnout. The best I hoped for was that Wiley would mellow into an evergreen sonic innovator like Lee Scratch Perry. Someone with enough success to keep working and paying the bills. But I feared a far worse outcome.

I often recall Wiley's generosity with wonder. He gave me half of his publishing cheque. He was constantly – much to my frustration – trying to get us to sign younger artists he'd discovered. He appeared to be literally incapable of seeing that most of them weren't nearly as talented as he was.[3] There was nothing in any of this for him and he wasn't pursuing a financial interest. I'll always remember a day in the Roll Deep studio in Limehouse, on which Wiley marshalled the young MCs to write their bars, to stop playing PlayStation, to stop rolling another spliff and write on their notepads. He was harrying them into the vocal booth and recording them himself – the older figure, the leader.

When Wiley comes up in professional conversations now, there's a blank-eyed uniformity of opinion. He's gone, done, cancelled, rejected. And after all, he did it to himself.

But there's something in the self-righteousness I find uncomfortable. The eyes aren't always blank. In some of them there's something close to glee. This look is often discernible in the people whose pronounced ethical sense should presumably make them sympathetic to people raised in some of the worst circumstances the UK has to offer.

And there's the rub. If black lives matter, as they so obviously do, then we might need to engage with some of this dark, difficult stuff. We might need to look a little deeper and wonder what circumstances could produce this outcome. We might need to ask ourselves why a brilliant black talent would get himself rejected by society in a blaze of self-destruction.

Generosity was one of Wiley's defining characteristics, and, as with all our rejects, perhaps some small quantity is due to him in turn.

---

3 As a result of this and a couple of other examples I've encountered, I've developed a pet theory that artists aren't much cop at A & R.

Mick Ronson, the Spiders from Mars

I've got God. Who's Mick got? – David Bowie

MICK Ronson was the original musical enabler. He made other people's work shine, but didn't quite have what it takes to be a solo artist. His initial sacking from the Spiders from Mars was as staged and performative as everything else about Bowie's first great guise – he may be the only reject in this book to have been in on his own demise. His second, more genuine falling from Bowie's favour was also more painful, drawn out and less straightforward.

Mick Ronson – Ronno to his musical friends – was born into a working-class family in Hull in 1946. This was the post-war north – a terraced house with no electricity upstairs, and a tin bath that was filled by kettle. Considering that Ronson played a key role in the shocking, sexualised glam of the Spiders, there would always be something of the northern sitting room about him. He had a handsome, chiselled face with an angular jaw and 'eyelashes like a cow', in Angie Bowie's words. 'Mick was a car door opener, a hand-holder as you crossed the street, the first one to get the young lady a drink. He was adorable.' He was honest and straightforward, perhaps a little naive.

Interviewed in later years, Ronson is often in fact sitting in a living room. He had a down-to-earth Hull accent and seemed sharply alert with a good memory. His speech was punctuated by short little 'y'knows' at the end of each sentence. When he related the stories of his career, he often did so with a dry humour that seemed to ask: 'Isn't it all odd?' This gives him the air of an observer of the pretensions and indulgences of rock stars, rather than that of an active force like Bowie. Where Ronson *was* active was in the work, in the craft. But a person without pretension isn't destined to be a frontman.

If anyone brings the splinter of ice in Bowie's heart into relief, it's Ronson. And it's not because he was treated particularly cruelly, but more because Ronno showed none of the self-preservation and drive of his bandleader. In fact, he completely failed to look after his own interests.

Before meeting Bowie, Ronson had already made a couple of abortive forays to London to try and make it in music. During these, he diligently wrote letters home to his younger sister. They reveal that he lacked the killer instinct shown by say, Brian Jones (see Chapter 6), in his move from the regions to the capital. He was too polite and proper to go and force his way in. He wound up back in Hull, working as a municipal gardener.

During one of these London spells, though, he'd met John Cambridge, who by 1970 had become Bowie's drummer. When Bowie was looking for more players, Cambridge suggested Ronson. The drummer travelled up to Hull and found Ronson painting the white lines on a rugby pitch. He persuaded him to pick up his guitar and come back down south for one more try.

Bowie was living with his first wife, Angie, in their flat in Haddon Hall, Beckenham. This bohemian environment would become the creative nursery for Bowie's career. The flat was very large, and there were wide landings, silver-painted ceilings and huge stained-glass windows. Ronson auditioned there for Bowie and his producer, Tony Visconti.

'We thought he was just a cool, silent type,' Visconti said. 'Later we found out that our apartment was very "big time" for him, and he was simply overwhelmed.' A terraced house in Hull it was not.

But Ronson's playing was brilliant, and the two men looked at each other and silently mouthed 'Wow.'

A couple of nights later, Mick was playing guitar for Bowie's session with John Peel on Radio 1. Ronson stood to Bowie's left, so he could watch his hands in order to figure out what to play. Bowie noted Mick's improvisatory abilities. He was rawer live than on record, playing the slashing lines from his Les Paul that would command attention on songs such as 'Jean Genie'.

'Are you going to be doing gigs with this band?' Peel asked.

'Yes, we're going to aren't we, Michael?' Bowie replied, laughter in his voice. 'Michael doesn't really know. He's just come down from Hull and I met him for the first time about two days ago.'

Ronson becomes Ronno, and a band called the Hype is formed. Visconti is a member of these proto-Spiders, and Ronno is dressed up as a gangster. Visconti teaches Ronson to score music properly, a skill that will enable him to arrange and write string parts – as he did for 'Life on Mars'.

Bowie releases *The Man Who Sold the World* to some acclaim in 1970, but it isn't until *Hunky Dory* at the end of the following year that things kick into gear. By now, Ronno's fellow Yorkshiremen have joined the band – Mick Woodmansey, or

Woody, on drums, and Trevor Bolder on bass. 'The lads from Hull,' as pianist Rick Wakeman would call them. They all live at Haddon Hall, kipping on the landings, immersed in the sleepy but upbeat creativity of the London suburb, with its art events and music clubs.

The project that would take Bowie into the big leagues begins to take shape: *Ziggy Stardust and the Spiders from Mars*. Bowie develops his persona, and Mick rocks him up, giving him an electric guitar and the band a 'heavier, more electric' sound. Ronson had joined Bowie at the embryonic stage, and this is the form that will propel him into stardom. Angie dresses the band in *Star Trek*-inspired boots, women's clothing and – gulp – make-up.

The gap between Bowie's myth-making and Ronson's bubble-popping begins to emerge. Bowie would claim that the Hull lads hated the make-up until the girls went wild for them. Ronson recalled hard women in rough pubs, wanting to attack them with their stiletto heels.

Nevertheless, Ronson liked the freedom the stage garb gave him: 'Just after *Hunky Dory* and before *Ziggy* there was a lull in the scene – it needed jarring and excitement. Bowie's dressing us up and the make-up was needed. It wasn't what I usually did but it was exciting. On stage I became someone else. I'd been very shy and nervous as a kid, but in costume I became another person, detached.'

The infamous guitar-fellatio performance takes place at Oxford Town Hall. Mick Rock photographs it, and a page is purchased in *Melody Maker* to promote this transgressive moment. Mick Ronson struggles with the homosexual over-tones, but not because he's homophobic, he's just a bit private.

Plus, he'd been raised as a Mormon and had been practising until adulthood.

'Personally, it was a bit of a shock, but Bowie manipulated the media again and again.'

And David's provocations cause problems back home. On the school bus, kids bully his beloved sister: 'That's your brother, that poof drummer.' They can't even get the instrument right. Paint is thrown over the white Mini that Mick has bought his parents.

No matter, history is being made. Bowie and Mick get on. Bowie likes Ronno's northern humour and dependability. 'Mick was a self-contained man. He didn't seem to need much to keep him going. His cigarettes, his guitar and a sturdy pair of shoes and he was ready to go. A less needy person you couldn't find.'

In the documentary *Beside Bowie: The Mick Ronson Story*, Cherry Vanilla, the Warhol acolyte and Bowie publicist, says that Ronno's innocent boy from Hull was a guise, too. Perhaps we all have them. Either way, the contrast with brash, energetic Angie and the dreaming, ambitious Bowie somehow works.

Ronson had a strong style, and the people that worked with him refer constantly to his 'tone'. He achieved this by setting a wah-wah pedal halfway open, to get what he called a 'honking, very middle' tone. The rest was classic blues rock – riffs that could have come from Muddy Waters or John Lee Hooker.

'One thing he adored doing was building up layered tracks,' Bowie said, 'so that there'd be a great wedge of sound in certain areas of songs, and from there he could fly off into his sinewy lines and riffs in a heartbeat.'

★　　★　　★

Ziggy is released in summer 1972. It peaks at number five in the UK and a lowly seventy-five in the US. Bowie decides he wants to crack America, and Ronno is along for the ride.

First port of call is producing Lou Reed's *Transformer*. Ronno loves the experience, and Angie and Rick Wakeman both claim that he did the actual work – arranging the music and manning the boards.

No-nonsense Hull comes up against the towering pretension of New York art music.

'I could very rarely understand a word he said,' Lou Reed said. 'He'd have to repeat things five times.'

'Lou used to say some funny things like: "Can you make it a little more *grey*?" Ronson said. 'I guess he was just trying to explain things in a more artistic way, y'know. It was going over my head a bit.'

'*Transformer* is easily my best-produced album,' Reed said. 'That has a lot to do with Mick Ronson. His influence was stronger than David's, but together, as a team, they're terrific.'

With *Transformer* in the can, it's time for Bowie to take America. A new manager – the clever, driven Tony Defries – is brought on board. In an echo of the Beatles' Apple Corps, he sets up a new business, MainMan, which employs all the freaks and alternative types in his and Bowie's orbit.

The US *Ziggy* tour makes a splash. Both David and Ronno see their duo in terms of the great rock archetypes: Mick and Keith, Daltrey and Townshend, Lennon–McCartney.

'He was very much a salt-of-the-earth type,' Bowie said. 'The blunt northerner with a defiantly masculine personality, so what you got was the old-fashioned yin and yang thing. As a rock duo I thought we were as good as Mick and Keith.'

But David, as ever, is giving a performance, deconstructing and playing with 'the rock band'. It's not something that – as an artist – he'll want to do for ever.

For now, the chemistry works. 'I'm like a bricklayer,' Ronson said, insightfully. 'I think I was more like a man, and he was more like a woman, y'know?'

'He was brilliant at divining what I meant when I'd describe in words what I wanted,' Bowie said.

Defries understands that the music industry is smoke and mirrors. He sends images back to the UK from the US tour, and the impression of stardom is created. Mick translates the vision into reality, directing musicians and arranging.

As so often, the fall when it comes is down to money. Mick has auditioned and recruited a pianist, Mike Garson, bringing him into the fold and advising him to 'make yourself indispensable. That's what David likes. Don't just be a session man.'

Garson mistakes Defries's high-rolling smoke and mirrors for reality. He innocently lets slip to Mick Woodmansey what he's being paid: $800 a week. Woody's face goes white. He and the other Spiders are on thirty quid.

They go to Defries, who tells David they're being difficult. Then they go to a lawyer – and that's full-scale treason. It could all have been resolved with a quick, overdue pay review. All that work, and not even a percentage point for Mick. Not even a half.

Defries and David calm Mick by telling him that after the tour he'll become the next MainMan solo artist. They'll kill Ziggy off at the Hammersmith Odeon.

It's all smoke and mirrors. Mick Ronson is in on the Spiders' doom. Trevor, Woody and much of the crew are not. Bowie had staged his great rock 'n' roll act, and now he was staging its demise – a key part of a band's life cycle. Everything takes place behind a layer of performance and artifice.

The Spiders only lived for eighteen months.

'The Spiders from Mars got me the kind of fame that I had in the early '70s,' Bowie graciously said later, 'and the lead guitarist in that band was Mick Ronson.'

Ronson is still working with Bowie in 1973 for *Aladdin Sane*, which is like a more American *Ziggy*. He's still there for the light-hearted *Pin Ups* later in the year. While they work on this, he gets together with his future wife, the Bowie camp's hairdresser Suzi. And then it's his turn as a solo artist.

'The criticism was it was like a Bowie concert without David,' Suzi said, years later.

Ronson's nerve failed him. 'He's not really a frontman,' Tony Zanetta, the MainMan president and sometime Bowie tour manager, said.

The cruel truth is that this solo outing exposed exactly how much David relied on Mick (finally, not so much) and how much Mick relied on David (a lot).

Mick begins drinking heavily. David and Defries are eyeing up their next *grand projet*: *Diamond Dogs*. Initially conceived as a musical adaptation of Orwell's *Nineteen Eighty-Four*, it morphs into an apocalyptic vision inspired by William Burroughs. Bowie and Defries consider everyone replaceable, and they now replace Ronson with Earl Slick, an American with a Keith Richards look.

If the sacking of the Spiders was in part artifice, the sacking of Ronson was all too real.

Diamond Dogs is *Ziggy* on steroids: big, ambitious, expensive and made in New York. Bowie is now on cocaine, and dealing with him is difficult. The relationship with Defries – so intense that he and Bowie speak for hours every day – burns out, and he too is sacked.

Earl Slick, who loves Ronson's style – 'melodic and ferocious at the same time' – credits Mick as having produced several of the songs. But David, and thus history, does not.

Mick and David make a final appearance together in October 1973, for NBC's *Midnight Special*. After each song, David pats Mick tenderly on the back, perhaps because he knew what was coming. After the show, Mick is out.

Ronson is in demand after his Bowie years, but it's never quite the same. He joins Mott the Hoople, whose 'All the Young Dudes' he'd produced and arranged. But Mick wants a limo, and the band are riding around in Transits. He becomes firm friends with singer Ian Hunter, though, and the pair decide to work on the latter's solo album together.

Mick might like limos, but his lack of financial acuity begins to catch up with him. He and Suzi are living in Hyde Park Gate like rock stars, but there's no money.

'Mick was a school gardener,' says Suzi. 'I was a hairdresser from Beckenham. We had no clue about royalties, or how much money was around.'

They begin to live hand to mouth. There are hints of trouble – Suzi refers to 'ups and downs' – and there are frequent references to heavy drinking. The ups and downs included infidelity, because Ronson fathered a son with another woman in 1990.

But there are highlights still to come: a spell with Bob Dylan, who recruits a drunk Ronson for his *Rolling Thunder Revue* tour in 1975.[1] Ronno produces the evergreen smash 'Jack & Diane' for John Mellencamp – you can hear the influence of Mick's guitar style. Glen Matlock (see Chapter 16) is thrilled to hear Ronno on the end of the phone one day, agreeing to produce his pre-Pistols band, Rich Kids.

'You only get one chance,' Ronson tells him. Matlock, recounting this, appears wistful, as if he wishes he'd listened.

In 1976, Ronno and David trade barbs publicly.

'David needs someone around him to say: "Fuck off, you're stupid,"' Mick said. 'He needs one person who won't bow to him."

'I've got God,' Bowie replies. 'Who's Mick got?'[2]

Mick is plagued by a sort of chipper guilelessness. He lets Tina Turner slip through his fingers, and almost does the same with Morrissey when he says can't meet the ex-Smiths star because 'I'm babysitting for me sister.'

In the end, he takes the job of producing Morrissey's *Your Arsenal* in 1992 – 'the last big cheque he got', according to Suzi.

---

1 Amusingly, Ronson had never liked Dylan, and thought he sounded like 'Yogi Bear'.

2 Of course, for all this bombast, David Bowie did need other people to make his music. As David Hepworth told me: 'Throughout his career, absolutely without fail, he depended on a right-hand man. Eno, Robert Fripp, Mick Ronson, Nile Rodgers – he never had any success other than with somebody else. And very often the other person was the one who could make what he did make sense. And Ronson was clearly hugely important to him. He's the person who gave shape to those records, and who made them commercial. Because, prior to *Ziggy Stardust*, he'd not been commercial at all really. 'Space Oddity' apart, which is kind of a one off. And then suddenly with *Ziggy Stardust* it was mainstream, meat and potatoes rock 'n' roll, underneath it all . . . He always wanted to be in a group, David Bowie. That's why he formed Tin Machine, for God's sake.'

'He was northern and glamorous,' Morrissey said. 'He asked me what kind of LP I wanted to make, and I said, "One people would want to listen to for a very long time," and he said, "Oh, all right then," as if I'd asked him to put the cat out.'

The parallels between Bowie and Morrissey are evident: both ruthless, ambitious, vain. Both made darkly romantic music that vaulted from the everyday to the elemental. One is a gay man, the other played at being one. Both fell out with an iconic guitarist.[3]

Despite Bowie's ill-judged comments about dictators at the peak of his drug use, one can't imagine him exploring the limits of free speaking as Morrissey has latterly done. But Bowie must have been a huge influence on Morrissey. When he enlisted Ronson for *Your Arsenal*, perhaps he was delighting in the chance to steal his hero's 'Jeff Beck'.

For these reasons, his views on Ronson are fascinating. In 2017, he spoke to Max Bell at *Classic Rock* about Mick. Whatever one thinks about Morrissey, he gives a great interview.

'Everyone who worked with Mick expresses devotional love for him, whereas people who worked with Bowie express admiration,' he told Bell. Mick had told him that 'he alone wrote the main guitar hooks for "Starman", "The Man Who Sold The World" and others – not just hooks, really, but grand choruses in themselves – but a share of publishing wasn't ever on offer for him.'

Morrissey went on to point out that Ronson was remarkably overlooked: 'Has Mick ever been on the cover of a major British

3 As a sidenote, there's a direct line from Bowie through the Smiths to Suede. Suede were often compared to the Smiths, though preferred to use Bowie as a reference (including in the anonymous ad in *NME* they placed when looking for a guitarist to replace Bernard Butler). Brett Anderson was another frontman who wrote yearning, darkly romantic songs, played with being gay as a marketing ploy, and fell out with his brilliant guitarist.

music magazine? Even when he died?' Mick was 'extremely humble. He was just happy to be there.'

There was a moment that, for Morrissey, said everything about Ronson's relationship with Bowie.

'There's a late clip on YouTube of Mick and Bowie discussing my song "I Know It's Gonna Happen Someday". The song ends very similarly to Bowie's "Rock 'n' Roll Suicide". This part was added on to my song by Mick, who said: "Don't worry, Bowie can't sue – because I wrote it in the first place."'

[However, in the YouTube clip, Ronson tells Bowie that the coda was already on the song before he started working on it.] 'The clip shows Mick to be not exactly afraid of Bowie, but overwhelmed by him.' For Morrisey, this seemed to reveal that Mick was unable to ask Bowie for what was due to him, because the risk of falling out might mean he'd 'miss his legacy.'

'I had met Bowie many, many times,' Morrissey continued, 'and the obvious conclusion to me was that he was an unashamedly ruthless person. Mick did not have that ruthlessness, which is why he is buried in Hull.'

What stands out for me is that, during the period Morrissey and Ronson recorded *Your Arsenal,* Bowie was writing to Ronson regularly: 'soldier-like letters,' Morrissey said of their frequency.

'One day at breakfast I asked Mick why Bowie wrote so often, and he said: 'He keeps asking me what you're like in the studio,' and then he exploded with laughter. I have no idea why this was so hilarious.[4] I think Bowie had interest in Mick only as much as it was in his nature to like anyone.'

---

4 It's wild speculation of course, but I wonder if Bowie had made a lewd or sexualised joke or comment of some kind.

When *Your Arsenal* was finished, Ronson yet again showed no interest in getting a valuable credit.

'This was Mick's unaffected Cinderella aspect,' Morrissey said, 'which I later saw in Jeff Beck when I worked with him on my *Years Of Refusal* album. Jeff and Mick were identical in the way that they would quietly pick up their guitars without fanfare, and they'd plug into the desk and a tingling earthquake would erupt without any discourse. And they both made their guitars sound like grand pianos.'

I think perhaps Bowie wasn't quite as cold and ruthless as he's sometimes made out to be, including by Morrissey. To my ear, there's a touch of jealousy colouring those words. Bowie having written so many letters might show a competitive interest in what Morrissey was up to, but it also suggests considerable warmth.

By the time of *Your Arsenal*, it was close to the end for Ronson. In the early nineties he'd begun to lose weight and to look ill. He was diagnosed with liver cancer in 1991, the year before he produced Morrissey's album.

His sister recalled driving him to the hospital, gripped in horror because she already knew the diagnosis he was about to receive. But Mick took it in his usual no-nonsense style.

'Typical Mick,' Ian Hunter remembered. 'Rang me up out of the blue. "'Ere, I've got cancer. Yeah, and it's inoperable."'

Ronson seems to have treated the diagnosis with the same unique blend of the down to earth and otherworldly with which he did everything else. He had one course of chemotherapy, and then resorted to alternative treatments.

'He tried various holistic therapies,' said Dana Gillespie, the singer and actress who'd known Bowie and Mick since the

Haddon Hall days. 'I gave him juiced carrots and vegetables. He was getting extremely thin.'

At the end of his life, Bowie ushered Ronno back in. They made the song 'I Feel Free' from Bowie's *Black Tie White Noise* together. And then came the crowning valediction: a performance with Bowie, Ian Hunter, Joe Elliott of Def Leppard and the remaining members of Queen at the Freddie Mercury Tribute Concert.

Mick came out and played guitar on 'Heroes', a song he 'should've always played on', according to Joe Elliott.[5]

He looked good on stage, despite the illness. His crisp white shirt rippled in the breeze, his hair was still blond, and his face looked sculpted, rather than gaunt. He appeared intent on what he was doing, lost in the music before a vast sea of fans.

A year later, in 1993, Mick Ronson would spend his last hours alive with Ian Hunter, Suzi and his sister Maggi at Tony Defries's house in Hasker Street, London.

When he died, at only forty-six, Ian Hunter was downstairs making tea. He refers to those final moments in his elegy for Ronson, 'Michael Picasso'. 'You turned into a ghost', he sings, lamenting the time spent sitting around in Hasker Street, pretending with Mick that there'd be a future.

Ultimately, Ronson was a huge talent, but one that needed to be harnessed to another in order to blossom. He was a workman, always in need of a project. He had none of the oceanic drive that it takes to get to the very top, to be a David Bowie.

---

5 Elliott is a Ronno partisan, and I think it's safe to say that 'Heroes' couldn't have existed with the guitar style that Robert Fripp brought to it.

'David pushed me forward,' he said. 'That was his thing. He made stuff happen.'

Those final four words sum it up perfectly. If there's one, defining characteristic in the musicians who succeed, it's that: they make things happen.

Mick Ronson could do it in the studio, but David Bowie knew not only how to write great songs, but to make an impact on the world itself.

But to do so – for a time at least – he needed Mick Ronson by his side.

Thank you, but we've got what we needed from you.

Anton Newcombe,
the Brian Jonestown Massacre

I never got paid for all the years I got fucked in the ass by
you, so why the fuck would I get paid now? – Jeff Davies

I t's all there in glorious celluloid, in the film *Dig!*.
    Anton Newcombe – messiah, addict, genius? I've never
been completely taken by the Brian Jonestown Massacre's
unashamedly retro garage/psyche rock, but the film does show
moments of greatness as well as madness – and a lot of embarrassing, youthful stupidity. *Dig!* captures the near rise and rapid
fall of the BJM, and their toxic friendship/rivalry with the band
they inspired, the Dandy Warhols.

Anton Newcombe is one of several bandleaders who rejected
or alienated so many bandmates that they found themselves
alone. The list of former members of the Brian Jonestown
Massacre is the stuff of underground legend. Wikipedia provides
a rundown of twenty, but this doesn't include Tony O'Neill
(see Chapter 18) or Billy Pleasant, a sometime drummer during
Tony's brief spell, and is contradicted on the same page by a
much longer 'comprehensive line up history'. Anton himself,
as part of statements made in a lawsuit over songwriting credits
filed by ex-guitarist Jeff Davies, claimed that the band has had

'a revolving cast of musicians over the years, numbering forty or more'.

Not all were sacked, of course. To Anton's dubious credit, most people to have departed the BJM seem to have been driven to quit, rather than fired. Some, such as Peter Hayes of Black Rebel Motorcycle Club, even benefitted from the experience. Escaping the often-monstrous BJM could be an eminently sensible move. Take Matthew Tow, for example, aka 'the Aussie'. A huge BJM fan, he contacted Anton via email and joined the band in 2003. He only lasted for one tour. 'I don't think the Aussie was freaked out by playing in Jonestown so much as he was freaked out by America . . . Well, maybe more like America's reaction to a Jonestown tour,' said BJM drummer Daniel Allaire (who himself left the band in 2018).

Even the BJM's tambourine/maracas player and jester, Joel Gion (who achieved something approaching an iconic status after *Dig!*), quit for a spell in the early noughties.

Nevertheless, Anton Newcombe sacked many musicians – sometimes after berating or even beating them on stage. There was Matt Hollywood, an original member and songwriter for the band, and the closest thing to a second creative force within it. Despite the onstage fighting and endless fall outs, he re-joined in 2009 and put in another six-year stint. When a twenty-fifth anniversary tour was announced in 2015, though, he wasn't included. Topically for the period, Hollywood tweeted that: 'At least The Donald has the balls to tell people when they're fired.'

Then there's the suitably gruesome massacre of members on Halloween 1994. Bassist Chris Dupré had already started to get on Anton's nerves: 'The reason I was kicked out was that I had a hard time playing simplistic drone two/three-chord songs, as I thought I was hot shit and wanted to play jazz,' he said.

According to Jesse Valencia's book about the BJM, *Keep Music Evil,* that Halloween at Slim's in San Francisco, Dupré was 'high on dope and started jumping around the stage, trying to get under Anton's skin'. He and Milo Warner Martin, the drummer, began goofing around together.

'Chris and the boys were being all heavy metal,' Milo recalled, and pulling faces like members of KISS. 'We get a great reception, leave the stage, and as soon as we get backstage, Anton announces the whole band is fired.'

Perhaps the most infamous firing took place during the band's first industry showcase at the Viper Room in LA in 1996. Jeff Davies wasn't playing guitar that night, so Robert Desmond stood in. In *Dig!* we see Anton kick Desmond in the leg, and then stop the band mid song to correct him. An argument breaks out, and Anton tells the crowd: 'Hey fuck that! No one's gonna say "fuck you" to me on my stage with my band! Fuck you, get off my stage!'

When Joel Gion begins kicking cables, Anton turns on him, threatening to have the bouncers beat him up, then tells him to leave too before punching and kicking him.

At this stage, the doomed Robert Desmond steps forward, points at Anton and valiantly shouts: 'STAND THE FUCK BACK MOTHERFUCKER!' Anton jumps him, and all hell breaks loose.

'This guy wasn't long for the Brian Jonestown Massacre,' drawls the Dandy Warhols' Courtney Taylor-Taylor, who narrated *Dig!*.[1]

1 'Poor Robert,' Joel said afterwards. 'He tried so hard. He was going to come in and help Anton. Be the right-hand man and organise everything.' 'At this point in my life,' Desmond said, 'I was hoping for nothing more than to finally get with a band that could make it big.'

Needless to say, the showcase did not result in the band getting signed.

Among these incidents, Newcombe is responsible for a perfect example of a rejection of taste. This is captured by Tony O'Neill in *Digging the Vein*, when Atom, the Anton character, recruits the narrator to play keys. The narrator says:

'You've got a keyboard player.'[2]
  'Not anymore. I had to let him go.'
  'Why?'
  'You know *Odessey and Oracle*? Like, The Zombies album?'
  'Yeah.'
  'He said the production on it was "faggy." That was the word he used – *faggy*." Atom shook his head . . .

It's all there in the film. The meltdowns live on stage, the blood on the hippie shirt and the broken sitar. Newcombe believed he was the chosen one, born to change music and the music industry. If you couldn't get with the programme – or be on the right drugs – you couldn't be in the band. In the middle stages of his descent, he began wearing 'Jesus robes' and making his followers wear white.

'I am here to destroy this fucked up system,' Anton says to the camera at the beginning of *Dig!*. 'I said: "let it be me." I said: "use my hands I will use our strength." Let's fucking burn it to the ground.'

You have to laugh at Anton and his cohort for this immature certainty. The scenes in which he rants about his holy mission

2 This is pure speculation, but given the timeline the musician in question might have been Christof Certik.

or gets into spats with jealous, humourless, long-suffering side-kick, Matt Hollywood, are quite simply childish.[3] But there is a real darkness in Anton, and a fevered obsession that plays out on the screen. He starts out relatively healthy looking, and by the end is gaunt, haunted, addicted. At a comeback gig at the Troubadour in LA, his 'genius' guitarist Jeff Davies throws down his guitar and storms off in disgust.

'Atom was a funny storyteller, and charismatic,' Tony O'Neill says of Anton's fictional counterpart. 'But there was an under-tone of malevolence that I found appealing and unsettling at the same time.'

When Anton's mother and father are interviewed, it's clear that his troubles – with substances, authority, mental health – are real and long term. His father, Robert, admits that he was an alcoholic, experiencing symptoms of schizophrenia, and left the family when Anton was one. His mother tells the camera that Anton was arrested 'fifty times' for breaking the Newport Beach curfew. Eventually, she refused to pick him up from jail, and he was sent to the adolescent unit.

We have the impression that his father has recovered. He refers to drinking in the past tense, looks tanned and has a neatly trimmed moustache. Nevertheless, there's a haunted look in his eyes. He laughs awkwardly at the title of the BJM album Anton had given him a copy of: *Thank God for Mental Illness*. This frame of Robert Newcombe – laughing in the California sun

---

3 On the *Tour Punisher* podcast, former BJM bassist Collin Hegna related a conversation with Hollywood in which, before joining, he asked what working with the band was like: 'Well, let's see. Anton's tried to stab me twice, he threw a flaming hot griddle with grease at me once and burned my face with it, and I've quit four times. So, what does that tell you?' Hollywood said.

– freezes, fades to black and white. A caption tells us he took his own life on Anton's next birthday.

Dig! also captures the parallel foolishness of the music business. After spurning/blowing their chances with a handful of major labels, the BJM were signed by TVT, which was once the US's largest indie label. A young A & R, Adam Shore, features in the documentary.[4] He grins in the back of a cab, casually reclined in the seat, listing their major label competition: 'Elektra and Sire and Capitol . . . I'm like, what's their problem? Within three weeks we had a deal. It's so easy. Why is everyone so scared? What's the problem?'

'Is this your first signing?' the camerawoman asks as he enters a building.

'Er, yes . . .' he says, still grinning, and not quite ironic. 'A & R, it's very easy, everyone should try it.'

Watching this, I winced inwardly in recognition.

The major labels in the film had backed off when they saw the BJM implode at various live shows. Perhaps some of them were more seasoned and could see what was likely to happen. Or perhaps they'd simply heard it all before.

Despite having signed the Dandy Warhols, it's Perry Watts-Russell of Capitol Records who talks the most sense in the film. He speaks of the Dandy Warhols having 'created a world of their own',[5] and the one-in-ten major label success rate.

Taylor-Taylor, the Dandy Warhols' singer, recounts a conversation with Watts-Russell.

---

4 I encountered Adam Shore myself, years later. He was more serious than he appears in *Dig!*, the music industry presumably having knocked him about a bit, as it tends to do. He was working for Red Bull, programming live events, and wanted to help get Wiley out to the US.
5 This is what we in the music industry really look for in an artist: the creation of an original world for a fan to escape into.

'I told him "I sneeze and hits come out,"' Taylor-Taylor says, 'to which Perry said: "Well then, if that's the case I'm sure that Capitol will have no problem finding the funds to finance your handkerchiefs."'

Perry-Watts provides a brutal appraisal of music industry dynamics: 'The odds are that the Dandy Warhols, like everybody else, will fail.'

As we move through our cast of characters, it's becoming clear to me that the rejects often break the trail for the bands that follow. They blaze brightly, create a vacuum around themselves, draw in attention and admirers, and then, their purpose fulfilled, they burn out. More calculating, professional musicians adopt their style and retool it for the mainstream. Perhaps Anton sensed this from the outset, because it's contained in the name of his band – it happened to Brian Jones via Mick and Keith.

'Anton created this kind of scene, and everyone else has built upon it,' says Adam Shore in *Dig!*.

'They continue to inspire us,' says Peter Holmström of the Dandy Warhols, towards the end of the film. 'They'll be remembered for ever. And who knows, we might just be forgotten.'

Way back then, he didn't quite seem to believe that this would happen.

31

Kim Shattuck, Pixies

The Pixies don't do that.
— Richard Jones, Pixies' manager

Often it boils down to aesthetics. After all, each member must serve the look of the band. And as we saw in the case of Jason Everman (see Chapter 12), one member who looks as though they're in a different type of group entirely can be disastrous.

In 2013, Pixies' brilliant, mercurial bass player and vocalist Kim Deal finally quit the reunited band. Kim Shattuck was hired as her replacement — a dream job for someone who'd previously played in minor LA punk bands the Pandoras and the Muffs. Joining a legendary — and legendarily difficult — band like Pixies can't have been easy. When they first disbanded in 1993, Francis Black, the group's leader, famously told guitarist Joey Santiago of his decision on the phone — then he sent faxes to the group's rhythm section.

The Pixies had always epitomised alternative cool — ironic, arch, detached. On tour in 2014, it seemed Kim Shattuck hadn't got the memo. Playing a show at the Mayan Theater in LA, perhaps excited to be in her hometown, she decided to perform a stage dive.

'I know they weren't thrilled about that,' she told *NME*. 'When I got offstage, the manager told me not to do it again. I said, 'really, for my own safety?' And he said, 'no, because the Pixies don't do that.''

Shortly afterwards, she was fired.

32

Ross Valory and Steve Smith, Journey

*They drove a dagger between band members . . . placed their
own greed before the interests of the band, jeopardizing the
future of Journey.* – Neal Schon and Jonathan Cain

B eware bad advice – and pity the poor rhythm section.
In the spring of 2020, an attempted coup took place
within the ranks of soft-rock titans Journey. Ross Valory (bass)
and Steve Smith (drums) launched a boardroom takeover to try
and gain control of Nightmare Productions, a business entity
they believed owned the rights to Journey's name and logo. The
pair didn't have much in the way of writing credits and resulting
publishing royalties, and perhaps they had their retirement in
mind, or simply a rebalancing of the group's finances. Either
way, they seemed to think that through a quick, clever board
vote, they could take full control of the band.

They were wrong.

Bandleader and guitarist Neal Schon and keyboardist Jonathan
Cain instantly fired their two long-term bandmates. Valory was
a founding member, and Smith had been part of the key line up
from 1978 onwards. (As we'll see, Smith and Valory had actually
been fired once before, in 1985, for 'creative differences'. They
re-joined the group ten years later.)

Schon and Cain's lawyers accused them of launching an 'ill-conceived corporate coup d'état', and wanting to 'hold the Journey name hostage'. They sued the hapless rhythm section for $10 million, and accused them of 'destroying the chemistry, cohesion and rapport necessary for the band to play together'.

The whole thing rapidly turned into the usual flurry of suits and countersuits in the time-honoured American style. Valory sought 'past and future compensatory damages' based on 'emotional distress'.

A year later, in April 2021, the debacle was settled out of court.

Journey's sometime management, Q Prime,[1] announced that everyone had 'resolved their differences and reached an amicable settlement. Neal Schon and Jonathan Cain acknowledge the valuable contributions that both Ross Valory and Steve Smith have made to the music and the legacy of Journey.'

Journey was no stranger to line-up changes – they'd lost their iconic singer, Steve Perry, for one thing. If that hadn't killed them, nothing would – least of all a lowly rhythm section. Journey had long since become a brand as much as a band, so the arena-rock colossus simply thundered on.

Nice one, lads.

But perhaps the story really starts with the exit of Perry. He joined Journey in 1977, when they were a progressive rock

---

1 Q Prime is a powerful US management company. One of the 'smaller' artists it once represented was Mark Lanegan, although they almost dropped him when they caught him shooting up Courtney Love – a bigger client at the time. As with almost everyone else who works with the band, Journey's Q Prime manager was later sacked.

outfit. He quickly brought about a change in sound, overcoming initial resistance from fellow members and fans to take the band in a poppier direction.[2]

And so began Journey's 1980s heyday, which resulted in towering, perennial hits including 'Anyway You Want It' and 'Don't Stop Believin''. In the second half of that decade, perhaps high on his own success, Steve Perry took over production duties, and decided to further modernise the Journey sound for *Raised on Radio*, the band's ninth album.

When Ross Valory and Steve Smith pushed back, Perry was the leading figure in having them sacked (for the first time). Perhaps this was where some of the real poison entered the Journey bloodstream. Certainly, relations had become so bad after *Raised on Radio* that Perry told Neal Schon and Jonathan Cain that he wanted a break from the band. As a result, Journey went on hiatus from 1987 until 1995.

According to Journey's Wikipedia page, and an article by industry veteran Paul Rappaport on his *Classics du Jour* site, Perry had a condition for coming back. In order to re-join the band for 1996's *Trial by Fire*, he now demanded that Journey's manager, Herbie Herbert, be fired. This duly happened, and he was replaced by management giant Irving Azoff. The poison apparently drained, Smith and Valory re-joined too, and Journey was back in business. *Trial by Fire* reached a more than respectable number three on the *Billboard* chart.

The problems came when it was time to tour. While on (another) break, hiking in Hawaii, Perry experienced pain in his

---

2 Early drummer Aynsley Dunbar resisted the changes, and was sacked and replaced by Steve Smith.

hip and discovered he had a degenerative bone condition. He'd need a hip replacement if he was to go out on the road.

At this stage, Perry must have thought he was indispensable, but he'd underestimated the ruthlessness of Neal Schon and Jonathan Cain. From their perspective, he'd delayed taking action on his hip for two years or giving Journey a decision on touring. According to an interview Perry gave to Melodicrock. com's Mitch Lafon in 2005, Schon and Cain issued an ultimatum: get the hip replaced, or we'll replace you.

Steve Perry announced he was leaving, and this time it was for good. Steve Smith followed suit, and Journey spent the next nine years undergoing more line-up changes and searching for a permanent vocalist. In 2007, Neal Schon found a Filipino covers singer called Arnel Pineda on YouTube and recruited him for the band.

For Perry's part, he became something of a recluse after 1997, and his story has become an intriguing mystery for Journey fans. In 2001, during an episode of VH1's *Behind the Music*, he claimed that he 'never really felt like part of the band'.[3] At first this seems unlikely, given the almost total control he had at that stage. But perhaps that explains it. Perhaps he always sat slightly outside or above Journey. Maybe that's what gave him the perspective on where the band should be going. Indeed, perhaps the visionary bandleader never truly feels part of the group.

If Perry had left the band, he hadn't given up all control. He appears to have signed a fruitful exit agreement to handle his

3 Ex-manager Herbie Herbert quipped in response: 'That's like the pope saying he never really felt Catholic.'

royalties and rights from his Journey work, which also gave him a place on the board of Nightmare Productions. Interestingly, he voted with Smith and Valory in their failed takeover bid. Given he'd left the band almost a quarter of a century earlier, perhaps he'd had time to reflect, and wanted to atone for his treatment of the rhythm section back in 1987. Or perhaps his resentment of Neal Schon and Jonathan Cain was the real motivation. Either way, it was a signal that, far from being drained, the poison had only spread further into the Journey bloodstream.

It seems that having fired Smith and Valory, Schon and Cain had no one left to turn on but each other. In 2022, Journey undertook a vast arena tour. Apparently suspicious (or paranoid), Neal Schon is said to have hired two off-duty police officers to guard his dressing room. *Consequence of Sound* reported that he and his wife then allegedly dispatched an assistant to go and snoop on Cain's own backstage quarters. The assistant proved ill-suited to subterfuge and was discovered. Cain hired his own guard, and arguments then broke out over whose security took precedence.

All this on a tour that had reputedly grossed $31.9 million. During the shows, Cain and Schon appeared to remain at least twenty feet apart at all times.

Schon was apparently livid that Cain had made an appearance at Donald Trump's Mar-a-Lago, playing 'Don't Stop Believin'' for a singalong. Cain is married to Paula White-Cain, Trump's 'spiritual advisor'. Schon issued a cease-and-desist order, and Cain blasted his bandmate in the press, saying he'd watched Schon 'damage the brand for years'.

The calamitous, not-so-behind the scenes fall outs saw the band's bank give up on them, and even their website cease functioning.

In an increasingly clownish atmosphere, Schon's wife, Michaele, seems to have become a prominent figure. Previously best known for gate-crashing an Obama dinner with her former husband, Tareq Salahi, Michaele is a sometime *Real Housewives of DC* cast member and long-term Journey superfan. During the collapse of her previous marriage, Neal Schon allegedly called Salahi and said: 'This is Neal. I am fucking your wife.' Neal and Michaele were later married in a pay-per-view ceremony that cost viewers $14.95.

More recently, *Billboard* reported that Schon was suing Cain for 'improperly' refusing him access to a corporate American Express card. Cain's response accused Schon of 'completely out of control spending' on personal expenses. According to unnamed industry sources 'who have worked with the band over the years,' Schon appears increasingly obsessed with controlling the band.

Billboard's industry sources are quoted saying that the actual conflict isn't Schon vs Cain, but rather Schon vs everyone. 'He's just an impossible human being,' said one such source. 'Jonathan, he's a good guy: "I wrote 'Don't Stop Believin'' and I'm blessed." Neal's just: "I'm a superstar."'

When Schon fired the band's team and he and Cain became their own managers, Cain reportedly gave a proportion of the resulting fees to Arnel Pineda.

Conversely, when the band performed a tribute to Aretha Franklin and were lauded by a journalist, Jay Cridlin, Neal Schon reportedly emailed Cridlin directly to tell him that it had been his idea alone and to change the article accordingly.

When Journey undertook another big tour in 2023, Pineda used Twitter regularly. Among celebratory videos and pictures of the dates, he posted references to his bandmates: 'If some of them are tired of me being with them, with all means, they can fire me anytime . . . and don't lecture me about spiritual BS,' he said in one. In another, reacting to a headline which claimed: NEAL SCHON BELIEVES ARNEL PINEDA WOULD BE A 'NOBODY' WITHOUT JOURNEY, Pineda wrote: 'He may be right . . . like I said, if they're tired of this #nobody? I'm just a phone call away . . .'

All this, while the band was playing together nightly. Perhaps Schon had found a new victim for his ire after all?

It's exhausting just writing about all this, let alone living through it. Might the colossus soon fall to its knees after all?

Given that it's survived thus far, I somehow suspect not. Perhaps this is simply how Journey rolls.

33

Martyn Ware, the Human League

Interviewer: Could you work in the studio with Ware again?

Phil Oakey: Oh yeah, I could do that at some stage.

Interviewer: What would the collaboration be called?

Susan Ann Sulley (laughing): It wouldn't be the Human League!

Phil Oakey: It wouldn't be a Human League collaboration because he can't be part of the Human League again.

— From an interview in *Digital Spy*, 2011

Martyn Ware: I was completely devastated. I was blindsided. The equivalent would be walking down the street and being hit with a brick from behind. There was absolutely no indication whatsoever that anything like that could have possibly happened . . . It was my idea to invite Phil into the band because he was my best mate and obviously he went on to be very good, but just the simple idea that your best mate could betray you in that way was incomprehensible; it still is.

— From an interview in the *Yorkshire Post*, 2022

34

This is the End, My Friends

One Monday morning in September 2019, I received a horrifying email. I'd finished the novel I was to publish the following January, and my publisher had sent it out to various other writers in the hopes of securing jacket quotes. I had asked that a copy be sent to one of my favourite novelists, Michel Faber. Several of his books – *The Crimson Petal and the White*, *Under the Skin* and *The Book of Strange New Things* – have strong claims to be masterpieces.

In the last of those novels, a priest travels to a distant planet to teach Christianity to aliens. The man must leave his beloved wife behind. Life on earth is unravelling, terrifyingly. The aliens are hard to read, and the company that's arranging the colonising of their planet seems shadowy. Over the course of the novel, every single expectation raised by this premise is subverted, powerfully and brilliantly. It's one of the most moving novels I've ever read, and one in which an entire world is invented – the hardest thing for a writer to do.[1]

I didn't have much hope of Faber giving me a quote. He's a great novelist, I hadn't come across blurbs from him previously,

1 The aforementioned Will Ashon, coaching me along one day, once said something along the lines of: 'If you say "London" most readers are already there. If you say: "a distant planet" then you've got a lot of work on your hands.'

and I knew that he'd recently lost his wife. I believe *The Book of Strange New Things* is partly based on that experience. I'd exchanged emails with him when I'd asked if he might write a piece for a magazine that, in my role at Ninja Tune, I was commissioning for Bonobo's *Migration* album. Faber's agent had put us in touch, and he'd sent a friendly reply saying he was too busy, and that he preferred the more leftfield music on the label, but thanks for asking.

I was thus not expecting the email I saw – with a sharp, ominous thrill – drop into my inbox that Monday morning. A good lesson in life is not to read emails in bed – at least until you've had a coffee.

Faber had written a little over seventeen hundred words breaking down all the problems with the first fifty-odd pages that he'd read of my novel. I sat upright in bed as I began reading, sweat breaking out on my brow, my heart thumping in my chest. My wife was still asleep beside me.

Faber would not be able to provide a cover quote, he told me, because my prose was not up to scratch.

It's hard to describe how bad I was feeling at this point. A skin-crawling horror, a sense of everything collapsing, but also the warm, flushing sense of the truth being told, of something coming out into the open. Despite having achieved the thing I'd wanted most in the world – the publication of a novel – this was not a very happy time in my life. The novel was semi-autobiographical, and I was worried about the implications of this. It was no longer a private thing, growing and evolving on my hard drive and in my mind. It was set – literally typeset – and finished and going to be out there in the world. I'd left my job. LA in the age of Trump had become a fraught, fractious place. I had two young children and was permanently exhausted.

Even if fairly soon afterwards, I'd recover – this was only a novel, after all; it wasn't a cancer diagnosis or the news of a loved one's death – Faber's email gave me the sense of my world imploding.

There was one awful moment in particular, at which I could barely stand to read on. Some would-be writers, Faber told me, were simply never going to make it. Regardless of how much effort they put in, or how much help they sought. They would never rise above their essential lack of ability.

Oh God, I thought, looking away for a long moment.

Back on the screen, the verdict came down: this did not apply to me. I was in possession of the basics, Faber said, going on to list a handful of positives. He included one striking compliment that still glows like a bright coin in my gloomier writing moments.

Oh Christ, I thought. *Oh, thank fucking Christ I'm not going to die!* By this stage I was sweating freely.

But this was the only good news, and Faber was unflinchingly honest. I was still a novice when it came to the craft, he said, and I had a lot to learn.

There were problems in those first fifty pages – a great many of them. Faber went on to quote extensively, laying the issues out in excruciating detail.

'So basically,' my sister wrote, after I'd forwarded the email, 'a free tutorial from an author you really admire.'

Which, of course, it was. A day or so later I was reeling less in horror, and more in amazement and excitement that one of the artists I admired most in the world had taken the time to send me a seventeen-hundred-word letter about my novel.

If you're going to try and make art, and put yourself out there, then you need to learn to roll with the punches. There are really just two skills required: to be honest with yourself about whether you – or your project – is or could be really any good; and the ability to just keep on going.

Now back to the point. I replied to the email, and this began an exchange that took place over the subsequent few days. It was something in this correspondence that lingered in my mind while writing *The Rejects*.

I had told Faber of a question to which I often returned, namely: whether it's really worth writing books if the writer is not truly 'great'? This question, or feeling, would often arise on finishing a masterpiece: *Lolita*, *A Handful of Dust*, *The Book of Strange New Things*. If someone out there can do that, to say everything I'd like to say better than I ever could, then what's the point? (This feeling, by the way, should never be allowed to diminish the joy of the work that inspired it – it must never turn bitter.)

Faber – well known as a music obsessive – responded to this by relating writing to music. He made the point that there are certain high-profile writers who've become too big to be edited. Their egos won't allow any feedback, with the result being that they write bad books. Incidentally, this exact problem plagues the music industry. If you've heard an over-long or self-indulgent record by a famous artist, this explains why. Being edited – or A & R'd – is a privilege, because it makes the work better.

Faber said that he thought the best approach to writing was to regard the work as a machine or a piece of furniture. If the core premise was a good one, it should simply be a case of working hard on it until you couldn't see the joints, or the machine ran smoothly. Sometimes, he said, enlisting expert help from other people could be useful.

And he didn't believe in great writers, he believed in great works. He gave an illustrative example of how the 'great artist' theory distorts everything: In a year in which Bob Dylan puts out a bad album, and Loudon Wainwright a brilliant one, the critics still obsess over the former because of the major/ minor artist delusion.

In an ideal world, the critics would approach each work based purely on its merit.

In short, Faber said that an artist worrying about whether they were great or not was a waste of time. The focus should be on making the best work possible, in the hope that some of it would be of 'enduring value.'

This, I think, gets to the heart of what makes musical rejects worth looking at. Perhaps we shouldn't think of great bands, either. Rather, we should think of great projects, the fleeting moments when characters shuffle together like a deck of cards to produce something beautiful – a great work. Perhaps this allows us to perceive the important thing – the music – more clearly. The rejects allow us to see into the craft, to crack open the myth of the great band and peer into its inner workings.

I set out on this book with the naive view that the original line up of a band was usually the best, and that it was wrong to excise a person from it. Actually, examples where this is true are the exception. Only in Steven Adler's case did the band lose something they'd never recover. Other groups – the Supremes, the Rolling Stones – carried on even without the very person who created them. Looking at a band like

Fleetwood Mac smashes the idea that the 'original' line up really matters; it's the optimal one that counts – even the one optimal for a certain era or a certain album. Whatever personnel it takes to get the sound right, to make the greatest albums and play the best shows.

The truth strikes me as more interesting, and its own way more reassuring.

We, the audience, play a key role in the mythologising of bands. We put their posters on the wall and imagine them to be the best of friends, the sort of closeness we'd love to experience for ourselves. As David Hepworth said during our interview: 'There they all are, together. And it's like they've put your life back together for you.'

But the truth is in something else Hepworth told me – that the key decisions in the lives of hit records are 'very often made by people who are not the star', but 'just want it to be good'.

This is what explains why any artist – from Bob Dylan to Steven Spielberg – can make something great once, or even several times, but not every time. They need help, and very often the person who helps create the important thing, the work, will then be left behind.

This is what unites Danny Whitten, or Mick Ronson – musicians who enabled a big star to achieve their vision. Ronson saw himself as a 'bricklayer' – he wanted to bring that machine or piece of furniture, to which Faber refers, into existence.

Pete Best and Jason Everman might never have been destined to be in the bands they played with, but they still played crucial roles. Best and his mother drove the Beatles forward, booked shows, retrieved gear and provided a space for them to form and evolve. Everman funded a crucial tour and, perhaps more importantly, his spell in Nirvana freed Kurt up to become the frontman he needed to be in order to take his vision to the masses.

As much as the alchemy of groups, the randomness of chance meetings plays a role. This is reassuring because it means the possibilities are endless.

Some of our rejects are tragic. Some burn out too quickly, often having blazed a trail for the consolidators that follow. The Stones couldn't have existed without Brian Jones, but they didn't reach their creative peak until after he was gone. Wiley created a space for the new breed of British black music that followed in his wake and achieved greater commercial success.

These rejects are the mavericks and pioneers that the thrill of popular music depends on. They're transgressive and exciting. After they're gone, in the professionalisation that subsequently takes place, some of the magic is lost. These rejects are the price of music being visceral.

But in the best cases, there's plenty more life to come. Being kicked out of a band isn't the end of the world. In fact, rejection opens up a whole new realm of experience that – forgive me the cliché – makes a person stronger.

The rejects have told us a lot about life and music and the bands they were in. They show how the craft is carried out, and how the personnel are always subject to the work itself.

Finally, they tell us that an experience is what you make of it, and that anything could happen. In all our lives, we might just be the right person for the job. With my own ruptures behind me, it gives me great hope to realise this.

And we'd all like to think, wouldn't we, that one day a light might be shone on the contribution we made?

So this is that moment.

Once more for posterity: here's to The Rejects.

Acknowledgements

For the second book in a row, thanks first and foremost to Jenny Parrott, who inspired *The Rejects*. Most writers will require the huge luck of finding someone like her along the way. To my brilliant agent, Matthew Hamilton, whom I fear knows more about music than I do (and certainly in the case of yacht rock). To my erudite editor, Andreas Campomar, for taking a chance on the book and bringing a dream to life. To Holly Blood for her consummate project management (a skill on which all creative arts are finally dependent), and to Howard Watson for copyediting this book – I can never get enough of this uncanny craft. To Jason Everman, Brad Thomas and Chris Cunningham, and to David Hepworth, Michael Hann, Craig Brown and all the other brilliant writers whose work I so enjoyed in researching *The Rejects*.

A special thanks to the inspiring Tony O'Neill, who began as an interview subject and ended up as a friend. His advice on my Danny Whitten chapter was invaluable.

To Felix Leather and Jessica Blackman for their reading and encouragement once again. To Andy Buncall for being a life-long musical compadre. To Dan Reisinger, for his belief, enthusiasm, and knocking that man's baseball cap off. To Michel Faber, for the kick up the arse.

To my family: Ian Collinson for suggesting I take a good look at Pete Frame's *Rock Family Trees* – an invaluable resource. My mum and dad for tireless moral support, my wife Marie for endless patience, and my kids for tolerating the writing spilling into weekends. To my amazing sister, Shura Collinson, for her reading and editing – not least in helping me hunt down Jason Everman.

And finally: a shout to anyone who's ever found themselves rejected.

This book is for you.

Hidden bonus material:

Survivalism with Jason Everman

It takes me months to track down Jason Everman. At first, it feels strangely appropriate that it's so difficult – he's a master of military subterfuge, after all. I tried to contact journalists to whom he'd given interviews previously. One of them followed me back on X/Twitter, but completely ignored both a direct message and an email. A second also never responded, and a third sent me a friendly reply telling me that 'Jason keeps a super low profile online, so the best way to get in touch with him is probably through his band, Silence and Light.'

This I duly tried, initially to no avail. Silence and Light are a grungy hard-rock band formed of special operations veterans, which Everman founded in 2017 alongside Brad Thomas.[1] They donate profits to veterans' charities, regularly play live, and recorded a full-length album in 2020.

At first, I heard nothing back. On a second attempt, Brad sent me a polite reply saying he'd ask Jason. For a few months, I'd occasionally check in, get another polite reply, hear nothing. 'Jason is a pretty private person,' Brad told me.

---

1 Brad Thomas fought as a Ranger in the Battle of Mogadishu in 1993, before going on to join Delta Force, the US Army's most elite Special Forces unit.

I'd vaguely hoped to see Everman in person and do something interesting. Something that might scare me a little and entertain you – treasured reader.[2] I'd had visions of the far-flung Pacific Northwest, perhaps climbing Mount Rainier, fearing for my life while asking Everman about his. Coming away with the rich, fresh ore of experience from which good writing can be mined.

But, as the months wore on, I gave up hope and slumped into despondency. I was clearly never going to get in touch with Everman.

Then, suddenly, Brad Thomas gave me his email address.

Nervous, I couldn't seem to get the tone of my email right. I enlisted my sister – a professional writer and editor – for help, and finally hit send.

Again nothing happened, again I chased. And then, just before Christmas in 2022, J. Everman's name dropped into my inbox – bold black, swollen with promise, unread.

We speak by Zoom, early in the morning my time on Christmas Eve. Jason had offered me a window that seemed to include Christmas Day itself. Perhaps he doesn't take Christmas very seriously, my sister and I speculated. While I'm drinking a coffee and waiting to start, the windows beyond my desk still black, I see that he's entered the call early, so I do too. He doesn't switch the camera on, though I think this is more to do with his unfamiliarity with Zoom than a reluctance to do so. Having had his privacy emphasised, I decide not to ask him to. I know that he's somewhere distant – UTC +13, he told me by email.

2 Something really Vollmannish.

'Are you in the Far East?' I ask, after a couple of pleasantries.

'Right now I'm on Tinian Island,' he replies.

I admit that I don't know where this is.

'I guess the best reference point – it's east of Guam, a couple hundred miles.'

'For something you're working on?'

'I'm helping a friend move a sailboat,' he says. 'So, it's been a good trip so far.'

He speaks in the clear, precise, polite way I associate with US military types, though with a slight hesitancy – ahs, ums and y'knows – that makes him sound thoughtful. I get the sense his answers will be to the point.

First things first, the music.

'Do your spells in bands feel a really small part of your life now, or do they feel like big, important moments?'

'No, they feel really small, and the older I get the more insignificant they are in a way. I mean months go by where I don't even think about that part of my life, for whatever reason.'

'They were quite brief periods, I suppose?'

'Yeah, when you look back on it. I think about this stuff all the time, not just music stuff. I was on Peleliu Island recently – I'm a big military history buff – and I was thinking about World War II. Both my grandfathers fought in it. And World War II, at least the US involvement, was four years.' He chuckles. 'It's so shockingly short, looking back on it now. This huge, huge event. It boggles my mind, at least.'

'And World War I, too,' I suggest. 'Only four years for all involved, but it changed absolutely everything.'

'Yeah, I think – and this is a tangent, so I'll make it quick – but you look at WWI, WWII and the interstitial wars that were fought in the twenties and thirties. I look at it like how the Peloponnesian War is considered one conflict, but it was really three conflicts with periods of peace built in between. I think in maybe a hundred years or more we'll look at WWI, WWII and everything in between as an ongoing conflict with hot and cold periods.'

This talk of history reminds me of a story I'd read about Everman making a model plane from a famous Special Forces battle.

'Yeah, I made a model of one of the C-130s from the Entebbe Raid.'[3]

'I hadn't heard of the battle until I read that interview with you. Was Benjamin Netanyahu's brother involved in it?'

'Yes, Yoni was killed in that operation; he was the only Israeli casualty.'

I want to dig deeper into the statement Everman made to the *New York Times*: that the bonds he formed in the military, and in the rarefied, heightened world of the Special Forces, were stronger than in any band.

'The personal bonds that have been created in my life are definitely with dudes I served with overseas, y'know. I'm sure there are bands out there where it's not such a superficial relationship or there's a sense of brotherhood with the people you're playing with. I unfortunately never experienced that. That being said, there are still people from those

---

3 Operation Entebbe took place in 1976, when the Popular Front for the Liberation of Palestine hijacked a passenger jet travelling from Tel Aviv to Paris, and diverted it to Entebbe Airport in Uganda. A hundred commandos, primarily from the Israeli Defence Force's SF unit, Sayeret Matkal, flew in two Hercules C-130s and landed in darkness. They killed all the hijackers, and 102 of 106 hostages were rescued.

days that I'm very close friends with and I love as brothers for sure. So, it's not entirely superficial, I guess is what I'm trying to say.'

I'm getting the sense that Everman will be more loquacious on matters military, and since we're on the subject, I take the plunge and ask him if there's an operation he was involved in that he can tell me about.

'Like, battles?' he asks, surprised.

'Yeah.'

'Um . . . I mean . . . No. I guess?'

There's a pause. Yikes, I think – for a moment I worry I've made a faux pas.

'I guess that's kind of indicative of the GWAT[4] in general – there really have been no set-piece battles. Like the Second World War or Korea or even probably Vietnam. Like my experience, and it's more of a function of just being in smaller units I guess, is there's been some intense firefights for sure, some crazy stuff, definitely moments where I was like "OK, we might not get out of this one." But I don't have any, y'know, motion-picture-style battles or anything like that. Maybe the Iraq invasion, watching the conventional military kind of do their thing was really impressive and awesome.'

'The scale and power of it?'

'Essentially watching a true combined arms assault in action. That was cinematic for sure.'

'I assume you're following what's happening in Ukraine. Are you impressed by what they're managing to achieve?'

---

4 The Global War on Terror, just in case you're having a slow morning, as I was when I asked Everman what this was. 'Jargon,' he chuckled, after telling me.

'Yeah. They're getting a lot of outside support, which is definitely a factor. But I guess what's been most stunning to me is how bad the Russian military is. I mean they're shockingly bad. The troops and the equipment. I honestly was expecting a lot more from them. The best quote I heard, from someone I know who was fighting over there, was the Russians were "worse than ISIS".'

'You've got friends out there working privately?'

'Yeah, I know a couple of guys who joined the Ukrainian – it's not called the foreign legion but it's something similar.'

'They must be brave and motivated.'

'Yeah, I understand the allure. Even now, post GWAT, there's this romantic notion of fighting the good fight or whatever. I can definitely understand the whole missing the action kind of stuff.'

'Did you do any private military work yourself?'

'I've taken some security consulting jobs here and there, but I think at this point my military days are probably behind me. Which is fine because I've got other stuff on the horizon that I'm interested in.'

I want to hear more about the way Everman has perceived and planned his life in archetypes; poet, warrior. Does he still look at things that way?

'Oh, absolutely, it's a work in progress, that I'm sure I'll die before it's even close to completion. Just being active in the endeavour, to me, I think is key in human flourishing. I've always been interested in historical figures who were these well-rounded human beings. So, you were talking about the SAS earlier – I just started watching the BBC mini-series, have you seen it?'[5]

5 I referred to the SAS in the Battle of Mirbat when trying to fish a story out of Everman.

'Yes.'

'Super good. Obviously I'm sure a lot of it's amplified for dramatic effect. But dudes like David Stirling and Paddy Mayne – these larger-than-life characters – are so necessary, at least in the evolution of special operations. They were all cut from that cloth, and I think that's really intriguing.'

There are a few controversies around Mayne, one of which is detailed in *SAS: Rogue Heroes*, the Ben Macintyre book on which the series is based. In one of the shock, desert night raids the SAS pioneered, Mayne machine-gunned uniformed but off-duty combatants.

'That's a tough one,' Everman says. 'The GWAT rule of engagement was that if they didn't have a weapon, you didn't engage, and so that was the whole thing. I, thankfully, was personally never involved in a situation where there were CIVCAS, or someone who didn't have a gun was shot. So I think that's an interesting ethical question – if it is still uniformed combatants armed or not. I'm not sure what the Geneva Convention says about that.'

So which aspect of Everman's life is he working on now?

'Near term, I've really fallen in love with sailing over the last five, six years. I have my own boat. Unfortunately I seem to spend more time sailing on other people's boats than mine. Have you ever heard of R2AK, Race to Alaska?'

I haven't.

'There's been a couple documentaries made. It's a sailboat race that starts close to where I live. It started out as the barroom joke gone too far, but now it's kind of an institution. But it's a boat race from Port Townsend in Washington to Ketchikan, Alaska. And basically, the only rule is you can't have a motor in the boat. So, it's either wind power or rowing, or some other human form of propulsion if you can design it. I've got some friends from the military as well as a buddy from the music days, and we're gonna do the Race to Alaska.'

'I assume the weather will be interesting?'

'Never underestimate the sea, for sure. The route we're gonna take will go west of the Strait of Juan de Fuca, and then north on the Pacific side, so open ocean, because I think the winds will be way more favourable out there. But from working in Alaska and other boat experience I've had, it's like, do not underestimate the sea, because the sea does not give a fuck.'

That Alaskan experience was on his father's fishing boat?

'Yeah, when I was a teenager I was a deckhand on my dad's fishing boat for four seasons up in Alaska.'

'That must've toughened you up,' I suggest.

'It was high adventure. And it was definitely a good step – that was my first step into the world, basically. Being more or less on my own doing hard work in an exotic place. It was a good evolution.'

I refer to the story that stuck with me from an SAS documentary, when a soldier describes a colleague in a photo, deep behind enemy lines, as being 'happy to be there'. I wonder when Everman realised he was capable of this.

'I wouldn't call myself fearless, because if you're not afraid in situations like that there's something wrong with you. But you manage it, and that's the key. Since I was a child, I was always a risk taker. A lot of stupid stuff really. I kind of had a free-range childhood in that, from a very early age I was pretty much left to my own devices, so that meant just going out in the woods and getting on my bike or whatever . . . Let's see – stupid stuff I did as a child. There were the train tracks that ran behind our house, one place we lived – and by house, I mean trailer. I would go up to the train tracks, and there was this corner where the train had to slow down to negotiate the corner, so I would jump on the train and just ride it for a few miles and then jump off and walk home.

'There were these high-tension power lines – like the big steel towers – I would climb those. Six or seven years old, so stupid. Climbing to the top, no safety gear, no idea of what electricity was capable of doing. Just dumb stuff, but it was high adventure.

'Riding my bike – it was nothing to put a four by eight-foot sheet of plywood over a picnic table and ride down a hill as fast as you can and launch off that ramp. No safety equipment, nothing. In retrospect it's a miracle I didn't die in childhood really.'

'Did other kids seem different, and impressed?'

'I mean, at the time it was just normal. And my parents – my mother especially – encouraged an adventurous childhood. We'd be camping on the Washington coast somewhere, on one of the big rivers that come down from the Olympic Mountains. And I had this twenty-dollar, piece of shit, K-Mart inflatable raft – something meant to be a swimming-pool toy. And my mum would drive me ten miles up the river, drop me off with my little raft, and I'd raft by myself down to the camp-site, ten miles down the river. And it would take a few hours to get down, but it was high adventure,[6] it was so fun. I look

6 Everman keeps coming back to this term, which is obviously something of a guiding principle for him. A life of high adventure – how many of us are lucky enough to experience this? How many of us want to?

at it now, and my mum would probably go to jail for doing that now.'

At this stage, Everman is talking a lot more freely, with enthusiasm and laughter in his voice.

'How old were you?'

'Six, seven, eight.'

'And is high adventure just as important to you now?'

'It is, but I do notice, as I get older, the notion of a calmer life, some stability, is becoming more and more appealing. So I don't know if that's another stage I'm entering or what, but for now, yes definitely. I still love travelling. I'm fifty-five years old and I still get excited when I get on a plane, and I fly a lot, but it's still kind of thrilling to me.'

I wonder if being in bands failed to live up to high adventure?

'My time as a professional rock musician . . . I don't think I looked at it as adventure in the traditional sense, I definitely looked at it as something interesting to do, and the travel component of touring really appealed to me. But really, being in a rock band, honestly it's kind of boring.[7] I would try to make the best of it. During European tours, I'd go out of my way to hit the museums and do stuff like that. OK, I'm essentially getting paid to travel around Europe, I'm gonna make the most of it. So things like that were fun.

'There were definitely some crazy stories that happened within the context of being a rock musician, but not necessarily

---

7 This is definitely true – a lot of music industry activity is: the hours spent on tour buses or planes, sitting around in studios, or answering the same questions from dozens of interviewers, or – worst of all – stuck on the tedious sets of music videos.

music related, so there were definitely adventurous moments for sure.'

When he sloughed off the shackles of cool, was he able to retain his passion? He still plays, after all.

'This has happened a couple of times in my life, where I got fed up with all the bullshit of the music industry and stepped away. I remember when I did the final break and went into the military, honestly it was years before I even touched a guitar, I just really had no interest in it. And when I finally did start playing again, I kind of recaptured why I did it in the first place, it brought me joy. So the music projects I've been involved with now, it's great. The only reason I do it is because it's fun, there's no other expectations. And honestly if it's a situation where I didn't derive joy from it, I just wouldn't do it. I love playing guitar now, I probably play it every day.'

I want to get to the question that's most burning for me. The leaders of both the bands that Everman played with ended up killing themselves: Kurt Cobain of Nirvana and Chris Cornell of Soundgarden. Listening back to the grunge era, the music and lyrics are very dark – think Alice in Chains, Screaming Trees, Pearl Jam – as well as Nirvana and Soundgarden. What was it about this generation of musicians? Why were all of these characters so apparently damaged?

'Someone asked me a very similar question recently, and this person posited that it was this gloomy Pacific Northwest, like a physical thing – geography and weather and things like that. And I was like, ahh, I don't think that's it. Conversely, the Pacific Northwest is beautiful. I've lived there basically my entire life, with a few exceptions, and I'm still struck by the natural beauty of Cascadia. I'll stop – I'll see the Olympic Mountains on a clear day, and I'll have to stop and take it in, it's like "Wow, that's amazing."

'I think maybe it's more – and this is my kind of counter-hypothesis I guess – is it's a Gen X thing. We're all the kids of baby boomers, and so many of those marriages were unhappy and ended in divorce – that was definitely true of my childhood. And most of my peers, it's a similar story, y'know. So I definitely had, at least when I got to my adolescence, a less than happy childhood. I still have my demons, and it's a full-time job grappling with them and keeping them in check. I think in the cases you're talking about, the demons won.'

I sympathise with his regional instincts, and his love of the Pacific Northwest. I tell him of how it reminds me of my beloved Scottish Highlands.

'It's a special place. When I was a teenager and I left for the first time to go fish in Alaska, I was like "fuck this place," vowed never to come back. I did go away for a good chunk of my adult life, but when I finally did boomerang back I was older and in a different mindset, and I was like "Oh, this place isn't so bad." And my home there now is wonderful, I've got an amazing group of friends – honestly a group of friends way more interesting and cool than people I knew in New York or more quote-unquote sophisticated places. Just really cool, creative, down-to-earth people. It's great.'

But going back to the demons. How does he grapple with them exactly? How does he win?

'I think that when I was younger I would kind of willingly give in to it, because I thought it was cool – y'know, it was cool to be melancholic and aloof or whatever. Whatever silly things a person in their teens or early twenties thinks.

'Now, it's like a constant process of self-examination and self-evaluation, where I can feel it coming on now, and I'm pretty good at cutting off before it even gets there. And this is gonna sound so hippie and silly, I'm almost a little embarrassed to say it, but I try to invest my time and energy in positive creative pursuits, you know, or sailing or cooking, things like that.'

And did Kurt Cobain and Chris Cornell get trapped in that romantic melancholy?

'This is supposition on my part, but yeah, I think that cliché of the tortured artist, there's an element of that I think. Maybe some people feel they need that in order to be creative, and so if it's not occurring naturally it becomes self-inflicted. And does it work or not? I don't know, I mean, I'm sure there's instances where it does.

'But to this day it makes me sad that both Kurt and Chris killed themselves, you know. Because if there's ever been people in a position to do whatever they wanted, they were. But everybody's fighting their own battle . . .'

Does he ever feel relieved to have escaped from these orbits?

'Yeah, for sure. And when I was younger, I was honestly on that edge a couple of times myself. I ultimately thought better of it, and obviously I'm still here. At the end of the day it was just feeling sorry for yourself, at least in my case. And it's like OK – it's that existential moment where you can just be passive and cast yourself in the role of being a victim of life and circumstance or whatever, or engage the will and make the effort to change things, as far as your personal situation goes.

'Most things in life you have zero control over, zero. Almost everything. But the things you do have control over, those are the things you can change.'

I wonder if he still listens to music from his former milieu.

'I don't listen to bands I played in, but that's just me. We did some recording this summer with one of the musical projects I'm involved in, and it's hard for me to listen to the rough mixes. I don't know why, it just is. It's not that I think it's bad, it's just weird to me. The analogy I've made, and I don't know how much sense it makes, is like – do you have cats?'

'Not personally, but my parents do, so I'm around them quite a bit.'

'I've had cats most of my life, and one thing I've noticed about cats, at least the cats I've had, is that if you hold a cat up to a mirror, they will not look at themselves in the mirror. They'll turn their heads and contort their bodies – they will not look at their own reflection, which always struck me as odd. So that's kind of the way I feel about writing prose or recording music or different creative things like that. Once it's finished, I just kind of leave it alone. And I guess I get kind of squirmish about looking at myself in the mirror, metaphorically, like that.'

These days, he listens to a lot of metal – Black Sabbath's *Vol. 4* is in his top three of all time – and American hardcore and rock music from the eighties and nineties. He spent a few years living in Argentina, where he fell in love with bossa nova. A trip in an Uber in Cyprus introduced him to the joys of Greek stoner rock – 1000mods, Planet of Zeus and Nightstalker – 'strongly influenced by Kyuss, but there are worse bands to emulate'.

I'm keen to hear which movies about special military operations he considers good portrayals.

'So with cinema at least I'm usually pretty good at suspending disbelief and just going along for the ride, so I'm not one of those people who are gonna nit-pick inaccuracies or whatever. I remember when I left the theatre after seeing *Saving Private Ryan*, I overheard some dude in the lobby saying how fake it was, like the German machine gunners didn't have their rear sights up. And I was like, "OK dude, come on . . . enjoy the narrative."

'My all-time favourite war movie – and I think it's only a war movie in broad strokes – is *For Whom the Bell Tolls*. I've always been obsessed with the Spanish Civil War for some reason, probably from initially reading the novel as a teenager. Super-interesting conflict, and I think there's probably some analogues to be made between that and what's going on in Ukraine right now.

'Something I think is good as far as like ringing true to me was the raid sequence in *Zero Dark Thirty*. I thought that was a great depiction of at least a modern special operations raid.[8] Because it's not this insane gunfight – it's slow and deliberate, and there's not a lot of shooting to be honest, and I thought they captured that really well.'

Some people complained that the soldiers talked more than they would in reality, I venture.

'The talking was a concession to the storytelling and propelling the narrative, and again I can go along with that. Most raids like that, they're slow and they're quiet and the pacing is very deliberate – it's not chaotic, it's very controlled. So I liked the way that was portrayed.'

8 I was glad Everman said this, because I love this scene.

I wonder how he feels about the well-worn hand-wringing over American political division.

'I think it's interesting and probably a bit concerning how polarised all these political camps have got in the US. I think it's something that, as a nation, will pass. You get these extreme pendulum swings, and then both sides recognise the insanity and it's like "All right, it's time to moderate a bit. Let's find some middle ground and sort this out."

'Some people talk about civil war and blah blah blah, but no one's gonna start shooting until their family's starving. That's the point you get to a civil war. And our country's so fat and happy, still, even with the economy kind of in the toilet and everything, we're so far from that.'

Finally, I'm surprised he hasn't written a book himself. He has the kind of story that could lead to a good book, both creatively and commercially.

'Yeah, it'll probably definitely happen. I actually flirted with that idea six or seven years ago, and it got to the point where I had a literary agent and everything, and I wrote the book proposal, and I kind of decided that the time wasn't right. Another factor was that I got accepted to graduate school, and it's like "OK, I'm gonna focus on the master's degree and put the book idea on the back burner." And so it's still on the back burner and it'll probably happen someday, but probably not anytime soon.'

And with that, I leave Everman on Christmas Eve in the tropics to 'try and find a place in town that's serving some kind of Christmas dinner, maybe'.

'I'm sorry it was kind of a convoluted process,' he says. 'Things have been kind of busy.'

I end the call. It'll soon be time to make breakfast for my kids. What passes for the midwinter sun is up beyond the windows, and I'm feeling quite inspired.

Who knows, perhaps life has high adventure in store for us all yet.

Notes

Chapter 1: Pete Best, the Beatles

12–13 *No other member of the group ever made any mention*: *Beatle! The Pete Best Story*, Patrick Doncaster and Pete Best, 1985.

14 *The news of the Decca turn-down . . . And George Martin doesn't think you're a good enough drummer*: Ibid.

17 *Once I had become stabilized*: Ibid.

17 *Nevertheless, feelings about Best's sacking*: *One Two Three Four: The Beatles in time*, Craig Brown, 2020.

Chapter 2: Steve Mann, the Mothers of Invention

21 *Steve Mann, who was one of the best guitarists*: *Pete Frame's Rock Family Trees*, Pete Frame, 1980.

22 *An airline made of snow*: *Snowblind Friend*, Hoyt Axton, Columbia Records, 1969. Written by Hoyt Axton.

Chapter 3: Bootsy Collins, the J.B.s

23 *Son, y'all the greatest band in the world*: Interview with *Bass Player Magazine*, 2018. https://www.musicradar.com/news/bootsy-collins -interview

23 *He kept me real close . . . Hard core*: Ibid.

23–24 *I mean, good Lord*: Interview with *Rolling Stone*, 2017. https:// www.rollingstone.com/music/music-features/bootsy-collins-on- what-james-brown-taught-him-why-he-quit-drugs-204108/

24 *Haaargh! You just ain't on it . . . He was on another planet*: Interview with *Bass Player Magazine*, 2018.

24 *He knew what he was doing*: Ibid.

24 *I was playing a lot of stuff . . . you my boy*: Interview with *Rolling Stone*, 2017.

25 *When we saw how stupid this stuff was . . . We knew we had it*: Interview with *Bass Player Magazine*, 2018.

25 *I promised myself I'd never do it . . . He had his bodyguard throw me out*: Interview with the *Guardian*, 2017. https://www.theguardian. com/lifeandstyle/2017/oct/28/bootsy-collins-lsd-was-a-big-part-of -why-i-left-james-browns-band?CMP=fb_gu

25 *He fired me, but I just couldn't stop laughing*: Interview with the *Guardian*, 2020.

25 *With him, you could just come as you are . . . you could just keep reaching and reaching*: Ibid.

26 *Now put that together . . . It can make you a better person*: Interview with *Rolling Stone*, 2017.

Chapter 5: Florence Ballard, the Supremes

28 *I always watched my mother . . . Just go back upstairs*: Autopsy: The Last Hours of . . . Florence Ballard (Podcast). Interviews originally recorded by Peter Benjaminson for the Detroit Free Press.

29 *Milton Jenkins, the manager*: Daily Mail, January 2007. https://www. dailymail.co.uk/tvshowbiz/article-431858/The-Supremes-killed- sister.html

29 *I think it should be the Supremes*: Dreamgirl: My Life As a Supreme, Mary Wilson, 1986.

30 *Flo was thrilled when they first made it big . . . I'll see you all later*: Daily Mail, January 2007.

31 *Diana had that pop sound*: Autopsy: The Last Hours of . . . Florence Ballard (Podcast). Interviews originally recorded by Peter Benjaminson for the Detroit Free Press.

32 *Thin is in . . . Pretty damn stacked . . . You're fired*: Ibid.

32 *Explosive*: Unsung: The Story of Florence Ballard (Documentary, TV One), 2009.

33 *She only got $160,000*: Daily Mail, January 2007.

33–34 *She didn't have a very good life . . . during these dark times in her life*: Autopsy: The Last Hours of . . . Florence Ballard (Podcast).

Interviews originally recorded by Peter Benjaminson for the Detroit Free Press.

34 *If something happens to me . . . A broken heart*: Ibid.

34–35 *All of a sudden . . . to be the star of her own funeral!*: *Paperback Writer*, Mark Bego as quoted in an article in the *Village Voice*, 2010.

Chapter 6: Brian Jones, the Rolling Stones

41 *Evil genius*: *Sympathy for the Devil: The Birth of the Rolling Stones and the Death of Brian Jones*, Paul Trynka, 2014.

42 *When we first started playing together*: *Shindig!* (TV show), 1965. https://www.youtube.com/watch?v=gWBS0GX1s9o

42 *The importance of a handsome English man*: *Sympathy for the Devil: The Birth of the Rolling Stones and the Death of Brian Jones*, Paul Trynka, 2014.

42 *The light that burns twice*: Blade Runner (Film), 1982.

43 *Oldham's PR partner, Tony Calder*: *Sympathy for the Devil: The Birth of the Rolling Stones and the Death of Brian Jones*, Paul Trynka, 2014.

43 *That's a wonderful song*: *Rolling Stone*, 1995.

44 *I held him up by the collar*: *Sympathy for the Devil: The Birth of the Rolling Stones and the Death of Brian Jones*, Paul Trynka, 2014

47 *Just pick up a guitar . . . Just go home, Brian*: Ibid.

48 *Free to become him*: Ibid.

Chapter 8: All the Musicians Kicked Out of Fleetwood Mac

52 *Emotionally fragile*: *Guardian*, Danny Kirwan obituary, 2018.

52 *So into it that he cried*: Show-biz Blues, CD liner notes, 2001.

52 *It was clear that he needed to be with better players*: *Play On: Now, Then and Fleetwood Mac*, Mick Fleetwood, 2014.

53 *Once we got Danny in . . . a number-one hit record*: *The Vaudeville Years*, CD booklet notes, 1998.

53 *The originator of all the ideas . . . we've got to rehearse*: *Fleetwood Mac: The First 30 Years*, Bob Brunning, 1998.

53 *Got the impression*: *The Vaudeville Years*, CD booklet notes, 1998.

53 *We just didn't get on too well*: Martin Celmins, *Guitar Magazine*, 1997.

54 *He suddenly said*: Pete Frame's Rock Family Trees, Pete Frame, 1980.

54 *The glue*: My Life and Adventures with Fleetwood Mac, Mick Fleetwood with Stephen Davis, 1990.

54 *The pressure . . . was tremendous*: Play On: Now, Then and Fleetwood Mac, Mick Fleetwood, 2014.

54 *There was one terrible . . . talked them back in*: My Life and Adventures with Fleetwood Mac, Mick Fleetwood with Stephen Davis, 1990.

55 *He suddenly turned to me . . . that was the last time I spoke to him for two years*: Pete Frame's Rock Family Trees, Pete Frame, 1980.

55 *It really did a number on them*: Play On: Now, Then and Fleetwood Mac, Mick Fleetwood, 2014.

56 *Not once did we take the stage knowing*: Ibid.

56 *We were scared stiff*: Peter Green: Founder of Fleetwood Mac, Martin Celmins, 1995.

56 *I was expecting they'd tell me . . . We basically got drunk and had a good time*: My Life and Adventures with Fleetwood Mac, Mick Fleetwood with Stephen Davis, 1990.

56–57 *Meticulous . . . say something in a guitar lead*: The Penguin Q&A Sessions, Bob Welch, 1999.

57 *Personality clash*: My Life and Adventures with Fleetwood Mac, Mick Fleetwood with Stephen Davis, 1990.

57 *Danny was a brilliant musician . . . don't feel he loved my stuff to death*: The Penguin Q&A Sessions, Bob Welch, 1999.

58 *Living mostly on beer*: Danny Kirwan's Wikipedia entry.

59 *Pissed out of his brain . . . I guess he was, in a way*: The Penguin Q&A Sessions, Bob Welch, 1999.

59 *Danny was fired . . . It got intolerable for everyone*: Pete Frame's Rock Family Trees, Pete Frame, 1980.

59 *I would say 'the guy doesn't . . . he was Peter's protégé*: Fleetwood Mac: The First 30 Years, Bob Brunning, 1998.

60 *You're gonna need it*: The Penguin Q&A Sessions, Bob Weston, 1999.

60 *We thought we'd try having*: Pete Frame's Rock Family Trees, Pete Frame, 1980.

60 *The light finally dawned*: http://www.fleetwoodmac.net/fwm/index. php?option=com_content&task=view&id=65&Itemid=79

61 *He was asked to leave after a strenuous*: Ibid.

62 *I used to live near London Zoo*: Ibid.

63 *I got a phone call early . . . Cost me a career, that did!*: http://www. fleetwoodmac.net/fwm/index.php?option=com_content&task=vie w&id=64&Itemid=78

64 *It didn't take two guitarists*: *The Rebirth of Fleetwood Mac*, Mark David Hendrickson, *Music Paper*, 1990.

65 *I needed to get some separation*: Fleetwood Mac's Blue Letter Archives.

65 *I snuck into concerts for years ... whole thing was just really scary*: *Rolling Stone*, December 2022.

67 *Things got weird ...They were a great band to be with*: Ibid.

68 *Used ... God, it's a hard one to top*: Ibid.

68 *Stevie never wants to be on a stage with you again*: *NME*, September 2021.

69 *Mick Fleetwood had happened to bump into*: *Pete Frame's Rock Family Trees*, Pete Frame, 1980.

69 *Stiffed out ... master a raunchy rock 'n' roll style*: Ibid.

70 *Went nowhere fast ... stamping his foot to the rhythm*: Ibid.

71 *At the time, we were ... knocked me down with a feather*: Ibid.

72 *The guys in the business were 'supposed' ...An ongoing battle*: https://www.theguardian.com/music/2013/dec/12/fleetwood-mac-stevie-nicks-christine-mcvie-nuns

74 *Ironically, nothing went down*: https://www.latimes.com/entertainment-arts/music/story/2021-09-10/stevie-nicks-lindsey-buckingham-relationship-timeline

74 *It was the straw that broke the camel's back*: https://www.poconorecord.com/story/entertainment/2020/10/02/moonlight-confessions-stevie-nicks/5892636002/

74 *It was time to get divorced from him*: https://www.latimes.com/entertainment-arts/music/story/2021-09-10/stevie-nicks-lindsey-buckingham-relationship-timeline

74 *It would be like a scenario*: https://www.latimes.com/entertainment-arts/music/story/2021-09-08/lindsey-buckingham-fleetwood-mac-stevie-nicks

Chapter 9: Bob Stinson, the Replacements

77 *He was throwing stones*: https://www.spin.com/2013/06/hold-my-life-bob-stinson-the-replacements-interview-june-1993/

77 *Raw-throated*: *Our Band Could be Your Life*, Michael Azerrad, 2001.

78 *Hang side by side*: *Swingin' Party*, the Replacements, Sire Records, 1985. Written by Paul Westerberg.

78 *Getting high in the bathroom*: https://www.rollingstone.com/music/music-news/inside-the-replacements-disastrous-saturday-night-live-debut-161765/5/

79 *Lori, ah, Mrs Westerberg*: https://www.spin.com/2013/06/hold-my
-life-bob-stinson-the-replacements-interview-june-1993/

Chapter 10: Steven Adler, Guns N' Roses

87 *I'm tired of too many people*: Axl Rose, onstage at LA Coliseum, 1989.

92 *Odd ambient blend of New Age*: *A Supposedly Fun Thing I'll Never Do Again*, David Foster Wallace, 1997.

94 *Really, emotionally Steven wasn't much older than a third grader*: *Slash*, Slash with Anthony Bozza, 2007.

96 *Wannabe gangster*: *My Appetite for Destruction: Sex & Drugs & Guns N' Roses*, Steven Adler with Lawrence J. Spagnola, 2010.

97 *I owe it all to Steven Adler*: *Slash*, Slash with Anthony Bozza, 2007.

99 *He never kept up the dedicated work ethic*: Ibid.

99–100 *That definitely stopped me in my tracks*: Ibid.

100 *Steven would watch my left foot*: Ibid.

100 *There's no way Steven gets twenty percent*: Ibid.

101 *Now you three, suck his dick*: *My Appetite for Destruction: Sex & Drugs & Guns N' Roses*, Steven Adler with Lawrence J. Spagnola, 2010.

102 *Steven could get very emotional ... keeping him company*: *Slash*, Slash with Anthony Bozza, 2007.

103 *Irretrievable*: Ibid.

104 *At this point I could see that his mental*: Ibid.

104–05 *Mom really went to bat ... one sweet gift to me*: *My Appetite for Destruction: Sex & Drugs & Guns N' Roses*, Steven Adler with Lawrence J. Spagnola, 2010.

106 *To Steven's credit*: *Slash*, Slash with Anthony Bozza, 2007.

106 *Our songs were written*: Interview with Izzy Stradlin in *Musician*, November 1992.

Chapter 11: Alan Lancaster, Status Quo

110 *Early on we got*: Interview with Dave Ling, *Classic Rock*, 2001.

111 *It would be like trying to get your*: Interview with *Classic Rock*, 1992.

111 *Like having your child abducted*: https://www.loudersound.com/
news/status-quo-francis-rossi-cocaine-take-over-alan-lancaster

Chapter 12: Jason Everman, Nirvana

112 *We wanted to make him*: Come as You Are: The Story of Nirvana, Michael Azerrad, 1993.

113 *Do you ever think about*: 'The Rock 'n' Roll Casualty Who Became a War Hero', Clay Tarver, *New York Times*, 2013.

115 *The collision of*: Got Your Six, Jason Everman speech, 2014.

116–17 *I'd have access to these bands in LA or New York ... All in*: Ibid.

119 *Early on, they began to realize ... he had long Sub Pop hair*: Come as You Are: The Story of Nirvana, Michael Azerrad, 1993.

119–20 *I hated them ... You don't move it at all*: Ibid.

120–21 *Kurt didn't have much experience ... financing the show*: Ibid.

123 *A little ridiculous ... history of the music business*: https://www.youtube.com/watch?v=R2x10zAalW0&t=202s

124–25 *Jason probably made a mint ... mental damages*: Come as You Are: The Story of Nirvana, Michael Azerrad, 1993.

126–28 *Yeah, Chad. You're the next to go ... 'cause I'm such a dictator*: https://www.youtube.com/watch?v=JePpMwL9Yb8

126–29 *I think that the ... Johnny Rotten complex*: Come as You Are: The Story of Nirvana, Michael Azerrad, 1993.

131 *Middle of one night ... just happy to be there*: SAS: The Soldier's Story (TV show), Goldhawk Productions, 1996.

133–34 *That's Afghanistan I think ... I felt free*: Got Your Six, Jason Everman speech, 2014.

137–38 *He was reading a magazine, when he ... a strange sense of kismet*: 'The Rock 'n' Roll Casualty Who Became a War Hero', Clay Tarver, *New York Times*, 2013.

138–39 *Fighting isn't like the movies ... blew up in front of me*: Ibid.

139 *The experience of war and combat*: Got Your Six, Jason Everman speech, 2014.

139 *They didn't approach like ... ran their suck constantly*: 'The Rock 'n' Roll Casualty Who Became a War Hero', Clay Tarver, *New York Times*, 2013.

139 *The deepest, most meaningful human*: Got Your Six, Jason Everman speech, 2014.

140–41 *Challenge leads to achievement ... I still get goose bumps on my arms*: Ibid.

Interlude: The Lodestars Cross Paths in the Sky

143 *My hair had started to fall out*: *Mind Wide Open*, Lily Cornell Silver, https://www.instagram.com/p/CDttflvgmtm/
144 *That he'd died*: https://www.youtube.com/watch?v=WFLlXFx9gZg
144 *Terrible premonition . . . guardian angel*: *Sing Backwards and Weep*, Mark Lanegan, 2020.

Chapter 13: Dave Mustaine, Metallica

145 *It's difficult for me*: *Some Kind of Monster* (Film), 2004.
145 *Impoverished, transient . . . check check check*: *Mustaine: A Life in Metal*, Dave Mustaine, 2010.
All other quotes: Ibid.

Chapter 14: Danny Whitten, Crazy Horse

171 *Did you ever feel like killing somebody?*: *Shakey: Neil Young's Biography*, Jimmy McDonough, 2002.
182–83 **[All lyrics]**: *Come On Baby Let's Go Downtown*, Neil Young, Reprise Records, 1970. Written by Danny Whitten.

Interlude: The Elephant in the Room

187 *We knew what we had . . . The destruction of Danny's life*: *Shakey: Neil Young's Biography*, Jimmy McDonough, 2002.

Chapter 15: Jimmy Chamberlin, Smashing Pumpkins

188 *A lot of tea in China*: *Rolling Stone*, 2018. https://www.rollingstone.com/music/music-news/smashing-pumpkins-band-drama-the-complete-history-198087/
189 *When Chamberlin awoke . . . 4.02 a.m.*: *New York Times*, July 1996. https://www.nytimes.com/1996/07/13/nyregion/musician-for-smashing-pumpkins-dies-of-apparent-drug-overdose.html

190 *Now they know ... well as the other individual*: *Los Angeles Times*, July 1996. https://www.latimes.com/archives/la-xpm-1996-07-16-mn-24734-story.html

191 *Jerry Garcia of the Grateful Dead ... possession in the last year and a half*: *New York Times*, July 1996. https://www.nytimes.com/1996/07/13/nyregion/musician-for-smashing-pumpkins-dies-of-apparent-drug-overdose.html

192 *Put down the needle*: *The Love We Make*, Prince, NPG Records, 1996. Written by Prince Rogers Nelson.

193 *Cold hotel room*: *Angel*, Sarah McLachlan, Nettwerk, 1997. Written by Sarah McLachlan.

193 *I've never done heroin*: *CMJ New Music Monthly*, August 1997.

193 *How I love you*: *Jonathan*, Wendy & Lisa, World Domination Records, 1998. Written by Wendy Melvoin and Lisa Coleman.

Chapter 16: Glen Matlock, the Sex Pistols

194 *Always washing his feet*: *Rhino*, 2014. https://web.archive.org/web/20110715180804/http://rhinomedia.com/rzine/storykeeper.lasso?storyID=779

195–97 *In our little ... It's always there*: Interview in *The Times*, January 2023. https://www.thetimes.co.uk/article/glen-matlock-why-i-really-left-the-sex-pistols-g38xxbbsc

Chapter 17: Adam Ant

198–99 *Job had come to an end ... turn them upside down*: *The South Bank Show* (TV show), 1984. https://www.youtube.com/watch?v=TC72833smbQ

199 *Hours and hours of philosophy*: *Louder Than War*, January 2017. https://louderthanwar.com/interview-adam-ant/

199 *Malcolm was a sort of ... surrogate father*: *Guardian*, April 2010. https://www.theguardian.com/music/2010/apr/21/adam-ant-malcolm-mclaren

199–200 *At the time it was devastating ... good for both parties*: *Louder Than War*, January 2017.

200 '*Ethnic beats*': *The South Bank Show* (TV show), 1984.

Chapter 19: Lemmy, Hawkwind

233 *It fell to me to break the bad news*: *Classic Rock*, January 2016. https://www.loudersound.com/features/remembering-lemmy-the-band-mate-dave-brock

All other quotes: *White Line Fever*, Lemmy with Janiss Garza, 2002.

Chapter 20: LaTavia Roberson and LeToya Luckett, Destiny's Child

244 *I came into class . . . nobody knows that though*: *The Grio*, January 2014. https://thegrio.com/2014/01/23/single-ladies-star-letoya-luckett-i-was-beyonces-bodygaurd-in-school/

244 *Weak without you*: *Survivor*, Destiny's Child, Columbia Records, 2001. Written by Beyonce Knowles, Anthony Dent, Mathew Knowles.

244 *Deliberate, disparaging . . . lawsuits to file*: *Billboard*, February 2002. https://www.billboard.com/music/music-news/ex-destinys-child-members-sue-over-survivor-76633/

245 *It was very difficult . . . no longer in the group*: *People*, December 2016. https://people.com/music/latavia-roberson-getting-dumped-destinys-child-led-to-depression/

Chapter 21: Gary Young, Pavement

All quotes: *Louder Than You Think: A Lo-Fi History of Gary Young and Pavement* (Film), directed by Jed I. Rosenberg, 2023.

Chapter 22: Ian Stewart, the Rolling Stones

268 *My little three-chord wonders*: *Guardian*, April 2004. https://www.theguardian.com/music/2004/apr/03/popandrock.shopping

268 *Alright my little shower of shit*: *Rolling Stone*, January 1986. https://www.rollingstone.com/music/music-news/ian-stewart-1938-1985-248898/

Chapter 23: Nick Oliveri,
Queens of the Stone Age – Part One

269 *If I ever find out this is true*: Interview with Zane Lowe on BBC Radio 1, July 2005. http://www.thefade.net/oldsite/transcripts/ radio12005.html}

276 *"Kings" would be too macho*: Josh Homme speaking at Ozzfest, 2000. https://www.radiox.co.uk/artists/queens-of-the-stone-age/meaning-story-behind-band-name/

277–78 *I would have axed me too . . . out there with you*: *Antiquiet*, 2012. https://www.youtube.com/watch?v=51dsoWRjOT8

280–81 *Always had an edge . . . To me, that's so beautiful*: Nick Oliveri, 'Rock & Roll Komodo Dragon' of Kyuss, Queens of the Stone Age, *REVOLVER*, 2018. https://www.youtube.com/watch?v=Cfvg_8L3UpU&t=17s

Chapter 24:
Siobhan Donaghy, Sugababes

282 *As young girls do, you have arguments*: *This Morning*, ITV, June 2020. https://www.dailymail.co.uk/tvshowbiz/article-8431407/Sugababes-Keisha-Buchanan-says-portrayed-bully-black-band-member.html

285 *It's like United Colours*: *Ponystep*, September 2009. https:// web.archive.org/web/20090922220945/http://www.ponystep. com/music/article/SiobhanDonaghyTheonethatgotaway_380. aspx

286 *There's no doubt*: Ibid.

287–88 *We met each other when we . . . naff band*: Ibid.

288 *That was back when A1 were out . . . it kind of suited us*: Ibid.

290 *It was clear that there was someone in the band*: Ibid.

291 *I hate her for running away and leaving us*: *Guardian*, June 2003. https://www.theguardian.com/music/2003/jun/24/artsfeatures. glastonbury2003

291–92 *I'm not good under pressure . . . insisted she sing lead' on 'Overload'*: *Guardian*, June 2003. https://www.theguardian.com/ music/2003/jun/24/artsfeatures.glastonbury2003

292 *McVey's got kids my age . . . They've got it on their conscience*:

Guardian, June 2003. https://www.theguardian.com/music/2003/jun/24/artsfeatures.glastonbury2003

292 *Rubbish . . . I didn't tell my mum at the time*: Ibid.

293 *She made my life a living hell . . . No one does. Even when you're fifty*: *Ponystep*, September 2009. https://web.archive.org/web/20090922220945/http://www.ponystep.com/music/article/SiobhanDonaghyTheonethatgotaway_380.aspx

293 *I was a bitch to Heidi*: *Daily Mail*, 2009. https://www.dailymail.co.uk/tvshowbiz/article-1253898/Being-Sugababes-unbearable-Keisha-left-The-girls-admit-better-known-rows-hits.html

293 *We never knew from one day to the next*: *Daily Mail*, February 2010 & 2015. https://www.dailymail.co.uk/tvshowbiz/article-1253898/Being-Sugababes-unbearable-Keisha-left-The-girls-admit-better-known-rows-hits.html; https://www.dailymail.co.uk/femail/article-3211427/How-life-stardom-went-sour-Sugababes.html

293 *Although it was not my choice*: *NME*, September 2009. https://www.nme.com/news/music/sugababes-37-1308066

294 *Some people had never met me . . . It felt more unified*: *Daily Mail*, June 2020. https://www.dailymail.co.uk/tvshowbiz/article-8431407/Sugababes-Keisha-Buchanan-says-portrayed-bully-black-band-member.html

Chapter 25: Wiley – Part One

296 *It's disgusting there are no words*: Twitter, July 2020. https://metro.co.uk/2020/07/25/wiley-dropped-management-shocking-tweets-no-place-society-anti-semitism-13036240/

297 *Sometimes I just feel cold hearted*: *Jockey Slut*, Autumn 2003. https://web.archive.org/web/20080216202712/http://www.xlrecordings.com/features/wiley-interview.html

299 *What? . . . Come on, Dyl*: *Conflict DVD*. https://www.youtube.com/watch?v=qqqwq9mxUPc

300 *Lisa Maffia report*: *Guardian*, July 2003. https://www.theguardian.com/uk/2003/jul/19/cyprus.travelnews

300 *If you didn't try*: *Metro*, October 2017. https://metro.co.uk/2017/10/09/wiley-ends-vicious-feud-with-dizzee-rascal-i-have-nothing-but-respect-6986206/

300 *Lisa Maffia was on stage*: Interview with Megaman, RTM Records, September 2023. https://www.youtube.com/watch?v=8-U0z61Guk8

300 **There was some fighting with another crew**: *Time Out*, June 2016. https://www.timeout.com/music/wiley-you-want-to-know-the-truth-im-gonna-tell-you-the-truth

Chapter 27:
Andy Nicholson, Arctic Monkeys

320 **You're gonna have to get**: *The Michael Anthony Show* (Podcast), May 2020. https://www.youtube.com/watch?v=kPBCddbPJvQ

321 **Fatigue**: *Independent*, May 2006. https://www.independent.co.uk/news/people/profiles/arctic-monkeys-too-much-monkey-business-479704.html

322 **No longer with the band . . . all the best**: *NME*, July 2006. https://web.archive.org/web/20071119022317/http://www.nme.com/news/arctic-monkeys/23380

322 **We sorta found ourselves . . . that's all that really matters**: *NME*, August 2006. https://www.nme.com/news/music/arctic-monkeys-544-1359043

324 **Shaking hands and chatting**: *Exclaim*, June 2018. https://exclaim.ca/music/article/arctic_monkeys_career_retrospective_from_rubble_to_the_ritz

All other quotes: *The Michael Anthony Show* (Podcast), May 2020. https://www.youtube.com/watch?v=kPBCddbPJvQ

Chapter 28: Wiley – Part Two

329 **Bum . . . Boy who stabbed**: Interview with Vlad TV, 2017. https://www.youtube.com/watch?v=Aa5USMeVvjk

333–34 **Both of ur parents . . . I hate u u tramp**: *Guardian*, Jan 2017. https://www.theguardian.com/music/2017/jan/24/wiley-godfather-grime

334 **Blow up**: Red Bull Music Academy Interview, May 2015. https://daily.redbullmusicacademy.com/2015/05/wiley-feature

335 **There are 2 sets . . . Cowards and snakes**: *Guardian*, July 2020. https://www.theguardian.com/music/2020/jul/25/wileys-management-firm-drops-grime-artist-over-antisemitic-tweets

335–6 **Talking to him privately . . . cut all ties with him**: Brooklyn Vegan,

July 2020. https://www.brooklynvegan.com/wiley-dropped-by-management-following-anti-semitic-tweets-report/

336 *I'm not racist . . . rather than the beginning*: *Sky*, July 2020. https://news.sky.com/story/wiley-hits-back-over-antisemitic-remarks-saying-im-not-racist-12038497

337 *If I want to turn*: *50/50*, Wiley, Big Dada, 2007. Written by Hallgeir Rustan, Lemar Obika, Marcus Miller, Mikkel Eriksen and Tor Erik Hermansen.

338 *Soldier of Allah*: *Guardian*, December 2013. https://www.theguardian.com/uk-news/2013/dec/09/lee-rigby-murder-accused-adebolajo-religion-is-everything

339 *I'm a weirdo*: *Weirdo*, Wiley, Big Dada, 2012. Written by Wiley.

339 *People say I'm bipolar*: *Dazed*, July 2011. https://www.dazeddigital.com/music/article/10867/1/wiley-is-back-on-the-beat

Chapter 29: Mick Ronson, the Spiders from Mars

342 *I've got God*: *Rolling Stone*, 1976. https://www.rollingstone.com/music/music-news/david-bowie-ground-control-to-davy-jones-77059/

342 *Eyelashes*: Ibid.

342 *Car door opener*: *Louder Sound*, Max Bell, April 2017. https://www.loudersound.com/features/the-rise-and-fall-of-mick-ronson

344 *We thought he was just a . . . overwhelmed*: Ibid.

344 *Wow*: *Beside Bowie: The Mick Ronson Story*, directed by Jon Brewer, 2017.

344 *Are you going to*: Ibid.

345 *The lads from*: Ibid.

345 *Heavier, more electric*: Ibid.

345 *Just after Hunky Dory*: *Louder Sound*, Max Bell, April 2017.

346 *Personally, it was a bit*: Ibid.

346 *That's your brother, that poof drummer*: *Beside Bowie: The Mick Ronson Story*, directed by Jon Brewer, 2017.

346 *Mick was a self-contained man*: Ibid.

346 *Honking, very middle . . . Lines and riffs in a heartbeat*: Ibid.

347 *I could very rarely understand a word . . . my head a bit*: Ibid.

347 *Transformer is easily my*: *Louder Sound*, Max Bell, April 2017.

347 *He was very much a salt . . . Mick and Keith*: Ibid.

348 *I'm like a bricklayer . . . Don't just be a session man*: Ibid.

349 *The Spiders from Mars*: *The Arsenio Hall Show*, 1993. https://www.youtube.com/watch?v=G-I4mOFM5yY

349 *The criticism was it was like . . . not really a frontman*: *Beside Bowie: The Mick Ronson Story*, directed by Jon Brewer, 2017.

350 *Mick was a school gardener . . . ups and downs'*: Ibid.

351 *You only get one chance*: Ibid.

351 *David needs someone around him to say*: *Rolling Stone*, 1976. https://www.rollingstone.com/music/music-news/david-bowie-ground-control-to-davy-jones-77059/

351 *I'm babysitting for me sister . . . the last big cheque he got*: *Beside Bowie: The Mick Ronson Story*, directed by Jon Brewer, 2017.

352 *He was northern and glamorous . . . put the cat out*: *Uncut*, February 2013. https://www.uncut.co.uk/features/he-had-been-very-loyal-to-bowie-morrissey-on-mick-ronson-25863/

352–54 *Everyone who worked with . . . grand pianos* **and all Morrissey quotes**: Interview with Max Bell, *Classic Rock*, 2017.

354: *Typical Mick*: *Beside Bowie: The Mick Ronson Story*, directed by Jon Brewer, 2017.

354: *He tried various holistic therapies*: Ibid.

355: *Should've always played on*: Ibid.

355: *You turned into a ghost*: *Michael Picasso*, Ian Hunter, Citadel, 1995. Written by Ian Hunter.

356: *Pushed me forward*: *Louder Sound*, Max Bell, April 2017.

Chapter 30: Anton Newcombe, the Brian Jonestown Massacre

357 *I never got paid for all the years*: *Dig!* (Film), directed by Ondi Timoner, 2005.

358 *Revolving cast of*: Massacre v. Davis, August 2014. https://casetext.com/case/brian-jonestown-massacre-v-davies-1

358 *I don't think the Aussie . . . Daniel Allaire*: *CityBeat*, October 2003. https://www.citybeat.com/music/music-casualties-of-rock-12176830

358 *At least The Donald*: Twitter, September 2015. https://www.phoenixnewtimes.com/music/matt-hollywood-doesnt-know-why-he-was-fired-from-brian-jonestown-massacre-7659731

358–59 *The reason I was kicked out was*: *Keep Music Evil: The Brian Jonestown Massacre Story*, Jesse Valencia, 2019.

359 *High on dope*: Ibid.

359: *Chris and the boys were*: Ibid.

359 *Hey fuck that! No one's ... STAND THE FUCK BACK MOTHERFUCKER*: *Dig!* (Film), directed by Ondi Timoner, 2005.

359 *This guy wasn't long*: Ibid.

360 *You've got a keyboard player ... shook his head*: *Digging the Vein*, Tony O'Neill, 2006.

360 *Poor Robert ... Make it big*: *Keep Music Evil: The Brian Jonestown Massacre Story*, Jesse Valencia, 2019.

361 *Well, let's see. Anton's tried to stab me twice*: *Tour Punisher* (Podcast). https://open.spotify.com/episode/5kzxXuPZXFST8Id9MzY5VN

361 *Atom was a funny storyteller ... and unsettling at the same time*: *Digging the Vein*, Tony O'Neill, 2006.

362 *Elektra and Sire and Capitol ... it's very easy, everyone should try it*: *Dig!* (Film), directed by Ondi Timoner, 2005.

362–63 *Created a world of their own ... Will fail*: Ibid.

Chapter 31: Kim Shattuck, Pixies

364 *The Pixies don't* and all other quotes: *NME*, December 2013. https://www.nme.com/news/music/pixies-39-1239648

Chapter 32: Ross Valory and Steve Smith, Journey

366 *Creative differences*: Consequence, March 2020. https://consequence.net/2020/03/journey-fire-sue-steve-smith-ross-valory/

367 *Ill-conceived ... to play together*: *Ultimate Classic Rock*, April 2021. https://ultimateclassicrock.com/journey-settlement-ross-valory-steve-smith/#:~:text=Journey%20fired%20Valory%20and%20Smith,said%20this%20belief%20was%20incorrect.

367 *Past and future ... legacy of Journey*: Ibid.

369 *Steve Perry ultimatum*: *Melodic Rock*, 2005. https://web.archive.org/web/20070517084119/http://www.melodicrock.com/interviews/steveperry-mitchlafon.html

369 *Like the pope saying*: Castle's Burning, Herbie Herbert interview, 2002. https://web.archive.org/web/20101115035157/http://members.cox.net/mrcarty/page3.html

370 *Off-duty officers, snooping*: *Consequence of Sound*, March 2023. https://consequence.net/2023/03/journey-feud-members-hire-off-duty-police/

370 *Damage the brand*: *Ultimate Classic Rock*, December 2022. https://ultimateclassicrock.com/jonathan-cain-neal-schon-cease-and-desist-response/

371 *This is Neal. I am fucking*: *Billboard*, March 2023. https://www.billboard.com/pro/journey-lawsuits-legal-fights-explainer/

371 *Improperly*: Ibid.

371 *Completely out of control . . . over the years*: Ibid.

371 *He's just an impossible human . . . I'm a superstar*: Ibid.

372 *If some of them are tired of me . . . I'm just a phone call away*: Twitter, April 2023. https://twitter.com/arnelpineda/status/1646209093928120320

Chapter 33:
Martyn Ware, the Human League

373 *Could you work . . . Human League again*: *Digital Spy*, March 2011. https://www.digitalspy.com/music/a311494/phil-oakey-id-record-with-martyn-ware/

373 *I was completely devastated . . . It still is*: *Yorkshire Post*, November 2022. https://www.yorkshirepost.co.uk/whats-on/arts-and-entertainment/martyn-ware-of-heaven-17-all-of-a-sudden-it-was-like-the-dam-bursting-3902003